THE BRIGHT PROMISE

RICHARD SHERMAN

THE

BRIGHT

PROMISE

Boston

LITTLE, BROWN AND COMPANY

1947

The author wishes to thank the following for permission to quote from copyrighted material:

Gershwin Publishing Corporation for two lines from "Summertime." Copyright MCMXXXV by George Gershwin. Published by Gershwin Publishing Corporation. Chappell & Co., Inc., Sole Selling Agent for U. S. & Canada.

Music Publishers Holding Corporation for six lines from "Bei Mir Bist Du Schön." Copyrighted 1937 by Harms, Inc. Used by permission.

Shapiro, Bernstein & Co., Inc., for two lines from "The Last Round-Up." Copyright 1933 by Shapiro, Bernstein & Co., Inc.

Published simultaneously
in Canada by McClelland and Stewart Limited

PRINTED IN THE UNITED STATES OF AMERICA

To My Mother and to the Memory of My Father

THE BRIGHT PROMISE

≫≫ I ≪≪

THERE WAS A RING ON MY FINGER
that I had never worn before and have never been without since.
There was a voice which I had never heard and now shall never
hear again. There was a new way of life beginning, not only for
me but for others, and I was both hopeful and a little afraid. Out
of the past, troubling and troubled, had come this future on whose
threshold I now was waiting, as for the opening of a door. It was
Saturday, March fourth, 1933. A day to remember, a day of change.

I woke early, and when I glanced over at the other bed I saw that
it was already empty. From the bath came the hiss of the shower,
and I lay listening to it, to it and to the intermittent rumble of the
El and to the halting, iron progress of a garbage truck along the
street below. This is the last time I shall wake here, I thought. This
is the last time I shall open my eyes to those orange curtains listless
in the sooty air, and the dead geranium stalks in the window box,
and this furniture so bright and cheap and filled with memory. I
had made and hung the curtains, planted the geraniums and seen
them bloom, stenciled the bureau and the bedsteads to their bold
red-and-yellow. Oh, the times I had waked here, and the many
moods of those wakings. . . . But this was the last time.

The clock on the table said seven. Yes, seven here, but six back
there in that big white house set far back on the deep lawn on that
quiet street. My mother would still be asleep, and my father might
or might not be, depending on how late he had sat up the night be-

3

fore reading and rereading accounts of Antietam and Chancellors-ville and Shiloh. Or perhaps even my mother wasn't asleep now, at this particular six o'clock on this particular morning. If she had been here or I there she would have been padding in, a big gray-braided figure still in kimono and slippers, to sit on my bed and take my hand and soothe back my hair and say, "Well, dear. This is the day." She had always loved those morning talks, and no doubt she still did. Once I had loved them too, and had looked forward to them, but in the past two summers whenever I had gone home they hadn't been quite the same. Too many questions on her part, too many evasions and silences on mine. And today of all days there would have been more questions. So maybe it was just as well things were as they were.

But lying there, I pictured that white house and its cupolas and the snowball bushes around its broad porch, and I suddenly found myself wanting it, missing it. This wasn't what I had once planned today to be, and it wasn't what my mother had planned. Instead of waking here in this cramped, shoddy, anonymous little room of India prints and candles in wine bottles, I ought to have been waking among girlhood's bird's-eye maple, with elms in full June leaf outside the open windows and with birds singing in them. Instead of those orange net curtains there should have been starched white ruffles with pink tiebacks, with Saint Cecilia on the wall and a yellowed palm frond behind her. And in place of that empty, glass-littered, cigarette-stale "studio" beyond the closed door there should have been a whole downstairs of big, square, high-ceilinged rooms already alive with preparations and bustle, neighbors knocking, cakes coming, peonies in vases, clatter in the kitchen. And above all, especially above all, in my closet there should have been hanging Grandma Pepperdine's sachet-scented, twice-worn, seventy-year-old dress of ivory satin and Irish lace with a veil, rather than a never-worn, week-old suit of gray wool with a hat. Even though the suit had a fashionably long and stunningly monkey-fur-trimmed coat to it, of which I was very, very proud.

All that I thought, the I that was, waking and wondering.

4

The door opened then, and Natalie came in from the bath, her dampened hair forming dark crescents against the pallor of her cheeks. She was a tall girl, tall and thin and sallow, with the peculiar attractiveness of one who never got quite enough sleep and to whom the out-of-doors was simply something to hasten through as fast as possible while en route from here to there. Opening the closet door, she began to toss things in and pull other things out. She didn't look at me.

"Well, this is it," she said.

"That's right."

"You'd better get up. We've got ten hundred thousand chores to do this morning. Including that living room. You ought to see it."

Getting out of bed, I went to the window and stood looking across at the chimney tops and clotheslines and fire escapes of MacDougal Street. A gray day, and cold. Even this early, the man on the roof opposite was waving his bamboo pole at his circling pigeons. The torn canvas of a faded deck chair, set among the tar and the pebbles, flapped a little in the slight breeze and then was quiet again. To the west, on Sixth Avenue, a train on the El went roaring past. I couldn't see it, but I could feel its vibration on the floor where I stood and on the window sill my hands were touching. It was part of me. More a part of me now than those birds in the elms back home would have been.

"Happy the bride the sun shines on," I said.

"Mm?" said Natalie, and stepped toward the window, peering up at the sky. "Oh, that. Well, don't worry. After all, it could be snowing." She moved back toward the closet. "Probably will be, too, I shouldn't be surprised."

"Not snow," I said. "Snow's too pretty — like Christmas or something. Rain would be better. A good, steady, dismal downpour, with the gutters running over."

I could hear her behind me, getting into the old blouse, too short skirt, and cracked patent-leather pumps that constituted her at-home-in-the-morning wear. Then she came toward me, fastening the snaps at her waist.

5

"Look," she said. "Don't go feeling sorry for yourself. Or if you do, don't expect any sympathy from me. This thing wasn't my idea, you know."

"I know."

"And from all I can gather, it wasn't exactly Lyle's either."

I didn't say anything.

"So whose was it?" she persisted. "Who does that leave?"

"I guess that leaves me," I said.

She nodded emphatically, snapping the last snap. "You bet. That leaves you. It leaves you with what you've got, which is trouble, and it leaves me with what I've got, which is a seventy-five-dollar apartment to keep up by myself, *and* the light *and* the gas *and* the phone." She inserted two fingers at her belt and ran them round to meet at the back. "So if you think I'm going to go all wistful and pathetic with you because you can't do it up with orange blossoms and stuff, you're crazy. You oughtn't to be doing it at all. Other people aren't, not to mention names, and they get along. And you could get along, too. After all, you did for quite a while, both of you. And although it might not have been legal, at least it wasn't plain lunacy."

I leaned my forehead against the cold pane. Looking down, I could see a man wearing a cap and no overcoat standing with his hands in his pockets outside Mr. Pestalozzi's grocery store with a mound of apples neatly pyramided up on a wooden box in front of him. Silly creature, I thought. No initiative. Didn't he know that the place for apple men was either uptown on Fifth and Park or downtown on Wall? Why pick MacDougal Street? And why at seven in the morning outside a grocery store that was probably full of apples?

"Well?" said Natalie. She was waiting. For what I didn't know, since we had been through all this several times before.

"Well what?"

"Well, are you going to change your mind and be sensible? You still could, you know. And I doubt if Lyle would object."

Oh, no. Not Lyle. Not he.

I shook my head, and kept looking down at the apple man. "I don't believe so," I said. "Thanks just the same."

6

There was a sigh, and a silence. Then she turned away, toward the door. "Come on," she said. "Let's get to work. The bridegroom cometh, and the gin's not made and the ash trays aren't emptied."

I took a shower and dressed, and as I did I thought a little, once more traveling that well-worn treadmill of pros and cons that went round and round and got me nowhere. Natalie was right. Everything she said was right, more or less, and she knew it and I knew it. Only . . . well, there were things she didn't understand and possibly never would understand. Herself, Ben, Mrs. Ellery, Mr. Kendrick at the office, my mother and father, everyone I knew, they all had reasons, and although most of the reasons were different the result was nevertheless the same: no, not now, better put it off till later, better wait, my-dear-is-this-quite-wise? Yes, even Lyle, who had reasons too. But my reason was best, or so it seemed to me. Nothing very definite or concrete. Just a feeling that if it wasn't now, it would be never.

Weekday breakfasts were a gulp and a rush — coffee drunk standing up and usually with our hats on — but on Saturdays and Sundays we went as domestic as the closet kitchen permitted. Since this was a Saturday, even if not a normal one, Natalie apparently saw no point in altering the routine, for when I came out into the other room there was the sizzle of bacon and the crackle-spatter of eggs frying. In the kitchen, where there was space for only one, she was bent over a memorandum pad, writing and muttering. "Ice, juniper juice, glycerine, cheese things, anchovies — " She broke off, shuddering. "How can I even think of anchovies at seven-thirty in the morning?"

I was straightening the pillows on the divan and gathering up last night's glasses. "Let's not make it too elaborate," I said. "And I wish you'd search them at the door for rice."

"Now listen," she said. "This isn't going to be a champagne and Meyer Davis business, but if we're going to do it at all we might as well do it right." She picked up her pad again. "Salted nuts, olives, ask Fran to bring extra glasses. . . . Do you suppose we ought to try stuffing a few eggs? A sprinkle of paprika here and there — I always think it lends a sort of tone. You know?"

7

"They won't all come. They'll think it means presents."

"Well, I certainly hope it means presents. Don't you?"

I skirted round her and edged her out and after that put the glasses in the sink and then reached for the eggs and bacon. "But most of them can't afford it. Elsa with no job, Ernie with his third wage cut, Hannigan on that half-day, half-pay schedule — "

"You wait. They'll be here anyway, presents or no presents — and with their tongues hanging out." She put the pad aside. "What about his mother? She coming?"

"I imagine so."

"Hm." Glancing upward, she gazed meditatively at the shelf on which stood a gallon jug of alcohol, and tapped her teeth with a pencil. "Well, I *suppose* that'll be enough. Especially as she'll no doubt be a little primed to start with."

"Let's eat."

We ate. Silence mostly, and now and then the sound of pages turning. But I let my section of the paper lie untouched beside my plate. I was wondering if Lyle was up yet, and if so what he was thinking and how he was feeling. I pictured him dressing in that apartment I knew as well as my own, that dank and perpetually murky basement apartment which looked out on a passing humanity that was all feet and legs. I saw him preparing coffee on the electric plate and probably running his finger down the "Help Wanted" columns to winnow out the calls for pantry workers and leather stitchers and the glittering opportunities available to anyone who happened to have five thousand dollars to invest — and all the time seeking the perfect opening which wouldn't be there, had never been there, might never be there.

"Isn't it wonderful?" asked Natalie.

"What?"

"This." She rattled the paper. "The *Herald Tribune* coming out today. I mean, it's so brave of them." She reached for a cigarette. "But maybe they decided that since the sun seemed to rise just as usual, they might as well try it out and see what happens."

I hadn't given much time to considering what that particular aspect of today meant. I was aware of what was going on all right, but it was too large for comprehension and in any case it didn't seem to touch me very closely. Also, I had other things to occupy my mind.

"What do you expect Mrs. Hoover's doing now?" she continued. "Looking under the beds to see if there's any dust, maybe? Trying to decide if it's worth while taking along the rest of that meat loaf that's left in the icebox?"

"Whatever she's doing, she's probably glad she's getting out. It can't have been too gay there lately."

"Ben says . . ." she began.

But I didn't listen to what Ben said, because I knew in advance that I wouldn't be able to understand it. Ben taught economics at N.Y.U., and he thought and spoke in terms of never less than ten million people. To him there was no such thing as one farmer or one lawyer — instead there were only "the agrarian workers" and "the professional class." A woman standing at a counter buying soap or sugar wasn't a woman to him, she was "a consumer," while the clerk who sold it to her was "the middleman." I was willing to acknowledge that Ben was very bright, very learned, but the fact remained that our languages were different. I never could visualize "Americans" or "New Yorkers" in whole masses. I could only visualize one American, or one New Yorker. Usually myself. Or for the past two years, and more than ever from now on, Lyle and myself. Ben was contemptuous of such an attitude. That was a woman's way, he said. Maybe — I didn't know. All I knew was that it was this woman's way and there seemed little likelihood of my ever being able to change it.

Natalie rose, smudged out her cigarette, and began to shuttle back and forth to the kitchen, clearing away the dishes. "Now let's get organized," she said. "Suppose I go out to market and get this junk we'll have to have while you pretty up the place."

I nodded, and reached for the paper and idly turned its pages. On the society page a pretty girl beamed up at me, coming out of St. Thomas's, all awash with white tulle and a triple strand of pearls and with a top hat and a frock coat at her side. At one time Lyle might well have been that top hat and frock coat — but who would have been descending those steps with him? Not I. Certainly not

I. . . . Quickly I shifted to an adjoining column. "I see they've had another of those treasure hunts," I said. "They managed to find a tattooed dwarf. Armenian."

"Mm. So I noticed," she said, heading toward the bedroom. "From Sutton Place to Hooverville — and back again. All in one mad romp. Isn't it cute? What will they think of next?"

She got her coat, went out, and I sat there at the table over cold coffee. I glanced around the room, observing it with the fresh view of one about to say farewell to it. The bedroom was a Macy's basement version of the peasant style — very quaint, very old-world and arty-crafty — but this was belligerently modern. Or "moderne," rather. The last word, the very newest thing in *décor*. Our landlady, Mrs. O'Hanlon, always referred to the room as "the studio," though the only thing we had ever painted in it was the furniture and the only writing ever done there were my weekly letters home and sometimes Natalie's "Lines for Ladies" shopping paragraphs for the back-of-the-book in the magazine.

I can still see it now, today. One good chair, a rep-covered and basically white overstuffed affair set on rockers of tubular chromium — a bit tricky, but comfortable once you got the hang of it. Setback bookcases which had begun life as packing boxes. A broad and bumpy divan whose trailing monk's-cloth cover concealed the fact that it was nothing more than a box spring and mattress propped up precariously on volumes of the encyclopedia. A fairly taupe-colored carpet with a pinkish blotch on it where someone had spilled a glass of New Year's Eve red-wine punch. A folding screen pasted up with old *New Yorker* covers. Some framed color prints from the magazine on the wall, and one original. . . . At night, what with the white light cast by the parchment-shade lamps, it was a passable room, even warm. But in the daytime it wasn't so good.

Yet when I had moved in, with Natalie, it had seemed a wonderful place — sophisticated, distinctive, unique. I had been twenty-two then, and straight from Iowa — almost straight from Iowa City and its university, too, save for a detour through business college and a restless, discontented year at home. I was in New York at last, I had a job which I was sure would bring me into contact with talented and creative spirits, and the whole experience was so exhilaratingly novel that I was certain it couldn't ever have happened before. I had no way of knowing that the room, far from being unique, could have been more or less duplicated perhaps a thousand times within a radius of twenty square blocks, from Sixteenth Street southward. I had no way of knowing that I could have been duplicated, too, and Lyle, and Natalie, and all of us. We were individuals, but we were also a type — Metropolitan Americanus, Middle Class, White Collar. Period, late 1920's, early 1930's. . . . No one even called it "postwar" any more, because the war was so remote that you sometimes forgot there had ever been one. And of course no one called it "prewar" either.

I knew all that now, though. The bloom was off the rose and I was twenty-six, four years older and more than four years wiser. There had been a crash and now there was a depression and almost everyone I knew had been touched by it in some way or other, including my father, who had never looked at a stock-market quotation in his life.

"Middle class, white collar . . ." I mused, sitting there at the breakfast table and cradling my empty cup. Or did Lyle's background and upbringing entitle him to be listed in some category other than middle class? And then I decided that I was beginning to think like Ben. It was time I got up and got going.

I washed the dishes, made the beds, dusted, straightened, re-arranged. Then I started to pack. Most of my things I had already moved uptown to the new place, going up on the subway with Lyle evenings after work, with each of us carrying two suitcases. Therefore, aside from the gray wool and its fabulous monkey fur, which I would be wearing, all I had to attend to were the things I would need for the week we would be away. ("Why only a week?" Lyle had asked. "I've got all the time in the world. Nothing else but. So why not a leisurely couple of years?" And I had said, "Now look. You've got to stop that.") Mr. Kendrick was lending us a car and we were driving to the Delaware Water Gap, to a place where we had once spent a week end the previous summer. And since the Poconos in early March were likely to be on the brisk and snappy side, I was relying chiefly on heavy things, a skiing outfit I had bought during the excitement of last winter's skiing craze (and never used), sweaters, a corduroy skirt, a bright plaid mackinaw, relic of my college years.

I packed them all, and the underthings, and a capestyle georgette dinner dress — just in case. In folding the mackinaw I felt something scratch my wrist, and looking down I saw that it was my sorority pin, neatly centered in one of the checks of the plaid. I unlocked the clasp and fingered the seed pearls that bordered the diamond-shaped edges. Time had been when that pin and all it meant ("Look, kiddo," Irmadee Tupper had said, herself in a pleasant agony of indecision brought on by an embarrassment of riches, "the Kappas have the best crowd, and yet the Tri Delt house is so cunning") had seemed to me to be the most important thing in the world. But now it wasn't important at all; only rather sad and very young. Put it away. Put it away, along with the high-school prom program, and the Campfire Girl uniform, and the eighth-grade diploma, and the last doll, and all the other milestones leading back down the dim, lost trail to childhood. Let them gather dust. . . . So I tucked the pin into one of the pockets of the mackinaw. Maybe I could sell it. The few dollars it would bring — they might come in handy. In fact they definitely would come in handy.

It was almost eleven o'clock now (Natalie must be buying out practically the whole of Bleecker Street, I decided), and so I went downstairs to see if there was any mail. Four flights, with Mrs. O'Hanlon vaguely industrious with whisk broom and dustcloth on one of them. I paused politely, knowing what was coming. The O'Hanlon was a good sort. We had had our little tiffs about the radio being played loudly after midnight and a somewhat more serious discussion concerning bottles crashed down into the areaway at four in the morning from what could only have been one special window in one special apartment, but on the whole we got along. "Nice girls," was her verdict on us, and her recommendation. "They go to business regular, and they keep no pets."

"Well," she said, "I expect somebody's a very happy young lady today."

"Yes, Mrs. O'Hanlon. Yes, I am." On and off, and all things considered. "Thank you."

She sighed. "Couples starting out in times like these — it's risky, isn't it?"

Surely not Mrs. O'Hanlon, too?

"Oh, I think we'll make out all right."

"I hope so. Indeed I hope so." The dustcloth glided back and forth over the scarred wood of the banister, and then her blue eyes looked at me. "Is it him?"

"Who?"

"The dark one. The one I've seen around."

Seen when? At what hour? I never could tell about Mrs. O'Hanlon, what she knew and what she didn't.

"Yes. That's right. Mr. Ellery."

"What does he do?"

I hesitated. "He's — he's an editorial associate. A writer, sort of." And why not, pray? After all, he had been an editorial associate, on three different magazines, all of which had folded catastrophically beneath him. And he was a writer, too, though nothing he had ever written had ever sold. And in any case it was none of her business.

"Well, he seems like a nice young man, I'm sure."

"Oh, he is." I edged around her, downward. "I'd better be getting the mail. I've a lot to do this morning."

"I wish you every happiness," she called after me. "Both of you. You're a very brave young woman."

"Thank you, Mrs. O'Hanlon," I said, rounding the landing. "Thank you. . . ."

Brave? That was a new word for it. Natalie said I was silly, Lyle said I was stubborn, and now it seemed I was brave.

I got the mail and brought it upstairs, passing Mrs. O'Hanlon on the same flight again, an anticlimax which we both treated with the silence and averted glances it deserved. There was nothing for Natalie, but there were two letters and a package for me. The package was addressed to "Mrs. Lyle Ellery," in my care, and when I looked at it I thought, "Something for his mother. But why send it here?" And then I looked again and thought, "Why, no — that's

13

me. *I'm* Mrs. Lyle Ellery, or I will be in five hours." I traced my finger lightly over the name. Funny, I thought. Funny. . . .

Then I sat down on the divan and undid the package. It was a gift from my Aunt Florence in California — a quite hideous object carved out of a redwood tree and of no discernible use that I could determine: it could conceivably have been a humidor, or on the other hand it might have been something to put dead hair in, for neither of which we were in any crying need. Still, it was sweet of her to have sent anything, especially as I hadn't seen her for fifteen years. But I concluded that she must have very peculiar ideas as to the basic requirements of New York housekeeping.

After that I opened the letters. I dreaded them, because one was from my father and the other was from my mother. I opened my father's first and from it fluttered out the familiar pink oblong Manila County Savings and Trust strip of the same sort he had sent me all through college and, until he couldn't any more, even after I had come to New York. It fell to the floor, and I picked it up and looked at it. Two hundred and twenty-five dollars. I put both hands to my face. Oh, he shouldn't have, he shouldn't have! The paper was barely managing to hold its own, he was still driving that awful old crate through country roads in all sorts of weather, my mother had been forced to violate the sanctity of the house by filling it with teacher roomers, and — well, he just shouldn't have. It was too much. Anything would have been too much.

I started to read. "My Dear Daughter," he began — and my hand holding the letter fell to my lap. I can't, I thought. I just can't. And then I decided that if he could write it, I could read it. I lifted the letter again, which like all of his was typed on the paper's letterhead — "The Ammon Argus, Ammon, Ia., John Hardin, Editor and Prop." — by means of that antique L. C. Smith which was already a museum piece, and went on:

March 1, 1933

My Dear Daughter:

Mother and I are each writing you a letter, trusting they will arrive on your wedding day. If circumstances were otherwise, we would be there with you — or, better still, you would be here in the house where

14

you grew up and where we had always hoped to see you married. But we talked it over and we agreed that it would be best to give you money instead. With it goes our fondest love. You have always been a good girl and a good daughter to us, and we only wish that we were in a position to do more for you at this time. But — *nil desperandum.*

I will not write at length, as am very busy. You may have read in the papers of the riots against farm mortgage foreclosures out this way and of the so-called Farmers' Holiday movement. There have been some increasingly serious disturbances and, I regret to say, some bloodshed, all of which is of course front-page news for each week's issue of the *Argus* — though hardly of a kind which I enjoy publishing.

Please give my affection to Lyle and tell him that Mother and I want to make his acquaintance as soon as conditions permit. Tell him, too, to be good to our girl.

Your loving
PAPA

I gazed sightlessly at the letter, and tears came. "Papa." It had been years since he had signed himself as that. When I had been little he had always been Papa to me, but as I had grown older I had discarded the name as being too embarrassingly childish and had adopted "Daddy" and sometimes "Father" and had trained him, not without some difficulty, to adopt them too. But now he was Papa again.

The tears kept coming, and now I looked at the other envelope. Well, go on, open it, I told myself. This is what you get for going away and growing away. This is what you get for growing up. And there's nothing anyone can possibly do about it, neither you nor they. There never has been anything anyone can do.

I took out my mother's letter, which at least had the virtue of seeming to be shorter. But still, short or long, it would probably prove even worse, even tougher, because she herself was tougher. And yet in a way, a surprising way, it wasn't.

Home
March 1

DEAREST AMY,

Although I can't agree that this is the time to do it, I must admit that I am very glad and even thankful that it is Lyle you are marrying.

15

Glad? Thankful? Why should she be either, I wondered. She had never even seen Lyle, except in photographs. And although I had once written a lot about him, when we had first met, I hadn't mentioned him much lately. I read on:

From your letters and from what you have said here while you were at home, and haven't said, I know how much he means to you. I only pray, my darling, that you will be a good wife and that he will be a good husband.

It has not been easy for me to write this, and perhaps it will not be easy for you to read it. But don't be sad on your wedding day. Remember, although we may not always understand you, at least we try — and we always love you.

God bless you, dear,
MOTHER

I stared at the letter, and read it again to see if I could have misinterpreted its meaning. But I hadn't. She knew. My mother knew, and no doubt had known all along, despite my carefully phrased letters and the hundred small deceptions I had practiced when at home. I sank back among the divan's pillows, and I wasn't certain whether I should burst out laughing or start to cry again — so I ended by doing a little of each. My mother was nearer and dearer to me then than she had been for a long, long time. In many ways she was a woman of great narrowness and little tolerance — I realized that, and accepted it — and it must have been hard for her to have kept silent. It must have been very hard.

I rose briskly, feeling better. "Don't be sad on your wedding day," she had written, and I wouldn't be. And I would keep those letters, both of them, to show to Lyle. I'd keep them even longer than that. Sometime there might be someone else to whom I might want to show them, or parts of them.

Just then the entry buzzer sounded from downstairs, so I went to the wall button and pressed it, knowing that it would probably be Natalie, her arms filled with bundles and without her key. I waited until I was certain the latch had caught the click and then, opening the door into the hall and leaving it ajar, went into the bedroom to put the letters away — and Aunt Florence's redwood curio too, far, far away. As I bent over one of the suitcases I heard someone entering the other room, and I called, "You back?" There was no answer. Curious, I moved toward the bedroom doorway. Beyond, standing in the center of the living room with his overcoat and hat still on, was Lyle.

"Look, darling," I said, without going toward him. "We ought to try to maintain a few of the conventions, anyway. You celebrated your bachelor party here last night, with me, and now you're here again this morning. It's not etiquette, and it's also probably unlucky. Don't you know we're not supposed to see each other until four o'clock?"

He took off his hat and sent it sailing across the room. Then he slumped into the white chair.

"This does it, I guess," he said. "It's all we needed."

There was a deadness in his voice and his face. I came into the living room and went toward him.

"What's happened?" I said.

He looked up at me. "Haven't you heard?"

"Heard what?"

"The banks are closed."

There was no particular news in that. For the past several weeks banks had been closing all over the country — in Michigan and Maryland and other states. But not in New York. At least, at least . . . Suddenly I went rigid.

"What banks?"

He shrugged, and fumbled for a cigarette. "All banks. The Governor shut 'em all up at four-thirty this morning. Calls it a holiday." His tone was dry. "Boy, some holiday. More damn fun."

"They — they didn't close the Bowery Savings, did they?"

He nodded.

"But they *can't* close the Bowery Savings. I mean . . ."

"They did, though. And the National City and all the rest. I went around this morning to draw out the money for the trip and — well, that's it." Putting his hand into his trouser pocket, he brought out some crumpled bills and some coins. He extended his palm toward me. "With my worldly goods I thee endow. Four dollars and thirty-eight cents. And a Canadian dime."

I walked to the divan and sat down on the edge of it, carefully. On the coffee table was my purse, where I had left it after giving Natalie my share of the grocery money. I reached for it, in a slow-motion fashion, and opened it. I hadn't bothered to draw out anything special for the journey because Lyle had insisted that he was going to pay all the expenses, every cent of them. "I'm prepared to live off you for the rest of my natural life," he had explained, "but this honeymoon, if you can call it that, is going to be on me. All of it, including gum and tips. After all, we men have our pride. Not much, but some."

I examined the purse now. A five-dollar bill. A fifty-cent piece. A dime. Four nickels. Three pennies. . . . It was odd how important pennies seemed. I pressed one in my hand, feeling its hard, cold surface.

"Five dollars and eighty-three cents," I said, looking at him.

He lifted his finger and did a sum in the air, his lips moving silently. "Hm. Ten twenty-one, all told. We're in clover. We're rolling."

I dribbled the coins back into the purse, and peered vacantly into its interior. Then I shut the purse and set it on the table.

"What are we going to do, Lyle?"

He got up, took off his overcoat, and tossed it onto the divan.

"Well, one thing we're going to do is not get married."

I didn't move. In front of me on the table lay my father's pink check for two hundred and twenty-five dollars, which wasn't worth the paper it was written on. But although I was looking at it, I wasn't seeing it or even thinking about it. Instead I was thinking of Mrs. O'Hanlon. She had known. She had known, and she had taken it for granted that I knew too. That was why she had said, "You're a very brave young woman." But what good is a very brave young woman without a very brave young man? And anyway, was I so brave, really — now that this had happened?

Rising, he began to stroll around the room, up and down, back and forth, restlessly. Finally he stopped in front of me.

"Well, why don't you say something?"

But what could I say?

He sat down beside me, taking my hand in his. "Don't you see?" he said. "It wasn't in the cards. I've told you all along it wasn't."

"Yes." So many times. Too many times.

"You've got a job, and I haven't," he went on. "O.K. — we knew that, and we decided to go ahead anyway. But that was when we each had some money in the bank. Now we haven't even got that."

"They — they may reopen." I didn't intend to argue or try to persuade — I'd done all that some time ago — but I wanted to have everything clear and straight.

"Sure, maybe. And maybe not. And if so, when? We've got to be sensible. This whole country is flat on its face at the moment, and there's nobody around to pick it up. They tell me marriage is a tough enough proposition under the best conditions. Why should we start with two strikes against us?"

I groped for my handkerchief. "But we've waited, and we've waited, and we've waited. . . ."

"I know, honey. I know."

I turned my face away. "Lyle. Lyle, do you love me?"

"Now why ask that now? Does it make it any better?"

"Do you?"

His voice was bitter. "Of course I don't. I had the banks closed simply so I could get out of it. Quite complicated, but worth it." And then his arms went around me, and his cheek was against mine. "Oh, darling, do I love you. . . ."

Turning to him, I pressed my head on his shoulder. "I don't want us to be like Ben and Natalie, and just go on and on," I said, talking into hard-finished worsted. "I'm a Middle Western girl, a small-town girl. I wanted to wake up beside you in a home of our own. I wanted to cook your breakfast for you — "

"Sure," he said. "And then go off to your office while I do the dishes and run the carpet sweeper."

19

I shook my head. "That wouldn't have mattered. You'd have found something sometime. You still will."

"What makes you so positive? Why kid yourself? Why try to kid me?"

"But —"

"We might as well face facts." His hand fell away and began picking at a raveling in the divan's cover. "I've got an education that probably cost about ten thousand dollars, maybe more. Prep school and Harvard and Europe with all the trimmings. I'm a Bachelor of Arts, *cum laude,* and when I got out of college everybody said, 'There's a Live Wire. He's Going Places.' And so what am I doing? I'm selling brushes from door to door. Or trying to. I'm the old brush man — brushed off."

"There are plenty of others like you." Which wasn't quite true, because for me there was no one like him. "And anyway, it's not your fault."

"Well, it's somebody's fault — or the fault of something. The system possibly. If there is a system." He shrugged. "I don't know. Sometimes I begin to think that Ben may be right. Maybe it's all got some sort of moral. Maybe if my father hadn't been allowed to make so much he wouldn't have been allowed to lose it all so quickly."

"Don't, darling," I said. He didn't speak of his father very often, but whenever he did he always got all excited and tense. "Don't talk about that now."

But he went on, unheeding or unhearing. "One day he was a millionaire, he thought, and a week later he was crashing through a roof skylight with forty-two stories above him and six inches of concrete below. We had to sell his clothes to pay for his funeral. Is there a lesson there and if so what is it? And how do I learn it? And who's going to teach me?"

"I asked you not to talk about it," I said.

With a gesture he flung himself back full-length on the divan, his arms spread wide, and stared up at the ceiling. There was a little vein in his left temple, and it was standing out now. I could almost see it pulsing, racing.

"I can't help it," he said. "Look at my mother. She wasn't always the way she is, you know. You'd have liked her once."

"I like her now," I said. And I did, sometimes.

"Sure — the lady barfly, the speakeasy queen. And those boys she trails around with. Oh, God, those boys. At fifty-three — forty-five, according to her. But when she really was forty-five she was a completely different person. You wouldn't have recognized her. She had a garden. Sometimes she'd go out in the kitchen and bake a cake. She was happy."

"Lyle, please. When you talk about your mother and father you always get so wrought up. It isn't good for you. It isn't — "

His arms made a sweeping movement, and he reached out and took my wrist, almost roughly. "Oh, the hell with it," he said. He pulled me downward, across him. "Come on, kiss me. Live with me and be my love and we will all the pleasures prove."

I kissed him, and for a moment there wasn't any world or any banks — good or bad, open or closed — for either of us. At least I know there wasn't for me.

"Did you get the ring?" I said, then.

"Yes."

"Let me see it."

"Why?"

"Oh — because."

"But what for? You aren't going to wear it."

"I know. I just want to look at it, that's all."

"No."

"Please, darling."

He sighed and then felt at his vest pocket and took out a small leather box. "There you are," he said. "And that isn't paid for either."

Opening the box, I lifted out a thin band of gold from its bed of satin. I looked at it and, revolving it, read aloud the tiny script engraved on its inner side. "Amy and Lyle. March 4, 1933." I circled the ring between my fingers, but I didn't put it on. "Oh, Lyle. It's beautiful."

"It could have been," he said, and took it and put it back into the box and after that snapped the lid shut and returned the box to his pocket. "Well, we'll use it sometime. I can always have that date changed. To 1934 — or '44 or whenever. It's probably better this way. In ten years or so I ought to have all the payments down."

The door opened then, and Natalie walked in, her arms laden with brown paper packages, and behind her came Ben, equally burdened. She glanced at us briefly as we half-sat, half-lay there on the divan, and spoke over her shoulder to Ben. "The country goes bang — and look at them. Talk about Nero. He fiddled. They neck." Bending over, she dumped her bundles onto the table. "I suppose we should have coughed or knocked or something, but after all at high noon on your nuptial day it's hardly the sort of thing one expects. For pity's sake, what would Mrs. Post say?"

Ben put his packages down, too. He wore the uniform of his trade — the baggy-shaggy tweed coat and the gray flannels, the horn-rimmed glasses, even the briar pipe at which he was wont to suck with the proper meditativeness. Now he rubbed his hands, briskly. He looked very much alive and alert, and his brown eyes glowed behind their lenses.

"Well," he said. "Pretty exciting, isn't it?"

Natalie flipped off the shallow, untrimmed bit of felt that was her hat. She nodded at him. "He's busy as a bird dog," she said. "This is just his meat. I ran into him in Sheridan Square, where he'd cornered some poor, benighted Italian woman and was asking her how the immigrant population was reacting. You'd have thought he was the *Literary Digest,* taking a poll."

Ben sat down in the white chair and removed his glasses. He blew on them, held them up to the light, and then began to polish them.

"Well, as a professor of economics — " he began.

"Assistant professor, I thought it was," said Natalie. She bent toward him and kissed him lightly on the brow. "That's all right, sweet. You just go right ahead. I'll bet you haven't had so much fun since the Panic of 1907."

"I was in rompers in 1907," he replied coldly. He replaced his glasses. "And at least you've got to admit that this is interesting."

She began to pick up the groceries to take them into the kitchen.

22

"Interesting? It's downright fascinating. But you don't have to be quite so enthusiastic about it, do you? If you were a doctor and somebody had cancer, you wouldn't say, 'Oh, boy! Some fun!' would you?" She started toward the kitchen. "Or on the other hand, would you?"

He got out his pipe and undertook the ritual of beginning to fill it. "Actually that's not such a bad comparison as you might imagine. It so happens that I can look at this from a scientific point of view —"

"Mm. How nice for you," she said. "I wish I could. But with a total of three bucks left on my person, it's a little difficult." I watched her through the doorway as she undid the bundles and emptied the bags. "Peanuts, anchovies, pickles — well, we won't starve. It may not be what you'd call a balanced diet, but it's food." Reaching upward, she brought down the jug of alcohol, swinging it from her knuckle. She extended it out into the living room, toward Ben. "And with food goes drink. Come on, Socrates. Make the gin, will you?"

He went toward the kitchen and, squatting, began to busy himself with a medicine dropper and vials of juniper juice and glycerine. "This is interesting, too," he said. "Intoxicants and their relation to periods of crisis. The eat-drink-and-be-merry theory."

"Well, we're going to have either a wedding or a wake," she said. And then she glanced over toward the divan, to Lyle and me. "What's the matter? You haven't opened your mouths."

"They haven't had much chance," said Ben. He looked up at Lyle. "How do you feel about it, Lyle?"

"Not so good."

"Yes. I know. But aside from that."

"The unemployed are not amused," said Lyle. "And you can quote me."

Natalie was looking at both of us, from one to the other. "What about that little ceremony you were planning? Are you going to keep to your schedule?" I had thought she might capitalize on the situation and cite it as proof that she had been right from the beginning. But she didn't. Her words were not a comment, but a question.

23

And it was a question which remained unanswered. I said nothing, Lyle said nothing. Lifting his wrist, he looked at his watch. Then, rising, he went toward the radio, sitting atop one of the setback bookcases. He switched it on.

"We're having a change of management," he said. "We might as well listen."

Natalie folded her arms and leaned against the wall. "Why not?" she shrugged. "It's free."

In a moment, the unnaturally subdued voice of a "color" commentator speaking against a background of movement and noise filled the room, along with some cracklings of static. ". . . gray skies," he was saying, "although it looks as if the sun is trying to break through. Here at the east front of the Capitol the crowds are thick. The Presidential party hasn't come out from the Senate yet, but in the meantime I'll try to point out some of the notables I can see from here. Over there is Al Smith, the Happy Warrior . . ."

"Who did you vote for, Lyle?" asked Natalie. "Who — whom. Well, you know."

He had his elbow on the bookcase and was cupping his chin in his hands. "I didn't vote for anybody," he said. "I voted against."

The others might not have understood what he meant, but I did. His father, his mother, his own condition — his reasons had been negative, those of protest and emotion, rather than positive. His vote for Roosevelt had been as instinctive and as simple as a reflex from pain.

"Who did you?" he said, addressing Natalie.

She reached for a cigarette, and tapped it on her wrist. "Well, you know, it's a funny thing. I meant to vote, I really did. Registered and everything. They gave us half a day off from the office, just so we could. But as I was on my way to the polls I decided that it was a God-given opportunity for me to get that permanent I'd been wanting and hadn't been able to find time for. So I got it." She touched her hair ruefully. "Except that it didn't turn out to be permanent after all."

"You, Ben?" said Lyle, glancing toward him as he knelt among the bottles and the jug.

"Me? Oh, I voted for Norman Thomas."

"Ben always votes for Norman Thomas," said Natalie. "You know that."

Ben took up one of the bottles and began to shake it vigorously. "How about the bride?" he said.

I eyed Lyle. It had seemed to matter so little to us that we hadn't even argued about it.

"Hoover," I said.

Ben looked at me scornfully. "Why? Certainly Roosevelt is conservative and wishy-washy enough, but *Hoover* — "

"It's a free country," said Lyle, quietly. "That's one of its charms. And she's of age and has a right to her own mind."

"Yes, but — "

"Well, I don't know," I said. "I guess it was my father. I mean, he's always voted the straight Republican ticket all his life — and so I did too."

Ben glanced triumphantly at Lyle. "You see?" he said. "She may have had a right to her own mind, but she didn't use it." Then he looked around at the three of us. "Hm. One for Roosevelt, one for Hoover, one for Thomas, and one for nobody at all. Quite a cross section." He put a deliberative, analytical finger to his chin. "You know, that's really very interesting. Now if you took a graph of the whole population, on all levels, I believe you'd find that — "

"Shut up, dear," said Natalie, and indicated the radio, whose volume Lyle was now turning louder. "I have an idea that this may be a moment in history."

And I had an idea it might be, too. I think we all did. We were all quiet, listening, a little self-conscious about the importance and significance of the occasion, even embarrassed. "Mr. Roosevelt has now ascended the ramp, on the arm of his eldest son, James," an announcer was saying in hushed tones, amid the orchestration of coughs and shufflings and the murmur of movement. "He stands at the dais desk, which is decorated with the eagle and stars of the national seal. To his right stands Chief Justice Hughes, who will now administer the oath."

There was silence then, silence on that thronged platform and among the thousands there present and silence in the room where we were only four. It was a tableau I shall long remember. Ben there among the half-filled gin bottles, his hands idle now, his eyes fixed on the radio dial as if it were a face and he were appraising it. Natalie leaning against the wall, the smoke from her cigarette curling upward. Lyle by the radio. I looked at him, but, like Ben, he too was gazing intently at the dial. He was waiting. We all were waiting. A hundred and twenty-five million people were waiting — and hoping for hope and, I think, some of us, praying.

Then the Chief Justice spoke the oath, and the voice repeated it. "I, Franklin Delano Roosevelt, do solemnly swear that I will faithfully execute the office of the President of the United States . . ." I had never heard that voice before. During the campaign, I hadn't listened to the speeches of either candidate, nor had I read them. At the time, I had been too much involved in my own relationship with Lyle — and also I had come to share his skeptical, even defeatist attitude: words, words, words, promises, promises, promises — we had had them before, and we would have them again. But when could we expect the deed behind the words, and the fulfillment of the promise? When would there be action? Never, we thought. Never, or too late.

But I was listening to the voice now, and so was Lyle. The phrases of the oath were repeated firmly, resolutely. Then there was a pause, and after that the voice again:

President Hoover, Mr. Chief Justice, my friends:
This is a day of national consecration, and I am certain that my fellow Americans expect that on my induction into the Presidency I will address them with a candor and a decision which the present situation of our nation impels.

"Candor . . . decision." I was still watching Lyle, but his face was still averted. Well, we had heard those words before, too.

This is pre-eminently a time to speak the truth, the whole truth, frankly and boldly. Nor need we shrink from honestly facing conditions in our country today. This great nation will endure as it has endured, will revive and will prosper.

The voice was becoming stronger and clearer with each syllable. There was feeling in it, and courage, and faith. Or so it seemed to me.

So first of all let me assert my firm belief that the only thing we have to fear is fear itself — nameless, unreasoning, unjustified terror which paralyzes needed efforts to convert retreat into advance. . . .

Slowly Lyle turned toward me, and looked at me. And he kept looking at me. Listening, I forgot the presence of Ben and Natalie — forgot much else, too, certain habits of thought and incrustations of belief. Like Lyle, though not to his degree, I was of a generation which was inclined to be cynical of the well-turned phrase. I had considered myself to be immune from oratory. Yet as I sat there listening, this seemed to be something more than oratory. There was the plasma of conviction in it, and gradually that conviction was transferring itself to me, strengthening the spirit as blood strengthens the body.

I got up from the divan and went over to Lyle and stood beside him. And I stayed standing there with him during the remainder of the address, throughout the lashing of the "money-changers" — and his father had been one of them — and all the rest. I felt his hand reach out and take my hand. . . . The actual ceremony came later, but in a way I think we were married then, at that moment.

Finally it was over.

In this dedication of a nation we humbly ask the blessing of God. May He protect each and every one of us. May He guide me in the days to come.

There was an upswelling wave of applause, a thousand-throated yes, and after that Lyle reached for the switch and turned it off. For an instant no one spoke or stirred. Then Natalie leaned over the table to crush out the last glow from her still-smoldering cigarette.

"Well, I don't know," she said, slowly. "It sounds all right. In fact it sounds good." She glanced toward Ben, who had risen and was putting the bottles away. "What was it he called it during the campaign? What was the phrase?"

"New Deal," he said.

New Deal, I thought. Well, we needed one.

She brushed her hands together briskly, as if to break a spell in which she, along with all of us, had been held, willingly or not. "So that's that," she said, heading toward the kitchen. "Now he goes to work and so do I. Each to his trade. He to the job of saving a nation and me to my canapés." She paused in the doorway, rolling up her sleeves, and looked at Lyle. "How about it now? Is this party going to celebrate the fact that you got married or the fact that you didn't?"

He waited a moment before speaking, and when he did he indicated me with a nod. "Ask her."

I hesitated, though not for long. "The fact that we did," I said. And then I turned to him, questioningly. After all, although we had both heard the same words, they might not have had the same effect. And in any case, how long would such an effect be likely to last? "Am I right?"

Again he waited. His eyes wandered toward the radio, the oracle that had spoken and now had ceased to speak. Then at last he seemed to make up his mind. He even smiled a little. "All right," he said. "We'll try it. We'll try each other — and him, too. We'll see what happens."

So we were married at four o'clock that afternoon among the potted palms of the Municipal Building's wedding chapel, kept open late by special prearrangement because Lyle had once covered City Hall for two months for the *World* and knew the magistrate, with Ben acting as Lyle's witness and Natalie as mine. I wore the suit with the monkey fur and had a corsage of gardenias (the last of Lyle's four dollars) pinned at my shoulder. Lyle's mother was present too, very sober — she more or less made up for it later, at the party — and very quiet, standing with her gloved hands clasped together and never taking her eyes off us during the whole ceremony. She had blue hair, the first blue hair I had ever seen on anybody, and afterward she kissed me and said, "Good luck, Amy. The best. I think things are going to be all right with you."

"I'm sure they are, Mrs. Ellery," I said. "We'll be fine." And I linked my arm more tightly through Lyle's, hugging it. "Won't we?"

"We hope we will," he said, smiling. "We'd better be."

It was a nice wedding. Nobody cried.

And after that there was the party: "reception" would have been a little too formal a word for it. I don't remember it too clearly, for there was such a crowd — upward of thirty people jammed in that small room and overflowing into the bedroom — and they all seemed to be laughing and talking at once. Yet bits and pieces come back to me as vividly as if it were yesterday. Some I taste and touch, and some I see and hear. The sweetish chill of the gin-and-grapefruit-juice cocktails, pinkened with grenadine and served in all sizes of glasses. The universal talk about money — how much were you caught with, which was your bank, do you think it'll reopen, do you think they'll issue scrip? Somebody coming in with a dark, pale, sad-looking Jewish girl, a stranger, and introducing her to me and then taking me aside and saying, "Be nice to her. She's a refugee." And my saying, "What do you mean? A refugee from what?" because it was the first time I had ever heard the word used in that sense. "From Germany," he said, whoever it was. "From the Nazis. From Hitler. They're having a national election over there too, you know. Tomorrow, in fact. Don't you ever read the papers?"

Yes, out of that blurred, dim room of that day and that hour fragments return which I can reassemble and thus, though never fully or wholly, re-create what is now gone. Fragments of music — a close-harmony quartette gathering in a corner and singing old songs which were admittedly classics then and new ones like "Night and Day" which have since become so. Fragments of faces — the rubber-aproned, olive-skinned, liquid-eyed, ten-year-old Tony, the iceman's son, lugging in his tongs with a fresh block of ice on them. (Tony would be twenty-two now. I wonder where he is, or if he is.) Fragments of talk, the talk of the town and the times — Mae West and the new silhouette, the forthcoming Century of Progress at Chicago, *The Good Earth,* would there be legal beer and if so when, would skirts go higher and if so how much. Brother, can you spare a dime? Sister, have you got a job?

And the people, those I liked and those I loved, those I sometimes still see and those I shall never see again. Mr. Kendrick discussing the increasing mortality among the magazines and still yearning wistfully for the days when he had worn a "Keep Cool with Coolidge" button. Ben gesturing with his pipe and becoming loquacious concerning the merits of Heywood Broun. Natalie moving about with the giant-sized pewter cocktail shaker, pushing her way toward the kitchen to get a new supply of canapés, greeting incoming guests, speeding outgoing ones. Mrs. Ellery growing progressively shriller and aggressively gayer, with her lipstick smudged and her mascara running a little and her blue hair like a blue night-light beacon in the haze of cigarette smoke. . . . Poor thing, I thought. Poor thing.

We left early, while the party was at its peak, going not to the Delaware Water Gap by car but uptown to the new apartment in Tudor City by subway — the Seventh Avenue I.R.T. to Times Square, the shuttle over to Grand Central, the tramping thud of hurrying feet on the wooden planks leading out, and then Forty-second Street and the walk eastward, past the shoeshine parlors and all-night lunchrooms and the signs saying "Lofts for Rent" and under the clangor of the two El trestles. Nobody had thrown rice, nobody had thrown old shoes, and as we sat there on the straw seats gazing up at the placards I doubt if anyone had recognized us as newlyweds, although my gardenias, already turning brown at the edges, might have hinted something. The suitcase at Lyle's feet contained blankets, sheets, pillowcases, and towels — a practical trousseau and possibly one well fitted to the times.

We had chosen Tudor City because of its location, which was near my office, and because we both had agreed that we had served our Village apprenticeship. Yet now that we were there and now that its dark bulk loomed over us, I began to wonder if its oak-beamed lobbies and uniformed attendants might not be perhaps a little grand and, for us, pretentious. Somehow the cluttered intimacy of MacDougal Street had seemed more friendly. Still, I reasoned, the rent here was only slightly more. We would merely have a little less space, that's all.

The ruddy-cheeked doorman didn't know us at first, but when Lyle said, "Our name is Ellery. We were moving into 6–C next week, but we've changed our plans and would like to move in now," he went and got the key and gave it to him.

"Thanks very much," Lyle said, and started to reach for his pocket and then stopped. "I'll be seeing you around. I'm a little short on change right now."

Smiling, the doorman touched the vizor of his cap, and the common bond of catastrophe gave us more courtesy than we could ever have bought for a quarter. "Yes, sir, Mr. Ellery. I guess we all know how it is today."

We stood together in silence as the elevator ascended. Although the people in the subway might not have known we were newlyweds, the towheaded, pimply-faced operator did. The very back of his neck was coy and smirking. But when Lyle lifted a shoe and pantomimed, "Shall I boot him one?" I shook my head and signaled, "Later, maybe."

The elevator halted, the operator slid the door back, we stepped out into the hall and started down it, hearing the gate slide shut again after a reasonably brief period during which the towhead no doubt stared speculatively at our retreating backs. Our footsteps tapped along the long, straight hall, turn right, go past the incinerator closet, stop.

At the door, Lyle put the key into the lock and turned it. He opened the door, pushing it a little, and made an ushering gesture for me to precede him.

"Well, here you are," he said.

I looked at him, not moving. "Isn't there some sort of little tradition?" I said. "Or are you above that sort of thing?"

He hesitated, and for an instant he seemed a little embarrassed, even shy, and much younger than his years.

"O.K.," he said. "Why not?" And he reached over and lifted me into his arms and carried me across the threshold, flicking the light switch on as he passed it.

He carried me to the center of the room and put me down. There was only one room, with kitchenette and bath and dressing room, and because the on-installments furniture was to have been delivered while we were away on our trip it was completely bare and empty save for two brown-paper-wrapped mattresses leaning against the wall. The single bulb in the ceiling fixture cast a strong, hard, white

31

light on the newspaper-strewn floor and the yellow walls, and the smell of fresh paint made my eyes water. Going to the casement windows, I opened one of them, letting in cold night air. By craning my neck, I could get a five-inch-wide glimpse of the East River.

"Look, Lyle," I said. "Look at the lights."

He joined me at the window, and we stood gazing out. A lighted tug was moving slowly up the river through the darkness. In the distance I could hear the faint toot of a barge whistle.

He circled his arm about my waist. "Are you happy?" he said.

I nodded, wanting to say "Yes" but not trusting myself to speak. Then I finally did. "You?"

He nodded also. "Yes. Yes, I think so."

Still with his arm around me, I turned and looked at the empty room, seeing it not as it was but as it would be, with the furniture we had picked out together and the pictures and the draperies. This was better than a Village walk-up, I decided, much better. Cleaner, more modern, more settled and substantial. A place for married people.

"It's going to be awfully nice," I said. "It's going to be a—a real home."

He smiled. "That's right." And then he bent and kissed me.

"I love you so much," I whispered.

"Darling. Amy . . ."

His arm tightened around me—the other arm, too. His lips were warm, and young, and sweet. Then he turned toward the double doors set in the north wall, his heels clicking across the bare floor. The night breeze touched one of the spread-out newspapers, and it drifted a little, rustlingly, and then was quiet.

"Come on," he said. "Let's go to bed."

He opened the doors and pulled down the beds, first one and then the other. Their springs made a twanging sound of vibration, and the vibration echoed thinly and then faded away.

After that he crossed toward the opposite wall and began to rip the twine and tear the paper from the mattresses.

"Well, one thing," he said. "We're starting from scratch. It's a New Deal for us, too."

I knelt at the suitcase, taking out the sheets and the blankets. As my hand reached toward them I noticed the unaccustomed ring on my finger — shining, new, symbol of so much that was past and so much more that was to come.

All that was so long ago. . . . Twelve years.

⟶⟩⟩⟩ II ⟨⟨⟵

Aʟʟ ᴛʜɪs ɪs ꜰʀᴏᴍ ᴍᴇᴍᴏʀʏ, ᴀɴᴅ ɪᴛ comes in waves, like surf, as I stand on the shore of the present with the past surging toward me. Some of the waves are days and some are years and some are merely minutes. Some boom against the shore while others only lap gently, but whether they crash or creep, each brings with it the accumulated sediment of time — a face forgotten, a name, a place. Here on the beach of now, gazing out at the tides of then, I try to assort the important from the unimportant and the significant from the trivial, as if they were shells or pebbles or a spar from some ship long since foundered. Yet I know that such an assessment is of no use, no point, because to me all of it is important, even though much of it might not have seemed to be so at the time.

The Hundred Days, for instance. I never thought of them as being of any particular consequence, certainly not as a period when the whole economic fabric of the country was being unraveled and rewoven. In fact I didn't think of them as "the Hundred Days" at all, for that was a phrase which history bequeathed on them long after they had ended. To me, at the time, they were just spring. There were an AAA and a CCC and an embargo on gold and a law against hoarding it, but such phenomena were less memorable than the sight of tulips blooming in the tiny patch of garden below our windows and sparrows hopping along the ledge to peck at the crumbs I placed there. Those were the really notable things, those and the way the room looked in the morning with the sun slanting through the Venetian blinds and the way it looked in the evening in the soft pink glow of the alabaster lamps that Mr. Kendrick gave us.

"There never was a spring like this one," I remember saying to Lyle. And I don't suppose there ever was.

Mr. Kendrick had not only given us the lamps but, what was even more welcome, he had given Lyle a job. Yes, at last the hateful blackness of that brush salesman's kit had disappeared, and we now rose together and went to the same office in the Graybar Building together, Mr. and Mrs. Lyle Vincent Ellery, Apt. 6–C, Woodstock Tower, Tudor City, who had every right by the laws of both God and man to be seen emerging side by side from the same door at eight forty-five each morning. I supposed that I would get used to it and that the time might even come when I would accept it as a normal, humdrum, everyday occurrence, but meanwhile — well, meanwhile . . .

The job Lyle got was something of an anticlimax, at least to him. Beer was back and Repeal was on the way, and in order to stimulate advertisers Mr. Kendrick had decided to inaugurate a wine-and-food department and Lyle was writing it. "Mr. Brillat-Savarin, Jr." was the way he referred to himself, sardonically. "The boy gastronomist. How to Get Plastered According to Form, or Recipes My Mother Taught Me." He was sardonic because although the job was certainly better than brushes, he was well aware that Mr. Kendrick had given it to him for my sake rather than his, and furthermore he had hoped to land something better than a column tucked away in the advertising section of a fashion magazine, even though it was a very glossy fashion magazine. "I thought maybe this would prove to be a leg up on something else," he said, disgruntled, "but I don't know. 'Lucius Beebe,' he keeps telling me. 'I want you to do what this fellow Lucius Beebe's doing.' Now is that a future to look forward to? I ask you."

"Just try it," I said, attempting to comfort him. "Just try it for a while, anyway. We'll see."

And he was trying it.

Mr. Kendrick stood in the doorway that separated the reception room from his office. He was a self-made man, Mr. Kendrick, and a

35

good one, who had started as copy boy almost forty years ago when the magazine itself had started and now was president of the board and a major stockholder. He had taught me much during the years I had been his secretary, and he was kind to me, and generous, and I liked him.

"Well," he said now, "and how's the bride coming along? How's married life?"

"Just fine, Mr. Kendrick," I said. "Just fine."

"He hasn't started beating you yet, has he?"

"Not yet," I said, smiling back at him. "We've sparred around a little, but there hasn't been any decision. And I think I can hold my own all right."

"That's good." He came toward the desk and leaned against it. We often had these little chats — "breathers," he called them. I would ask him about his wife and her Westchester gardening club, and his golf and his bridge, and he would ask me about the Village, which he still regarded as a spicily Bohemian and interestingly off-color neighborhood. In fact I think he had been somewhat disappointed when I had moved uptown, for until then I had provided a vicarious glamour.

"Lyle's not very happy here, is he?"

"Oh, but he is," I assured him hastily, lying. "He loves it." I hesitated, nervously. "Why? Isn't he satisfactory?"

"Enough." He took out a cigar, bit off the end, and began to chew on it. "But he seems to consider himself too good for what he's doing."

And so he is, I thought. But all I said was, "Well, naturally he's — ambitious."

"Hm!" He grunted. "Maybe his friend Roosevelt that he voted for can do something better for him." In a random and ill-advised moment I had chanced to remark that Lyle had voted for Roosevelt, and he had never forgiven it. He was still chewing on the cigar. "Thought they were going to put 'em all to work, fix everybody up. Looks to me as if they've forgotten their Forgotten Man pretty quickly."

"Oh," I said, "I don't suppose we should expect a miracle."

"Why not? A miracle was what they promised, wasn't it? And where is it? Here we are almost in the middle of June, and unemployment's still going up."

"But they have accomplished quite a lot," I said, earnestly. "I mean, look at the banks — they're open again, and we've still got our money. And those dams and reforestation things they've started are steps ahead. At least they seem to be." I didn't linger long on that, for I was very vague about them.

The cigar was being lighted and sucked at furiously. "What's a dam that won't be finished for five years and will still be two thousand miles away when it is, have to do with you and Lyle right here and now?"

I didn't try to answer that one. And I found myself wishing he would go away.

"What this country needs," he continued, "is a practical businessman to run it. And that's certainly what we haven't got."

I smiled, and groped for the light touch. "At least we have beer now." I knew he liked his beer. "And we didn't even use to have that."

"Beer," he said scornfully, with a gesture of disdain. "They ask for bread, and he gives 'em beer."

"It's better than a stone, isn't it? And if Hoover could try to comfort them with apples, I don't see why — "

He shook his head, sighing, and I realized that he hadn't even heard me, which was probably just as well. "I don't know," he said. "I've been willing to give him a chance. I've played along with him, just the way Congress has. All right, I've said to myself, he's got a lot of programs, a lot of projects — let's try 'em, let's see what happens. But *nothing's* happening. After all that legislative hoorah and all that alphabetical abracadabra, we're still just where we were." He turned and went in toward his office. "I'm getting pretty fed up with it, I can tell you that. The honeymoon's over, and people won't wait forever. They get tired."

And at the door he paused. "Oh, and you might tell Lyle that if he doesn't want to handle that Connoisseur's Column, there are plenty of others who do."

"Yes, sir." I knew that he was being serious, and so I used the "sir" to prove it to him.

"You're a nice girl, Amy," he said, "and the best secretary a man ever had. But why you had to go and pick out that particular . . ." And then he was gone.

I fingered the keyboard of my typewriter, and watched him as he disappeared. I wasn't thinking particularly of what he had said about Lyle and the column. I would fix that up, or at least I would try. What I was thinking of was that word "honeymoon" he had used. Honeymoon? Whose honeymoon? And then I thought again. Nothing was happening, he had said. But that wasn't true. Lyle had a job, and we were married. Wasn't that enough? After that I started to type, industriously. . . . Somewhere down the hall someone was humming a song which was heard constantly then, blared from radios and whistled pipingly in the streets. "Who's Afraid of the Big Bad Wolf?" asked the song. And who was, who was?

So the summer began, that Blue Eagle summer of the NRA.

Ben had a new job, too, and one night we sat with him and Natalie celebrating it in a restaurant in Yorkville, which was undergoing a renaissance that spring and summer. Oh, those rollicking evenings amid the ornate steins, with the hairy-legged waiters in their velvet shorts and embroidered suspenders and those sweet Bavarian hats with the feathers in them, and with the rolled-down chart that had the little drawings on it — "*Ist das eine Schnitzelbank?*" and the answering roar, "*Ja, das ist die Schnitzelbank!*" — and that atmosphere so gay and so German.

"It's so different up here," I said. "It's like a little world all its own, another country."

"*Gemütlich,* that's what it is," said Ben, who with his pipe and tall stein was trying to appear like somebody out of *The Student Prince.* His head moved from side to side, to the brassy bray of a Viennese waltz, and his brown eyes were soft with nostalgia. Ben's name was Liebermann, and he was both German and Jew, but mostly he was West End Avenue, the Ethical Culture School, and Columbia University. "Ah, this Hitler. This — this clown. At least I hope he's a clown. Now when I was at Heidelberg . . ."

Good old *gemütlich*.

Ben was enthusiastic about his job, not only because it was taking him to Washington but also because he felt it to be the gate to wider and more fertile fields. "It isn't that I haven't been happy at N.Y.U.," he said. "But — well, as a Columbia man my heart's never really been in it. Now everything will be different, though. I mean, with men like Ray Moley and Rex Tugwell and Berle, it'll be kind of old-home week — and also quite an opportunity."

"Our Ben," said Natalie, gazing at him with a studied fondness. "Our Ben in the Brains Trust. Imagine."

"Just what are you going to do down there, Ben?" asked Lyle.

He was shrewdly silent for a moment. "Mm, lots of things. I can't very well go into them now, of course, but we'll be pretty busy, I can guarantee you that."

Natalie lifted her stein, and sipped. "They're going to take a map of the United States and divide it into little squares," she said. "Every square will represent so many million population, and then they'll just sort of shove them around and see what happens. It's going to be terribly amusing. Like chess, only with people."

Ignoring her, Ben turned to Lyle. He was serious, earnest, and there was a subcurrent of excitement in him. "You know me, Lyle," he said. "You know how I felt about Roosevelt. As Governor he wasn't anything, this or that, black or white — just namby-pamby. But I've changed my mind about him. He's going to be all right."

"Meaning all left," interpreted Natalie, again. There was something more being needled here than just the beer, I decided, and I wondered why.

"It's extremely stupid to attach importance to labels, my dear," he said, annoyed and impatient. He went on with expanding fervor, addressing Lyle. "The point is that at last we've got somebody who's willing to make changes. Yes, radical changes, if you like — though by 'radical' I'm certainly not trying to scare you. Still, I think that with the proper nudging we can lead him the way we want to go."

"Who is 'we'?" said Lyle, with a bland innocence which should have been sufficient warning in itself. "And which way do we want to go?"

39

Ben eyed him with sharp suspicion. "But you know, don't you?" he said, in surprise. "After all, you wanted a New Deal, too."

Lyle nodded, half serious and half amused. I knew what he was doing. He was engaging in that parlor pastime which we always called "Ben-baiting." I had seen him do it often before, and I had sometimes done it myself, and of course Natalie did it constantly, though usually with more good humor and less venom than she was displaying tonight. Yet now, as he spoke, there was an inner core of content which was revealing itself for the first time; or at least it was the first time I had happened to notice it. It was — well, it was a little curious, that was all. Strange. Not because of its political aspects — I had no opinions on those, and neither did he, really — but because of something else.

"A New Deal, yes," he said. "Sure I wanted one, and I still do, though I haven't got it yet. But presumably it'll be with the same old cards, won't it? That's what I'm counting on, anyway." He smiled, pleasantly. "And I'm afraid I don't necessarily want it for a hundred million people I've never even seen. I want it for me, Ben. For yours truly, the undersigned."

Nobody said anything. He glanced around the table, lifted his stein, and then turned toward me. "Do I seem coarse? Possibly crass?"

I edged a little closer to him. "Of course not. Just sensible and both-feet-on-the-ground, which is the way you should be." And then I added lightly, to remind him, "But you want all that for me too, don't you?"

"Oh, naturally." He was quick, very quick. "I meant you too. That goes without saying. *Cela va sans dire.*"

Ben was looking at him contemptuously, dismayed and disappointed. "But you of all people. After what happened to your father — ?"

Lyle stiffened. "My father is my business, not yours." His voice was tight. "He had no luck, and he was in a gambler's game. Wall Street. What can you expect of Wall Street? It could have happened to anybody."

Ben stuffed and prodded at his pipe. His face was the face of a man betrayed. "I see," he said. "It's a bit different, now that you've got a job, isn't it?"

"I hope so. Not that what I've got at present is a job. It's not even a living. Not a real living."

Natalie was lighting a cigarette, and although her words were for Ben she wasn't looking at him. "Just for a handful of silver they'll leave you," she said. "And don't ever think they won't."

Ben was silent. Then, with an eloquent lift of his eyebrows, he took off his glasses and began to polish them. For him the episode was over. "Well," he said, "no matter how you may feel about it, we're on our way. Give us five years. You won't recognize this country."

"I'll bet," said Natalie, into her beer.

They talked on, and I sat looking at Natalie across the table. There was something in my mind which I didn't want to think about. So I didn't think about it. Instead, I leaned toward her.

"Lyle will be away for a while this summer, too," I said. "He has to go out to Chicago, to this Century of Progress thing. So we'll both be widows. We'll have to be mutually consoling. Tatting doilies with each other, and things like that."

Her eyes wandered to the ring on my finger. "You'll be a widow," she corrected. "And you'll have papers to prove it." She glanced down at her empty stein, and flipped its metal lid shut. "I'll just be . . ." And then she looked up, and added defensively, "But mind you, I'm not complaining. In view of everything."

Then she went on, as if to forestall any words of sympathy. "We're a fine pair, you and I. Ladies with no luck. I have a man who never thinks about anything except coal miners in Harlan County and jute pickers in Czechoslovakia, and you've got one who never thinks about anything except himself."

I looked away. "He thinks about me," I said quietly.

"Does he?" she said. "Does he?"

I ignored that, and I offered no rebuttal because it so happened that at the moment I could think of none. Anyway, I preferred to center the conversation on her, not on me — and not on Lyle. I put my hand out across the table, toward hers. "I didn't know," I said.

"You've always been so — gay about it. I had no idea that . . ." And then, because she showed no inclination to accept my hand, I withdrew it. "If that's the way you feel, why don't you marry him?"

She shrugged. "For a very peculiar and no doubt fascinating reason. You see, he's never asked me."

That night as we moved about the apartment, preparing for bed — a complicated series of maneuvers involving alternate exits and entrances into dressing room and bath, but one which by now had come to be timed to a split-second exactness — Lyle's thoughts were still of Ben. He supposed that Ben was thoroughly disillusioned with him now, he said, but the fact was that he couldn't sit by and listen to those impractical and crackpot notions any longer. So he finally had had to tell him where to get off, and he had told him.

I turned back the coverlet on his bed, which he had already pulled down from its niche in the wall, and then on mine. Where Ben got off? I was thinking. Ben and who else? Or had I ever been on?

"Don't you agree?" he said, coming out of the dressing room and going toward the light switch.

"Of course I do. You know that."

He glanced at me. "What's the matter?"

"Nothing. Nothing at all."

The room was dark. I heard him settle down into his bed. I heard him sigh. And I lay there, thinking.

"Ho-hum," he said, yawning. "Another day, another dollar — and it is just about a dollar, too." He pummeled his pillow. "I wish I could wake up tomorrow morning and be something besides the Connoisseur. I'm getting mighty fed up on being the Connoisseur. I have immortal longings in me."

It seemed like a convenient opening, one which might possibly lead me toward where I wanted to get, so I took advantage of it.

"For what?" I said.

Again he yawned. "Oh, for a lot of things I haven't got."

There it is once more, I thought. Always the "I." Never the "we." Merely a trick of speech, of course, and probably I was overemphasizing its importance. Certainly I had never been conscious of it before. It must be a sudden self-hypnosis on my part, I decided. You

42

walk along a certain street for years and never notice the pattern of the pavement on the sidewalk, and then one day — and from then on — you find yourself unable to see anything except that pattern. You look at the palm of your hand for a lifetime and never happen to discover a certain crease there, and then suddenly the crease is everywhere.

And yet, and yet . . .

"You know," I said, and I said it with an elaborate casualness, for although it was only a part of what I wanted to say it was at least a start, even if a circuitous one, "maybe you ought to try to pretend to be a little more enthusiastic about your job. Mr. Kendrick — well, he spoke to me about it."

"Mr. Kendrick," he announced, from the muffled depths of his pillow, "is a four-star drip."

"Possibly. Yes. But that's not the point, is it?"

"What is the point? If any."

"Well, you're not contented. And I want you to be."

"Why? Contentment is for dopes, and dead people. I'm neither. I hope." He shifted, restlessly. "Don't you see? I'm just a hack now. But if I had an idea, just one good, eighteen-carat idea, I could be off to the races." He was lying on his back now, and in the shadowy gloom of the room I could see that he was gazing up at the ceiling. "Ford had his Ford and Edison had a light bulb, and Henry Luce had *Time*. And all so young. But what have I got? Nothing."

Me, my darling, I wanted to tell him, but didn't. Me, that's what you've got. Must I shout it? Must I spell it out?

I too lay gazing up at the ceiling, and began to count the bars in the diagram of stripes made by the upcast shadow of the Venetian blinds. Now is the time, I decided. You've waited a long while, and now is the time to say it and find out what the answer is, one way or another. So I said it. But I didn't look across at him, because I didn't dare.

"Lyle," I said, "don't you think it might be nice if we had a baby?"

A silence. Then: "Sure, I guess so. Sometime. Most people do."

"I mean now. Soon." I had it all very neatly worked out in my mind, and to me it seemed as simple and solvable as a problem in higher mathematics — human calculus. One plus one obviously hadn't succeeded in forming a united and cohesive one, but one plus one plus another one might. . . . I know now that it was a romantic and adolescent conception, but I didn't know it then. I know a lot of things now that I didn't know then.

"A baby here?" he said. "In a one-room apartment? Where would we keep it — in the Frigidaire?"

"We could manage, couldn't we? And we won't always be living in a one-room apartment."

"We will unless I start to get going somehow."

Out of the corner of my eye I saw him turn over, drawing the sheet with him so that it shone pale against his rounded shoulder. His tone was kinder than his words. He was merely making a statement of indisputable fact, that was all. Elementary, my dear Amy. Elementary.

"Seems to me I've got enough to worry about without a baby," he said.

I, and I, and I . . . oh, please, I thought, isn't there any plural form in your grammar? Didn't you ever learn it? Suddenly I realized that my hands were clenched, and I forced them to unclench and relax. I lay very still. This was all very silly, I told myself. I was developing a monomania, that's what I was developing.

"It's an idea, though," he said, and yawned for the third time, yawned mightily. His voice was becoming drowsy. "I'll keep it in mind. And if you have any other bright notions, let me know, will you? I need one. I could use it. Oh, boy, could I use it. Oh, boy, and how. . . ."

So he slept, and later on I slept. But our dreams, if we had any, were different. Maybe they had always been different.

It was a summer of parades and banners, with white-garbed marchers trudging up the soft asphalt of Fifth Avenue beneath flags which bore the Blue Eagle emblem and its slogan "We Do Our Share." Why did they march, and what was our share, and what did marching have to do with it? I wasn't sure. Perhaps some of them weren't sure, either. ("NRA, hm!" snorted Mr. Kendrick.

44

"Well, I suppose it's no worse than a bad code.") But they marched nevertheless. And the months were marching, too. It was August now and Lyle was in Chicago, and while he was gone I depended chiefly on Natalie for companionship and now and then on Mrs. Ellery, whom I began to see fairly frequently, sometimes at our place, sometimes at hers. She had a small, frowzy apartment in the West Seventies, near Riverside Drive, and she was living on an insurance policy which Lyle's father had left and which was one of the few things his creditors hadn't been able to get away from her. It was a furnished apartment, and classically dreary, but here and there were relics of the past, the Good Old Days: a single, simple chair, a mahogany chest of great luster and great age, a silver tray from eighteenth-century England sitting inharmoniously on a much-whorled cocktail table from twentieth-century Ludwig Baumann. "I'm always promising myself that some day I'll tidy this place up," she said, looking at the dusty billows of overstuffed velours. "But after all, I'm out so much."

Yet she herself was always immaculately and studiedly *"soignée,"* a word she applied to others as the greatest of tributes. She even made a practice of sitting in her own living room with her hat on, though whether that was intended as an evidence of chic — she was the first person I ever heard use the phrase "chi-chi," and with one exception she herself was more chi-chi than anyone I have ever met — or because she wanted to be ready and on-her-mark if the telephone should ring, I don't know. She was out much, as she said, and there were few midtown speakeasies of the better sort with whose bartenders she was not on terms of an intimate and long-standing acquaintanceship. She went out with women and she went out with men, more or less. I met some of the latter, and they were very witty and amusing, if somewhat maliciously so. Most were young, several were handsome, and all were extremely well-dressed in a suède-shoe, tab-collar fashion. They were prone to gay shrieks, private jokes, and mysterious exclamations of "Get *him!*" and they referred to her as "Evie-Pie," though her name was Eva. But "Eva" didn't come naturally to me, and I already had a use for "Mother," so I always called her "Mrs. Ellery."

"Who are they all?" I asked her once. "They're very entertaining, but what do they do? For a living, I mean."

"Oh, various things," she said. "Bobbie's a salesman at De Pinna's, and Billy's in the chorus of *Blossom Time,* usually, and Glen has some sort of job in a gallery on Fifty-seventh Street. They're all nice boys. They're harmless."

"I'm sure of that."

She glanced at me quickly. "That sounds like Lyle," she said. "Don't be intolerant, dear. Or superior. Remember, you won't always be young and you may not always — have what you have now."

"I'm sorry," I said. And I was. It was her life, not mine — and she was of an age where she was perfectly capable of deciding how she wanted to live it.

I remember one evening in particular, because it was Lyle's birthday, the twenty-second of August. She had phoned me at the office, asking me to come to dinner. "I'll get in some cold cuts and things," she had said, "and we'll have them here in the apartment, just the two of us. We'll be very sentimental, and I'll show you Lyle's baby shoes. I'll be a real mother-in-law — if you can bear it."

"I think I can bear it," I said. "I think I'd like it."

The day turned out to be hideously sultry and muggy, but when she met me at the door she looked fresh and lettuce-crisp in a flowered print that was a little more on the formal side than my own rather wilted white piqué. The cracked green shades in the living room were drawn against the still-hot sun, and a small electric fan had been placed on the floor in a position where it would do the most good. The place certainly wasn't what would be called cool, but she had done what she could to make it so. And somehow it looked neater and cleaner — spruced-up, as if it bore an invisible sign saying, "Don't Touch. Guest Expected." There was even a tall spray of gladioli in a vase in a corner.

I went with her to the frayed-linoleumed kitchen and stood there while she busied herself with ice and ginger ale and gin. On a shelf was a tray stacked with gleaming white gold-banded plates, silverware, and a folded damask cloth and napkins, and beside the plate stood her "cold cuts" — a chicken in aspic, beautifully molded.

46

"But this looks divine," I said. "You don't mean to tell me you made it yourself?"

"Oh, but I was a housewife once," she said, replacing an ice tray in the refrigerator. "A long time ago."

I fingered the heavy brocade of the napkins and touched one of the plates. "And such wonderful china."

She had gathered up the two drinks and now turned to head back into the living room. "Just some things I had," she said. "I seldom get them out any more." She extended one of the glasses. "Here you are. Let's go in, shall we?"

She was so nice that evening, at first. She looked distinguished, her blue hair done in an expensively simple style, and she was somehow more composed than I had ever seen her. She was — well, she was a lady, and watching her I understood what Lyle had meant when he had said, "You wouldn't have recognized her then. She was happy."

We talked — the usual comments on the weather — and then, getting up my courage, I said, "Tell me about Lyle. I mean, about when he was little."

She smiled at me. "You really do want me to be the mother-in-law, don't you?"

I nodded. "Yes," I said. "I do."

Reaching for her handkerchief, she slowly wiped the pebbled moisture from her glass. "Actually, there isn't much to tell. You see, until Mr. Ellery made his money and — lost it, it was all so . . . average. And it was so long ago, and I've forgotten most of it, and . . ."

But there was a lot to tell, and she told it, and it was evident that she hadn't forgotten any of it. They had lived in Essex County, in New Jersey — first East Orange, where Lyle had been born, and after that Montclair — and for a while there, sitting opposite her in that stuffy room, I lived with them. I suppose it was what she said it was — "average." But that didn't lessen its interest for me. She wasn't being "chi-chi" any more now: just easy and natural and in her own way wonderful. Lyle's baby illnesses, his first report card and the extraordinary but indeed flattering comment which the teacher had

47

written on it, the first girl he had ever had a crush on ("Her name was Veronica, and she was very pretty, in her fashion," she said, and I've hated the name "Veronica" ever since), his years at prep school and at Harvard — she retraced them all, even to his Commencement Day when she had watched him ascend the platform, tall in his black gown and with his mortarboard on a little crooked so that its tassel kept brushing his face. . . .

"Did he have any little — peculiarities? Idiosyncrasies?"

She looked at me. "Why?"

"Oh, I just wondered."

She hesitated. "A few, perhaps." She was silent, thinking. "Yes, he could be difficult."

"Oh." And he still could. Then: "Have you any photographs? An album, maybe?"

Her glass had been empty for a long time. She revolved it between her palms, and looked down into it. "No," she said. "No photographs. No album." And then she rose, reaching for my glass. "Let's have another — hm? After all, it's Lyle's birthday and we haven't even toasted him."

"Surely," I said, and thought, "Well, it'll be all right, really."

She headed toward the kitchen. "I shouldn't have gone on like that. I never do. I suppose it's what Bobbie calls 'total recall,' and a sign of senility. But you asked for it, you know."

"I know. And I want more."

"Very well. You shall have more."

I heard her in the kitchen, the tinkle of bottle against glass, the rattle of ice cubes. . . .

Well, I got more — but it was drinks mostly, left untouched on the table by my elbow, drinks warming and their bubbles dying. The transformation was like the snapping of a magician's finger: now she was herself, and now she wasn't. Or I don't know, which was herself? The one who had greeted me when I came in, or the one who now dabbed at the flowered print where she had spilled her glass and said in a slurred voice and with an increasingly unsteady gesture, "This is the best part of the day, I always think. Don't you?

The cocktail hour, I mean. So — you know, relaxing. It sort of takes you out of yourself, I always think."

"Don't you suppose perhaps we ought to eat?" I asked. "All those nice things out there . . ."

"Oh, later," she said airily, expansively. "Plenty of time for that. And they can't very well get cold, you know," she giggled, "because they already *are* cold."

We sat on. The sunlight faded behind the green shades, and for an interval the room was filled with a kind of aqueous light, neither day nor night. The city summer twilight, hot and humid and murmurous with street noises. Upstairs, a baby whimpered. On the other side of the wall there was the repeated click of poker chips being tossed onto a table. In an apartment across the court a radio was playing: "*I — got — rhy-thum. I — got — sweet-dreams.*" She tapped her white-shod foot, small, well-shaped, and slim-ankled. "Let's call up the boys, shall we?" she said. "Billy or Glen or somebody. We might go out to dance."

"Oh, I think I'd rather we just sat here and talked," I said. "And had dinner. If you don't mind."

"Oh, I don't mind," she said, docilely. "I don't mind at all."

So we talked, or rather she talked — wanderingly, with digressions and irrelevancies. There was no continuity to what she said. At one instant she would be in the recent present speaking about Lyle, and at the next in the faraway past speaking about her husband. It developed into a monologue on her part, a monologue interrupted only by her frequent excursions into the kitchen. Those finally ceased when she brought in the gin bottle and placed it on the floor beside her, without benefit of ginger ale.

"Vincent and I used to go to Pasadena in the winters," she said. "We'd stay, oh, for a month, maybe, and our rooms at the hotel overlooked a steep canyon, arroyo I think they called it. . . . When Lyle was little he brought me a hummingbird and he said, 'Look, Mother. It isn't really dead, it's only hurt,' and, well, I knew all along it was dead, but I just said, 'All right, dear. You go get a medicine dropper and we'll . . .' I had my own charge accounts, both at Arnold Con-

49

stable's and Bamberger's in Newark, and Vin always gave me a blank check the first of every month and he said, 'Now I don't want to know how much you spend, Eva. I probably couldn't bear it. So all you have to do is . . .' Our first car was a Studebaker, and it was a sight, it really was, a great, high-busted thing with brass trimmings and a bulgy rubber horn you squeezed. But Vin never really cared much about driving. He always said . . . I was working out in the garden when it happened. It was mid-November and I was putting burlap around the rose roots when Bonny, the upstairs girl, came running out, her face white as a sheet, and she said, 'Oh, Madam, you're wanted on the phone. It's about Mr. Ellery. Something awful has . . .' Twenty-nine years ago today it was, yes, twenty-nine years ago this very day. I didn't have him at a hospital. He was born at home. My grandfather's name had been Lyle, so we decided to . . . He planned to retire completely when he was fifty-five, and he would have been fifty-five in another three months. We were going to sell the Montclair place and just travel for a while — Europe and Hawaii and places like that. . . . So that first Christmas when Lyle came back from Lawrenceville we gave a dancing party for him. Some of the boys wore dinner jackets, but I said, 'Lyle, you're too young for a dinner jacket. Now you put on your blue serge and you'll look just as nice as any of them.' And he did. . . . When they brought him home, Lyle wouldn't even let me go in to see him. 'No,' he said. 'I don't want you to.' And I knew why. It was because all that was left of him was a pulp and a jelly. Vincent. My Vin. Just a pulp and a jelly. . . ."

She sat in silence, her body weaving. The room was dark now, full night. The radio across the court had stopped, and most of the other noises too, for it was late, and there was no sound except the whirr of the fan and its creak as it revolved jerkily — *squ-eek, squ-eeek*.

Suddenly she looked at me, her eyes straining through the dark, as if she were trying to focus not only on me but on a thought. "But you know, it's funny," she said. "All those years, and yet in a way he never really loved me at all. He kept himself to himself, always. 'I,' he always used to say, not 'we.' What is it they call it — ego?

Well, that's what he had. So much ego. Too much. And so when the crash came and he was wiped out, I wasn't enough for him. Nothing was enough for him, because he felt that he himself was nothing. And so he . . ." She let her words drift away, and then after a long pause she said, "Do you understand what I'm trying to say. Do you?"

"No." I repeated the word, almost defiantly. "No."

She lurched against the arm of her chair. "You do," she insisted. "You know you do, but you won't admit it. That's why you were asking about Lyle. Because Lyle is the same and I've always known he is the same and now you know it too. That's one reason I wanted you here tonight. I wanted to talk to you. I wanted to try to tell you —" Breaking off, she held her head between her hands and shook it wearily. "Oh, but I didn't mean to do it this way," she said. "Not this way." Then, struggling up from her chair, she came toward me, knocking over the gin bottle which lay in her path, though that didn't matter now because the bottle was empty. I felt her hand on my shoulder, the sagging weight of her whole body as she leaned downward. "There's an old saying about a dog. 'Never give your heart to a dog to — to —' What is it? 'Tear'?"

"Yes."

"You know it?"

"Yes."

"Well, it's true about men, too. Some men. And it's true about Lyle." She was kneeling on the floor beside me now, though I tried to stop her. "You're a nice girl, such a nice girl, so warm and so willing. Don't love him too much. Try to love him as little as you can, and still get along. Because you'll never get as much as you give, never in a million years. I know. I know . . ."

Then abruptly she sank back onto her heels, and it was all over. She sighed, and passed a vague hand over her forehead. After that she looked at the fan and for the first time seemed to become aware of its eternal *squ-eeek, squ-eeeek*. She looked at it for a long time.

"Needs oiling," she said at last, pursing her lips speculatively. "Must do that. Get Glen or the janitor or somebody. Remind me."

I undressed her and put her to bed in that bedroom which was

51

violently pink with ruched taffeta spread and baby pillows and lamps with dolls as their bases. When I started searching in the drawers of the dressing table to get her a nightgown I opened one from which the set, self-conscious faces in a group photograph stared up at me — herself, Lyle when he must have been about ten, wearing knickerbockers and a Norfolk jacket, and a mustached man whose dark eyes told me that he could only be Lyle's father. I lifted the picture and stood looking at it. Then as I was about to replace it I saw that underneath in the drawer there was a thick album and on it in gold leaf was stamped "Eva Ellery: Her Book." I ruffled its pages — snapshots of picnics, of Lyle on a pony, a colored postcard with "Yosemite, 1921" scrawled on it in a handwriting I had never seen. . . . I laid the picture back and closed the drawer

From the bed came the sound of a groan, a moan, and her voice calling faintly as she started to sink toward oblivion: "Amy. Amy, where are you?"

"I'm here."

"Don't ever tell Lyle about this. He'd be so ashamed. He's ashamed of me anyway. Promise me you won't ever tell him. Promise me . . ."

"I promise."

Then I went home.

When I got home there was a letter from Lyle waiting for me. He had been away for three weeks and would be gone for several more, and when he wrote it was on the wineglass-decorated letterhead of the Connoisseur's exhibit which he had been sent out to set up and manage.

Darkest Chicago
August 20, 1933

DARLING:

Well, my in-laws have come and gone, as per schedule. They claimed they came to see the Fair, but I have a hunch it was to size me up. I met them at the station and your mother announced that she would have recognized me anywhere. They're very nice, both of them, and you would have blushed to hear us talking about you. I blew them to dinner at the Blackstone and gave them a fling at the Fair, including Sally

52

Rand, of whom your mother most decidedly and most articulately did not approve. In fact your mother strikes me as being a pretty strict customer and I doubt if she and I would ever be what you'd call sympatico. However, she's a different type from my own sainted mother, certainly. Your father and I hit it off a little better, though I must admit that I did a double-take when I first saw that alpaca suit and that William Jennings Bryan collar and that black string tie. He's sort of cute though, at that — and he seemed to like Sally Rand just fine.

Oh, lest you forget, happy birthday to me. . . .

I had started to read the letter while seated on the sofa, without even taking off my hat. Now I let the pages flutter to the floor. I pressed my hands to my face and buried my head against the pillows. Darling, I thought, I need you, I want you, why don't you come back?

And then it was October and he was back, and I sat beside him in a taxi heading away from Grand Central, with his bags at our feet and my cheek on his shoulder. It was a Sunday morning, sparkling and sunny. "October," he said, his arm circled around me. "October. New York. It's wonderful." He inhaled deeply. "Smell it."

"That's just carbon monoxide, dear, and it's bad for you."

"It's nectar and ambrosia, after a summer in Chicago. Oooh, that Chicago. I died. The lake was right outside the building the exhibit was in, and you could have boiled an egg in it."

"Did you miss me?"

"Intermittently."

"Much?"

"Mm . . . Oh, God, did I miss you. Every day and every hour. Nights and noons and all the time."

Well, this was a change, and a welcome one.

"Darling — darling . . ."

Then:

"Darling — stop. The driver . . ."

"Stop? I've barely started. And the hell with the driver."

"But Lyle, really. Here in a public conveyance in broad day-light — "

"So what? Broad daylight — high noon in Macy's window — who cares? You're just an Eastern prude, that's all. I'm fresh from the great open spaces where men are men and are accustomed to proving it."

"I guess maybe you ought to go away oftener."

"I guess maybe I had. Absence, abstinence — whatever it is, it makes the heart grow fonder and its effect is remarkable, it really is. Something for the medical profession to take up and ponder. Drugstores would make a fortune if they could bottle it."

There was a buoyancy to him that he hadn't had when he went away. Something had happened to him out there. What had it been, I wondered, and I wondered it gratefully, for his presence dispelled so many thoughts I had been having, so many small doubts and secret misgivings. Did he love? Of course he loved, and his words and his warmth proved it. And then my gratitude became streaked with uneasiness as the thought suddenly occurred to me that instead of wondering "what" it had been which had changed him, I ought possibly to be wondering "who."

But I soon learned that I needn't have worried, even momentarily. For what had happened was that at last he had hit upon the idea — the Open Sesame, the magic wand, the lamp to be rubbed — for which he had so long been searching.

He told me about it as he unpacked, shuttling back and forth between dressing room and main room and the bags that lay between. "I'd like to be able to say that it came to me in a vision," he said, opening drawers and shutting them, "but it didn't. It came to me when I was prowling around the Art Museum out there one Sunday, bored stiff and with nothing to do. There was a special photographic exhibition on and I was standing there looking at it and all at once I said to myself, 'Well, here it is, you numskull. Here it is right under your nose. If it was a bear, it would bite you.'"

"What?" I said, sitting tense and expectant on the sofa. "Don't build it up so. What is it?"

He paused dramatically in the dressing-room doorway, his arms piled high with shirts and underwear. He was whoever it was who first struck tinder to fire at the instant of its striking, he was the

Curies announcing the discovery of radium, he was an unsilent, unstout, aggressive Cortez on a peak in Darien.

"A magazine," he said. "An entirely new kind of magazine." He waited, extracting the last ounce from my anticipation. "A picture magazine."

I looked at him blankly. "Y-yes?"

"But of course yes," he said impatiently, sweeping aside my uncertainty. He was in a ferment, the yeast of his inspiration having set and being ready to explode. "Don't you see? There's never been anything like it in this country. In Europe, yes — I've done some research and there's a thing called *Vu* in France and a couple of others in Germany. But there's none here." He was dumping the shirts into one of the drawers in his bureau. "And it'll go like a house afire. It's bound to. A magazine — a weekly, probably — filled with nothing except photographs and captions. All kinds of photographs, and maybe drawings and reproductions of paintings too. The news told visually instead of just through words. My God, it'll be a sensation!"

I began to understand now and to glimpse the possibilities, for his enthusiasm was contagious.

"Darling," I said, "it's — it's terrific. I'm awed. Really."

"Well, about time."

"And where do you come in?"

He was closing and locking the bags now and storing them away on a shelf in the closet.

"Me? I'm the editor."

"It'll take money, won't it?"

"You bet it will. Lots of it. It'll take it and make it. It's a bonanza, baby. Believe me."

I believed him. "But where will you get your backing?"

He was withdrawing a sheaf of papers from his briefcase. "Where else but from your pal Kendrick? He's a publisher, isn't he? Well, this is his chance not only to publish but to be a pioneer. He'll make more out of this than he's ever made out of his patterns and those high-style, slick-finish Paris Openings issues. And so, I may add, will I."

I rose and went toward him. He had settled himself in a chair and was beginning to square up the papers, balancing them on his knee. I sat on the chair's arm.

"I'm excited already," I said. "We're rich already. And you're famous."

"Mm." He smiled. "I can't wait to see Kendrick's face."

"When will you tell him? Tomorrow?"

"Oh, no." He was separating the papers into individual groups now — pages torn from magazines, photographs from rotogravure sections, scribbled designs on a yellow pad. "I've got a lot to do first. I'm going to paste up a sort of dummy and make it fancy — you know, what the advertising boys call a 'presentation.' It's going to take a little time, but it'll be worth it." He glanced up at me, still smiling. "Up until now I've just been your boss's secretary's husband, as far as he's concerned. But from here on in, you'll be my wife."

I placed my hand on his shoulder. What I wanted to say was, "And it's all I've ever wanted to be, too. You know that." But I didn't. That would have been sentimentality probably, certainly sentiment, and I always had to be cautious about that with him. Sometimes he was in a mood to assimilate it, sometimes he wasn't. And, as I had reason to know, those times when he wasn't could prove to be unfortunate for me, like a kick in the stomach or a slap in the face.

Gently I ran my hand across the back of his neck, stroking it. "It's funny," I said. "I knew something had happened to you the minute I met you there at the station. You were so assured and kind of — happy." I paused. It was a confession and I owed it to him, but it wasn't easy making it. "I thought it might have been . . . some girl, some woman."

"Silly." He had returned to his papers. "Since when can a woman make me as happy as work?" The pages went on being sorted, this one here, that one there. "Present company excepted, of course."

"Of course." I smiled down at that bent head. "Turn around, will you? I want to kiss you."

And he did and I kissed him. "You're very smart," I said. "I'm proud of you."

"Are you?"

I nodded. "Yes."

"Will you always be?"

Again I nodded. "I think so. Yes."

That picture-magazine idea and the inner glow it gave us made our autumn, if a New York autumn can be said ever to need making. Which of the city's annual rebirths I prefer, the one in spring or the one in fall, I have never been able to decide. But I do know that that particular fall had its own unique excitements, even aside from our personal one. There was an election, with La Guardia becoming mayor on the Fusion ticket, and Repeal was in the air. Somehow it seemed to be an autumn when everything was new. New fashions in the shop windows — evening gowns very formal in the grand style, and the vogue for tiaras. New streamlined designs for cars, making it difficult to tell back from front, and a new school of decoration for bars — the red-leather, brass-studded stools and the hard glitter of chromium, which Natalie predicted would be to our generation what antimacassars had been to our fathers.

Yes, all that was new that fall, in addition to the customary miracles of the Palisades turning from green to gold and doormen's liveries from cream to plum, and a once-wilted humanity reviving.

But newest and most stimulating of all, both for me and for him, was the idea inside Lyle's head, that foetus of fancy which we carried within us wherever we went, which we slept with and ate with and lived with, and which as the weeks went on was developing from an intangible into an elaborate "prospectus," immaculately typed by me and pasted and planned and written by him and treasured by us both.

Then at last it was done, finished, as much as a masterpiece can ever be finished, and we had to decide on the most propitious moment at which to present it. We had already selected the day. It was to be the day of Repeal, for Mr. Kendrick's magazine was fat with liquor advertisements, and to celebrate the new era he was giving a party that evening and he was likely to be in an expansive mood. Yes, the day was set. But after that — careful campaigners, we — we had to narrow it down to the hour and the instant.

"When?" said Lyle. "You probably know him better than his own mother does. When?"

I pondered. "Well, not before lunch, because then he's too empty, and not afterward, because then he's too full." I hesitated, and the die was cast. "Along in midafternoon, I should say. Around four."

So now it was four and I sat in my accustomed secretary's chair beside Mr. Kendrick's desk while Lyle stood in front of it. The prospectus was there, and Mr. Kendrick sat fingering it. Lyle's words were there, too, and Mr. Kendrick was tilted back in his leather chair listening to them. As was I. Not that I hadn't heard them before, from beginning to end. I had coached him and cued him and I knew where the introduction left off and the climax started and I knew what part was intended as "sales talk" and what as plain documentation. "Not that this thing really requires a sales talk," Lyle had said, "any more than a good wine needs a bush. Either he'll buy it or he won't buy it. But he'll buy it. Who wouldn't?"

Yet although I was listening, I was hearing the voice rather than its message. And although I was watching, I wasn't watching what I probably should have been watching, which was Mr. Kendrick, to gauge his reaction, to divine his mind. Instead, I was watching Lyle. That's a nice face, I was thinking, and it's a nice voice, too. And those are nice shoulders and those are nice hips. No matter what he was trying to sell, he could sell it to me, at any time and at any place. . . . But maybe I was prejudiced, I decided, just a wee bit prejudiced.

He was finished. Relaxing a little, he leaned against the desk. His eyes were on Mr. Kendrick's, and Mr. Kendrick's were on the dummy.

"Well?" he said.

Mr. Kendrick placed the dummy on the desk.

"Very interesting," he said. "Very interesting indeed."

Lyle glanced at me. We had discussed many possible reactions, ranging from a whoop of delight to a quiet "We start tomorrow," but not this one.

"Is that all?" said Lyle.

Mr. Kendrick steepled his well-manicured fingers. "I'm afraid it's all for the present, yes," he said. "The idea has great potentialities. I realize that. But this is no time to be launching a venture of this size, not with that man in the White House doing what he's doing." He reached for his cigar. "I'm having enough trouble with one magazine, what with the way these nonsensical codes of his are snarling me up. I certainly don't want to take on another until things simmer down to some reasonable normalcy."

Lyle's face had gone white. "But look at the advertising in your current issue. It's thick enough to choke a horse."

"That's not Roosevelt. That's rum." Mr. Kendrick shook his head. "No, Lyle, you've got something here, but it'll have to wait. Now later on —"

"Later on?" Lyle's temper was rising, which was exactly what I had warned him against. He placed both of his hands on the desk's edge, and leaned forward. "This thing is in the air now. It's inevitable. If we don't grab it, somebody else will."

"Oh, I imagine it'll keep for a while," said Mr. Kendrick. His hand went out toward his "Urgent" folder. The interview was over. "Well," he said cheerfully, "I'll be seeing you both at the party tonight, won't I?"

I knew what Lyle was about to say. He was about to say "No" — and probably several other things, too. Quickly I signaled him.

"Of course," I said.

"You better leave early, Amy. I expect you'll want to do a little primping."

I rose. "Thank you, Mr. Kendrick," I said. "Thank you very much." Thank you for nothing.

Well, I did a little primping all right, though not very enthusiastically. I had bought a new dress for the occasion, black with a V-back, and to set it off Lyle had given me a lapin evening jacket. It was a nice jacket, too, although when I had previewed it for Natalie's benefit she had said, "Rabbits, hm. Very pretty. But wouldn't it have been better to get live ones? Then you could eat them, if worst came to worst — and it might."

It might? It had.

Lyle stood at the window of the apartment, wearing the tails and top hat which he hadn't had on since 1929. They had smelled a little of moth balls, but I had fixed that up. He wasn't saying anything. In fact he hadn't been saying anything for the past several hours, ever since we had emerged from Mr. Kendrick's office together and I had sat down at my desk and he had gone out the door in the direction of his. I had expected him to erupt in violent protest, and in a way I would have felt better if he had. But he hadn't. He was silent, that was all. Grim and bitter and silent. . . . It didn't promise to be the most hilarious of evenings.

"Well," I said, coming out from the dressing room, "I'm ready."

He turned. "This is silly," he said. "Why are we going?"

I smiled, and attempted lightness. "You're the Connoisseur, aren't you? Don't you think that on Repeal Night the Connoisseur ought to — "

He groaned. "The Connoisseur! Oh, God!"

I went toward him. "Darling," I said, "don't take it so hard. You told me that if he didn't snap at it, somebody else would. You said you'd go to a bank, you said you'd go to the Luce people or somebody."

He shrugged, and stared down at his patent-leathered toe. "I said a lot. Too much, I guess."

I took his arm. "Now, please. Come on. You've got to forget it for tonight. You've got to forget the whole thing."

And he tried, I will say that. It was a large and lavish party — otherwise I don't suppose we would have been asked, but with such a guest list a few more didn't matter — and it was given at the Central Park Casino. Natalie was there and Ben too, for he had come up from Washington especially for the event and had even gone so far as to don a non-proletarian stiff shirt and dinner jacket, the one rumpled and the other shawl-collared and rusty. Ben and Mr. Kendrick had never been formally introduced, and Natalie had been looking forward to their meeting, which she had said ought to turn out to be quite a thing — "like a get-together between the Guelphs and the Ghibellines. Or Winchell and the Shuberts. I can hardly wait." Lyle and I had been looking forward to it also, and when it came we tried to derive what enjoyment we could from it. But there wasn't much.

"Oh, Mr. Kendrick," said Natalie, circling her arm through Ben's and leading him gently out of his corner and into the ring, "I'd like to present Mr. Liebermann."

"How do you do, Mr. Liebermann?" said Mr. Kendrick, extending his hand and being the hearty host. "Glad to have you with us."

"Nice of you to let me come," said Ben. He was sipping a port which he had judged to be "quite sound," and either it was mellowing him or he wasn't fully aware of what Mr. Kendrick represented.

The preliminaries over, Natalie briskly sounded the gong. "Mr. Liebermann is just up from Washington," she said. "He's one of Mr. Moley's Bright Young Men."

A pause from Mr. Kendrick — rather long, and definitely eloquent. "Oh."

She turned to Ben. "Mr. Kendrick is interested in politics, too. He's a member of the Republican Campaign Committee, and he once caught a fish at Rapidan."

Another pause and an equally significant "Oh," this time from Ben.

"Well, I'm sure you both have lots to talk about," she said, and retired to the bar, where Lyle and I stood watching and waiting. "Round One," she said, reaching for her glass, which was champagne — everyone was drinking champagne, and pretending to act as if it were no novelty. She glanced over toward the two of them. Mr. Kendrick was already slightly flushed, though not yet at the apoplectic stage, and Ben was slightly pale. "What a pity," she mused. "I mean, one's the host and the other's a guest, so those tiresome conventions of politeness interfere and each is at a disadvantage. I'd much rather have staged it in the Garden."

I smiled, and hoped that Lyle might be able to smile too. And he did, but with an effort. From the adjoining main room, the circular one, came the sound of the orchestra, Eddy Duchin's piano, and a vocalist singing:

I'm headin' for the Last Round-Up,
Gonna saddle old Paint for the last time and ri-i-de. . . .

"Come on," I said, placing my hand on his sleeve. "Let's dance."

We danced. The style that year was for couples to shuffle casually arm-in-arm, their bodies tangent, while they engaged in earnest conversation. But Lyle always maintained that if he just wanted to go for a walk and a talk, he would do it outdoors — and that when he wanted to dance, he wanted to dance. And he was a good dancer, with rhythm and flair. Usually. But tonight neither his heart nor his feet were in it.

"Poor Natalie," I said, thinking to divert him from his own troubles to someone else's. "She's no nearer first base than she ever was. Did you notice the way she was looking at Ben?"

"She might make a try at using sugar instead of salt for a change," he said.

"Sugar? Natalie? She wouldn't know how."

He was silent again. Well, I thought, that seems to wipe that up. And now what? Books? Music-and-the-arts? The current state of the theater?

"We have Celebrities with us," I said, again as a diversion.

"Who?"

"Over there. Mr. and Mrs. Royal Archer III. Themselves, in person."

"So?"

"Yes." I was looking at them over his shoulder. "What a dress. That's the kind that has to be called a gown. Did you see her photograph in last month's issue?" And then, wishing that I had mentioned neither "photograph" nor "issue" at a point when I was at last coming along so nicely, I went quickly on. "Cecil Beaton did it. She looked wonderful."

I laid my head against his satin lapel.

"She doesn't look bad now, either," he said.

The music ceased, and I watched them as they started to leave the floor, passing in our direction. I had seen her pictures often, but this was the first time I had ever seen her herself. This indeed was "chi-chi," an international and cosmopolitan chi-chi — London and the Lido, Antibes, and all those things I'd read about. Quite tall, very slender, a heavy tan even in December, greenish eyes, and dark hair which appeared to be sculptured to her narrow skull. How old is she? I wondered. Thirty? Thirty-two? Younger than he is, anyway, and taller. He's nice-looking, though. And I've always loved that silver-at-the-temples effect. He's debonair, elegant, and what small hands and feet. Mr. and Mrs. Mammon, of Manhattan — and of the *Europa* and the *Ile de France,* and of Scotland in August and Mayfair in June and all the rest.

"They say she's very intelligent," I whispered. "They say — "

And then I stopped, for they had stopped also. Right in front of us, not two feet away. She was smiling. And he was not only smiling but speaking.

"Aren't you Mr. Ellery?" he said. "Mr. Lyle Ellery?"

"Yes, I am," said Lyle. My arm was still linked through his, and I tightened it, automatically. Now what? What was this?

"My name is Archer, Royal Archer." How embarrassing and superfluous and even screamingly funny it must seem to him to have to say that, I was thinking. It's like having to say, "My name is Rockefeller, John D. Rockefeller." Or "My name is Field, Marshall Field." He paused. "And this is Mrs. Archer."

"How do you do?" said Lyle. He gestured toward me. "My wife."

"How do you do?" she said, and her voice was made for her body, a curious combination of lightness and huskiness and somehow shimmering.

"How do you do?" I said.

Archer was looking at Lyle. "Mr. Kendrick pointed you out to us," he said. "He was telling us that you have an idea for a new kind of magazine. A picture magazine."

Lyle nodded. "I did have, yes. But he didn't seem to be much interested. At least not right now."

"Well, Mr. Archer is," said the shimmering voice. "And so am I."

I could feel Lyle's arm suddenly press close against mine, electrically, galvanized; so close that it hurt.

"Oh, Lyle," I said, weakly. "Oh, Lyle."

III

How do you record the passing of time? The ticking of a clock marks the hours but not their content, the succession of seasons measures the months but not what they mean. So how do you record time? By a move from one room to five and from one street to another, from Forty-second off Second to Sutton Place off First? By extra digits joining others in a bankbook balance? Can you chronicle time by new faces and new friends, or should it be reckoned by the daily count of meals eaten, sheets changed, teeth brushed, and shoes resoled?

Or can it be chronicled at all, except in the diary of the mind and the ledger of the heart?

It was Laura Archer who found the new apartment for us. I don't suppose she even knew what or where Tudor City was, but in any case she phoned me to say that there was a new building about to open on Sutton Place and that if Lyle and I were interested in moving, as she understood we were, there were units in it which would seem to be ideal. Not large, of course. Five rooms, two baths; that sort of thing. Still, it was all in the best of taste and certainly very reasonable and something really quite charming could be made of it. Did I want to talk it over with Lyle when he came home, and ring her back? She happened to know of a little man who could decorate the place beautifully.

Laura always knew of a "little man."

Yet that isn't fair to her, because it makes her out to be a snob and she wasn't a snob. If she had been, she probably wouldn't have bothered with me at all. No, it was simply that she seemed unaware that there might be social and economic levels other than her own. In her way she was extremely kind and extremely generous, and had been ever since that first evening when, with Archer, she had abducted Lyle and me away from Mr. Kendrick's party and had taken us to the privacy of the Rivera-muraled library in their house on Sixty-third Street where we had discussed — or at least she and Archer and Lyle had discussed — the new magazine until four in the morning. I grew a little sleepy, and so did Archer, but she didn't and Lyle didn't. And when we finally came away, we both knew that although the money for the project was going to be supplied by Archer, the ideas and the directing force and even the inclination to sponsor a magazine at all were hers. Obviously he was presenting it to her as an expensive toy, like a bangle on her wrist or an additional pearl.

"I don't know," said Lyle, as we sat in the cab heading homeward. He was still dazed, and he had already asked me to pinch him so that he might be sure he wasn't dreaming. "I hope she isn't going into this thing as a fad that she'll get tired of. This patroness business is all very well, but it can be risky."

"Well, she may be a patroness," I said, "but she certainly isn't patronizing. As a matter of fact, I think she's really very serious about it. You can tell. And she's terribly bright. I guess she's just about the brightest woman I've ever met."

"She's got some good ideas," he agreed. "I liked what she said about Roosevelt. You know — that he's our 'strong man' and that he can be just as strong as old Musso or Hitler too." He yawned. "But she can handle the political end, if it'll keep her happy. Me, I want a lot of crime and cheesecake. Machine-Gun Kelly and Betty Boop. That's what's going to get the circulation."

I giggled. "She asked me to call her 'Laura.' Isn't that wonderful? Me calling Mrs. Royal Archer III by her first name? Wait till I tell Natalie. She'll die."

Burying his hands in his overcoat pockets, he stretched his legs out on the jump seat luxuriously. "You can wait for that if you like," he said. "What I'm waiting for is to tell Kendrick. Oh, boy! Zowie and bam."

And he did tell him, the very next day. There could be no denying that Mr. Kendrick was both surprised and disappointed, and he made no attempt to conceal it. But it was his surprise which was most evident. "*Archer?*" he said, as Lyle and I stood by his desk awaiting his reaction. He was silent for a moment, drumming his fingers on the blotter in front of him. "Well, that's gratitude from a guest, I must say. You invite a man to dinner and he steals business from right under your nose. Right off your plate, practically. Isn't there such a thing as ethics?"

"But you weren't interested," said Lyle, mildly. He was enjoying this. "You told me so."

Mr. Kendrick nodded. "What I told you was that I wasn't interested right now," he admitted. "That's what I told Roy Archer, too. But I didn't say that I wouldn't be interested eventually."

"Eventually is too late," said Lyle. He turned as if to head toward the door. Although his manner was courteous and pleasant, there was also a note of triumph in it. Already, overnight, he had acquired a touch of the Executive. "Well, I'm afraid you'll have to get yourself another boy. Another Connoisseur."

Mr. Kendrick smiled. "That I can bear," he said.

At the door, Lyle paused. "And another girl, too," he added, nodding toward me.

I looked at him in astonishment. This was something quite new to me.

"What do you mean?" said Mr. Kendrick. I could see that characteristic apoplectic flush start to mount slowly upward from his collar line.

Lyle shrugged. "We're going to be branching out a bit from now on. You know — larger apartment and all that. Amy will have enough on her hands being just 'Mrs. Ellery.'" He grinned. "It'll be a full-time job, and I think it'll pay her better than you've been paying her."

Mr. Kendrick's fist banged on the desk with such violence that the leather accessories jumped like Mexican beans. "Damn it!" he said, roaring. "God damn it! I can stand losing you, I can even stand losing that idea of yours, even if it makes a million dollars, which I suspect it won't. But I *won't* stand for losing Amy!" His cheeks were purple. "I can't do business without her! I can't even live without her!"

Lyle's hand was on the knob. "Neither can I," he said, which was a tribute he had never happened to have paid me before. "And she's my wife." He beckoned toward me. "Come on, honey. Get your rubbers."

For the first time in my life I was experiencing the most delightful situation a woman can ever find herself in: the exhilarating and dizzy satisfaction of being fought over. I turned to Mr. Kendrick, although I didn't like to face his imploring, pleading eyes. . . . He was a fool in many ways, but I loved him. I still do love him.

"I'm sorry," I said, gently. I didn't mind leaving the job — in fact I welcomed it, for I had never been a career girl anyway — but I did mind leaving him. "If he doesn't want me to keep on working — well, I guess I'll have to stop."

He had sunk back in his chair, and he was chewing on his cigar. "Caesar had his Brutus," he said, looking at Lyle, "and Christ his Judas. I have you."

And so we went out together, and as we closed the door behind us — it wasn't quite as dramatic an exit as it appeared, for of course I intended to stay on until a replacement could be found — Lyle said, "Sweet is revenge. Especially to employees."

I had never been a lady of leisure in New York before, and I liked it. I had never had an opportunity for such prosperity in New York before, either, and I liked that too. I liked phoning Lyle at his office in the rivet-ridden pandemonium of Rockefeller Center, where he was gradually assembling a staff and preparing what was to prove to be the first of a long series of experimental dummies, and being respectfully shuttled from switchboard to secretary and ultimately saying, "May I speak to Mr. Ellery, please?" and then hearing the alert response: "Oh, yes, Mrs. Ellery." I liked Saks, and I loved Bonwit's, and I enjoyed giving the address "Sutton Place" at each. I liked being listed on the Plaza exchange rather than on the more workaday Mohawk, as at Tudor City, or the undeniably prosaic Watkins, as on MacDougal Street. Yes, I imagine if anyone was ripe for snobbishness, it was I. . . . And I liked standing in the living room of the new apartment with Laura Archer and her decorator, with a judicious finger placed across my chin, and saying, "Chintz? Yes, I think chintz would do very nicely."

"Glazed, I should imagine," pronounced Laura. "With box pleats."

"And now," said the decorator, who was a little man and no mistake — about five feet two — "all that's left is the other bedroom. Have you any notions for that?"

I had plenty of notions for that, though no one knew them. Not even Lyle. Nor would he until he himself volunteered similar notions. I had asked him once. That was enough. . . . After all, I didn't want to be a bore about it.

"Just a spare room," I said, and then, because that sounded too Middle Western and Laura was listening, corrected myself. "Guest room, I mean. You know."

"Padded headboards there, too?"

"Oh, yes. Of course."

I was Laura's protégé now, and a willing one. At first I had been more than a little awed and afraid of her, but as time wore on my initial bedazzlement wore off, or at any rate eased to the point where I no longer had to restrain an impulse to curtsy whenever she entered a room or to throb in quiet ecstasy when I found myself seated beside her. I had no illusions that we would ever become very close, of course; not really intimate. I doubt if she had ever been very close with any woman, or had wanted to be. One of the privileges — and possibly one of the penalties — of goddesses is that they are under no obligation to associate with mortals. Mortal women, at least.

Yet if she was a goddess, and to me she was, she had sprung from origins which were somewhat less than divine. I don't believe many people knew that, and I probably wouldn't have known it either if it hadn't been for a chance remark on my part and a moment of weakness, or laxity, on hers. When the apartment was finally completed I had phoned her rather timorously to ask if she would care to stop in some afternoon to see it, and on the day she arrived — an hour late, and silky with sables — I took her on a tour and then brought her back to the living room and asked her if she'd like a drink of tea or something. She chose tea, and after an interval during which I disappeared into the kitchen to make it we sat sipping.

"You're not trying to take care of this place yourself, are you?" she said.

I felt a little embarrassed, for it seemed almost degrading that she should have to be aware of such menial concerns.

"So far, yes. With the aid of cleaning women. It's been so torn up and in such a mess that it didn't matter. But now I'm scouting around for someone permanent."

"Remind me to give you the name of a little agency I know," she said. "Up on Madison. They're very efficient."

Still in the first glow of pride, I glanced around the room. It was a nice room, the nicest I had ever lived in. At Tudor City we had thought we had a river view, but here we had a real one — the whole web of the Queensboro Bridge, with the snow ridged on it. "Sometimes I can't believe it," I said. "Me sitting here in Sutton Place." I almost added "With you," but didn't.

She gazed into her cup, and then put it back on her saucer. She placed the saucer on a side table. "Yes," she said. "I know."

"You?" I laughed. "How could you?"

"Where do you suppose I came from?" she said, reaching for a cigarette.

"Well, I don't know. But not from Ammon, Iowa, certainly."

She lit her cigarette with a Cartier lighter that worked. "No, not from Iowa," she said, snapping shut the lighter and rubbing its encrusted brilliance contemplatively between her fingers. "From Butte, Montana. The wrong part of Butte, Montana. Slag Hill, they called it. It was a very rich neighborhood, but all the riches were under the ground."

It seemed incredible, and I said so. "Why, it's like a fairy tale!"

"Not quite."

"Is that where you met Mr. Archer? That is, Roy?" I wasn't yet accustomed to referring to him by his first name, although he had asked me to.

"No."

"But how did you — ?"

She smiled, and then tossed her lighter deftly in her hand and after that put it back in her bag. "That's a long, long story, and I've never told it to anyone. So I don't think I'll tell it to you, if you don't mind." She rose, gathering the sables around her. "I'm not sure why I told you that much."

I wasn't either, but I was glad she had. It made her more human.

"Yes, I am too," she said, abruptly. "It's because you're simple. And I like people to be simple. Either very simple or very strong. And between you and Lyle you have both qualities."

"Thank you," I said. I was touched; touched and flattered too. Should I have been? Well, anyway I was.

Accompanying her to the foyer, I stood watching her while she finished putting on her gloves, smoothing down each finger. That has always seemed to me to be the most elegant of feminine gestures, and she was the most elegant of women. I was trying to visualize a little girl from the wrong side of the tracks in a mining town. But I couldn't.

I hesitated. "You must have a great sense of achievement," I said. "To have come so far so quickly."

She had reached the final finger. "There have been times when it hasn't seemed quick."

"But now you have everything."

Her voice was matter-of-fact rather than boastful. "I suppose I do, don't I? And yet — " She started to open the door, and then paused. She smiled. "Did you ever hear of Alexander?"

"Alexander?"

The smile widened, and I felt the soft brush of perfumed kid as her hand came out and lightly touched my cheek. "Still, you need no other worlds, do you?" she said. "You're satisfied with the one you have. And that's as it should be."

Then she was gone.

I wandered back toward the living room. That was very interesting, I thought. That was very interesting indeed. I would have to repeat all that to Lyle. And I did, that evening, and after I did he said, "Hm. So that's where she gets that bulldog grip of hers. I didn't think she could have got it from the Finch-Spence setup or Rosemary Hall. My God, you ought to hear that woman argue! She's got an office up there with us now, and she's on a regular ten-to-six schedule. Rolls up her sleeves and gets her pinkies all inky and yammers about type sizes and pictures in relation to text and everything else. If I ever said she was a dilettante, I take it back. She slaves like a stevedore. And she's got most of the staff scared to death of her."

"You too?" I said.

"No, not me too. She may be a pain in the neck sometimes, but I'm not scared."

She knew them all. She knew Bernard Baruch, and she called him "Bernie." She knew General Johnson, and she called him "Hughie." To her a telephone conversation with Washington and its most sacred and innermost sanctums — save one — was as commonplace as a chat with my butcher was to me. Occasionally I would stop in at Rockefeller Center to pick up Lyle for dinner, and I would find the two of them closeted either in his office or hers, alone or with lesser members of the staff — and usually wrangling. Sometimes Archer was with them also, and when he was he had a habit of lounging in a deep chair — a dapper and fastidious figure who somehow always reminded me of a lean, unjuvenile Prince of Wales — and gazing at Laura with a fond and even amused benevolence and pride, as if more and more on him the wonder grew that her one small head could hold all she knew. What was it like, being married to such a Luther Burbank amalgam of beauty and brilliance? I wondered. Did he ever get nervous about it? Did Croesus ever pause to realize how unique it was that he should be mated to Cassandra?

"My dear Lyle," she said, fingering one of the gardenias which she was never without, "page spreads of Carnera and Dillinger and college boys eating goldfish are all very fine. We want them, naturally. But that's merely the icing, don't you see? It's the other thing that really matters. We want to give this magazine importance and *size*."

72

"The hell with size," said Lyle. "That kind, anyway. Who wants to look at six pages on the life of Mussolini? It's dull."

"To you, possibly. But it's significant. Here you have one of history's great men and you want to ignore him. And we could get exclusives. All I'd have to do is cable Edda. We had cocktails with her on the Lido last summer, and — "

"Oh, nuts. Look, what I'm thinking about are our A.B.C. figures and J. Walter Thompson. And that's what you ought to be thinking about, too." He glanced toward Archer. "And you. After all, it's your money we're going to be tossing around. Are tossing around."

Archer smiled, but for the moment said nothing. Such lovely white teeth, I thought. True or false? Then, looking at his watch, he rose and reached for Laura's coat. "Come on, dear. We have to dress."

She stood as he helped her into the coat, and she kept flicking one scarlet nail against the other, nervously, irritated. But not petulant. She was too self-controlled for petulance; it was undoubtedly one of the things she had schooled herself to and against, among many others. "Well, all I have to say, Lyle," she said, "is that there's an opportunity for a very interesting and stimulating parallel spread there. Mussolini on one side, Roosevelt on the other. Italy's leader and ours. And ours can be just as great as theirs is. Even greater."

"Who cares?"

"I care, and you ought to. This is an era of strong men, giants, and it so happens that we're fortunate enough to have one of them. And the magazine can make a very sound point about it. It can — "

"Please, Laura," said Archer. "We'll be late."

Lyle smiled at her. "We'll go at it again in the morning. Bare knuckles, and no holds barred."

They left, and he leaned back in his chair and stretched his arms ceilingward. "I'm tired," he said. "Sparring with Il Duchess all day. It gets a man down." Flexing his hands, he then let them fall to his lap, relaxedly. "But not out."

I was standing by his desk, turning over the pages of the latest tentative dummy. "I don't think you should have said 'Oh, nuts' to her like that," I said. "I mean, it wasn't very polite. And she is your publisher's wife. In fact she's really your publisher, as far as I can see."

"Oh, nuts," he repeated.

He stared moodily at the dummy, as if both saddened and inspired by its riches. "Look at that thing," he said. "Look at those stories. Beebe in a bathysphere, Sam Insull, Roehm and that purge — good blood-and-guts stuff. And what are we doing? We're getting out sample issues of a niggardly hundred copies that trickle out only to the newsstand people and the agencies." He shook his head, sighing. "It's criminal. Like a barbecue served to a ladies' bridge foursome."

"There'll be other stories," I said.

Again he sighed. "Will there? Let's hope so."

Closing the dummy, I traced my finger over the lettering on its cover. "Today" it was called at the moment, but that was only the most recent of the names suggested. "Panorama" it had been once, and at another stage "Now." Today and now, I thought. Well . . .

"It takes almost as long to have a magazine as it does to have a baby, doesn't it?" I said, but not looking at him.

I heard the squeak of his chair as he pushed it back.

"Yeah," he said. "Even longer. But I want to have it right. And with Archer backing me I can afford to plug along until I get it right." He was heading toward the closet where his coat and hat hung. "Come on, let's go out and get some dinner. I'm starved."

So that, I thought, is that. I went toward the door, where I stood waiting. "Your mother phoned," I said. "She wanted to know if she could join us, and I told her yes."

He groaned. "Oh, God! Not with one of those little friends of hers, I hope."

There really was no reason for him to have asked the question, because she had never yet brought any of her friends to see us. She probably knew better. Not that I would have objected. I would have welcomed and even have enjoyed them, if only for her sake. But he . . . "I don't think so," I said. "It's just that she's sailing again tomorrow, and she wanted to say good-by."

He was shouldering himself into his coat. "Oh. Well, that's different. Where is it this time?"

"Nassau, I believe."

"You know," he said, as he came toward me and we stepped into his outer office, "I wish she could pick herself up some nice, widowed, retired capitalist on one of these junkets, and marry him. It might be the best thing in the world for her."

"I think she's doing all right as it is," I said. "I'd let her alone, if I were you."

And she was doing all right, in fact she was doing far better than I had ever been able to hope or than anyone had ever had a right to expect. I didn't see her often — I knew that she was still self-conscious about that evening in August, which neither of us had ever mentioned — but when I did see her I had to admire the change which her own therapy, self-conceived and self-administered, had wrought in her. In January, without a word to anyone, she had consulted one of her husband's friends and through him had obtained a position as a cruise directress on a line which operated a series of brief, medium-priced winter voyages down into the Caribbean. When I had first heard of the proposal my reaction had been the same as — though less explosive than — Lyle's, who had said, "Her? In the middle of the ocean and with nothing to do but hang around the ship's bar with a bunch of lushes? Well, this *will* be the end, believe me. I know her."

"Let her try it," I had said. "It'll be something for her to do, anyway. And it can't be any worse than sitting around that awful apartment." I knew her, too. In certain respects, I thought privately, I perhaps knew her even better than he did. And therefore I was even more uneasy.

Yet I needn't have worried, for the first time she came back — from Jamaica — she was very brown and very clear-eyed and in better health and spirits than she had appeared in a long time. She had called at Tudor City one afternoon when we were getting ready to move and had displayed her tan and presented me with a native beach hat which she had brought back as a souvenir. Her tales of her travels were varied, and often hilarious. "I think it's

75

going to be all right," she said, "though if I ever see another quoit or shuffleboard, I may scream. Still, it's fun in a way, and certainly educational. I like it."

"I suppose it's apt to be pretty — gay sometimes, isn't it?" I said archly, probing. Lyle was at the office, and I had decided to find out what I could.

If she noticed my archness and deduced the reason for it, she gave no sign. She was holding the hat in her lap, and she smoothed its floppy brim placidly. "Oh, yes, there are mornings when we have hangovers by the deckload, poor things, and when we dole out aspirin as if it were corn flakes." Lifting the hat, she held it at arm's length and examined it critically. "Of course that doesn't apply to me," she added casually. "As directress I can't take a drink while on the job. It's in the contract."

I was both relieved and embarrassed. How good for her, I thought, and yet how humiliating, too.

"Oh, really?" I said. "They — they insisted on a clause like that?"

She didn't look at me as she answered. "No," she said. "I did."

So we met her that night to say good-by, and that was only one of many nights. All that winter she went out and came back, went out and came back, always browner and with a trunk filled with dresses that were ever whiter and more sports-minded. On the first evening of her return she invariably had dinner with us — and we rarely saw her after that until it was time for her to sail again. What she did during the remainder of her intervals ashore, whom she was with and where she went and how she amused herself when she got there, I didn't know and didn't ask. What a sailor does while in port is the sailor's own business. . . . But sometimes as I lay in bed listening to the foghorns on the river I would picture her standing at the bar in a lighted liner floating over a moonlit-mirrored sea with a prop glass of untouched lemonade or soda in her hand, smiling brightly and professionally and determinedly while around her the champagne corks popped and the confetti swirled and the paper-capped joviality grew louder — her own Ancient Mariner with her own albatross.

She was so lonely, she was so lonely. . . .

And now, strangely, I was beginning to feel a little lonely, too. Or useless, rather. The novelty of my leisure had begun to pall. Everything that could be done to decorate the apartment had been done — each china ash tray stood neatly in its appointed place, each crystal pendant dangled motionless and dustless from the mantel candelabra — and I no longer even had the time-filling chores of housekeeping, because by now I had Callie.

Callie. Callie. Time out for Callie.

I hadn't got her through Laura's "little agency," for the silent Swedes they had sent seemed too stupefying and the Finns too formidable. I had got her through a want ad, and I was hoping for someone ample and aproned, with a rich laugh and a flashing ivory smile on her ebon face beneath her bright bandanna, and with the general air of one who is accustomed to slap her broad thighs and chuckle "Honey chile" while engaged in tossing pancakes over a griddle. A mammy, so to speak. But Callie didn't prove to be like that at all. She was more or less ebon — the color of a good cigar, actually — and although she could toss pancakes, and very expertly too, I don't believe she had ever owned a bandanna; and when she laughed, which was seldom, she had to be very certain that there was something to laugh about. As for her addressing me as "Honey chile," that was a wistful dream which I soon learned to put away. To her, I was "Mis' Ellery." The way she spoke them, the words were indistinguishable from "Miss Celery."

She was in her fifties and thin to the point of scrawniness, stringy-necked, bony-ankled, huge-footed, and as she sat in the living room the first time I interviewed her the first thing she said was, "Peace it's wonderful, Mis' Ellery. Peace it's the lamb of God."

"Yes. Yes, isn't it?" I said, a little nervously. What I was seeking was a maid, not a maniac. I glanced down at her well-thumbed references. "Your name *is* Callie, isn't it? Callie Potter?"

She folded her knob-knuckled hands on her lap. She was arrayed in complete and unrelieved black. A widow? I wondered. Mourning?

"That's what they call me," she said. "My true name's Flowin' Balm."

"Oh." Somehow I couldn't picture Lyle arriving home and saying, "What's for dinner, Flowing Balm?" Or even "Screaming Wrath." "Well, I think perhaps I'll just call you Callie too, if you don't mind." I paused, uncertainly. "You're married?"

She nodded, not too enthusiastically. "Everett, he is. He's a Home Reliefer." She said it as one would say "He's a carpenter," or "He drives a truck."

Whatever her eccentricities, her references were admirable, too good to be discarded. And although she frightened me a little, she didn't frighten me nearly as much as the Finns had.

"Suppose we try each other out for a while," I said, in the conventionally diplomatic phrase.

She was wearing octagonal, rimless spectacles, and she peered at me over them. "Do you drink?" she asked.

I hesitated, thinking of our nightly martinis. "Why, ah — yes. Now and then. That is, Mr. Ellery does. And occasionally I join him, just to keep him company."

She brooded. "Liquor's a sin," she said, "and I'm against it. That's why I had to leave my last two places. They drank too."

I smiled with what I hoped was both charm and persuasion. "With us it's mostly medicinal," I said. "It isn't as if we actually enjoyed it."

She rose. "Well," she said, "we'll see. Peace it's a cooing dove," she observed, and went out.

Wonderful, wonderful Callie. She ferreted out dirt from places where I had never imagined dirt could penetrate, she completely reorganized the geography of the kitchen (and tacitly implied that I was to keep out of it), and she informed me that the eggs I was paying seventy cents a dozen for were less fresh than those she could bring down from Harlem with her each morning for fifty-five. We had our troubles with her, yes. The key to the liquor cabinet was always mysteriously disappearing, leaving it in a sealed state, and there were times when Lyle would emerge from the pantry looking cowed and furtive and saying, "I'll be God-damned if I see why a man should be made to feel like a dipsomaniac just because he likes to have a drink in his own home now and then." But that bitter we took with the sweet, and gladly. Through her I learned of a Harlem I had never known. There were no stompings at the Savoy (I was never brave enough to tell her I had been there) in that Harlem, no Count Basie, no numbers lotteries, and if there were black reprobates who stumbled through it they were no less contemptible to her than the white. Wonderful, wonderful Callie, who was often a bore and always a blessing: a black thread of finest quality which ran through my life and bound it together. She had said her "true" name was Flowing Balm, and I think it must have been, because for me she was always balm and it flowed generously, selflessly, and unendingly.

Yet now, and partly because of her efficiency, I found myself idle, slackening, time on my hands. Spring had come — a faint fuzz of green over the Park, sunlight washing Sutton Place, brilliant and unexpectedly warm, hyacinths in the Vanderbilts' window boxes, the days growing longer and the sky bluer. For the first time hotels and restaurants began to blossom forth with outdoor cafés, and people enjoyed the novelty of eating and drinking behind hedge boxes and beneath striped awnings and picking particles of soot off their lettuce and saying, "It's just like Paris, isn't it? So continental."

But this restlessness I was feeling, this — this uneasiness, this yearning. Was that spring, too?

It was a morning in May, and I loitered in the sketch-strewn, paper-littered cubicle which Natalie occupied, a circumspect distance down the hall from Mr. Kendrick's office. (I had stopped in there too, maneuvering myself past my old desk where sat a mature but pleasant-looking woman who knew not Joseph and being greeted by Mr. Kendrick's rather glum and pouting "Oh, it's you, hm.") I hadn't seen Natalie recently, and at first she was inclined to be a trifle cool. "Ah, Mrs. Tycoon," she said, when I appeared in the doorway. "And to what do we owe this honor? Have you come to investigate conditions among the working girls?" She swept a pile of fashion drawings from the one comfortable chair. "Sit down. Let me tell you all about child labor."

But her rancor didn't last. It couldn't. Not with Natalie. Not with me.

She was at work on one of her monthly Modes-and-Manners articles, and she sat hunched at her typewriter with her chin cupped in her hands and gazed morosely at what she had written. " 'Why don't you try rinsing your hair out with dead champagne, to give it that moonglow luster?' " she read. Snatching the paper out from its roller, she crumpled it into a ball and threw it into a corner, where it joined a dozen others. "Oh, for God's sake. Why don't I try taking a running jump at myself?" She tilted back in her chair and swung her long legs onto her desk. "Imagine me sitting here and dreaming up things like that. It's embarrassing, indecent, obscene. I guess it's time I got out of this racket."

"Are you planning to?"

"Oddly enough, yes," she said, examining her fingernails.

"Ben?" I said, and I hoped it was. It wasn't that I liked him so much: it was that I knew she loved him.

"No, dear. Not Ben." She shrugged. "Life's too short. I mean, he's down in Washington all the time now, and — well, he obviously doesn't want to tie himself up with one woman anyway. He's interested in women as a sex, because they vote or they're downtrodden or they're useful in perpetuating the proletariat or whatever, but he's not interested in a wife. That's too bourgeois. And I'm getting no younger."

Hers was the sensible attitude, of course, and yet in a way I couldn't help regretting it. Still, she probably regretted it more.

"Who is it now?"

"Well, it's — " Suddenly and swiftly she put her feet down from the desk as she glanced over my shoulder, toward the doorway. She smiled, and her whole manner seemed to change. It was a remarkable and instantaneous transformation. "Oh, good morning, Freddie," she said. "Come in, do."

I looked toward the door, where a man was standing. A blond young man, and good-looking; almost handsome, in fact, in an even-profiled, unspectacular way. Certainly he was much better-looking than Ben.

"You're busy," he said. "I'll see you later. How about lunch?"

"Adore it," she said, and there was something in her voice which caused me to swivel toward her again, almost startled. If I hadn't known who she was, I would have sworn that she was on the verge of simpering. And I began to notice other things about her. Always before, she had been severely though becomingly tailored. Now I saw a flounce at her throat, frills at her wrists. Ah, I thought, so at last she was trying sugar. Saccharine even. And it seemed to be working.

"This is Mr. Wheaton," she said, introducing him. "Mrs. Ellery. Mr. Wheaton writes our Connoisseur Department. And writes it so beautifully, too. It's marvelous. I just don't see how he does it."

"Oh, really?" I smiled at him. "How do you do?"

He smiled also, and very winningly. "Hello." The smile lingered as he looked at Natalie again. "One o'clock O.K.?"

"Whatever you say, Freddie."

He disappeared, and she returned her feet to the desk top, relapsing into normality. She said nothing. She didn't need to.

"He's nice," I said. "Cute."

"Isn't he, though?" She was once more enrapt in her fingernails. "Intelligent, too. And you know what? He thinks I'm pretty. All my life I've been 'striking' or 'unusual' or even 'an awfully good sport.' But I've never been 'pretty.'" She sighed. "It's such a relief. Divine."

"Is it serious?"

"Well, I shouldn't be surprised if he asked me to marry him one of these days — and that will be a novelty, I must say." Rising, she went to the window, where she stood looking down into Lexington Avenue, her back toward me. "This time I'm playing it a bit more cagily. There's been a certain amount of scuffling in taxis, but aside from that — well, you know."

I nodded, soberly. "I think you're being very wise, too."

Turning, she strolled back toward her desk and perched herself on it. "Let's talk about you. How's Madame Récamier?"

"Who?"

"You know. The awesome Mrs. Archer."

"Oh." I had had her to dinner with the Archers once, and to say that she and Laura had clashed would be an understatement.

Theirs had been the friction of steel against diamond. "She's fine."

She waited a moment. "And Lyle?"

"He's fine, too."

She began to kick her heels idly against the desk bottom. She was looking at me. Then she looked away. All at once I became aware of a great silence, and of the ticking of her little ivory desk clock. Its ticking rose above the hum of the street traffic below. The sound was more like hammer blows than ticking.

"What are you thinking about?" I said.

"Nothing." Quickly and casually, yet not too quickly and not too casually, she glanced down at the morning's *Times,* which lay outspread on her desk. "The most amazing thing," she said. "Did you see this? Some woman up in Canada has had five children."

I seldom smoked, but there was a package of cigarettes on the desk and I reached for one. "That's not so very amazing. Women used to have them by the dozen. My own grandmother had eight."

"Yes, but this one had them all at once. Five baby girls. Quintuplets. Imagine!"

"I'd rather not, frankly."

She looked at me. "The other end," she said, nodding. "That one's cork."

Reversing the cigarette, I struck a second match. There was a burnt and bitter taste in my mouth. The clock was loud, so loud.

"I asked you what you were thinking about just then," I repeated.

"And I told you 'nothing.'" She paused. "Why? What were you thinking about?"

"Well, not that, I assure you." I got up and smudged the cigarette out on an ash tray. I didn't want it after all. "It's certainly not his fault that she's up there at the office all the time, is it? He doesn't even like her. They fight like cats and dogs. He can't even be civil to her."

"Listen," she said. "Did I say anything?"

"You looked so — so sly. So *knowing.* I hate that sort of thing. It's so cheap." I picked up the ash tray, which was full to overflowing, and started to empty it in the wastebasket. "She happens to be the

82

wife of his publisher, and she also happens to be very much interested in the magazine. She — "

"Better not do that," she said. "You'll start a fire."

I put the ash tray back on the desk. I suddenly realized that I was trembling. Why?

"Well," I said, turning toward the door, "I guess I'll be on my way."

She had the *Times* in her hand now, and she was creasing it. She looked down at it, then over at me. "I'm not trying to pry," she said. "Into anything. But by any chance you couldn't happen to be — ?"

"What?" I said, challengingly, defiantly. Let her say it. Just let her dare say it.

"Pregnant."

Oh. "No," I said. "I couldn't happen to be. Not by any chance at all. Thanks just the same." I went out. "Good-by. I'll be calling you."

I walked down the wide corridor, over the silver crescents embedded in the mosaic of the black marble floor, toward the elevator bank. Pushing the button, I waited. As I stood there, one of the stenographers passed by, a girl I used to know, a pert and pretty little girl.

"Hello, Amy," she called. "How are you?"

"Just fine, thanks, Millie. How are you?"

"Oh, swell. How's Lyle?"

"He's fine, too."

The elevator came, and I stepped into it. It was an express, and we plunged swiftly downward. I suppose there were other people in the car, but I don't remember noticing them. Arriving at the ground floor, I got out and edged my way through the crowds in the lobby and then went down the steps into the arcade and after that turned toward the Lexington Avenue exit. I pushed at the brass rail on the glass door and then at another brass rail on another glass door. Then I emerged into the bright sunshine of the street.

And it was then and only then, finally and at last, that I faced it; faced what I had been refusing to face for months, had been refusing to admit even to myself, had been refusing to think about, to wonder about, even to dream. I was jealous. What had been smoldering was now in flame, and I was blazingly, tormentedly, and possibly unreasonably jealous. I had probably always been jealous, from that very first evening when I had met her and had seen them together. And the strange part was not that I was acknowledging it now but that I had been unwilling to acknowledge it sooner.

It was a weakening, sapping, subversive thing, as relentless and deadly as a cobra's coils, and I hated it. Yet it was there, it was there, and as I stood gazing sightlessly at the rushing traffic I knew that from now on it would always be there and that it would lie down beside me at night and awake with me in the morning and that I would drink it with my water and eat it with my bread.

And I did. They say that jealousy is a color, green, and I don't know, perhaps it is. But to me it was a swamp. Or maybe a silt, a fine, gritty silt that powdered everything with the film of suspicion and fear. A color, a swamp, a silt, whatever it was it had its distorting and corroding effect on all my five senses — sight, hearing, smell, taste, touch. I sat in the cool Regency formality of Laura's drawing room — a classical background for a modern beauty — and saw not Laura but Lilith. I waited in Lyle's office while they quarreled over the magazine's policies, and as I listened to his disparagements, even insults, and to her apparently meek acceptance of them it seemed to me that I was hearing the language of love. I looked at the carnation in his lapel, and smelled a gardenia. Food lost its flavor, and I tasted mistrust. I touched his hand and felt it still warm from hers.

There were times when I tried to be detachedly analytical about it, and to argue rationally against my own inner convictions. I tried to concentrate on Archer, who had managed to run an inheritance of ten million dollars up into fifteen plus and who was therefore presumably, though not positively, no fool. I even tried to be self-satirical about the whole situation, and to deny that there was a situation. I of all people to be disturbed by the threadbare threat of the "office wife," I told myself. I knew offices and I knew maga-

84

zines and I knew the close co-operation essential to both. Surely in this day and age it was possible for a man and a woman to unite in a common intellectual enterprise and yet not necessarily . . . But I thought that only when I was alone, and even then only with an effort and never successfully. When I saw them together I realized that although it might be possible, it wasn't very probable. Not with that man and that woman.

And I remembered a remark he had once let fall. "Since when can a woman make me as happy as work?" he had asked. Well, since now. Because now he had both the woman and the work in one, and both were big league.

It isn't fair, I thought, it isn't sporting. If I had to have a rival, why couldn't it have been somebody my size? Somebody human, anyway — not this international paragon who has brains and beauty and everything else, including green eyes. How can I be expected to compete with her in anything? Why match Braddock against a mouse?

But there is no point in my attempting to trace the origin and in-tumescence and pathology of my disease — the hours I spent alone, which were bad, and the hours I spent with the two of them, which in a way were even worse. The diagnosis was plain enough. What the prognosis might be I didn't know and was afraid to imagine.

It was summer now, midsummer, July, and I sat by the open window in Mrs. Ellery's ovenlike little room at the Barbizon watching her pack for another of her cruises, while outside the city lay sweltering and steaming in a haze of heat. Steaming like — yes, like a swamp. . . . Hotels, almost any hotel, were where Mrs. Ellery stayed now whenever she was ashore, for she had given up her apartment and had turned over to me the few personal possessions she had had in it, the mahogany chest and the silver tray and the rest. Rootless, she now was also homeless, a not-so-merry widow. Both Lyle and I had made offers to her — he to set her up in another and better apartment and I that she feel free to occupy the extra bedroom in ours whenever she was in town, but she had declined each with thanks. To him she had said, "No, I'm probably a hotel

85

type anyway," and to me, when I had pointed out that our guest room was vacant, "Well, it won't always be vacant. You'll find a use for it." And I had said, "Sometimes I wonder."

Playing with the cord on the window shade, I looked over at her as she knelt at the trunk rack, expertly arranging the sleeveless white sport frocks and evening gowns which were her working clothes.

"Where to this trip?" I said.

"Oh, messing around off Florida. Havana eventually. They'll probably be rumba-ing all over the place on my way back. I'll bring you some maracas." She tucked at a fold. "And one of those pink shirts with the ruffles on them for Glen. He's mad for one."

I gave the cord a final flick and, rising, walked over to the bed, where I cleared an island for myself among its litter and sat down. "I think maybe I'm going away too for a while," I said.

"I thought Lyle was too busy."

"He is. I'm going alone." I fingered the high heel of an evening slipper. "That is, I think I'm going. I haven't mentioned it to him yet." But if when I did, he should protest, "You can't. I need you here," oh how wonderful, how wonderful. . . .

"Oh," she said. She reached for another sheet of tissue paper. "You're leaving him here alone?"

"He'll be all right. Callie will look after him."

Crinkling the paper, she wadded it into the toe of a canvas brogan. She glanced up at me. "I assume you've considered this from all angles, haven't you?"

I nodded. "Yes."

She went on packing. "Well, that's all that matters. . . . Where are you going?"

"Out to Iowa. To Ammon. My mother and father have been wanting me to come out for a long while, and this seems as good a time as any."

"I'd like to meet them sometime," she said. "I wonder how we'd get along."

For an instant I tried to visualize her and my mother together, and couldn't. "Well, you might not get along with my mother, but I

86

think you would with my father. He gets along with almost everybody."

She smiled. "I'd probably be the acid test for him. You know, I believe I'll make a point of that. Meeting them, I mean. I'll write it down."

I hesitated. She had already provided me with a transition into what I wanted to say, the real reason for my call, and I had foolishly let it pass. Now I had to start afresh. "Mrs. Ellery," I said, "there's been something I've been intending to ask you." And it wasn't going to be easy, either. "If you think I'm being too inquisitive and too personal—or even too morbid—I wish you'd tell me so."

She sat back on her heels, in front of the trunk. "Would it have anything to do with Laura Archer?" she said. It was the first time that she or anyone had been so direct, and hearing the name I felt as a patient must feel when at last vague hints about "malignancy" give way to the outright word "cancer."

"No." Then I began again. Because of course in a way it had everything to do with her. "That is, yes. I mean . . ."

"What is it? Go ahead."

I took the plunge. "It's about Mr. Ellery. You and Mr. Ellery. Did he—was he ever—?" I rarely blushed, but I could feel myself blushing now. I stopped, unable to go on. Why had I ever been so impertinent as to start?

But I didn't have to go on, for she understood me. "Oh, I see," she said. For a moment she was silent. She smiled, faintly. "You've never forgotten that—that little evening of ours, have you?"

"There was something you said."

The smile faded. "I said much too much."

"There was one thing especially."

"About Vin and Lyle being so alike?"

"Yes."

Slowly she circled her thumb and forefinger around the bottle of sun oil she held in her lap. She looked down at it. "No," she said, at last. "So far as I know, he never did and he never was. I'm not sure why. Perhaps it was—the ego again. He might not have needed me, but he didn't need anyone else either." The smile came back, more brightly, encouraging. She put her hand out and patted mine. "So cheer up. Lyle may be like him in that way, too."

"Thank you," I said, and I tried to derive what relief I could from it. "And I'm sorry. I didn't want to ask you, but I had to."

"You don't have to thank me, and you don't have to be sorry. You've been good to me, Amy — and for me." She resumed her packing, and her voice took on that old note of brittle banter which at times must have been such work for her. "You know, I've been thinking lately. Maybe at my funeral they ought to sing a spiritual — 'Nobody Knows the Trouble She's Been.'"

So I felt a little better and then later on, when I told Lyle that I thought I might go out to Ammon for a month or so, I felt a little worse. Quite a lot worse, in fact. Because what he said was exactly what I had been hoping he wouldn't say. "Fine," he said, and "Good idea," and "No reason why you should be cooped up in this heat just because I have to be. When do you want to go?"

"Oh, I don't know," I said. "Around the first of the month, I guess. August."

"That'll be a good time for me, too," he went on briskly. Far, far too briskly. "We'll be starting to get ready to go to press for the first issue along about then, and I'll be up to my ears. So you probably wouldn't be seeing much of me anyway."

"Not that I have been."

"What?"

"You certainly have been spending an awful lot of time in that office."

"Oh, that." He laughed easily, apologetically. Was this man going to turn out to be what they called "suave"? I had never considered him to be suave before. "I have, haven't I? But the bud's just about ready to blossom. And you know how I am when I get hot on a thing."

"Yes," I said. "I do know."

He glanced at me curiously. "Look," he said, "you're not going to be the abused wife, are you? The one whose husband sets out to make a mere lousy fortune."

88

"Oh, don't be so — jocose," I said. "I don't know what I'm going to be. I haven't made up my mind yet."

His eyebrows elevated. "Hm." But he wasn't looking at me any more. "Maybe it's time you had a change of scene. Maybe you need one. August, you said?"

"Yes."

And now it was August, the month, the day, almost the hour. Five hours from the hour, to be exact, for my train was to leave at midnight and it was now seven. Packed, dressed, ready, waiting, I stood at the window watching evening sunlight filter through the lattice-work of the Queensboro Bridge. I wasn't likely to have been in the most cheerful of moods anyway, and the fact that Lyle was late and hadn't even bothered to phone made me feel no better. For it was my fate that before going on to the station we were scheduled to attend a dinner party at the Archers'. Yes, that too, in addition to everything else — irony's crown of ironies. I hadn't wanted to go, if only because I knew that I would feel foolish climbing into a Pullman in a cloud of black chiffon, but Lyle had insisted. "She's having several useful people," he had said, "some of them even coming up from Washington especially. And she's been planning it for a long time. I don't see how we can very well get out of it."

"Oh, no," I said. "Of course not."

"Now why take that attitude? As a matter of fact, when I told her you'd be leaving she spoke of you particularly. She said it would be a nice send-off for you. A celebration."

"Oh, she did, did she?" I said. "Well."

Standing at the window, I foresaw every detail of that dinner party, the very prospect of which would once have thrilled and awed me. I saw the cocktails and canapés being served in the bamboo bar, while the cockatoos squawked in their cages, with Laura wearing something magnificent and new — inevitably new because I had never seen her in anything that wasn't — and surrounded by a musical-comedy supporting cast of black ties and white shirt fronts. I saw the candle-lit, flower-decked, damask-laid length of the table in the green-and-gold dining room, or possibly a covey of small tables in the lantern-hung garden, and myself allocated to some neutral position somewhere below the salt — that nice little Mrs. Ellery who had to be invited because she was her husband's wife. I saw Archer's slim silk-clad ankles above shiny patent leather as he sat in the card room playing bridge. I saw Walter Lippmann, James A. Farley, John L. Lewis, Dorothy Thompson, and perhaps Dwight Fiske as an after-dinner entertainer. Maybe even Louis Howe and Dr. Wirt, because through motives of either sadism or hospitality Laura was a firm believer in mixing opposing factions at her dinner parties. "It makes them go," she said.

But mostly I saw Lyle and a pair of green eyes.

"Simple" she had called me, and oh God had I been simple.

"Mr. Ellery not home yet?" I turned. Callie stood in the dining-room archway. Rusty black hat with the roses on it, shopping bag in her hand, newspaper-wrapped bundle under her arm. She was ready for the bus, Harlem, and Father Divine.

"Not yet, Callie."

"Well, you have yourself a good time."

"Thank you."

"And a good time out there in Iowa, too. You get yourself a real rest."

"I will, Callie."

She started to retreat toward the kitchen. "And you needn't worry about Mr. Ellery. I'll look after him."

I watched her as she disappeared. You do that, Callie, I was thinking. And if you should happen to come across some hairpins that aren't mine, or lipstick stains of a shade called Flamingo, or even a few tired gardenia petals, you might drop me a line.

Then there was the scrape of a key in the lock, the sound of steps in the foyer, and, turning, I saw Lyle.

"Sorry I'm late," he said, as he headed toward the bedroom. "It was those God-damned proof sheets again. They never get 'em right."

"She said seven-thirty."

"Well, she'll be late, too. She was helping me with the dummy. In fact she dropped me just now from her cab."

90

He went into the bedroom, and I remained standing at the window. The dummy? Who is the dummy? I am the dummy.

I picked up a book and put it down. I turned on the radio and turned it off. From the bedroom I could hear the bustle of movement, drawers opening and closing, a door shutting, then the spray of the shower.

"Amy?"

"Yes?"

"Help me with my studs, will you?"

Even that, I thought. The patient Griselda. The little wife.

I went toward the bedroom, and I glimpsed him through the bathroom doorway as he stood in front of the medicine chest mirror, combing his hair. He was wearing slippers and shorts and nothing else, and drops of water still pebbled his bare back, for although this was the summer of *It Happened One Night* he had been accustomed to going without an undershirt long before Clark Gable had.

I saw the reflection of his hand as it speculatively rubbed his chin.

"You think I ought to shave?"

"It's up to you."

Seating myself on the bed, I began to press the studs into the starched, stiff shirt.

"Guess not."

Then he came out and went toward his closet, where he lifted out his evening trousers on their hanger and, reaching for a brush, stood brushing them.

"Well, so you're off, hm?"

"Yes."

"I'll miss you."

"Thanks."

The whish of the brush went on, slowed, and then gradually stopped. I didn't look up at him. I kept my eyes on the studs and on the whiteness of the shirt. There, one more and then the cuff links.

"Amy."

"Yes."

"What the hell's the matter with you lately?"

"Nothing."

I heard the soft plop of the trousers being tossed onto a chair and then the pad of his slippers as he came toward me. Two bare legs appeared within the range of my vision.

"It's Laura, isn't it?"

I did look up at him then, and finally it came out. At last. I suppose it must have been like the eruption of a festered sore with the pus spurting forth, yellow-green and ugly.

"Yes," I said.

He stood with his hands on his hips, looking down at me. "I thought so," he said. "I've thought so for a long time." He paused. "You're a fool. You know that, don't you?"

"Am I?" I looked away again, and reached for one of the cuff links. "Well, we can't talk about it now. We haven't time."

Putting out his hand, he took the shirt from me and threw it onto the other bed.

"Oh, yes, we have," he said.

Very well. If that's the way he wanted it.

"She's a predatory woman," I said.

He made a gesture. "Oh, for God's sake! 'Predatory woman.' Where do you pick up phrases like that? What have you been reading?"

"I don't have to read anything. She told me herself that she was looking for new worlds to conquer — and she's conquered you."

I could see the cords at his throat tighten. "You're an even bigger fool than I thought you were," he said. "Don't you understand? She meant politics. She's got this power complex, this bee in her bonnet. That's what she meant. I ought to know. I have to fight with her enough about it to keep it out of the magazine."

"I don't believe you. You're either sleeping with her now, or you're planning to."

There was a second then — just a second — when his open palm came out and I thought he was going to slap me. But instead, the palm knotted into a fist and after that relaxed, his hand falling limply to his side. He sat down on the bed beside me.

"Look," he said, "you're going away. Is this any way to say good-by?"

"You haven't answered me."

"What?"

"Are you?"

He waited, and he looked at me. "No," he said.

"Will you swear it?"

"I'll swear it on anything you like. A stack of Bibles ten feet high. Your mother's heart. My father's grave."

I have stood in the street and watched an eclipse pass and the sun come out, dazzling and brilliant and strong. I have seen surf break over a beach and cover it with dark, roiling waters and then wash away, leaving the sands bright and clean and golden. This was like that — only more so. . . . I pressed my hand over my eyes, because for a moment I was blinded by joy. It is a big word, "joy." I don't use it often.

Then his arms went round me, and I could feel the smooth shower-cooled warmth of his body through the thin net of my chiffon. His lips were on mine.

"You should have slapped me," I said. "I deserve it."

He held me close. "What will I do when you're away?"

"I won't go. I can't go."

"Darling."

"Oh, Lyle, Lyle."

"Amy. Amy Ellery. My love. My wife."

I had sunk back against the pillows, and for an instant — or how long is an instant? — I lay there. Then gently I tried to push him away.

"Darling, my dress. It'll be all rumpled."

"Darling, please."

"Lyle, you've got to dress. You — "

"Please, darling. Please. Please. Please."

"But dearest, we have to go."

"Please."

"They're waiting. They'll be — "

"The hell with them. The hell with him and the hell with her."

⋙ IV ⋘

THERE WAS SUN HOT ON MY FACE, and my eyes were closed. In my ears there was the muted hum and drone made by the quick click of the ties. Yet above it there rose another higher, thinner drone, a sort of singing. Yes, somewhere a fly was buzzing. Lazily opening my eyes I watched the fly, a blue-bottle crawling up the spattered glass which separated it from the passing landscape of Indiana in September. Or was this still Indiana? South Bend and Elkhart had already gone by — that I knew, because I had still been awake then — and perhaps by now we were in Ohio. Yawning, I turned my cheek against the stubbly green velours of the Pullman seat and gazed out at the flat farmlands, gold in the sun of late afternoon. The racing, receding telephone poles and their wires that dramatically sagged and then dramatically swooped up again. Trackside goldenrod with the dust of a summer thick and gray on its fronds. Cows. A straight ribbon of pavement and a wagon inching sedately along it. . . . Well, Indiana — Ohio — who could tell? And who cared, really? The main point was that I was heading east again, I was heading home.

Home? Once, and not very long ago either, home had meant where my mother and father were. But not any more. I guess maybe I'm growing up a little, I thought. And high time.

Sitting up in my seat, I reached for my compact and flipped it open. Napping, me napping. And people always look so silly when they're asleep. Silly and vulnerable. But when I glanced across the aisle I saw that I needn't have worried, for the haughty lady with

94

the ankle bracelet and the hennaed bangs was still deep in her *Anthony Adverse.*

I relaxed back and looked out at a fleeting and somehow familiar group of neat farm buildings set toylike in a grove of willows. I had traveled this road many times, but now I was remembering the first time. That had been in September too, a September six years ago. I remembered my not having been able to sleep at all then, even at night, and my lying awake in my berth with my head propped up on my elbow and my nose pressed to the pane, checking clusters of passing lights against a timetable. Sandusky, Cleveland, Ashtabula, Erie, at last I was on my way east. The East, the East, that fabulous, magic land whose residents were sure to be cleverer, handsomer, richer, and in every way superior to those of my own Middle West. And when the train had stopped at Buffalo I had hardly been able to keep myself from getting up and dressing and going out to set foot on hallowed ground. New York at last. Only the state as yet, of course, but already the excitement had begun, and I liked the taste of the words on my tongue, "I'm in New York, I'm in New York." . . . Sometimes I pity young people who have been reared on the metropolitan eastern seaboard, for there is a dizzy instant of discovery which they can never know. When you have been born in Mecca, then where do you turn?

"New York City?" my mother had said. "I don't see why you're so set on New York City. You don't know a living soul there. If you must go away, why don't you go to Des Moines? Or even Chicago?"

"But Mama, Daddy says it's all right," I had pleaded. I was still in the "Daddy" stage then and often "Daddy, dear," and given any encouragement I would have been using "Mummie." "Daddy says if that's what I want, that's what I ought to have. Or Daddy says I can try it, anyway."

"Oh, well. . . . But there's no sense in it. There's not a bit of sense in it."

Mama and Papa. . . . I put the compact back in my purse, and snapped the clasp shut. They were getting old, both of them. Mama moved more slowly, and less often. There were mornings when Papa didn't get down to the *Argus* office until as late as eight-thirty, and his neck seemed to be shrinking within the circle of his string-tie collar.

As I placed the purse on the seat beside me my hand touched the green cover of the first issue of Lyle's magazine (and to me it would always be "Lyle's magazine"), which finally, after long and earnest debate and a harrowing series of changes of mind on the part of all concerned, had been permanently titled *Panorama*. Once more, for at least the twentieth time since I had bought it at the newsstand in Chicago, I leafed lovingly to the contents page. Vol. 1. No. 1. Yes, and there it was, bold and beautiful — "Editor in Chief. Lyle Vincent Ellery." And above it, equally bold though less beautiful, "Publisher. Royal Archer III."

Proudly I caressed the name, my name. When you are alone and on a train, to whom can you tell your delight? And I had so much delight.

Picking up the greenness and clutching it ostentatiously to my suit jacket, I rose and started back toward the club car, directing a reproachful glance at the lady with the bangs, who didn't bother to look up. How could she sit there bovinely engrossed in *Anthony Adverse* — or even Shakespeare or S. S. Van Dine — when she might be reading *Panorama?* I marched past her more in contempt than in anger, and then brightened as I saw that a man in a section farther up the aisle *was* reading it. To me he looked like an unusually intelligent and discerning man, obviously a person of considerable taste, and I restrained my impulse to pause and pat his head and congratulate him on his discrimination.

Well, I thought, tugging at a door lettered "Aloma" and stepping across the roar of the vestibule and pushing at another lettered "Verde Grande," that makes eleven of them I've seen so far. Five in the Union Station and six in the La Salle Street. Not counting that boor who had lain stretched out disgustingly asleep on a waiting-room bench with a copy of it over his face. And the club car ought to yield at least several more.

It did. Three, in fact. I seated myself in the chair next to the nearest one — held in the fat but sensitive fingers of a portly man (a leading industrialist, perhaps? an influential magnate?) — and casually placed my own copy in my lap, cover side up. I looked at the man out of the corner of my eye. Why don't you just turn back to that contents page? I was thinking. You certainly have no idea who's sitting right here beside you. And would you be surprised, surprised and impressed and no doubt dumfounded.

Gradually I realized that the man was no longer studying the magazine, but instead was studying me. He was tentatively smiling, and I believe that in another moment he might have winked. Quickly I turned away. . . . Not quite the type to whom I hoped *Panorama* might appeal, I decided. Still, it takes all kinds to make a public.

There was a crumpled newspaper at my feet and, stooping, I reached for it. The *Toledo Blade*. Well, probably that meant we had passed Toledo, anyway. Straightening out the paper, I smoothed its first page and glanced at the headline — "Ship Disaster, *Morro Castle* Burning." Idly I let my eyes wander down into the lead of the story, sampling it with the detached, impersonal horror with which I usually read of any mass catastrophe — a famine in Armenia, an earthquake in Tibet, what were they to me? And then suddenly my hands clenched the paper and I stared again at the black streamer across its top. *Morro Castle, Morro Castle.* And I could recall Mrs. Ellery kneeling in front of her trunk in that room at the Barbizon and saying, "It's going to be a new ship for me this time. The *Morro Castle*. They say it's very nice."

I began to read.

Can words swim before the eyes? They can. And images of people can swim before the eyes, too, and struggle through oily waters in the black of night, and cry out, and drown. They can try to fight their way up a flaming staircase and not succeed, they can be trapped in a locked stateroom with tongues of fire licking in beneath the door, and they can pound on that door and scream and not get out. Bewildered, frightened, sobbing, they can run in frenzied desperation through a maze of corridors and never find the right corridor. With hysterical fingers they can scratch futilely at the hot iron of a lower-deck passage. They can be scorched and seared, and their flesh can shrivel and blister and blacken. They can die.

97

I looked at the occupants of the chairs on the opposite side of the car, and now I noticed that they seemed to form a solid wall of outspread *Toledo Blades,* each with that headline, each with that name. Above the steady rhythm of the speeding ties I heard scraps of conversation: "Did you read this part? They say the captain was found dead in his bath just before the alarm sounded. . . . Someone smelled smoke in the library. . . . It's still burning. Isn't it incredible to think that while we're sitting here it's still burning and they don't even know how many are lost and how many are saved?"

Rising, I fled, my *Panorama* falling to the floor behind me.

I don't remember much of anything about the remainder of that journey, and what I do remember is confused and blurred. I remember standing in the rattling clangor of a between-car vestibule and staring out at the oncoming dusk and at the lights which were beginning to flash on in the towns racing past. I remember huddling in my section and wishing again — but for a different reason — that I had been able to get a compartment, and gazing across at a braceleted ankle and not seeing it. I recall sitting before an untouched plate in the swaying diner at a table for four where the other three seemed to be able to talk about nothing but the *Morro Castle,* using it as a pleasant and convenient conversational gambit for strangers and enlarging upon its final agonies with an ever more clinical imagination. Once I started to break my silence by saying, "My mother-in-law — " and then I stopped before speaking, realizing that the words "mother-in-law" were inevitably comic, a joke. And so, rising, I fled from there, too.

When you are alone and on a train, to whom can you tell your sorrow?

I finally told mine. Seeking refuge in the women's room, I sat in a stiff little chair until two nuns came in, their black robes rustling and their beads clicking, and when they saw my face and the wadded handkerchief damp in my lap one of them said, "May we help you?" And although I wasn't certain whether or not they could help me, I told them, and I think that in a way perhaps they did help me. "We'll pray for her," said one, and "Yes, we'll say a prayer," added the other. "And you say a prayer, too." And I did, although it had been a long time since I had prayed and I never had been very good at it even then. And after that I went back to my section and I lay in the tomb of my berth throughout the night while the ties clattered by and crossing bells tinkled loud and then faded away and far ahead there was the most mournful and melancholy of all the sounds on earth, the sound of a train whistling at night. That was the first time I realized how sad it can be. There was to be another.

She can't die, I thought, the pillow wet against my cheek. Not yet. Not now. She can't, she can't, she can't. She has to live at least until she knows. Because next to Lyle, she is the first of all the people I wanted to know. I didn't even tell Mama and Papa.

But when I saw Lyle standing there waiting at the gate at Grand Central the next morning I knew there was no hope, and I felt that he knew it too, although he didn't say so. I kissed him and I held him and there was nothing I could say. His eyes were dry, and his voice was controlled.

"I went down to the Ward Line and checked the survivors' list myself," he said. "She's not on it."

"Maybe she's been picked up since," I said. I was well aware that I was deceiving neither of us. "The *Monarch* and those other boats are around there. Maybe she's —"

"Maybe." He took my arm. "Come on, there's a job ahead of me. We've got a crew of photographers out, and I want to make sure that they cover all the angles."

"The angles?"

"Yes. This is the first big news story we've had. It's really a break, coming just in time for our second issue, though it's a pain, too, because I'm having to rip out six pages. And I've arranged for a camera plane to get air views."

"But Lyle —"

"What?"

"Nothing."

I waited as he signaled for a redcap. "Can I go with you?" I said.

"Sure. If you want to."

I did. He could go because of the magazine, if he liked. I would go because of his mother.

99

So I accompanied him down to Asbury Park the next morning, Sunday, and stood with him and the photographers and several thousand others watching the still-burning, still-smoking hulk of the liner as it lay grounded offshore. As he was jotting down his notes and conferring with the photographers, he made only one personal remark. "Sea Girt and Bay Head and Asbury Park — this whole Jersey Coast," he said. "She knew every yard of it, because we used to come here summers. And she had to die within sight of it. Just a few more miles and she would have been safe."

I looked out at the twisted, blistered ruins of the decks, and I thought of the reason — and I had always been certain that it had been the chief reason — why she had chosen to isolate and quarantine herself on them. Yes, I thought. Yes, she had been almost ashore and almost safe. Just a few more miles and a few more months.

He turned to one of the photographers, and snapped his fingers. "Come on, Rocky," he said. "Let's get on with it."

Late that night in New York I was with him when he was directing and assisting others of the staff in interviewing some of the first bedraggled, weary, excited survivors. One of them was a girl about seventeen, grotesque and almost ludicrous in the makeshift clothes her rescuers had given her. She talked on garrulously, with a Southern accent. "Oh, it was terrible," she said. "It was awful. My girl friend and I, we were positive we were going to die, just positive. But there was a woman there, she was the ship's hostess, and she'd been teaching us contract bridge on the way up, and she was just about the nicest person you ever heard tell of. 'You won't die,' she kept saying. 'Stop screaming like that, and do what they tell you. You won't die.' Oh, she was such a *lady*. And so — well, so sort of aristocratic and refined looking. You know? She had hair that was kind of a peculiar color. Kind of blue."

Lyle's pencil paused only briefly. "What was the last you saw of her?" he said.

She was probably no more callous and bloodthirsty than any other girl of seventeen, but now that she had solid ground beneath her and was filled with hot coffee and surrounded by a flatteringly attentive audience she warmed to her theme. "Well, it was just after we'd got into the boat and were being lowered — we were in one of the last of them. She was standing at the railing looking out in the dark toward the coast line. I could see her just as plain as if it was day, because she was lighted up by all those flames around her. My, it must have been simply stifling for her up there. Anyway, after that she turned and went away — I don't know where. Probably to get more people out of their staterooms. She'd got a lot out already." More personal concerns began to stir her. "My girl friend and I, we'd bought some perfume in Havana. French perfume. It cost us, oh, so much money, and now I don't suppose we'll ever be able to . . ."

The pencil resumed its work.

In the early morning, almost dawn it was, we were back in the apartment, the notes sent on to the office, the job done. Coming out from the bathroom, undressed and ready for bed, I was surprised to see that he wasn't where I had expected to see him, which was in his bed and asleep. He wasn't even in the room. I went toward the living room, and there I found him. He didn't hear me enter, nor did he see me, for he was seated on the sofa wearing pyjamas and robe, in the small pool of light from a single lamp, and his back was toward me, only the top of his head showing above the sofa's rim. I went forward and looked over his shoulder and I saw that he was slowly turning the pages of the charred remains of an album, its leatherette cover half burned away but with the tracings of gold-leaf letters still faintly legible: "Eva Ellery: Her Book." And on the table in front of him lay the singed shell of a broken maraca.

With my hands in the pockets of my dressing gown I stood there looking down at him. I felt better, so much better; for now I knew that he felt worse. Yet as I watched him I felt sorry, too — even sorrier than I would normally feel — for I was thinking of him and his mother and of how she had eternally rasped and grated against him, and I knew that he was thinking of that also. I was remembering his impatience with her imperfections, the withering scorn with which he had used to speak of "you and those boys of yours," his embarrassment on those occasions when she had become too gay, his ill-disguised exasperation when she had become too giddy. "Good

God," I had heard him say, and he had said it more than once, "the least she can do is to try and act her age."

Gently I placed my hand on his shoulder.

"Darling," I said, "you mustn't torture yourself like this."

If he was startled by my presence, he gave no sign of it. He didn't even look up or around, and he made no answer.

"You couldn't have been any different from the way you were," I went on, "and she couldn't have been any different from the way she was. You just weren't able to understand her, that's all. And she wasn't always easy to understand, either. So you mustn't be remorseful."

Then, turning and lifting his head, he did look up at me. "What?"

I leaned toward him, my arms folded on the sofa's edge. " 'I wish I hadn't done that, I wish I hadn't said that' — now where does that get you?"

He was fingering the album again, which still smelled of smoke.

"That is what you were thinking," I said. "Wasn't it?"

He nodded. "Yes."

I touched the lobe of his ear and began to deliver a homily which, though it might have been trite, at least was true. "Well, that's wrong. It's human enough, but it's wrong. Everybody does that when someone they love dies. They think, 'Oh, I wish I'd been kinder, more sympathetic, more — more tolerant.' But you see, that doesn't help either you or her now. After all, you only behaved the way you had to behave, didn't you?"

"Yes."

Straightening, I smiled and looked down at his head. I smoothed his hair and let my hand rest on it a moment.

"Come on, dear," I said. "You ought to get some sleep."

"In a minute."

I left him there, and went back to the bedroom. It was much more than a minute before he came in, and in the meantime I could picture him sitting on the sofa reviewing those snapshots which were a record of his early years and her best ones. Then as I lay in bed I saw his silhouette in the doorway and the glowing tip of his cigarette, which moved with him. I heard the springs creak as he got into his bed, and saw the sparks of the cigarette shower away as he crushed it out on the ash tray beside him. For a time he was silent, and in the dim light I could see that he was staring at the wall.

"I never knew she kept a thing like that," he said. "I never would even have imagined it."

I said nothing, because there seemed to be nothing I could say.

His hand roamed restlessly over the blanket. "There are so many things I'd like to tell her that I didn't tell her. I always meant to, I suppose, but I never did. I mean, about things she did for me when I was a kid and that I've never forgotten." He paused. "I remember once I found a hummingbird and I brought it in to her and she — "

"Now don't, Lyle," I said. "I told you not to. Go to sleep."

He shifted on his pillow. "All right." And then a moment later he began to talk again, and I realized that he was excusing his soliloquy on the assumption that he was theorizing generally rather than being personal.

"I never knew I'd feel like this," he said. "I never had any idea. But I suppose a mother is like light or air or the ground you walk on. It's always been there, and you think it always will be." He waited. "And then suddenly it isn't there. It's gone, and you're alone."

I was looking at the wall now, too. "You're not really alone, though. I mean — well, there's me."

"I know."

It wasn't all I could have desired, but it was something.

We lay there, not speaking, for quite a long time. Then I said, "Lyle."

"Mm?"

"Are you awake?"

It was a question I had sometimes asked before and to which he had usually replied, "No. I'm sound asleep and snoring." But now he merely said, "Yes."

"I'm going to have a baby, Lyle. At least I think I am. And I went to Dr. Herkle out in Ammon just before I left, and he thinks so too."

There was no answer, and I thought, "No, I shouldn't have told him now, at this time. I had a notion it might help him. But it hasn't. Maybe — maybe he's even angry." And I left off looking at the wall and turned my head away from him, to gaze at the profiled furniture, black against the windows in the first gray light of daybreak.

Then I heard his hand reach out from the other bed, across that inches-wide chasm which could be either a thousand miles of separation or none at all, and which at various times and for various reasons had been each. He took my hand. "That's fine," he said. "That's — well, fine. I'm glad."

Again I faced him, and I smiled. "Are you? I hoped you would be, because I am too. But I was a little afraid you might be — "

And after that with a single throwback of the covers he was out of his bed and sitting on mine, sitting beside me and holding me, or rather letting me hold him, and burying his face in my shoulder and hair. The tears which hadn't come, and which I had taken for granted would never come, came now. No words at first, just tears.

I soothed his cheek, and felt it wet. I cradled him. "Go ahead — cry." Weep for your mother, weep for women.

His voice was muffled, and he brushed his wrist against his eyes. "I'm sorry I'm making such a damned fool of myself," he said.

"You're not. You're really not. Please cry. Get it out and get it over."

And he did cry and then later he slept, even though I still lay awake until shafts of bright September sunlight began slanting into the room. How curious it was, I thought, how odd. He had never been so weak before — and yet to me he had never been so wonderful.

Because he needed me.

That was the winter of my content, a winter when there was richness everywhere, within me and without. There have been numerous picture magazines since, but none ever created that first sensation that *Panorama* did, and none has ever equaled its success. "There'll be other stories," I had told Lyle, and there were; in fact there were so many that occasionally it seemed as if time and events were co-operatively conspiring to produce their most lavish harvest in order to fill and feed those glossy white pages. Dali and surrealism were a novelty, and Lyle crammed a portfolio of color reproductions of limp watches and ladies with snakes in their stomachs into half an issue. Hauptmann and "Jafsie" were giving their testimony at Flemington, and he established a permanent crew in the courthouse there whose cameras clicked constantly and the results of whose labors were published for the edification of an avid if deplorable public week after week after week. The Rainbow Room opened, and subscribers in Altoona had the vicarious pleasure — and only for a dime, too — of seeing a much-tinted Ethel Merman standing in the center of its revolving dance floor and singing "You're the Top." Even Europe was gracious enough to contribute its quota of photogenic entertainment — a king of Yugoslavia assassinated in Marseilles, a tiny Austrian chancellor lying dead on a couch with his blood running out. And each trip of the *Conte di Savoia* brought sandscapes of handsome, bearded Italians cantering briskly, romantically, and possessively over the Ethiopian desert.

"It's really astonishing how the thing has caught on," commented Natalie, admiringly. "You know, if Lyle keeps on like this it won't even be necessary for Americans to learn how to read any more. All they'll need to do is know how to open their eyes and look. And great grief how the money rolls in!"

"What does Kendrick have to say about it?" asked Lyle, grinning. He was a little complacent — and why not?

"Oh, boy! He's livid. Speechless. Every week it comes out he slams a copy down on his desk and sits there glaring at it and probably thinking, 'There but for the grace of God is what belongs to me.' "

"It could have," said Lyle. "It could have."

We saw a lot of Natalie that winter, and of Freddie Wheaton, too. I liked him. He was fun, and kind, and — well, nice. And I could see that Natalie liked him also. More than liked him. At the beginning I think she had looked upon him calculatingly and even cold-bloodedly as a potential husband, a port in a subsiding storm, but gradually I could see her changing. She was a trifle more adroit in the employment of her sugar now, and certainly she was far less tense and even in a way tender. Less brittle, more benign. She never spoke of Ben at all, and I doubted that she even ever thought of him.

She spoke of Laura, though, and when she did I had to smile as I recalled how once I would have winced at her outright mention of the name.

"You had a pretty bad case of the jitters back there for a while, didn't you?" she said, on a Saturday afternoon in late autumn when I had taken a bus ride down Fifth Avenue and had stopped in to see her in MacDougal Street.

"Did I?" Those months had been a nightmare which I didn't like to think about, much less talk about.

"Look, you needn't be coy with me," she said. "You were a female Othello, and you know it."

I looked at the tubular chair which had once been white and which she had now had re-covered in a lemon-yellow. "Yes," I admitted. "I was."

"Well, why aren't you now?"

I sat abstracted, bemused, in a reverie. Even though I had been there many times since moving out I never could get over a strange sense of duality whenever I returned to this apartment. I was not only a visitor who would be spending an hour or so here and then leaving, I was also someone else — a girl, or the ghost of a girl, who lived here, slept here, had head colds and washed her stockings here. I could lay my coat on the red-and-yellow bed in the bedroom, powder my face in the oval mirror which had reflected it back at me so often, and sit here on the monk's-cloth divan and be two people, myself-past and myself-present. . . . And now I found my hand going automatically and gently toward what was still more or less my waist, to feel the life that was stirring beneath it. There was a time when I was so unhappy in this room, I thought. But out of the nettle danger I have plucked this flower safety.

"Why aren't you now?" a voice repeated; Natalie's voice. I turned toward her. I was back again.

"Why aren't I what?"

"Jealous of Laura. Why shouldn't she still be the same old green-eyed monstress she was then?"

"Oh." Letting my hand fall to the divan cover, I pulled at a raveling. Always raveling, it was: how did it ever manage to hold together? "Well, things have changed a little. The situation and — attitudes."

She was standing in the closet kitchen preparing a cup of coffee, and she peered at me round the doorjamb. "Attitudes? Whose? Yours or Lyle's?"

"Both."

She came out and extended the coffee toward me. "How about hers?"

"I'm not really interested in hers. Whatever it is or was, it doesn't make any difference now."

She seated herself on the other end of the divan and, lounging there, looked at me speculatively. "I hope you're not depending too much on the baby. I know they're supposed to be practically as effective as a ball and chain, but still — I'm told that this period you're going through has its elements of risk."

I shook my head, and smiled. She was perverse, she really was; perverse and contrary. When I had had what I believed to be genuine reason for jealousy, she wouldn't discuss it. Now that I knew for certain that I had no reason, she wouldn't discuss anything else.

"The baby is a result, not a cause," I said. "It's the — aftermath, not a preventive." How to tell her about a vow? Yet, after all, why should I tell her? . . . I sipped my coffee. "So you needn't worry. He doesn't even speak of her any more. He still has to work with her, yes — of course. But he hardly ever mentions her."

She munched at a cookie. "So? Very interesting. And what does that prove?"

It wouldn't have proved anything if I hadn't happened to have had other proof already, in the form of words which were engraved on my mind and carved in my heart. But those were a secret, my peculiar treasure.

"Enough," I said. "For me."

"You know," she said slowly, meditatively, "silence can sometimes mean — "

"Yes, yes. I know."

I had stated that I wasn't interested in what Laura's attitude might be now, and I wasn't, but that didn't mean that I disliked her or that we saw any less of her and Archer than we had previously. The memory of a lightning flash remains whether the lightning has struck or hasn't struck, and therefore I was unable to recast her in my mind in her original role of lady bountiful and rescuing angel. But she was still an indefatigable hostess, still an unpublicized though potent factor in the formation of the magazine's policies, and — there was no doubt about it — she could still momentarily enslave and enchant me whenever she took the trouble to do so. She didn't take it often, and I don't suppose there was any reason why she should have. I probably wouldn't have either, had I been in her place.

Yet when she did she was irresistible. I hadn't mentioned my pregnancy to her because I didn't believe it would interest her greatly, and also because I had an idea that she might even consider it to be rather peasantlike of me, but when I did — with studied matter-of-factness, over the phone — I was both surprised and pleased by her warmth and cordiality. "A baby?" she said. "Oh, my dear, how wonderful for you! How simply wonderful!"

"Really?" I said. "Do you really feel that way about it?"

"Of course I do," she insisted. I could sense that celebrated charm zooming toward me with the speed of light crosstown from Sixty-third Street to Sutton Place. "Anybody would. It's what you've needed."

She talked on at length, intimately and with an unexpectedly detailed lore of obstetrics, for some seven minutes of her valuable and strictly rationed time, and when I rang off — or when she rang off, rather, because it was always she who rang off — I was in a glow of good-feeling. She was nice, I decided, she really was nice. And it was only later that I realized that during those seven minutes she had not spoken the name "Lyle" once or even hinted at his existence. If I was going to have a baby, in her opinion I apparently was going to have it through the process of parthenogenesis and all-my-own-work. . . .

"If" I was going to have a baby? It was becoming increasingly evident that I was going to have one. For the first several months I had been conceited enough to imagine that I was destined to explode the whole doctrine of the fruits of Original Sin: I was going to defeat nature and be the first woman in history ever to bear a child in a dignified, abnormal, and completely unobtrusive manner. However, I knew now that that was not to be — and I knew it even more as the weeks went on. The possibility of my proving a miracle was past, long past, and I was going to be like everybody else who was as I was and look like everybody else.

To say that I enjoyed those middle months would be to exaggerate. Yet surely I wasn't unhappy during them, either. There was discomfort and distress, yes, but not unhappiness. In a way I went from one extreme to the other, for instead of attempting to conceal my state I now began to flaunt it. Along with my sisterhood, of whom I had never believed there could be so many in one winter, I sat in whimsically named department store specialty shops and hesitated gravely between the pink and the blue. I presented myself at regular intervals for inspection at my doctor's office, and dutifully took slow, ponderous walks in the Park, and gradually transformed the anonymous "other" bedroom into a nursery. During the long white afternoons — it was a season of much snow — I reclined knitting in the living room while Callie ironed in the kitchen, intoning mournful melodies. "*They's comin' to carry me away, oh Lord,*" she sang, "*they's comin' to carry me away. . . .*" Occasionally I said, "Couldn't you sing something a little more lively, maybe, Callie?" and she always said, "Yes, Mis' Ellery." But she seldom did.

Days of quiet, days of growth, days of peace, the snow falling, the pavements slippery (be careful, be careful), slabs of ice drifting in the river, a coal barge with its black load frosted white, the girders on the bridge ridged with white too, and little puffs of smoke white against a gray sky. A loom of days, weaving in, weaving out, each much the same and each furthering an ultimate pattern and design. . . . There was a lull in my life, and it was a lovely lull.

And then that one day, the long day.

It was March and it was noon and I was seated with the tray lunch which Callie had brought in to me in the nursery, where I had formed a habit of often sitting, as if trying to acclimatize myself. There were times when I couldn't seem to eat anything, and there were others when I couldn't seem to eat enough. This was one of those when I couldn't seem to eat enough. I had a chicken bone in my hand and I was gnawing at it with a serious and sensual concentration when I became aware of someone looking at me and, glancing up, saw Lyle in the doorway.

"Hello," I said, a little embarrassed and ashamed that he should have been standing there watching my solitary wolfishness. . . . He was home in the middle of the day? Why? I wondered.

I soon learned why. Coming into the room, he walked toward the chaise longue and looked down at me, nervously jingling the keys in his trouser pocket. Even if I hadn't been able to discern it from his face, the jingling of those keys would have been ample warning that storm signals had been set. It was and always had been a mannerism whose message was as unmistakable as the running up of a distress flag.

"There's been a row," he said. "I've quit."

"Quit?" The word meant nothing to me. "Quit what?"

"My job. The magazine." He went toward the window and stood with his back toward me, the keys going furiously. "The bastard," he said. "The dirty bastard."

I put the bone on my plate, carefully. "Who?" I said.

"Archer." He turned, and I had the feeling that for him this particular moment was not so much a crisis as it was the anti-climactic continuation of a crisis, the fag-end finale to something that had gone before. There was a savage irony in his tone. "Me getting the freeze-out now, just when the presses can't even keep up with circulation," he said. "My God, can you imagine it? It's rich, it really is. I suppose it's even funny."

It might be rich and it might even be funny, although the humor escaped me, but I certainly couldn't imagine it. Or at first even grasp it.

"I don't understand," I said. "You mean you and Archer have quarreled?"

"Oh, boy. Have we. They probably could hear us in the top gallery of the Music Hall." He paused. "I hope they didn't, though."

"What did you quarrel about?"

Wearily he rubbed his hand across his forehead. "Oh, the same thing. It's always been the same thing. What sort of magazine we're running, and who's running it. I'm all for pictures. He's all for pictures plus propaganda." Shrugging, he made a gesture and then, sighing, sank into a boudoir chair, his tension apparently easing a little. "Well, at least it's finally over, anyway."

"But Lyle," I said, "Archer doesn't care what goes into the magazine. He's never cared. Laura, yes. But not — "

Taking out a cigarette, he tapped it on his wrist with fingers which were shaking slightly. "He cares now." He struck a wavering match. "'A leader,' they say. He says. 'Other countries all have a leader, we've got to have one too. We've got to get behind this man Roosevelt and build him up.'" He flicked the match toward but not into the flowered wastebasket. "Well, let 'em build him up if they like. He can build up Harry Bridges or Huey Long too, for all I care. Or Mickey Mouse. I want no part of it. It's not my dish."

I sat there listening. It wasn't new to me, any of it. Only I knew — and I knew it with increasing certainty — that Archer couldn't have said it, because so far as I had been able to discover he rarely said anything except "Six spades" and "Double." It must have been Laura. In fact I was sure it was Laura, because I had been there in that office time and time again and I had both seen and heard her. I could see and hear her now, through Lyle. "'A leader we can look up to,'" he was saying. "'A leader who'll be as strong as any other.'" He blew at his own smoke, dissipating it. "Mm, boy, am I sick of talk about leaders!"

"Was she there?"

"Who?"

"Laura."

He reached for an ash tray. "Oh," he said. "No, she's home, packing or something. She's sailing for Europe or someplace tonight, I think." Disregarding the interruption, he leaned toward me, urgent and earnest. "You see how it is, don't you? All I'm interested in is putting out a magazine that will be newsy and entertaining and that people will pay ten cents for and advertisers buy space in. That's all I've ever been interested in. I'm no crusader. Whether he's right or wrong, I'm no crusader."

I understood now. It hadn't been Laura in person. It had been Laura the ventriloquist, with Archer as her mouthpiece. As usual she was content to remain behind the throne rather than to appear openly on it.

"And so you've resigned," I said.

"Well — call it that."

"He fired you?"

He hesitated. "Yes." Then he went on, quickly. "Now look," he said, "I realize it's bad, but it may not be as bad as we think. It isn't as if people didn't know my capabilities by now. I can probably go out in the street right this afternoon and get backing for another magazine just by holding out my hand."

"But *Panorama* is established. It's — "

"And who established it?" he said. "I did." Gradually the elixir of his ego was beginning to work within him, and this was one occasion when I was thankful for it. "And I can do the same thing again, and better. If I find the right angel, I can come up with something that'll make *Panorama* look like a grocery store giveaway."

I gazed at the little that was left of my lunch. I knew him when he was in this state of ascendancy. It was the peak after the valley, the hot after the cold, the sudden mirage of the green oasis after the sudden fright of the barren desert. And, knowing that, I also knew that I would have to choose my words with care.

"Lyle," I said, "don't you suppose you ought to — think this over? Sleep on it, anyway. And then after that talk it over. With Archer again, maybe. Or with — "

He was crushing out his cigarette. "No," he said, sharply. "No, it's finished. That's over — and it's out. And I'm out, too. I just told you — I'm fired." Then abruptly his hand remained immobilized on the cigarette stub, and after that he twisted it again, almost triumphantly. He smiled. "I've got it," he said. "Kendrick! Now there's an idea. Why didn't I think of it sooner? He'll jump at it."

I was a little apprehensive. He wasn't as well acquainted with

Mr. Kendrick as I was. Few people were. "I don't know," I said. "He might — "

He had risen. "Don't be silly. It'll be a second chance for him, and it's not everybody who's lucky enough to be offered one." He stood there, grinning. "Say, you know I feel a hundred per cent better. Two hundred per cent." And he started toward the door. "Excuse me. I've got to see a man about a million dollars."

I watched him as he went, and I couldn't help smiling. In like something wounded, I thought, out like something rampant. Yes, it was Lyle. . . . But he wasn't out yet, because before reaching the door he paused and then, after an instant, came back toward me. He looked down at me.

"How you feeling today?"

"Fine." Though hardly as well as I felt ten minutes ago, I didn't add.

Leaning over, he kissed my cheek lightly. "You're not — sore about all this, are you?" he said.

"Sore?" I smiled up at him. "Of course not. I may be a bit — dubious, and it seems to me you're being more than a bit hasty. But I'm not sore. Why should I be?"

He patted my arm. "No reason. I just thought you might be, that's all. You're entitled to a few whims along about now." Then he straightened, and turned toward the door again. "Well, here I go. And don't stew about it. Everything'll be O.K." And he was gone.

After he left I remained there on the chaise longue for some time, tracing my finger thoughtfully around the oblong of the tray. Mr. Kendrick? I was thinking. Yes, Mr. Kendrick might and Mr. Kendrick mightn't, but even if he did it wouldn't be quite the same as *Panorama*. Not to Lyle. Nothing could ever be quite the same to Lyle as *Panorama*. And all those drudging months of preparation to be gone through again. And meanwhile the knowledge that *Panorama* had been the first in the field and that it had been his creation and that it had been taken from him. No dog like the dog that died. No jewel like the one that was lost. . . . No. No, it couldn't happen, it mustn't happen. And maybe — just maybe — I was the one who could keep it from happening.

Rising, I navigated myself through the door and down the hall and into our bedroom, where I stood at the phone, looking at it. Finally I picked it up and began to dial: R — H — 4. . . . Her number was an unlisted one, like movie stars' and bookies'. But before I had reached the final digit, I had replaced the instrument in its cradle. You invite people to dinner by phone, you discuss the weather over it and the price of fish and other topics. But when you beg, it is better to beg with the eyes.

I reached for the top button of my smock, and at that moment Callie passed by in the hall, en route for the tray.

"I'm going out for a while, Callie," I said.

"Yes, Mis' Ellery," she said. "You goin' for a walk?"

"That's right." A walk and a talk.

But I didn't walk. I went by cab, and it was only when the butler opened the bronze-grilled door that I wished I had at least taken the precaution to phone for an appointment, for until then I had been too busy rehearsing myself in strategy to pause to consider tactics.

The butler was Pierce, rotund, bald, baby-faced, and genial. "A personality boy," I had once heard Laura remark, "but we try to overlook that because otherwise he's so efficient."

"Good afternoon, madam," he said, and the door opened wider.

"Is Mrs. Archer in, Pierce?" I said. "I'd like to see her, if I may. Just for a minute."

"Won't you come in, madam?" There was no catching out Pierce, I thought, edging past him. Mrs. Archer might prove to be in or might not, but in either case he wasn't the one to leave a woman in my condition standing waiting on Mr. Archer's marble steps.

He ushered me into the drawing room, and after he disappeared I tried first one chair and then another, but I found the Roman-striped hardness of each a little uncomfortable. Ultimately I arranged myself on one of the sofas, which at least had the virtue of being broad. It was a nice room, a lovely room, beautifully proportioned and chaste and cool. I had never been in it alone before, and I had never realized how really large it was. Or how quiet it was. Outside was the city, but here was peace. Expensive peace, and elaborately simple. No gilt or gewgaws or gimcracks here. A high, white, fluted colon-

114

nade flanking the mirrored mantel. The long curve of a sofa back. A crystal chandelier foaming down like pendent ice. This was the Empire.

And upstairs was the Empress.

Lady Hamilton would look at home in this room, I decided. She could be quite happy here. She'd fit right in.

"Madam will be down in a moment, Mrs. Ellery." Startled, I turned. Pierce was standing in the archway.

"Thank you, Pierce."

He hesitated, politely hovering. "Is there anything you wish?"

Poor man, I thought. He's not used to pregnant women. And neither is this room and neither is this house. It makes them all nervous.

"No, thank you."

He left, and I sat on. I began to feel nervous too; or more nervous, rather. It was as if the room and the house were hostilely attempting to get back at me, to put me in my place. . . . Well, she was taking her time, she certainly was taking her time. Getting up, I began to wander around the room, to wander and to waddle. I went out into the oval entrance hall again, and there, near the stairs, I saw a mound of luggage, all leather and all in the same aquamarine shade of green. Trunks, suitcases of graduated sizes, round hatboxes, shoe containers, a typewriter case, even a golf bag. I went toward them and stood looking at the geological deposits formed by their labels. The freshest, with the gum barely dry, were those of "Hapag-Lloyd. Bremen," and some said "Wanted in Cabin" and some not, and all were neatly typed "Mrs. Royal Archer III. Suite 3. A Deck." Beneath and around were other strata, relics of other journeys — the *Ile de France,* the *Rex,* the *Paris,* the *Aquitania,* Imperial Airways, Air France, Pan American. And hotel stickers — two Ritzes, both London and Paris, Claridge's, the George V, the Royal Hawaiian, the Castle Harbour, the Adlon, the Royal Danieli, the Cap d'Antibes, and (a homey touch) the Everglades in Palm Beach and El Mirador in Palm Springs. No doubt about it, she had been around. I twirled one of the tags that said "Bremen." . . . By these shall ye know them.

"Amy?"

There was a scent of gardenia, and, looking up, I saw that she was coming down the stairs. I saw her first from the feet up, as if a curtain were rising on her: alligator pumps, flesh hose, tan skirt, tan sweater with the gardenia on it, brief pearls, and then her face with that black hair above. It was a simple costume, and she looked like a coed in it. Surely it didn't take her all this while to climb into that, I thought. I'd been expecting at least lamé.

"Hello, Laura," I said.

She had reached the foot of the stairs. "I'm sorry to keep you waiting, but this place is a madhouse today. You've no idea."

For someone who has just maneuvered my husband out from his own magazine, I thought, that is quite an airy greeting. Still, I knew that it was only a preliminary, and that she was waiting to take her cue from me: undoubtedly she had visions of a scene. But I would spare her that. There would be persuasions, even pleas, but no scene.

"I probably oughtn't to be bothering you at all," I said, "but I knew you were sailing tonight and so I — "

She smiled, the cue assimilated and accepted. "It's no bother." She nodded toward the library, on the opposite side of the hall. "Let's go in here, shall we?"

I followed her. I was glad we were getting out of the Empire.

But I was less glad after the double doors closed behind us, for I had forgotten the Rivera murals and those stocky, thick-limbed peon women toiling among the symbolic maguey plants in various advanced stages of fertility. Their saucer eyes seemed to leer down at me as if to say, "Well, look who's here. You too?"

"Sit down, Amy," she said. "I think you'll find that chair over there the most comfortable."

I sat, while she leaned against the desk, her ankles crossed, her arms folded. Her pose reminded me of something, but at the moment I couldn't think what.

"I suppose you know why I'm here," I said.

Reaching for a silver paper cutter, she began to toy with it. "I'm not quite sure."

"It's about Lyle."

"I thought it might be."

She was making things no easier for me, and I decided to get it all out at once. "Laura, the whole idea of the magazine was his, right from the beginning. He first told you about it here in this very room. And it doesn't seem fair that he should be forced out now."

There. I hadn't planned to put it that baldly — in fact I had had an artful brief worked out, complete with peroration — but there it was.

For a moment she was silent, drawing the paper cutter back and forth across her palm. Then she said, "I didn't know that Lyle was leaving the magazine until Roy told me. Believe me. It was Roy's idea entirely."

I looked at her, and oddly enough I did believe her.

"But you can get Roy to change his mind."

"No," she said, "I can't." She began to slap the cutter lightly against her palm. "And even if I could, I wouldn't."

For the first time I thought I detected a note of anger in her voice. Anger at whom? At Roy? Or at Lyle? Or at me?

"You wouldn't?"

"No."

"Why not?"

The cutter was going whip-whip now, and the anger was slowly but steadily mounting.

"Because Lyle doesn't deserve to be editor of a magazine as potentially influential as *Panorama*."

Ah, it was anger at Lyle. But why?

"But why?" I said.

"Because it's an instrument and he doesn't know how to use it the way it should be used. And even if he did know, he wouldn't dare."

Now was the time for pleas. "Oh, I realize that you and he disagree in theory — "

"More than in theory," she said. "In fundamentals. He's weak."

"Lyle?"

"Yes."

I was becoming a little confused. "How can you say he's weak when he talked up to Mr. Archer the way he did? When he tried to argue for his point of view."

There was a metallic noise as she tossed the cutter onto the polished desk, and the next day some maid probably wondered how that scratch got there. "You're his wife," she said. "Would you say that he had a point of view?"

"Well, I —"

"I'll tell you then. He hasn't. He's a little man, and he's afraid. I misjudged him completely." Her arms were folded again, and she was rubbing each of them with the opposite hand, digging her scarlet nails into the softness of tan cashmere. "He could have been a great man, a strong man, a leader. But when the opportunity was right there in front of him, he was afraid to take it."

"Opportunity?"

She shook her head impatiently. "You wouldn't understand. But I understand. And I'm thankful I discovered what he's like before it was too late."

She was right. I didn't understand. And the more she talked, the less I understood.

"Too late for what?" I said.

"For the magazine, of course. What else?"

I wasn't sure what else, but as I looked at her I suddenly remembered what her pose brought back. It was the memory of the big girls in grade school who had always ordered the other, smaller girls around, me among them, backing us up against a fence and standing there with their arms folded and saying, "Now, are you gonna or aren't you? You better, if you know what's good for you." And I knew too, now and for certain, that I didn't like her. I had never liked her, although her charm had often seduced me. But she wasn't bothering to use her charm now, and even if she had been I think I would at last have been immune to it.

"I don't want to fight with you, Laura," I said.

"You?" The derision in her tone was unmistakable. "You couldn't."

That stung me, and instinctively I reached out for the first weapon that occurred to me.

"You've come a long way from Butte, Montana, haven't you?"

"You mean all this?" she said, lifting a hand from her sleeve and

118

gesturing at the room. "It's not even the end. Not for me anyway. For Roy maybe."

Anger at Archer then, too, I thought. Contempt, anyway. . . . I got up from my chair.

"Well," I said, "I guess I'd better go."

I headed toward the door, and I was conscious of her watching me as I lumbered past. The Mexicans on the wall were watching me also. I felt awkward, heavy, reduced to a physical absurdity.

There was a small, straight chair in my path, and she stepped toward it with a swift litheness so marked as to be almost a parody of litheness. She swept the chair aside.

The gesture might normally have been interpreted as helpful, but as I looked at her I knew it wasn't meant to be. It was hateful. She didn't like me much, either. There had been anger at Lyle and anger at Archer, but all the time I had been in this room there had been mostly anger at me. And never more than now, when her inverted courtesy was turning me into a caricature. . . . Yet when I had told her about the baby she had said, "How wonderful." But she didn't think it wonderful now. It enraged her. Why?

Why? All I seemed to be able to think of was Why? and of answerless questions which I couldn't even formulate. Why? Why?

I turned, hesitatingly. "Laura —" I said.

But she had moved toward the doors, and had opened one of them. Only she could have managed such a gesture without appearing to be ridiculous.

So I went out, past her — she opened the other door too, again with that courtesy which wasn't courtesy at all — and past the slim white pillars circling the entrance hall and over the checkerboard of its floor and out toward the main door, and all the time I knew that she was standing there looking after me.

"I'll think of you," I heard her say, and because the entrance hall was severely unadorned her voice echoed a little. "Often."

I went out, closing the heavy door behind me, and I stood on the steps for a moment, trying to summarize something which seemed to have no summary. What had I accomplished, really? Nothing. The whole interview had been curiously unsatisfactory, from every aspect. When I had stood on these steps an hour ago I had been nervous, but at least I had had a plan. Now I had no plan. It was as if I had reached for something and it hadn't been there, as if I had attempted to draw aside a curtain and had found only another curtain, and another, and another, a mesh of curtains — and I had groped among them and had never got through.

Now where? Now whither? Now what?

There was a taxi passing, and I hailed it. It swerved up to the curb, and I got in, while the driver regarded me speculatively. Maybe he was a little worried, I don't know.

"Sutton Place, please," I said.

He started west, and I settled back. Settled? Sat stiffly, my gloved hand clenched on the upright rod. But by the time he reached the corner of Park and Sixty-third, I leaned forward and slid back the glass. "No," I said. "I've changed my mind. I'd like to go to Rockefeller Center, please. The Avenue side."

"Yes, ma'am," he said.

Sitting there on the edge of the seat, I felt him cautiously slow down to a crawl for a red signal. He was driving with loving care.

Yes, a mesh of curtains, I thought. Or a nest of boxes, one within another. Or a monkey puzzle. . . . Somewhere there is a link missing. Either I got too much from what she said or I got too little. It's like a game, and I've been out of the room and while I've been gone another conundrum has been substituted in place of the original one.

They were excavating for the new Italian building at the corner where I got out, and in company with scores of others I stood looking down at the huge dredges scooping up their great mounds of earth, clawing and scooping and swiveling and dumping. I saw them, yet didn't see them. I heard the clamor of the rivets and the staccato stutter of the compressed-air drills, yet didn't hear them. Then, turning, I went on. As I walked along the promenade I glanced down into the sunken plaza and noticed a cluster of models poised in front of Prometheus, wearing gauzy summer evening dresses and shivering in the March wind while a photographer knelt before them to get an angle. What was it that Natalie had said about Prometheus? Oh, yes, that he was the greatest boon to fashion photographers since the birth of Mrs. Harrison Williams. And there was a rumor that they were planning to install an ice rink down there, too. Silly. Crazy.

It's nice that I can think of things like that, I decided. It shows that it really isn't serious after all. And I went on. On and in and up, many stories up, my eardrums contracting.

I might merely have been imagining it, as well as imagining other things, but as I advanced amid the blond Swedish wood of the reception room and approached the receptionist's desk, which was large and completely bare except for the presence of six telephones, it seemed to me that I could feel a subtle alteration in her manner. Word gets around quickly, I thought. The king is dead, and so is the king's wife. Long live the new king, whoever he may be.

"Hello, Miss Roarke," I said. "Is Mr. Archer in? Could I see him?"

She smiled her receptionist's smile, which displayed more teeth but less warmth than her usual one. "He may have gone out, Mrs. Ellery," she said, reaching for one of the phones. "Just a moment, I'll see." I waited while she cupped the instrument to her lips and purred into it. Although I was separated from her only by the breadth of myself and the desk, I couldn't distinguish a word she was saying. She really was a very good receptionist, worth every cent they paid her. Replacing the phone, she shoved it into formation with the others. "Yes, you may go right in, Mrs. Ellery. He's free."

Free? I thought, starting down the hall. He was always free. "Why he feels he has to have an office here I can't imagine," Lyle had once said. "He never does anything in it except play solitaire and read Culbertson."

But he did have an office, and it was larger and more ornate than any of the others, including Lyle's or even Laura's. It was much-paneled and filled with deep chairs of cream leather which made sucking, sighing noises when you sank into them, and although I had never seen either the lounge in a gentlemen's club or the office of a Hollywood producer it fitted my conception of both. For a change he was neither playing solitaire nor reading Culbertson when I came in. He was seated at his desk, finishing a telephone conversation. "We're going to try Lambert, in News, for the present," he was saying, "but I doubt if he can handle it permanently. I want someone who—" Glancing toward the door, he saw me and motioned me forward. "Well, look around, will you?" he continued, into the phone. "Let me know. Call me back. It's a good chance for the right man."

Lucky Mr. Lambert, I thought. Lucky now. Unlucky later.

"Hello, Amy," he said, putting the phone aside and rising. "It's nice to see you. Sit down."

"No, thank you." I was a little afraid that if I ever sat down in one of those chairs I might never be able to get up again. "I'm only going to stay a minute."

He had come around his desk and was standing beside me. I had never known him well and had never understood him at all — perhaps because I could never have understood any man who was the possessor of fifteen million dollars — and now, as always, I wasn't even certain how to address him. Mr. Archer? Roy? I wished I could finally settle on one instead of using them interchangeably, and always with the feeling that whichever I chose was wrong.

"Well?" he said.

He was watching me, and waiting, an elegant figurine of a man with an aquiline nose and delicate features and with small, tanned wrists showing below monogrammed gold cuff links — I was sure everything about him must be monogrammed, and most of it gold — and with hips as narrow as a dancer's. "Dapper" would have been too vulgar a word for him, but he was debonair. Yes, debonair, fastidious, even exquisite. He was a silvering Eros dressed in a fine pin stripe.

"Well?" he repeated.

I used neither "Mr. Archer" nor "Roy." I just went ahead. "You and Lyle quarreled," I said. "What about?"

"Didn't he tell you?"

"Was it policy?"

"Yes."

"It wasn't."

There was a gold chain across his vest, and he plucked at it. Then he turned away and went back toward his desk chair. "I like you,

Amy," he said. "And I wish you'd go. It doesn't do anyone any good for you to—"

"Please. I want to know."

He shrugged, and he sat down in the chair. "Well, obviously you do know. Otherwise you wouldn't be here now."

So the last curtain parted and the inmost of the nest of boxes showed itself, and the puzzle was solved. I knew the conundrum now, and the answer.

He was looking at me, and his voice was kind, really kind. "Why didn't you believe him?" he said. "It would have been easier for you, wouldn't it?" He paused. "And for me."

One of the deep chairs was beside me, and I found myself sitting on the broad roll of its arm. "How long?" I said.

"Now look. I don't want to discuss it. It's over and finished and—"

"No. I want to know for how long."

He hesitated, and then he shrugged. "A long time. Months. Maybe even a year. I only discovered it myself last night. That is, for certain. I've been—wondering for quite a while."

Months. Maybe even a year. . . . The baby kicked then, hard. Whatever it was, boy or girl, I knew now that it was false merchandise. It's a bootleg baby, I thought. I suppose today I would have thought "black-market baby," just as I might have thought of that interview with Laura as a "booby trap." But neither of those terms had been popularized then.

Rising again, he came toward me, still fumbling at the gold chain. His voice was as gentle as a woman's; some women's. "I told you, Amy. It's over. I'm sending her to Europe, and he—well, where he goes and what he does is up to him. But he can't stay here. I'm sorry, but he can't stay here."

All that impassioned rhetoric there in the nursery about what he wanted the magazine to be and not to be, it had all been a blind, a lie, I was thinking. And "your mother's heart, my father's grave," that had been a lie also. How many lies had he told that I had believed? When he said "I had shrimps for lunch today," was that a lie too? When he said "I think it may rain," was that a lie?

Looking down, I saw a small, well-shaped brown hand on my

sleeve. He was bending toward me. "He was the one who ended it," he said. "She made him an ultimatum — you or her — and he chose you. So you see, in a way you're better off than I am. Because she was ready to give me up and everything I have." The hand pressed my arm. "That should be some comfort to you."

Comfort? Cold comfort.

Suddenly I looked up at him, and for the first time I began to think of him, of how he was feeling, must be feeling.

"Yet you still want her?" I said.

He had straightened. "Yes," he said. "I bought her. She's the most expensive property I own. The most — the most beautiful. And I'm going to keep her." He was silent and I saw a grimness there that I had never seen before. He might be a figurine, but he was cast in steel. "So far as I know, this is the first time. It will be the last."

No, I thought. I don't think so. You may think so, but I don't.

I stood. "Good-by, Roy," I said. It was strange how easily the name came now.

He extended his hand. "You understand why I couldn't let him stay on here, don't you? It wouldn't work. It just wouldn't work." He halted, and then he made his last admission — and perhaps his most difficult one. "You see, I'd always be afraid. Maybe not of him — but of her."

I nodded. After that, I moved toward the door, and he remained where he was. "Good-by, Amy," he said.

And then I went out, and down, my eardrums once more contracting.

And now I was in another cab and again saying "Sutton Place, please," but this time not countermanding the order, and the driver of this cab was driving with loving care also. In fact the drivers of all the cabs I took that day, and there were several, drove with loving care, taking corners slowly, not attempting to beat the lights, keeping their fenders even a superfluously safe margin from other fenders, as if they were carrying a precious and unique cargo.

But it isn't, I thought, looking at the bristly back of the driver's neck. It isn't precious at all. It's paste, fraudulent. And possibly it isn't even unique. For I suppose this has happened before, many times before. . . . Only it has never happened to me.

I got out and paid my fare, at least I must have paid it, and smiled at the doorman, at least I suppose I smiled, and again I was going up, but now there seemed to be no effect on my eardrums whatsoever. There was only a vacuum there, an emptiness, an emptiness everywhere. And I so full. Standing at the door, I inserted the key in the lock. I hope he isn't here yet, I thought. I need a little time, a little time. . . .

He wasn't there, but Callie was. I had barely passed through the foyer and into the living room when I heard the pantry door swinging, and there she stood in the dining-room archway, her hands dusty with flour, a sort of beige color.

"Miss Ism phoned," she said. "She phoned four times."

"Who?"

"Miss Ism."

Oh. Natalie. Her name was Chisolm, though not to Callie.

"She say you to call her. It's very important, she say."

Whenever Natalie phoned and whatever she wanted — advice about Freddie, analysis of their last evening, surmises on their next — it was always important, it couldn't wait. But it could wait now.

"Thank you, Callie."

She was washing her hands with her apron. "You feel all right, Mis' Ellery?"

"Oh, fine."

"You sure? You better let me get you a — "

I turned toward the hall and the bedroom. A cup of tea, that would be, because a cup of tea was her panacea for everything. "No, thanks, Callie. I really don't want anything."

Going into the bedroom, I sat on my bed, still in hat and coat. Then, pulling off my hat, I lay back with my head against the padded headboard. What I was feeling now wasn't jealousy or anything like it. I had been through all that a long time ago, and in retrospect — and in comparison with this — it seemed to have been a schoolgirl emotion, flighty and trivial. That had been a bad dream, but you wake from a dream. This wasn't a dream, and I wouldn't be waking from it. The difference was that between shadow and substance.

I closed my eyes.

There was a ringing. The phone. Well, let it ring. And I did let it ring. . . . Then, without opening my eyes, I reached for it and picked it up. I knew who it would be. It would be Natalie.

It was. But it was a Natalie I had never heard before — more excited, uncharacteristically burbling, and, it seemed to me, not quite lucid.

"I've been trying to get you for *hours*," she said, accusingly. "Where have you *been*?"

"Out."

"Thanks. Listen, can you be down at the Municipal Building by five o'clock? We're going to be married."

"Married?" And then I did open my eyes.

"I know. I feel the same way. But we only decided at noon. Am I in a dither!"

That makes two of us, I thought.

"Will you?" she said.

"What?"

"Stand up with me."

I wasn't sure that I could stand up at all, with or without her.

"Oh, Natalie, I don't believe I can. I mean . . ." I tried to devise a reasonable excuse. "You'd practically have to bring the Municipal Building up here. It would be simpler."

"Now don't quibble, Amy. And don't make me coax. You've *got* to do it. You've just *got* to."

And of course I did have to. I knew that.

"All right," I said. "I'll be there."

"Lyle, too, of course. Is he home?"

"No."

"Well, he's not at the office, because I tried there. So send out tracers or something." There was a slight sound of panting at the other end of the wire. "You know, I think I'm running a temperature. Is that normal?" And then she rang off.

Slowly and with difficulty I sat up, to face Callie's stern eyes as she came toward the bed with a cup and saucer in her hand. I smelled hot tea.

"Mis' Ellery, you're not goin' out again today, are you?" she said. "You been out once, and it didn't do you no good. I can see that."

I reached for the saucer. "I have to go, Callie. It's Miss Chisolm and Mr. Wheaton — they're being married."

She was unimpressed. "That don't make no matter. You tired. You —"

And I began to realize that I was tired, very tired. I stirred the spoon in the cup. "Callie, go get me some rum to put in this, will you?"

Her face stiffened in disapproval. "Now, Mis' Ellery —"

"Please, Callie." I made my voice authoritative. Sometimes I had to.

She turned toward the door.

"Oh, and if Mr. Ellery comes in," I added, "will you tell him please to go directly to the Municipal Building? He's supposed to be there by five o'clock." I lifted the cup, and I found myself smiling. I was glad I still knew how. "Tell him — tell him I'm going to be a matron of . . . honor. Be sure to say that. Honor."

"Yes, Mis' Ellery," she said coldly, and went out.

So again I sat in a cab. It is a long ride from Sutton Place to City Hall, a ride of several miles and several years, and I don't know why I should remember that when you get there the meter reads "$1.45"; but I do. However, that is about all I do remember, except for gazing dutifully up at the driver's license and noting that his name was Joe Appoloni and deciding that his photograph bore no resemblance at all to his actual face and wondering why such photographs never did and probably never would. It must be those caps they wear, I thought. It's an occupational hazard. Put a cap on a man and set him at the wheel of a taxi and he looks like every other man. You have no way of knowing what he's really like. You can't tell anything by his face or his voice . . . or his smile or the touch of his hand. Like every other man. Yes, like every other man.

Arriving at the Municipal Building, I walked up a corridor which was somehow familiar and opened the door to the anteroom and when I entered the first person I saw was Ben, with Natalie beside him wearing orchided mustard tweed and an expression which was not quite of this world.

Ben? I thought. Ben? You could have knocked me over, though not easily.

His greeting was warm and, for him, frivolous. "Well, well, well," he said. "My, how you've changed."

"Hello, Ben." I turned to Natalie, politely but confusedly. "I — ah — I guess I've made a mistake."

She was blithe, but vague. "Who knows? Maybe I have too." She jerked at her suit jacket. "I'll explain later," she added, hastily. "Or at least I'll try."

And later she did try, although I doubt if her explanation was much more satisfactory to her than it was to me. "I suppose I have Freddie to thank, if I should thank anybody," she said. "I mean, apparently it had never occurred to Ben that anyone else might be interested in me, and when he found out that someone was it sort of needled him into proposing, which had never occurred to him before either. Or maybe it had, because it seems that most of the Brains Trust boys are married and some of them even have children. Anyway, when he did of course I said yes."

"Why?"

"I'm not sure why. Freddie has a lot that Ben doesn't have, and he's sweet, I realize that. And Ben isn't sweet, exactly, though he can be at times. However — he's Ben, and I'm used to him. I'd never be used to not being used to him."

But all that was later.

We stood there in the unnatural, strident silence which precedes only weddings and funerals, and then the corridor door opened and we all turned toward it eagerly, with a sense of relief. But my relief was short-lived, because it was Lyle who entered. If he was surprised to see Ben, he gave no evidence of it. In fact he glanced at both Ben and Natalie only briefly, and all he said was "Hello, Ben." Meanwhile he was looking at me. I knew he knew I knew. I wasn't certain how — perhaps it was that word "honor" which I had left with

Callie, or perhaps my eyes were enough — but he knew I knew. . . .
I turned my eyes away.

"Well, here we are again," said Ben, with the groom's spurious
air of confidence and well-being. "Same old stage. Same old troupe.
Same old act." Somewhere outside and above us a bell began to toll,
heavily — one . . . two . . . three . . . four . . . five. Again Natalie
tugged at the hem of her jacket. Ben wet his lips.

"Well," he said, "shall we go in?" He started, stopped, and fumbled
at his pocket. "Oh, I almost forgot. You'll need this." Withdrawing a
ring, he thrust it at Lyle. "Shows how the church is all tied up with
the gold syndicate. Damn tribal nonsense. Voodoo business, that's
what it is."

"Come on," said Natalie, taking his arm. "Come on."

So we went in. The same gray-haired little man wearing what
appeared to be the same pepper-and-salt suit stood on the same
varnished oak dais surrounded by the same potted palms, a little
taller now and maybe a little dustier. Side by side in the background,
I was with Lyle yet not with him, away and aloof. Where Ben and
Natalie were standing, he and I had once stood, with me all monkey-
furred and nervous. As I watched them I thought, "Well, good luck.
Better luck, anyway. You'll need it."

The same fussing with the tie, the same preliminary clearing of the
throat, and then: "Do either of you know of any reason why you
both should not be legally joined in marriage . . ." No, I thought.
I suppose there is no reason, except they're taking an awful risk.
". . . or if anybody is present who can show any just cause why this
couple should not be legally married let them now speak or here-
after . . ."

I could speak and show cause. I could cite cases, too.

The drone of phrases spoken and repeated began to filter through
to me, the old phrases, the timeless phrases, with only the names
altered: "Do you, Benjamin, take this woman . . . Do you, Natalie,
take this man . . ."

Looking straight ahead, I nevertheless was aware that Lyle was
looking at me. I was starting to cry, and I was hating it. Why was I
crying? I hadn't cried at my own wedding. Nobody had.

". . . Will you love, honor" (oh, honor) "and keep her as a faithful man" (oh, faithful) "is bound to do . . ."

Despite myself, my mind went back to another March. Yes, Ben was right. This was the same old act on the same old stage with the same old troupe, only with the roles reversed — and with one of the troupe missing. For then there had been five gazing up at this droning man, and now there were only four. I seemed to feel the perfumed brush of rouged lips against my cheek, and to hear the echo of a voice: "Good luck, Amy. The best. I think things are going to be all right with you."

". . . in health, sickness, prosperity, and adversity and forsaking all others keep you alone to her . . ."

Lyle's arm was slowly creeping under mine. I could edge away, I thought. Just a fraction of a step would do, for this is an instance where an inch would be as effective as a mile. A thing like this — it isn't fair. (". . . have consented in wedlock and have acknowledged it before the face of this company," and mine began to tingle.) This time, this place, this reminiscence, it's merely sentimentality, and he of all people has always been the first to ridicule sentimentality. . . . But I didn't edge away, and when his hand came to rest on my sleeve I let it stay there. I even linked my arm a little closer with his. But I didn't look at him, because I didn't dare. For although I wanted to smile, I didn't think I was quite up to it yet.

". . . by the laws of the State of New York I now pronounce you husband and wife. May God bless this union."

May God bless ours, or what's left of it.

Then at last it was all over, and I was glad. It is wearing enough to go through that particular ceremony once. I shouldn't recommend doing it twice. At least not with the same man.

There was no wedding feast, because they had a train and they had to catch it. Standing at the curb, we saw them off to MacDougal Street, where they were to collect their luggage and then proceed to Niagara Falls. "Believe it or not," said Natalie, as she leaned from the cab, "we've never been there, either of us. Still, better late than never."

"It's a part of American folklore, you know," added Ben, good-naturedly, his foot on the running board, "and for some reason she wants to go." Then his eyes narrowed shrewdly, and he rubbed his chin. "As a matter of fact, now that I think of it I wouldn't be surprised if the whole custom was contrived by those Vanderbilts. Did you ever stop to connect this Niagara Falls custom with the New York Central? Did you?"

"Oh, Ben. Please," said Natalie, and her hand came out, yanking at him. "God help me," she murmured piously, from within the cab. "God help me."

And he got in, and they were off.

We stood watching the red tail light as it was swallowed up in the rush-hour traffic.

"Well?" said Lyle, as a second cab moved up in the rank and waited in front of us.

"Well, I guess we go home, don't we?"

"Yes," he said, reaching for the door handle. "Sure."

We rode in silence at first, and I think we both felt a little lost, for Natalie and Ben had provided not only a diversion but neutral ground. I sat in my corner, he in his, and outside the windows the lights sped by.

"A nice wedding," he said. "Wasn't it?"

"Yes. Very."

"She looked nice."

"He looked nice, too. That was a nice suit. His pants matched his coat — did you notice? That's quite unusual, for Ben."

Blocks and more blocks, the signals green and red, the taxi pausing and gasping convulsively and then starting forward again with a shudder.

"By the way, I dropped in to see Kendrick. He — he's not interested."

"No? Oh, that's too bad. But someone else will be."

"Oh, sure. Bound to be. It's simply a question of time."

And the screech of the brake being plunged down and the violent honking of the horn.

"Shall I tell him to slow down a bit?"

"No. He's doing all right. He's being careful."

Then, quickly:

"Amy."

"Yes?"

"I lied to you about why Archer fired me. The policy thing was part of it — that is, I did feel that way about the magazine and I still do. But that wasn't the real reason."

"I know."

Another silence, and it lasted and it lasted. Then I heard him as he slid across the leather, heard his arm come out, felt it around my shoulder. . . . I leaned against him, even gratefully. I was tired.

"But when you asked me, you know. That night last summer. The night you went away. Remember?"

"Yes."

"Well, I wasn't lying then. Because it hadn't begun then. It began while you were gone. She — "

Reaching out, I put my hand on his and pressed it, to indicate silence — and a lot of other things.

"You believe me, don't you?"

I shifted my head slightly against his shoulder.

"Of course I believe you," I said. "I knew you weren't lying then. I knew you couldn't have been."

That was the long day. Except for one which had gone before and another which came after, that was the longest day.

V

How do you record the passing of time? I asked, and I ask it again. The lying down and getting up bridge the nights but not the dreams dreamed in the night, the calendar tallies the days by their number but not by their final score. So how do you record time? By deaths? An English king in his castle, quietly from heart stoppage, a Southern demagogue in his legislature, noisily from heart stoppage and an assassin's bullet. Or by births? War Admiral to Brushup, my Johnny to me. Which is the proper metronome, the decrease in a baby's feedings or the increase in his weight? Can you chronicle time by a tune that is an agreeable novelty at one hearing and a pest at another (*"The music goes round and round . . . raound and raound"*), or should it be logged by a *Leviathan* docking for the last time and a *Normandie* sailing for the first? Can it be clocked by a move from Sutton Place to Jackson Heights, or should it be computed by the accumulation of check stubs and the steady subtraction of the figures on them, the zeros once added to a bankbook balance now chipping slowly off?

Perhaps time can never be tracked and traced, at least never completely, never wholly. Perhaps you're doing well if you just live it.

In Cleveland there were speeches on a platform and processions up aisles and the wailing chant of "for three long years," and beside my desk in the Graybar Building stood Mr. Kendrick, ready for a breather, a broad and beaming smile upon his face and a large celluloid button in his lapel lettered "Win with Landon." Mr. Kendrick was happy, Mr. Kendrick was hopeful. Hopeful? Mr.

Kendrick was sure. For the trump of the elephant was being heard in the land and he was preparing to emerge from bondage, led by the Liberty League.

"The latest poll of the *Literary Digest,*" he announced, smoothing its pages tenderly, "says that he hasn't a chance. Not a chance." Putting aside one sibyl, he opened another which lay beneath it. Two doves returning with bits of branches in their beaks. Two harbingers of peace after the Terror. "And *Panorama* says so too."

"Yes?" I said. I didn't know, and I didn't care.

"Yes." He was flipping through the leaves of that glazed stock whose contents had once meant everything to me and which now meant nothing, or worse than nothing. He paused, chuckling. "By George, this is rich! They've reprinted a whole column of this Pegler fellow on 'My Day' — and look at the photograph of Eleanor they've run with it." He held the magazine up outspread for me to see, and I looked. "How's that for a candid camera shot?"

"Is that what they call candid?"

"Guess they got her when she wasn't looking, all right. It's a pip, isn't it?"

"Wonderful." It was a very funny photograph. If it had been of me when I wasn't looking, I would have died.

His eyes wandered appreciatively through the surrounding type, and he was still chuckling. "The man certainly has a command of invective, doesn't he?" he said.

"He surely does, Mr. Kendrick. He surely does."

Tossing the magazine onto my desk, he chewed meditatively on his cigar. "You know, sometimes I wonder. What made 'em come to their senses? What made 'em change?"

"Who?"

He pointed at the green cover. "The Archers. *Panorama.* They used to treat that man in the White House like a little tin god. And now — well, now they don't. Now they're willing to call a spade a spade. A dirty spade, even."

I shrugged, and I smiled. "Maybe someone has decided he's . . . weak. Not a leader, or at least not their kind of leader. Maybe they — misjudged him."

The cigar was clamped firmly between his teeth. "How could they ever have misjudged a man like that? They ought to have been able to see right from the beginning what he stands for. I did. It was as plain as the nose on your face." The cigar began to waggle dangerously, always the barometer. I wished he wouldn't. I really wished he wouldn't. It was so bad for his arteries. "A 'breathing spell' he claims he's given us!" he said. "My God! After practically smothering us to death." And then he relaxed a little as he glanced fondly at the *Literary Digest*. "But it's all over now. Or it will be in November. No more Fireside Chats. That'll be something."

November, I thought, touching the bar on my typewriter. Where will we be in November? What will have happened by then? Or will anything have happened?

"How about Lyle?" he said, as if he had read my mind. "He found anything yet?"

"No."

"Still on that boondoggle?"

"Yes."

Again he began to fume. "I don't know what this country's coming to, I swear I don't," he said. "When I was Lyle's age, nobody ever coddled *me*, I can tell you! I made my own way. It wasn't easy, but I made it. And I didn't have the educational advantages Lyle's had, either."

I let my finger rest on the bar, and it jumped a space. "Perhaps the ways weren't so crowded then. Perhaps . . ." But why try to defend something about which I wasn't any too convinced myself? I tapped another space. "Well — times have changed."

"And people, too," he said. "They've got no initiative any more. They think all they have to do is stick out their hands and some Santa Claus will come along and drop dollars into 'em." Irately he turned toward his office. "And you know whose fault it is, don't you? One man's. One single man's."

I looked at him. What he had to say or think about Roosevelt didn't matter to me, didn't even interest me. What he said or thought about Lyle did. "Lyle isn't doing what he's doing because he likes it," I reminded him, meaningfully. After all, he had been willing and even anxious to have me back, and that was good and I was grateful, but his ears remained permanently deaf to any hint — and there had been several — that he might be able to help my husband. "He's doing it because he can't get anything else."

Halting, he turned. "Lyle's too big for his boots," he said. "Too cocky. He always was. He always will be."

I started to speak — and then stopped. I could have told him a thing or two about that, what Lyle was and what he wasn't, how he felt and how he didn't. But I decided not to.

"He had a good thing in *Panorama*," he continued. "A smart up-and-coming outfit like that. Go-getters. Why did he leave 'em?"

Yes, why? That was what they all had asked, wherever he had gone. Why?

"Stubbornness it was, the way I hear it," he said, answering his own question: apparently his pause had been purely histrionic. "Sheer obstinacy. Wanted to run the whole show." Again he headed toward his office. "What he needs is a good swift kick in the sit-spot." And he slammed the door behind him.

Possibly, I thought. Yes, just possibly.

Reaching out, I picked up the copy of *Panorama* he had left and idly leafed to its contents page, for I always found it an interesting if morbid speculation to guess who its current editor might be and what other new names might be listed below the unchanging one of "Publisher. Royal Archer III." Ah, still Tremaine? Congratulations. He had lasted quite a while. An entire six months. Much longer than poor Lambert, who had been in and out again within a meteoric but speedy six weeks, and longer than Hartwick and Corey, too. In fact it looked as if he were taking on the aspects of a Fixture. . . . Tremaine. Tremaine. I vaguely remembered having met him once at one of Laura's dinner parties. A nice-looking man, splendidly blond and highly articulate. "Dear Stan," I recalled her saying, "he's so able and so ambitious, but somehow he's never had a real break."

Well, he was having a break now all right. And a good one. He was walking around in a dead man's shoes.

Hastening on from that page as from something too poignantly

136

painful, I glanced at others. There was no doubt about it, the tone of the magazine had been much altered since Lyle's departure, not only in the increased space devoted to politics but also in what went into that space. He who had been a potential Messiah was now Lucifer, and the general plea was now for Rugged Individualism: rugged and as spiked with barbs as a cactus. The very type bled venom; the photographs were etched in gall. . . . I closed the magazine and dropped it into the wastebasket. She had wanted it to be an influence, and now it was. Why she had so dramatically reversed the direction of that influence I again didn't know and again didn't care. Maybe, as I had remarked to Mr. Kendrick, it had had something to do with "weakness." But whatever it was, it had little to do with me.

I sighed, stretched, and looked about the room. Like the other rooms around it (the organization occupied the whole floor), it was appropriately fancy and deceptively unbusinesslike — soft gray carpet, bright curtains, sofa and easy chairs of glazed chintz, fresh flowers in bowls. It was more spacious and elegant than many homes — certainly more so than my home — and whenever I left it at the end of the day to return to Jackson Heights I felt a sense of anticlimax.

It was the end of the day now and, rising, I hooded my machine with its cover. I was thinking of what Mr. Kendrick had said and why he had said it, and thinking too of what he had said on that morning some months ago when I had first told him — hesitantly, because I was fairly sure he wouldn't approve and I wasn't sure that I myself approved — that at last Lyle had found a job.

"Good," he had said, and I knew that what he had meant was that it would be good for me. "Glad to hear it. What is it?"

"It's — ah — government work," I said. "A federal project. They're planning on putting out a guidebook to New York and they want writers for it."

Suspicion had begun to cloud his eyes. The word "project" was the clue. "They?" he said. "Who's 'they'?"

I had gulped. "The WPA."

"Great Jumping Jupiter!" he exclaimed. "You mean to tell me they're putting *writers* on relief now?"

I had been standing by his desk in his office, and I had looked down at him. He was taking the words right out of my mouth — the very words I had said to Lyle, except that I hadn't said them so explosively and indignantly. Yet then, perversely, I had begun to repeat to him the words that Lyle had said to me. "But writers and editors are human too, aren't they? And painters and actors and musicians and people like that. They have to eat just like anybody else. Only this is the first time anyone has ever done anything about it."

He had snorted. "Thought they were supposed to starve in attics."

"Well, I don't think anyone ever claimed that they're *supposed* to, exactly."

My hands rested on the typewriter's cover, and I turned toward the file cabinet which was disguised as a highboy and on which I had laid my hat. It was difficult to realize that there had been a time when Lyle had been enthusiastic about the project, and even in a defiant way excited. And yet he had been.

The defiance was understandable enough. For months he had futilely made the editorial rounds, but according to him Archer had spread the word that he was taboo and every magazine in town cried "Unclean, unclean!" the moment he showed his face. If it was true, and it seemed to be, I suspected the subtle radiations of Laura's aura rather than Roy, for hell's usual fury was likely to be doubled and even tripled when the woman scorned was she. In any case, all doors were closed and had remained closed. All doors save one.

"All right," he said, "if that's the way Archer wants to play it, O.K. I'll take this thing. It's better than nothing."

"But isn't it a little bit like a — dole?" I said.

"Of course it's not a dole. I'll be paid for services rendered. Not paid much, but still."

"Well," I said, at least relieved that constant discouragement hadn't worn him down, "if it's what you want, why don't you try it?"

And he had tried it, was still trying it. That had been in early winter, and all through those raw, disagreeable months and on into the spring he had prowled from way below the Battery to way above the Bronx, collecting information and later writing it up. On Satur-

days and Sundays I sometimes went with him, and at the beginning
we had felt ourselves to be our own Columbus, for each of us discovered that although we had taken pride in what we believed to
be our thorough acquaintance with New York, it really wasn't thorough and never would be, never could be. We began to find that
there were worlds outside our world, and that there was more than
Manhattan — much more. We went to Riker's Island, then still rat-
run and not yet penal. We watched the giant arms of the Triborough
Bridge slowly feeling their way out. We roamed the jungles of Flat-
bush, and the bleakness of Mott Haven, and in the thin, pale light
of a winter sunset stood on a Flushing meadow which at that time
was mostly a dump for ashes and garbage. "I expect Peter Stuy-
vesant was the first to say it," observed Lyle, "but it's still true and I
suppose probably always will be true. This is going to be quite a
town, when they finish it. If they ever do finish it."

Yes, for a time it had all been very fine, very educational, even
exhilarating. But that time was long since past for both of us. For me
as well as for him. Especially for him.

Picking up my bag, I went out into the hall and stood waiting by
the elevators, toeing one of the silver crescents.

"Hello, Amy."

I looked up. It was Freddie Wheaton, and with him was the pretty,
flaxen doll who in a few weeks was scheduled to leave off modeling
in order to become Mrs. Freddie Wheaton. He had gone through a
decent period of heartbreak, but on the whole he had been quite successful in rallying from the jilting Natalie had given him.

"Hello, Freddie. Hello, Blanche."

"Another day gone, hm?"

"Yes, another day."

I eyed them as we rode downward. So young and so in love: the
current in their glances lighted up the car and made it glow. And
Freddie had been successful in other ways, too. He was no longer
the Connoisseur — there was no Connoisseur any more, because time
had proved that although Repeal might have varied people's drinking habits the basic staples were still whisky and gin — but instead
was one of the more enterprising solicitors in the advertising de-

partment. Onward and upward, Freddie. *Bon voyage*. And good luck to you.

Normally I used the subway, but this was late June and the day was warm and so, deciding to take the bus, I became part of the tide that flowed through the arcade and into Grand Central. I have always had more of a feeling for Grand Central than for any other station. Here, in one of the towers that loomed over it, was where I had first worked and now was again working, and I passed and repassed over this marble floor and under these zodiacal ceiling stars at least four times daily, usually more. The information booth in the center had been the scene of a thousand rendezvous, most of them with Lyle, and I had waited by it both while the dust-moted beams slanted overhead and while the great windows were dark. When younger, much younger, I had even danced here, coming out very gay and foolish from the Biltmore Cascades in the early morning hours and waltzing with Lyle while the cleaning men leaned on their mops and stared. If a public place can be home, and it can, Grand Central was home to me.

Yet not now, not this evening. This evening either it or I seemed alien, and it was much too big and much too crowded.

Maneuvering myself across the swarming beach, I ascended the stairs and, going out, dodged among the taxis and headed westward, toward Fifth Avenue and the bus. For once my timing was good, and a bus was waiting at my corner. Mounting to its upper deck, I expertly finessed a seat next to the rail, let the conductor suck in my dime, and sat gazing down at a human river of hot, tired city faces. Down at the faces and up at the buildings and ahead at the long straight street which, in the distance, was fringed with green on one side and with cliffs of stone on the other. Had there ever been a time when I had considered New York to be glamorous? I thought. When had I so considered it, and why? It wasn't glamorous at all. It was dirty and uncomfortable and inflated both economically and physically and there were far, far too many people in it. It was sucker bait, a trap for fools. I hated it.

Like a travelogue of disillusionment, my way unwound before me. Here was the Plaza district, as meticulously and showily groomed as an expensive woman — and just as hard and just as mercenary. No pity, and its charms regulated by the amount of your cash: and when the one was cut off, the other was cut off too. And here were the art-laden windows of Fifty-seventh Street: beauty for sale, if you had the price — and the price was seldom a bargain. And there the canopied canyon of the tall apartments, with their uniformed doormen stationed at their portals like so many watchdogs. You are expected? Oh, yes, sir. Follow me, sir. You are not expected? Then keep out, on your way, no loitering please.

We turned off, onto the ramp. Who says Fifth Avenue is always at its best when you're going up? It isn't. Because when you're on your way up you can also be on your way out.

We were trundling over the bridge now, and I knew that by a mere twist of my head I would be able to glance down toward those streets marked "Dead End" and up at the glint of a familiar row of windows high in a building on Sutton Place. But I didn't twist my head, for I was at my own Dead End and I had no desire to see the building. Instead I gazed at the cables as they flickered past. Who is looking out those windows now? I thought. What sort of curtains decorate them in the place where mine were? Who sits in that broad and spacious living room, and sleeps in that airy bedroom, and what have they done with the Aesop characters which used to be stenciled around the walls which Johnny was too young ever to notice and now will never see?

The bus lumbered onward. Over the river, I thought. Over the river and through the wood. . . . And so we bid farewell to Manhattan, miraculous and magic isle, rich and roseate in the pink wash of the late sun of Daylight Savings.

My elbow on the railing, I felt for my hat and, removing it, let the breeze blow at my hair. Placing the hat on my lap, I looked down at its white crown. Well, it was all our own fault, completely our own fault. We had spent so much; so much too much. All those Sulka ties of Lyle's and his Wetzel suits and that Charvet dressing gown, my own accounts at Bergdorf's and at Bendel and the rarely resisted enticements of I. Miller. Even Sutton Place itself. The leap from one room in Tudor City to several on Sutton Place had been too theatrical, even though at the time it had seemed no more than adequate and logical. Why hadn't we had the foresight to take it by easier stages? Why Sutton Place so suddenly? Oh, yes, I remembered now. Laura. That had been Laura's idea, as had been many of the others. "I'll think of you often," was the last thing I had heard her say, and no doubt she did. . . . But squirrels have the sense to store and save. Why hadn't we?

Over the river and through the wood and into the wastes of Queens. . . . The factoried litter of Long Island City and then out into Northern Boulevard to Jackson Heights. It is a comfortable and even an attractive section, Jackson Heights, a "garden development." But it is likely to seem more comfortable and more attractive when it is a preface to Sutton Place rather than a postscript, and after Eden probably no garden appeared quite the same to those who had once lived there.

Even after eight months I still sometimes became confused as to which of all these identical buildings was ours. But not this evening. This evening beacons were out, and neither the blind nor the deaf could have missed them: the sound of piano scales being practiced in 5-H above and the rich odors of pork chops being wafted out from the windows of 3-H below. From the left came the blare of the Morrisons' daily Amos-and-Andy vespers, to the right was the gilt cage set out to air on Mrs. Rauch's cerise afghan on Mrs. Rauch's window sill and the cheepings of Mrs. Rauch's canaries inside it. Also, somewhere there was a baby crying. Whose baby? My baby. Yes, I was correct. This was where the Ellerys lived.

I went up and on and in, and although my heart should have lightened it didn't. "No matter how humble"? Well, I'm not so certain. Sometimes yes and sometimes no. Maybe it all depends on where you've come from and where you're going — if anywhere.

Lyle was sitting at the secretary-desk in the living room, his portable typewriter set in the midst of an array of papers and maps. Laura's little decorator would probably have been not only surprised and chagrined but even insulted to see that desk in its present environment, and to see where the rest of his efforts — at least those which we had been able to squeeze in, and hadn't sold — had ended up. Mrs. Ellery would have been surprised, too (I was glad she couldn't be), for her mahogany chest and silver tray were there also And Mr. Kendrick's alabaster lamps, which had been the only possessions the decorator had permitted us to keep when we had made the move from Tudor City. The room was Sutton Place, or what was left of it, in Jackson Heights. But the blend had not been too successful, and at times it even made me uneasy, as if it were either a woman in a house apron wearing a tiara in her hair or one in an evening gown with a broom and dustpan in her hands.

"Hello," I said.

I had been unable to hear the typewriter at all from the hall — and in this building the walls were something less than soundproof — and yet now he was pecking away industriously. He glanced up briefly. "Hello."

"What's the matter with Johnny?"

He went on working, or at least through the motions of working. "The same thing that's been the matter with him all afternoon, I suppose," he said. "My God, what lungs."

"Did Callie give him his supper?"

"Mm."

There were two letters lying on the silver tray, one postmarked Ammon and the other Washington. My father and Natalie. Picking up the letters, I started toward the bedroom, and then I paused. "Thursday's the first," I said. "Have you spoken to her yet?"

Peck-peck. "Spoken to who?"

Who indeed. "You know who. Callie."

Peck. "No."

"Oh, Lyle. You told me you would."

"Well, I didn't."

I sighed, audibly. . . . I imagine there are few things more irritating and exasperating than a woman's sigh, and I meant it to be. If I was to be a martyr, I wanted him to realize that I was a martyr.

"All right," I said. "I'll do it."

I didn't stay long in the bedroom — just long enough to toss my hat onto the closet shelf and to repair my face. I never liked that bedroom. The oversized, padded bed headboards which had looked so smart in their original setting now looked simply silly. Either they were too big or the room was too small. Both, possibly. Screwing up my lipstick, I stood in front of the mirror, while Johnny continued to cry. It didn't alarm me, because he cried a lot; though normally he granted us an interval of peace after feeding.

"What lungs," I thought, tracing the lipstick. A fine one he was to be complaining about lungs. He might not know it, but he himself had done his share of crying too when he was Johnny's age. I knew it, though, because I could remember sitting in his mother's apartment there on West Seventy-seventh Street and listening to her tell me about it. "Such tantrums he used to have," she had said. "Cry, cry, cry — and half the time I never knew why. Mostly it was because he wanted something, I expect. And usually he got it."

Well, I thought, he certainly can never deny that he's the father. They look alike, they act alike, and as far as Johnny is able to think they no doubt even think alike.

Then I went through the connecting bathroom — part bathroom and part laundry and part pharmaceutical display, the whole smelling slightly sour — and into the other bedroom and there he was, squalling in his crib, my baby, my Johnny.

"Hello," I said, and I bent over the bar. "What's wrong with you?"

Nothing was wrong, obviously. He wasn't a mere infant any more. He was fourteen months, two weeks, and one day old, and he was healthy but not at the moment happy. Reaching for a wooden block, I extended it down toward him. "Knock-knock. Who's there?" I said. It sometimes entertained him, and why not? It seemed to entertain people much older. "Mr. Pat," I prompted, pantomiming, and waited for the crying to subside. It didn't. "Pat who? Pat your hands and . . ." He was not amused. Well, since this was getting neither of us anywhere, there was always "Handies." I forked two fingers astride my nose and fanned five others up behind my head. "Do you know what this is? It's an Indian in a — "

That did it. It was a newer dodge, though one he had fallen for before, and he was attracted, interested, and ultimately captivated. He smiled. The sun came out.

144

"Oh, Johnny," I said. "Oh, Johnny," and I leaned closer toward the crib. . . . It was the children's hour. For me, the best. Would I have felt differently if I had been with him all day? I suppose so. But the fact remained that I would have given much to be able to have been with him all day.

At first we had been undecided what to name him, though we were both agreed that he wasn't ever going to be "Butch." I had said, "How about Lyle?" and Lyle had said, "No, that seems to be unlucky." And after that I had said, "Well, there's your father's name, Vincent," and he had said, "No. That was unlucky too." So we finally had settled on my father, who was "John." But because that sounded too solemn and adult for one who looked neither we rarely used it, and instead said "Johnny."

I said it now, again. "Johnny. Oh, Johnny." And I stood there and I smiled and he smiled and by the time I left him he was gurgling.

All right, I thought, now for Callie. And I dreaded it, not for her sake but for mine.

She was tugging at one of the ice trays in the refrigerator when I entered, and I sensed immediately that her mood was not auspicious, for she hated that refrigerator with a bitter, personal hatred and had ever since she had first been faced with its treachery and malice. Either the trays stuck or there was the smell of ammonia leaking or the defroster refused to operate, and occasionally all happened together. Theirs was a feud, with the Machine usually winning. And it was evident from the way she was struggling with the tray that it was winning now.

"This thing," she said, panting and yanking. "This thing." Finally the tray gave up the fight, sulkily. In quiet triumph she bore it toward the sink.

"I understand Johnny's been acting up today."

She was holding the tray under the faucet. "Him? He's just restless, that's all. It's natural." Whatever Johnny did was "natural" to her. In spite or because of the fact that she had never had any children of her own, he was her sun and stars and she would tolerate no criticism of him, even from me. And often she could pacify him when I couldn't. Maybe it was as she had once explained it — "The

Lord never blessed me with no children, Mis' Ellery, but you don't have to be a seed to know how to grow grass."

Fingering the knob of the small radio which stood on the shelf of the cabinet, I watched her as she plopped ice cubes into a jug of cold tea. "Callie," I said, "Mr. Ellery and I have been talking it over and I'm afraid I have bad news for you — or for us, rather. We're going to have to let you go."

There were times when she was capable of a disconcerting and even questionable naïveness, and this was one of them. "Let me go where, Mis' Ellery?"

"You know what I mean. You'll have to — leave."

"Now Mis' Ellery," she said, placidly enough, "you don't want me to do that."

"Of course I don't." Who would? "But we can't impose on you any longer, really. You've already taken two cuts, and — well, we just can't afford to pay you even what you're getting now. I'm sorry."

Stooping, she peered into the oven and at the Swiss steak casseroled within it. "You quitting your job?"

"No."

"Who's going to take care of Johnny?"

"Well, Mr. Ellery does most of his work at home now, and I thought maybe we could get a high-school girl to come in and — "

She shut the oven door with a slight bang, and straightened. "You think I'm going to leave Johnny to any high-school girl? Or to Mr. Ellery either?" She shook her head. "No, Mis' Ellery. I ain't going to go."

"But Callie — "

She took up a skillet and put down a pot. "Now Mis' Ellery, you can just owe it to me, or pay me what you can. Everett gets his Home Reliefer check every week and what he don't drink up keeps me in church money. I got no call to spend much anyhow."

I hesitated, and then I turned my head aside, to gaze fixedly at a calcimined wall. Maybe there are ways of saying "thank you" when both heart and eyes are full, but I didn't know them and so I didn't even try. But I think she understood. I moved toward the door. "All right, Callie," I said. "All right. Forget it."

"You forget it, too," she said.

We ate the steak, we drank the tea, sitting across from each other in the dinette while on the other side of the swinging door Callie scraped at tins and beyond the screened windows the shadows lengthened and then blurred, the fading sun clouding over with something which looked as if it were going to turn into rain. Outside, on the playground below, there were shouts and sounds of running and the hard thump of bat against softball. Meanwhile I had read my letters, for I had thought that they might be useful as table talk. But they weren't, particularly.

"Natalie still keeps asking if we can't come down to Washington sometime," I said. "She says they have plenty of room."

"She offer to pay our fare?"

"Now, darling. Really." The clink of forks on plates, the tinkle of spoons against glasses, the click of the salt shaker, the clack of the pepper. "And Papa's peonies are in bloom. They must be beautiful."

"Is there any more butter?"

Well, that seemed to exhaust the letters fairly well. I turned to his more immediate interests — if they were interests.

"How did the work go today?"

"O.K."

"Are you still on the Bronx?"

"Um-hum."

"Somebody was telling me the other day about a place up there called Throg's Neck. It seemed to me to be such a funny name. I mean . . ."

My sentence drifted off, because now that I had spoken it the name didn't sound so very funny after all.

We sat on in silence until Callie came in to clear away, and then we moved into the living room, where he seated himself with the *Telegram* and immersed his face behind its widespread pages. The sun had gone now and twilight had come, either twilight or the prelude to a shower. Yes, it was a shower. Standing at the window and leaning against its frame, I could see a sprinkle starting, large drops spattering on the dust of the baseball diamond. The boys below were

147

gathering up their bats and heading homeward. A nondescript terrier trotted after them, its ears laid back.

Suddenly I turned. "What's the matter with you?" I said.

A page crackled. "With me? Nothing. Why?"

"Why don't you talk, then? It's not very pleasant for me to sit in an office all day and come home to a man who can't say anything except 'Is there any more butter?'"

The paper lowered, revealing his face. "What do you expect me to say?"

"I don't care what you say, just so long as you say something. You could talk about your work, or —"

"My work, hm."

"Yes, your work. Or anything else. Only don't just sit there and —"

"Now that's a fascinating topic, isn't it?" he said, throwing the paper aside. "I go down to the Battery and count the number of fishes in the Aquarium and then I come back here and list 'em. I spend all day typing out descriptions of the Mosholu Parkway and where you'll get if you take the Woodlawn Express. Oh, yes, that's wonderful material for conversation, that is. I'd like to see what Noel Coward could do with it."

"You needn't complain to me about your job," I said. "I was against your taking it in the first place."

He stretched his legs out, his hands in his pockets, his keys jingling. "What else would you suggest?"

"I went out and found work." That was a bit below the belt, and I knew it.

"Oh, yes. Sure. The little heroine. The good provider."

I let that go. "Nevertheless, if I could find it, you can find it."

"Can I?" He rose. "Where? Name just one place."

"I don't know of any place, at the moment. But I saw Freddie Wheaton today, and I couldn't help thinking that if you had stayed where he —"

"Oh, the hell with Freddie Wheaton." He began to pace the carpet. "You were right. You're always right. You said it was a dole and it is and I'm on it — along with sixteen million other people. I'm no

148

better than Callie's Everett." He uttered a single, sardonic laugh. "Ha! For this Relief, much thanks." And then he stopped and looked at me. "And this is the marvelous New Deal you were so sure was going to lead us into the land of milk-and-honey." He kicked at a chair. "New Deal! Good God, what's new about it?"

I went toward him. "*I* was so sure?" I said. "Whose idea was it to get married in the first place?"

"It was yours. You nagged at me about it night and day. You were hell-bent on it." Again he kicked at the chair. "Well, you're married all right. And so am I."

That was more than a bit below the belt, but it didn't even faze me: I guess I must be toughening up, I thought. "You didn't answer my question," I persisted. "Who was the one who said, 'Let's go ahead and try it, let's see what happens'?"

"I don't know. But anyway we've seen what's happened, both of us. This Roosevelt! He's made us what we are today. I hope he's satisfied."

There was a strip of *Panorama's* shiny green showing beneath the mass of papers on the desk, and now I noticed it and I knew what he had probably been doing all afternoon when he should have been working. He had done it before. I snatched at it. "*He's* made us?" I repeated. "You mean you've made us. You yourself and no one else. Whose fault is it that you are where you are? You can't blame it on him, you can't blame it on me, you can't blame it on anyone but you."

There was a silence, and he looked at me. "I've been waiting for you to throw that back at me. I've been waiting a long time."

I had never mentioned her name and I had sworn to myself that I never would, but now it was too late. I thrust the magazine toward him, and I was surprised to see that it was shaking a little. "Maybe you're wishing that you hadn't been so loyal now," I said. "If it was loyalty. She would have been able to feather your nest for you somehow. Maybe you wish you'd gone with her."

He was still looking at me, and it was a long, long moment. "Maybe I do," he said.

Again there was a silence, and during it I began to realize for the first time that it wasn't really a silence but that Callie's radio was on in the kitchen and that from it a voice was speaking. The words came toward me, from Philadelphia into the kitchen, through the panels of the kitchen door, through the dinette, into where I stood. It was a familiar voice now, and I had heard it many times before. But I had heard it one time especially, the first time. We both had.

I cannot with candor tell you that all is well with the world. Clouds of suspicion, tides of ill-wind and intolerance gather darkly in many places. . . .

And darkly here in this room and darkly over Jackson Heights, too. Rain was falling, swirling in the gusts of a summer storm. Turning, Lyle walked to the window and stood there with his back toward me, gazing out. I turned too, because I didn't want to stay, I didn't want to hear. Passing through the kitchen, where Callie was seated on her ladder-stool in front of the radio, her hands folded attentively on a dishcloth in black reverence — she didn't even notice me — I went into Johnny's room, to close his window against the rain. But although I fled it through the night and down the hall, the voice followed me, amplified from the Morrisons' on one side and from Mrs. Rauch's on the other.

Governments can err, Presidents do make mistakes, but the immortal Dante tells us that divine justice weighs the sins of the cold-blooded and the warmhearted in different scales. . . .

Mistakes, I thought, shutting the window. Many mistakes. And surely the erosion of the human spirit was one of them, no matter what the intention. I turned toward the crib and, straightening a coverlet and displacing a thumb, stood looking downward. The voice went on:

To some generations much is given. Of others much is expected. This generation of Americans has a rendezvous with destiny. . . .

"Generation — rendezvous — destiny." They were all grandiose words, platform words. Convention words. What did they mean? I

150

thought. Nothing. And yet perhaps they did mean something, though not for me. . . . And you, my darling, I thought, looking down, what and where will be your generation's rendezvous?

I stood by that crib for a long time.

Then I went back toward the living room, through a kitchen which was spotless and empty now, for Callie had gone home. Lyle was still by the window, and I looked at his back and it told me nothing. The room was almost fully dark, but I made no move to turn on the lights because I felt that what I had to say could be said better in darkness.

"Lyle."

"Yes?" But he didn't turn.

"We've got to do something. About you and me, I mean. Haven't we?"

"Yes. I suppose so."

"Well, I've been thinking. When my vacation comes in the fall, why don't we go down and visit Natalie and Ben for a while?"

"What for?"

"Because Ben knows Washington inside out — or says he does — and maybe he could find something for you there. And Natalie's invited us so many times and — "

He did turn then. "Oh, that's stupid," he said. "What could Ben possibly do?"

"I'm not sure. But he could try. And I know that he would try, too."

"I don't want to go crawling to Ben. And we'd be spending all that money, and — "

"It wouldn't cost much, and we could leave Callie here to take care of Johnny."

"But what's the point to it?"

"Maybe there isn't any point. But at least it's a straw."

"It's silly. It's — "

"Look, let's not argue about it now. We've argued enough for one evening, probably. But will you at least please think about it? Will you?"

He made a gesture. "O.K."

151

I started back toward the bedroom. "I believe I'll go to bed," I said. "Good night."

There was a moment before he answered, and glancing over my shoulder I saw that he had turned and was looking out at the rain again.

"Good night," he said.

Although Lyle had been there often, I had never seen Washington before, and I don't suppose I could have chosen a better season in which to have its splendors first unfold before me — in the bright blue-and-gold of October, when the winding gorge of Rock Creek Park was a polychrome wonder and flags hung tranquil from a hundred flagpoles and the dome of the Capitol glistened white against azure. To me it was magnificent, all of it. There seemed to be more and bluer sky than in New York, the air was cleaner, and the very sight of trees bordering city streets — trees all red-and-yellow — was soothing in itself. I loved the long green sweep of the Mall and the oblong peace of the reflecting pool and the view from the Monument, and when I strolled with Natalie past the embassies on Massachusetts Avenue I felt cosmopolitan and international. There was an atmosphere of tradition and yet the bustle of growth also, for the ubiquitous hand of PWA–WPA was at work here too, just as it was all over the country. Scaffolds soared, hammers sounded, and along Constitution great masses of marble were slowly rising, iridescent and dazzling in the sun.

"It's more than just impressive," I said. "It's beautiful."

"At the moment, yes," admitted Natalie, grudgingly. "But come around in the dog days sometime, when the thermometer gets going, and see how it strikes you. You know, I often wonder. Did they *have* to build the nation's capital in a swamp?"

Actually, as I soon discovered, she loathed the place — and for a variety of reasons. In New York, she maintained, streets and avenues were laid out with some degree of sense, and you could be reasonably sure of where you were at any given time; but here she was likely to head out from some circle and walk for half an hour only to find herself right back where she had started from. "And calling streets by the letters of the alphabet and the names of the states," she said. "Now there's a smug, inane notion for you. What makes them so all-fired certain that everybody knows the letters of the alphabet and the names of the states?" Also, according to her, the residents were either complacent because they knew their jobs would last their lifetime or in a perpetual tremor of the fidgets because they knew they would end with the next change in the Administration.

"Provincial may be a snob's word," she said, "but it's the word for Washington all right. Honestly, sometimes when I'm shopping along Fourteenth Street I try to figure out where some of these people come from. The Ozarks maybe, at least they've got that hillbilly look. They look like something Major Bowes would give the gong to. It's a hick town, believe me. It's crowded and it's cliquy and it's corny — a white-marble dump and you can have it. Only I'm the one who has it. Me, Miss Manhattan of 1923, who was born and bred to the sweet music of the Sixth Avenue El and never wanted to hear anything else."

"Isn't there *anything* you like about it?" I asked.

She deliberated. "Well, yes. You can get good soft-shell crab here, and when you blow your nose it doesn't come out black."

She and Ben were occupying a narrow slit of a green-shuttered, yellow-bricked house in Georgetown, and when I first saw it I was polite but embarrassed, because it looked like — and was — a remodeled stable and the neighborhood seemed to be not only a slum but a colored slum. I was well aware that Ben's ideas were "advanced," and yet . . . However, I needn't have tried to be so tactful. "Don't worry," she said. "It's really very stylish, as you'd know if you had to pay the rent. Personally I'd have preferred some nice unimaginative apartment that was based on hygiene instead of horses, but the fate of the nation is being decided in these Georgetown breakaways and Ben had his heart set on it. Oh, and that reminds me, I'd probably better warn you about the plumbing. I think it must have been installed along about the time of Rutherford B. Hayes, and confidentially it stinks."

Ben professed himself to be very optimistic about Lyle's chances of "finding something," and on our first evening we sat together in front of the Dutch-tiled fireplace in their slope-floored living room and planned the campaign. Or rather Ben planned it, mostly, while Lyle and I listened and Natalie, who was sewing on something, interrupted at intervals to offer what Ben genially termed her "two cents' worth."

"Now just exactly what did you have in mind, Lyle?" he began briskly, and I had a vague impression of a gavel falling.

"Well, nothing in particular," said Lyle. Unlike Ben, he wasn't confident at all, but at least he was open to conviction. And ever since we had arrived his attitude had been one of almost — could it be humility? In Lyle? Or was it only desperation? Whatever it was, it did curious things to my throat whenever it showed itself. "That is — anything that's available, I should say. And which happens to be up my street, of course. I suppose the main qualification is the ability to read and write."

"Not necessarily," said Natalie, biting off a thread.

"Hm." Ben sucked at his pipe. "Let's see now. Let's run through a few possibilities so that you can get the picture." Head back and crossed leg bobbing tweedily, he gazed up at the antiqued ceiling beams. "SEC, AAA, CCC, TVA, EIB, FHA, FHLB, REA, FCA, FDIC, FCC." He looked at him inquiringly. "Any of those appeal to you?"

"Ah — they sound pretty complicated."

Natalie unrolled a new spool and began to jab at the eye of a needle. "My dear," she said, "you've no idea." There were times when I wondered, and had long wondered, why Ben didn't rise up quietly and strike her dead, or at least dumb. And if his skin had been a little thinner, I think he would have. Or maybe he was a masochist and liked it, I couldn't be sure.

"You know what I think would be the best scheme?" he said. "We'll give a party for you and Amy — a big party."

"And me with my fall drapes up?" said Natalie. "Well, I should hope so. We'll give a real hoedown."

He had withdrawn a notebook and was beginning to jot something in it. "I mean a party with a purpose, so that Lyle can look the field

154

over and take his pick. He'll get the picture better that way." He held the notebook out in front of him. "Now how does this sound to you as a starter? Erd Phelps, Sid Mowitz, Herb McGonigle — "

"Oh, *Ben!*" She was brushing lint from her lap. "'Erd Phelps. Sid Mowitz. Herb McGonigle.' Lyle doesn't want a job in Moscow. He wants one here in Washington."

Each of his syllables was encased in ice. "Well, whom would you ask? Representative Fish?"

"Simply because it's a party doesn't mean that you have to stick exclusively to the Party Line, does it? Give him a break. Mix 'em up."

He relaxed a little, and smiled at Lyle. "She reads a lot, you see," he explained, charitably, "and she's got herself hipped on the Red Menace."

"That's not it at all," she said. "I think Communism is perfectly lovely, especially for Russians. But Communists aren't. Not those I know." She turned to me, as if in supplication. "I'm his ever-loving wife, finally, and I always will be, maybe, but really he manages to get himself tied up with the God-damnedest people. I swear that sometimes I think that if I have to hear the word 'liberal' again, I'll scream."

"Look," interjected Lyle, "we don't want to put you to any trouble. Maybe we'd better just — "

But Ben had returned to his notebook. "No," he said. "As a matter of fact, she may have something there in that mixing-'em-up business. After all, you ought to get the broad view. And I certainly don't want to seem intolerant."

Natalie opened her mouth, and I think she was about to say something; he thought so too, evidently, for he hastened onward. "So we'll include some of the Old Guard, too. Republicans, Democrats, New Dealers — we'll put 'em all in and let 'em stew."

"Democrats — New Dealers?" I said, confused. "But aren't they the same?"

"The same?" said Natalie, and glanced at me pityingly. "Are you kidding?"

Ben was busily writing down names. "I don't want to promise anything," he said, "but there's a possibility — just a possibility — that I can pull some strings and get Harry to come."

"Harry who?" said Lyle.

"Harry *who?*" repeated Natalie, aghast. "You don't mean to sit there and tell me there's anybody *else* named Harry?" She began to pile her sewing into a basket, and looked at Ben. "Let's give them their milk and let them toddle on up to bed. They've had a hard day."

There was a subtle change in Ben's manner, and I noticed it that first evening and noticed it even more as the days went on. Always before when he had come down to New York he had spoken profusely and intimately about his work — Mr. Moley was "Ray" and Mr. Tugwell was "Rex" — but now he referred to it very rarely. I assumed it was because the composition of the Brain Trust was altering, and undoubtedly that was part of it: Mr. Moley had gone ("No vision," Ben said), and Mr. Tugwell was going. Yet there seemed to be an additional reason for his reticence too, though I became aware of it only gradually.

"How's your Fascist friend, Kendrick?" he asked one evening when, despite his and Natalie's objections, Lyle and I had pooled our resources and had taken them to dinner at the Occidental. "You know, the eminent Liberty Leaguer."

"Is he a Fascist?" I said. To me he was just somebody who had once been one of the ins and now was one of the outs, a disgruntled Republican with a bad temper who remembered 1928 and forgot 1929.

"Well, isn't he?"

"I don't know."

"Sure he is," he said. "He's as dangerous in his way as the Archers are in theirs. Maybe more. At least they make no bones about — "

"Ahem," said Natalie. The name "Archer" was one which wasn't often mentioned in our presence. I never could decide whether or not she knew the true cause for Lyle's leaving the magazine, but I think she did. "Careful of your cuff, darling. It's in the butter sauce."

He took it out of the butter sauce, dabbed at it with a napkin, and looked across the table. "Wouldn't you call Kendrick a Fascist, Lyle?"

"I'm not sure I know what a Fascist is, unless he wears a colored shirt. I'd call him a jerk."

Those owlish brown eyes moved from Lyle to me, and back again. "Still middle-of-the-road, aren't you? Both of you. You'll never get anywhere that way, you know. The time's going to come when you'll have to choose your side."

"Why?" said Lyle, and momentarily it was the voice of the old Lyle, the unhumble and belligerent one. "I should think the middle of the road would get you farther than being stranded in either ditch, right or left."

Natalie cracked a lobster knuckle. "The trouble with metaphors, my dearest," she said mildly, "is that they have a way of exploding right in your face."

"Nevertheless," said Ben, who could be self-mocking when he wanted to, which wasn't often, "come the Revolution. . . ."

"But the Revolution's come," she said. "Didn't you notice?"

"I'm not so sure any more." There was only a trace of satire left in his tone now, and his eyes were grave. "To tell you the truth, I've been wondering lately. Are we headed for the promised land, or aren't we? Is there going to be pie in the sky, or is what I see the same old chicken in every pot?"

Natalie paused in her attack on the lobster long enough to glance at me. "There were twelve disciples," she said, "and one of them was Thomas. He doubted."

Could it be that Ben's zeal was about to cool? I asked myself — and asked Lyle later. Was cooling? Had cooled?

"I wouldn't know," said Lyle. "I really wouldn't know. About him or about practically anything else. We've been here four days, and I'm dizzy."

Harry didn't come to the party, but a lot of other people did, a steady stream of them. It was a cocktail party — specifically a mint-julep party — and they swarmed into the house and overflowed out onto the rickety, trellis-covered veranda and into the small back garden. I wore my wine satin, and as guests of honor Lyle and I stood at the head of the narrow stairs and with Natalie and Ben formed a receiving line. I had protested that a receiving line seemed rather too formal for two people whose main objective was to find a job, but she had said, "Protocol, you know. We have to follow protocol. Remember Dolly Gann. And you'll be in a strategic position. You can see them as they come up, and we can give you the low-down on who's who."

They gave us the low-down all right, and most of it was low down. Neither of us was completely a wide-eyed innocent or a babe-in-the-wood, for we both had had experience with the competitive chicanery of the New York magazine world, and there had been plenty of it. But that was child's play compared to this. These people were not maneuvering and manipulating in one profession or one city, even a profession as laced with intrigue as the editorial one and even a city as large as New York. Their stakes were those of an entire nation, sometimes several nations. This was the Big Time.

We got them as they came, we got them as they went, by means of Natalie's *sotto voce* vignettes and Ben's behind-the-hand digests, and even allowing for certain distortions induced by her excess acid content and the particular brand of ideological binoculars through which he assessed everyone and everything, a sort of vista or image began to emerge: what Ben had probably meant when he spoke of "the picture." A Washington Interior. But it was a confused picture, a chiaroscuro, as bewildering as a jigsaw puzzle. The pieces were there. But how to fit them together?

This center-parted hair coming up with the pretty lady in jet? He's made half a million dollars selling defective cement for WPA projects. This one with the hearty laugh and the corporation? He is a corporation. He's a lobbyist. For what? For whatever pays him most. This leonine figure with the white mane falling around his collar *à la* Garbo? He's a senator and he represents ten million constituents; that is, when he's not representing his son-in-law's metal interests. That one? He used to be a Townsendite, but now he's a Share-the-Wealther, with just a touch of a Silver Shirter. This chubby cupid who looks like a well-fed Boy Scout? He's a Brain Truster too, and he's supposed to have a two-way pipe line straight into the Kremlin. That one over there with the martyred expression and his eye on the hot hors d'oeuvres? Oh, he's labor. He has a marvelous old house down the Potomac. You can't see it from the road, on account of the wall, but it's lovely. Him? He's a committee chairman, and he's also in oil — oceans of it, from here to Mesopotamia. That one? Oh, he's a Senator too. But better give him a wide berth, because they say he has a fondness for pinching little girls' bottoms.

The babble was mounting higher now and the haze of cigarette smoke was growing denser and the mint sprigs in the juleps drooped and wilted.

"Well," said Natalie, "I think it's time you began to Circulate. Both of you. But not together."

"I don't believe I'm going to be very good at this," I said. "Maybe I should have done some boning up."

"Just select a suitable background and look pretty," she said. "It's never hurt yet, either in Washington or Walla Walla."

I tried that, but nothing much seemed to come of it. Lyle went in one direction and I in another, and I found myself on the edge of a dozen different groups but somehow never a part of any one of them. Abstract ideas were being bounced about like ping-pong balls, and proper names improperly, and I heard more concentrated talk — much of which I didn't understand (a CAF 4? what was a CAF 4?) — than I had heard in years. The main topics seemed to be the permanent one of the New Deal, the domestic affairs of the younger Roosevelts, a Congressman named Zioncheck, the cessation of League of Nations sanctions against Italy, and the situation (Civil War? Revolution? Which?) in Spain. Everything I heard appeared to be all pro and con and muddled, much as I was beginning to be. The words "Red" and "Reactionary" were used deftly as two-edged weapons, and I gathered that although "extremists" were a nuisance, "moderates" were worse. In fact as far as I could discover there were no moderates. Apparently it was bad form.

Sighting Ben's familiar face in a group in a corner, I edged toward him and stood listening. An intense young woman in a gold lamé blouse was talking about the bombing of Madrid, and I tried to follow her discourse with a show of intelligence, although as always I had to stop and think: now which are the Loyalists and which the Insurgents? And sometimes she used "Nationalists" and sometimes "Falangists," which made things no easier. Then she started to discuss Italy's annexing of Ethiopia, in lamentation.

"Ethiopia always seems so far away," I said, with what I hoped was the air of one offering a witty yet apropos generalization. It was high time I began pulling my oar. "In fact I can't imagine any place farther — unless it's China."

She was a striking and modish young woman, and as she looked at me I suddenly felt eight years old, three inches high, and as if I had braces on my teeth and acne on my face.

"Farther away how?"

"Well," I said, and wished I had kept silent, "geographically and — practically every way, I guess."

She employed a rather set smile as her best expression of eloquence, but the tennis-tanned man next to her didn't. He glowered. "It may be closer than you think," he said. "And China may be, too. There's been a little trouble there also, in case you haven't read about it."

The tactful host, Ben tried to realign the conversation, though not much. "And yet he does nothing," he said. "Absolutely nothing. The fact is, and we might as well recognize it, that essentially the man is too conservative, too bound by tradition."

"From that background, what could you expect?" said a man who was nibbling at a spray of bacon-wrapped olives. "Groton. Good God! Blood tells, you know. It always comes out."

Ben nuzzled at his julep. "Oh, you'll have to grant that he's instituted some reforms domestically. But even those aren't enough, not nearly enough." He shrugged. "I'm beginning to realize that we've misjudged him. He's afraid. Weak, really."

Oh, I thought, so then I was right. He has cooled, after all. And I turned away. "Weak." There is an echo in this room, I thought. . . . Behind me I could hear the main topic being resumed by the modish young woman: "Now you take this man Franco . . ."

I looked for Lyle, and finally found him on the veranda, leaning against its railing and making designs out of toothpicks.

"You oughtn't to be hiding like this," I said. "You're a guest of honor."

He squared one toothpick against another. It was quite a complex design. "I thought I'd take a little time out. Sort of a recess."

I looked down into the garden and onto its bobbing crop of new fall hats and tailored shoulders. Waves of conversation were coming at me from two directions, out from the house, up from the garden, and ripples of it washed over me: ". . . a traitor to his class. Ought to be tarred and feathered and put on a rail . . . until four o'clock this morning reading *Gone With the Wind*. I simply could not put it . . . Hitler . . . at Campobello for a week end and says he's a secret drinker. Old-fashioneds . . . which has branched off from the A.F.L. Congress of Industrial Organizations, you know. They call it C.I.O., for short. So these sit-down strikes . . . not officially known yet, but I got it straight from a man in the Embassy who's just back from London. He's insisting she'll be Queen. Imagine. A Baltimore girl . . . Hitler . . . Jack Garner told me himself that . . . this week's *Panorama* points out that 80 per cent of the press is against him . . . can count definitely on all the New England states as well as Pennsylvania, California . . . Hitler . . . adorable house out in Chevy Chase, right near the Club . . . no, you never should muddle them. Just mince them slightly, and be careful to use metal goblets and have them *ice-cold*. . . ."

Reaching for one of his toothpicks, I began to break it into small splinters.

"It's a very interesting party, isn't it?" I said. "Stimulating."

"Yes, it certainly is."

"Have you made any contacts yet?"

"Well, not exactly. One man was very nice. He offered to take me through the Bureau of Engraving and show me how they make money."

I tossed the splinters away. "You know, I've been thinking," I said. "We really ought to keep up better than we do. Study more, I mean. Maybe when we go home we should join Town Hall or something."

"Mm." He put his hand on the design, and when he took it away there wasn't any design: only the bare railing. "They use the word 'democracy' a lot, don't they?"

I nodded. "And 'Fascist,' too. I counted 'Fascist' eighteen times, and seventeen for 'Communist.' And that wasn't including either 'Reactionary' or 'Red.'"

He too was gazing out over the garden now. "They're so sure," he said. "All of them. Whatever they think or say, they're so sure." And then he looked at me. "Amy. Are you scared?"

I knew what he meant. He didn't mean was I scared of either Fascism or Communism. He meant was I scared of democracy, which was something I had never even thought about because I had always taken it as much for granted as the color of my own skin, and how it worked and if it was working. Neither of us had ever seen its inner coils and springs and countersprings before. But now we had.

I hesitated. "It isn't fair to judge from a cocktail party, is it?" I said. "And Natalie warned us that we'd be seeing the lunatic fringe. And . . . Yes. Yes," I said. "I am scared."

"A fine thing. Deserters. Welshers. Both of you." We turned. Natalie had come out from the house and was heading toward us. "I ask you. Is this co-operation?"

"We — ah — we were just admiring the view," said Lyle.

She stood beside us. "Um-hum. It's quite a view, isn't it?" She drummed her fingers on the railing. "There's nothing like Washington in October, which is just before November. I don't say that it's necessarily to be enjoyed, but I do say there's nothing like it."

The buzz of voices continued, the buzz and the babble.

"Well," she said, looking at him, "now that you've seen the circus are you still so sure you'd like a job in this wonderful city of wonders? That is, assuming you could get one."

"I don't know," he said. "But right now I think that what I'd like most is another one of those juleps."

"Me too," I said.

Linking one of her arms in his and the other in mine, she turned toward the house. "It's funny," she said. "So many people make that very same remark."

And that was all there was to that, because in the two days that remained to our stay all we did was go sight-seeing, sometimes with Natalie and sometimes without her. We stood in the tall rotunda and looked up at Lincoln, and went to Mount Vernon, and to Christ Church in Alexandria, and bent to decipher the inscriptions on the pedestals and monuments of the only men in this whole city who seemed to be judged impartial and just by all, the dead men whose bronze and granite stares slanted down unwaveringly — though if they had counsel to offer, they never spoke it. And one afternoon we went out to Arlington and walked slowly among the crosses there, but although some of the tombs were large and some of the words carved on them were sonorous, what I kept thinking of was what I always think of when I find myself in such places — which I usually take care not to do — and what I probably always will think of:

> This quiet Dust was Gentlemen and Ladies,
> And Lads and Girls;
> Was laughter and ability and sighing,
> And frocks and curls . . .

And then it was our last afternoon, a beautiful and golden afternoon with Indian summer in it, and we sat on a bench in Lafayette Square, the two of us, watching the pigeons waddle along the walks and the squirrels scampering through the falling, drifting leaves. I think we both were tired then, physically as well as mentally, and it was good to sit there in the sun beneath the elms and the waxy, yellowing magnolias and to toss peanuts at the squirrels and see them dart and run. So tame they were, those squirrels, so friendly, and bronze Jackson on his horse seemed friendly too. Despite the hum of the city and the honking of the cars and the clang of the trolleys, it was somehow a quiet, peaceful place.

I looked across the street. "It's really quite a small house for such a large country," I said. "Isn't it?"

He kept breaking peanut shells and flicking their kernels out onto the pavement. "Yes. I suppose so."

"And yet in a way it's hard to imagine anybody actually living there. I mean, getting up and going to bed and dressing and undressing. And sometimes not being able to sleep. . . ."

"Well, a lot of people have lived there," he said. "In their time."

"I know."

Crumpling the bag, he threw it into a wire basket which stood beside the bench. He dusted his hands together.

"Well," he said, "so here we are. Like practically everybody else, we came to Washington trying to get something. But unlike some of them, we didn't get it."

"That's because we didn't want it. Did we?"

Leaning his elbows on his knees, he rubbed his hands against his face. "I don't know. I've got to — get myself reorganized. Straighten myself out. I'm all confused."

I watched him. There are more poses for the Thinker than the one Rodin chose. Reaching out, I plucked a dead leaf from the shoulder of his topcoat.

"Lyle, do you ever wonder what's going to happen to us? To you and me and Johnny?"

For a moment his hands were still on his face, and he didn't move. Then he lifted his head and sat up. "Now don't go getting panicky," he said. "Things'll work out all right."

"I wasn't being panicky. I was just — wondering." I twisted the leaf, and it crumbled in my hand. "I guess I was thinking mostly about Johnny." And I was. I haven't seen him for eight whole days, I was thinking. Has he changed? Will he know me? He could say twenty-six words when I left. Can he say any more now, and what is the twenty-seventh? "Babies — what happens to them?"

He took my hand and put it with his into his topcoat pocket. "They grow up, that's what happens to them," he said. His voice was deliberately brighter, consciously cheerful. "And he'll grow up, too." With his other hand he made a flourish. "Gentlemen, I give you the celebrated John Ellery, son of the late, great ex-editor of — "

"Don't say 'late.' Even in fun. It makes me shiver."

"Celebrated for what, though, I wonder," he continued. "John Ellery, television idol of millions. The handsome, dashing heart-breaker who —"

"Oh, no," I said. "Dashing, maybe, and certainly handsome, and even a heartbreaker. But not a television idol, please. I don't think I'd like that."

"It's not going to be a matter of what we like. It's going to be a matter of what we get." He was silent for an instant, and then he nodded across the street. "Maybe he'll grow up to live over there. How would that suit you? Let's see. Along about 1990, say, or 2000. President John Ellery."

"You're getting maudlin, dear. And anyway, they may not have Presidents then. They may do it with capsules."

"But if they do have them, whoever it's going to be — he or she — must be looking right now just about the way Johnny does, a roll of fat on a potty." He squeezed my hand, within his pocket. "It wouldn't be bad, would it?"

My eyes were on the white pillars. "It wouldn't be easy," I said. "It probably isn't easy now. I don't know as I'd want him to live there."

Taking his hand out of his pocket, he reached for a package of cigarettes. The energy of his movements seemed to me to be a little calculated. At any rate, his mood of prophecy was over. "Well, so it's back to the dear old Writers' Project for me, it looks like," he said. "Back to dear old WPA for the winter semester. For the whole course, and maybe post-graduate work, too."

"You hate it so, don't you?"

He inhaled deeply, and blew out smoke. "Oh, it may not be so bad. I think I'll be able to — adjust myself now. Who knows? I may even get to like it."

I was silent. Now that he had said it, now that he had even mentioned the possibility of it, I knew that that was what I was most afraid of, even more afraid of than his rebelliousness — that he might come to like it, to be contented with it and desirous of nothing else. And I remembered something he had once said: "I have immortal longings in me." I had objected then (how silly, how young) be-

165

cause it had never occurred to him to add, "for us, for you as well as me." That didn't disturb me any more, because now I was certain that he did mean for us, for me as well as for him. . . . But where were the immortal longings? What would become of them?

The meek shall inherit the earth, I thought, and swarm over it, and parasitically feed on its fruits, and accept as their due what was meant to be earned. No, I didn't want that. And he didn't want it now either. But he might come to, he might come to. . . .

He glanced at his wrist. "I suppose we'd better be getting back," he said. "By the time we get through our good-bys and thank-yous we'll have to be heading for the station."

I was looking upward at one of the elms, some of its leaves already gone and its branches bare against the blue. I knew of an elm much like that. I knew of an elm a great deal like that. And I had seen it in all seasons.

"Lyle," I said, "do you like my father?"

"Well enough. What little I've seen of him. . . . Why?"

I realized now what had made me think of it. It was partly the elm and partly my sitting here in this small square of green from which the rest of the country radiated out to north and west and south. It was this white house I was looking at, and another white house I had lived in. Such a big country, and we had tried so little of it. . . . And yet of course it was impossible, impractical. It wouldn't work, couldn't work. In certain ways he would find it even less agreeable than WPA.

I rose. "Come on," I said. "Let's go."

He was looking up at me, curiously. "Why did you ask me about your father?"

"Oh, no reason. I just had a crazy idea. A brainstorm. But it's over."

"Well, if it has anything to do with me, I wish you'd tell me. Or with us. I'm not — " he got to his feet, and again there was that note in his voice which did something to my throat — "I'm not so choosy as I once was, you know."

"It has nothing to do with you," I assured him, "and even if it did

166

you wouldn't like it. You wouldn't like it at all. You're not the type."
And I took his arm. "Come on, we don't want to miss that train."
And so we started walking, over the winding pavements across
which the leaves drifted, under the elms, past the pigeons and the
people, among the frisking, frolicking squirrels.

➛➛➛ VI ⫷⫷⫷

You can leave and go a long, long way and stay a long, long time. You can acquire and cultivate new and strange tastes: the taste for sea food, the antennae of a mound of undulating crustaceans weaving gently on a bed of ice in a restaurant window; the taste for the faint salt smell of the near-by sea itself, even though adulterated by the fumes of gasoline and asphalt and the million other of the city's odors. You can educate yourself to the devious paths of subway and bus, and to the vertical necessity of elevators, and to walking beneath the juggernaut terror of the El without even noticing it, and to many other things too: to the sight of massed violin bows shuttling instead of just their sound; to live actors on a stage instead of their images on a screen; and to the knowledge that if you should want to see such images you need not hurry to see them tonight, or at the most within a space of three or four nights, but can always catch them on any of a hundred other screens on any of a hundred other nights. You can go away and discover the sea, any sea, and the mountains, any mountains, and a new world (and lose it), and forget the flat farmlands.

Yes, you can do all that. But if you are from a small town in the Middle West and were born and bred there, you are always from a small town in the Middle West. It's in the blood, it's in the bone, and no mere manicure of metropolitanism will remove it and no enamel of sophistication — no matter how arduously bought or tenaciously cherished — conceal it. For although you may think you return as

Mrs. Ellery, Amy Ellery, you really return as Amy Hardin, John Hardin's girl, the one who went east to New York City and married and is now back living with her folks. Her and her husband and their youngster and a nigger woman they call Callie. Kind of a caretaker for the little shaver, she is. And hired girl too. Or maid.

We arrived in the grayness of an early morning in the rainy rawness of early winter, at an hour that was neither day nor night — the bare bulbs on the station platform were still lighted — and as we waited there amid our bags I thought, "Well, if he can stand it when it looks like this, if he doesn't say, 'You were right. This isn't for me. Let's turn around and go back,' then I guess he probably ought to be able to stand it at any time." Because there wasn't even fresh snow to make it pretty; just the rain slanting on the dirty, porous ruts of old snow. Just the black dripping eaves and the clicking of the telegrapher's key, just the dark skeleton of the ladder on the water tank, just the wet Bull Durham sign on the barn in the corn-cribbed field across the tracks, just the departing whistle and diminishing red lights of the train as it disappeared down those tracks, whistling again for the trestle beyond and then rounding the bend.

We were alone.

But not alone. Crunching over the gravel came footsteps, a little tired and a little slow, and then the slight, stooped, and once-wiry silhouette of a familiar figure, and after that the straggling gray of a familiar and once-glossy mustache, and then the frailness of familiar arms around me. And the reediness of a voice which squeaked slightly.

"Hello, Amy."

"Hello, Papa."

"Well, and Lyle."

"Hello, Mr. Hardin."

"Papa, this is Callie."

"How do you do, Callie?"

No response to that. The gleam of somewhat nervous and apprehensive eyes in the semidarkness, a brief glimpse of teeth in something which might have been a smile.

169

"Well, sir. And I'll venture I know who this young man is. This is Johnny, isn't it?"

No response to that either. Only the shifting of leggings against Callie's coat, the move of a mitten, and the flutter of sleepy lashes. Perhaps there was apprehension there, too: I couldn't tell. Will he remember this morning, this platform, this moment? I thought. Will he?

"Johnny, this is your grandfather."

"Well, sir. What a fine boy. What a fine, big boy. . . ."

There was a quality about that ride from the station which I shall never forget. We rode through the gradually lightening day, with the chains flapping and the windshield wiper swishing in its arc and my father driving the sedan with his usual abandon — accentuated because he was pointing out the sights for Lyle's benefit — and with me seated in front beside him with Johnny on my lap and with Lyle and Callie wedged in back among the bags. On previous visits I had long since accustomed myself to the fact that a strange metamorphosis had come over the town since I was a little girl in it, that it had not only grown shabby but that certain buildings had actually shrunk, and I' had even come to regard it as picturesque, dear, humorously and lovably ridiculous. That was when I knew that I would always be leaving it again. The others stayed, not I. For me there had always been the return half of that ticket in the purse, that reservation in its envelope. . . . But this time my ticket had been one-way, for this was no visit. This time I too was staying — at least for a while. So now I saw the town through new eyes — and through Lyle's also.

A muskrat-gloved hand pointed. "That's the ice-cream plant over there. Up-to-date in every way. Best ice cream in the state of Iowa." An undistinguished brick building with a tall chimney on it. It looked like an ice-cream plant.

"Careful, Papa. The curb."

"You can see that it's all being built up out here. Not the way it used to be at all." I looked and saw, or believed I saw, two new houses which had been added in the last five years. No more.

"And this here right along in here is where a lot of the young married folks live. The well-to-do ones, that is. California Street. Some people call it Gold Coast Row." A gabled brown brick of more or less Norman origin. A Tudor arrangement in stucco. A very Spanish-style white plaster with its speared awning rods dripping, though the awnings themselves had been stored away. A grimly authentic Cape Cod cottage with a cluster of milk bottles at the brass-knockered door. That one undeniably did look new since I had last been here; in fact it would probably always look new.

"Know who lives there, Amy? Fern Hauberg. Remember him?"

"Yes, Papa."

Did I remember him? He had taken me to my Junior-Senior banquet and we had daringly danced the Camel Walk together and if I had played my cards right I could have been Mrs. Fern Hauberg this very minute, and asleep beneath that salt-box roof. But I was just as glad I wasn't, because it would have meant that Fern would be asleep beside me, and I didn't think I'd care for that. I had never thought I would care for that, though apparently Zelda Scheidt didn't mind.

"And this is the new swimming pool. All concrete. Cost twenty-nine thousand dollars. PWA." I turned away from it — it was a handsome pool, at the moment overflowing with rain water — to glance back at the black earth and bare saplings in front of the Cape Cod cottage and at the series of brown-patched lawns beyond. Gold Coast Row. Well, that was probably where we would be living if we were going to be here permanently — and if we ever attained that happy state of being well-to-do. But whatever Lyle might think, or think he thought, it wouldn't be permanent. Three months, five months — if that long. That would be enough for him.

"That's the grade school. The Harrison School. That's where you'll be going one of these days, Johnny."

No, I thought. I don't believe so. It's a nice, modern building — far less gloomy-looking than its predecessor — but he won't be going there. Where? I don't know. I wish I did know.

"And there's Mother's church."

It had always been "Mother's church" to him, because he seldom entered it. I looked at the glistening rough granite and at the cornerstone lettered "First Episcopal. MCMII A.D." and at the colored glass window, and I could visualize the rows of vacant pews on its other side, their veneered oak gleaming in the perpetual violet-tinted dusk. Oh dear, I thought, I suppose she'll expect me to start going again and maybe Lyle too. Well, I can't. And he won't.

We were turning onto Main Street now, broad and empty in the downpour, with only a few cars angled at the curb. The Baker Block, with Dr. Anderson's giant rusty-rimmed eyeglasses streaming and with Dr. Meltzer's giant tooth a gilt mist. The blue Rexall sign, the red and yellow of the A & P, the green-trimmed Conoco Super-Service station on the corner, the rivulet-run wide plate glass of the Liquor Store (if you bought anything, there was no possibility of passers-by not being able to see you buying it), the Ammon Hardware Company, the Manila County Savings and Trust, the Smoke Shop, the barber pole outside the Ammon Hotel, the Elite Café, all green tile and stainless steel and with goldfish swimming in its window, and a half-finished structure where the post office used to be.

"What's that, Papa? Where the post office used to be."

"That is the post office. Or will be. Eighty-seven thousand dollars. PWA."

The gushing cascade of the marquee on the Hawkeye Theater: "Bank Nite. $190. MacDonald-Eddy *Maytime*."

"Look, Amy." It was Lyle's voice from the back seat: the first words he had spoken. "That was playing in Jackson Heights when we left."

"Oh, they get 'em quick here," said Papa. He cheerfully ignored a red "Stop" signal — and he might as well have, since there was no other moving vehicle in sight. "Almost as soon as Des Moines, sometimes. So I'm told, anyway. I don't go very often myself, though I'd give a lot to see a good stage show. I used to go to Will Rogers whenever he came along. Poor Will. Mother, she goes now and then. That Shirley Temple. She never misses Shirley Temple."

And then again he pointed, with special pride. "Well, there she is, Lyle. That's where you'll be. And your desk's all ready for you." And there she was and there was where he would be — within that

one-story red-brick building with the sign above it which said THE
AMMON ARGUS. The sedan slowed. "Like to stop in and take a look
around now?"

"Oh, I don't believe I . . ."

"No, Papa. Not now. We'd better be getting on."

"I suppose so. And Mother will be waiting."

So the sedan went on, past the elaborate ugliness of the courthouse
— the clock in the turret was just striking its single chime for the
half-hour — past the neon-trimmed Welsbach Funeral Home, past
the Sillman Brothers' Garage, Body Repair and Fender Work, and
finally onto Manila Street, our street, the oldest street, and — despite
its age — still the best street, Gold Coast Row or no Gold Coast Row.
The black, wet limbs of the elms, the elms. . . . Irmadee Tupper's
house, where I used to go for Friday night slumber parties. The
young (in their sixties) Art Bruers'. The old (in their eighties) Art
Bruers'. The iron stag I had so often straddled on the Netchers' lawn,
or on what would be the Netchers' lawn again by next summer. The
Diederdocks' porch, which was the first porch I had ever been
kissed on. Judge Morley's, which was still Judge Morley's even
though he had been dead for fifteen years and some people named
Alton lived there now. Dr. Herkle's, who had brought me into the
world and who had been the first to confirm my suspicion that I was
to bring someone else into it. The Pete Schaufflers'. The Paul Schaufflers'. The Misses Trost's, who sewed. Myrtle Gannett's, in the attic
of which Myrtle and I had taken a solemn vow that we would join
the Catholic Church and become nuns. . . . And then at last that one
house, our house, white, cupolaed, the scrolls of latticework above
its wide porch and the sodden brown tangle of snowball bushes
around it. The upper bay windows which were to be ours and the
glassed-in sleeping porch — a modern addition, twenty years ago —
which was to be Johnny's and the oval third-floor windows which
would be Callie's. "The place is certainly roomy enough," Mama had
written. "We won't have to worry about that."

"Well, sir, here we are."

"Yes, Papa."

Out of the car and onto the flooded cement in which was still embedded a finger-daubed "A.H. 1915." That had been me, and I had got spanked for it. Quite rightly.

"Come on, Lyle."

"O.K."

Up the straight walk, with Johnny in my arms and with Papa beside me and with the splashing steps of Lyle and Callie coming after.

"Better wipe your feet, folks. You know how Mother is."

"Yes, Papa."

Amy Hardin was home.

Papa was aging and he wasn't too well — in the Ammon phrase, "his health was failing" — and he needed help with the paper. Lyle was aging too, in a different way, and he needed help also. Those were the two main reasons why we had come, in addition to the fact that we had nowhere else to go. For this was during that period which was termed, maybe justifiably and maybe not, the "Roosevelt" Recession. As Papa remarked, "Well, whether it's a 'recession' or a 'depression' or whatever it is, at least they can't pin this one on Hoover." Papa had been quite a Hoover man, though he was even more a Roosevelt man (the first one, that is: Teddy), and more than either a McKinley man, ever since he had cast his first vote in 1896. Papa was a grass-roots Republican.

I'm not sure what Lyle had expected Ammon to be — aside from a retreat and a refuge and perhaps, miraculously, the beginning of something better. It was a small town (pop. either 5000 or 4326, depending on whether you accepted the Chamber of Commerce's statistics or those of the Bureau of the Census), but it was different from any of the few small towns he had known, which were the summer towns along the Jersey shore. And it was in the Middle West, and except for that brief interlude in Chicago the Middle West was to him what it is to many others, a stretch of monotony which speeds past Pullman windows or under wing tips while you are en route to California. I imagine he expected it to be partly quaint, like a verse out of James Whitcomb Riley, and partly deadly, like a chapter out of Sinclair Lewis: an object of either sentiment or satire.

And I suppose there was still a residue of each in it, but there was more of something else. Something new had been added. A lot new.

Neither the house on Manila Street nor the *Argus* office provided much clue to it, however. Inside, the house was a cavernous, black-walnut, plush-portiered, high-ceilinged mausoleum, which Mama kept spotlessly and even fanatically clean, and although I understood and loved it, loved every inch of it, from the preserve room in its cellar to the lightning rods on its roof, I didn't see why Lyle should, or even could. The *Argus* office was as disordered and dusty as the house was neat and immaculate, but it seemed only remotely connected with the twentieth century. There was a halfhearted attempt at modernity in the front part — the circulation-and-advertising counter — but by the time you reached Papa's sanctum, which he now shared with Lyle, you were back in the 1890's. There was an ancient cracked black-leather couch, with the horsehair stuffing shredding out, suitable for naps, and a large brass cuspidor (though Papa didn't smoke), and a Globe-Wernicke sectional bookcase whose bound volumes of the *Argus* were available to anyone who had the guile and strength necessary to open its glass doors, and that early L. C. Smith set amid the decades-deep litter of the roll-top desk whose top wouldn't roll, and many paperweights, the whole being coldly surveyed from the wall by the glassy eyes of a stuffed pike which had a brass plate beneath it engraved "Lake Okiboji, Aug. 18, '04. J. Hardin." Presumably the room received an occasional cleaning, though I had never been able to find any evidence of it.

"Well," I said, when he returned after his first tour of inspection — and I said it almost challengingly, for after all I had given him ample warning — "what do you think?"

"They need a new linotype," he said. "The one they've got's all out of whack. And the folding machine doesn't fold."

"Is that all?"

"It's all for now."

"Oh, Lyle, why be so stubborn? This isn't going to work. You know it isn't going to work."

"You like it here, don't you? The house is comfortable, Johnny will have that big yard to play in when spring comes — "

"Of course I like it. I love it. But I was born here, and — "

"Look," he said, "give it a chance. Give me a chance, and yourself too. I told you I wanted to try it. Well, we're here — and I intend to try it. If you'll let me."

I was silent. "All right," I said, then.

"But if you could possibly see your way toward doing something about your mother, I think we'd stand a better — "

I shook my head. "I can't," I said. "Nobody can. She comes with the dinner, and she always has."

He sighed and shrugged, but even that prospect didn't wilt him. "I probably started off on the wrong foot with her," he said. "But maybe she'll come around. I hope so, anyway."

I hoped so too, though I doubted it. In any case there could be no denying that he had started off on the wrong foot with her. It so happened that the day of our arrival was also the day of the abdication, and we had all sat together at the radio listening to the broadcast proclaiming it. Hearing those quietly uttered, precisely spaced words, I had cried, almost, but Mama had just tchk-tchked and said sadly, " 'The woman I love' indeed. His poor mother. I keep thinking of his poor mother. He ought to be *ashamed*." And when Lyle, who should have known better, had asked, "Why? I should think she'd be pleased that he's going to do right by the lady and make an honest woman of her," she had glanced at him with quiet dignity and had said, "You wouldn't understand, Lyle. You've never been a mother."

Mama. Mama. She was a good woman, none better, although I knew that she wasn't going to be good for us, any of us. I knew it even before we came, for when I had written that I would have to bring Callie — chiefly because Callie declined to be detached — she had answered, "Callie will be very welcome, as I find I cannot do as much about the house as formerly. But I am not sure I will like to have a black woman in my kitchen as they always seem to me to be so dirty. And she will be the only one of her race in town, as you know, so there may be talk. Can she cook?" (Could Callie cook!)

Yes, I was well aware in advance that we would be a problem for Mama and she for us. And now that we were here I was even more aware of it. Because she didn't approve of Lyle, and never had. After the first night, during which neither he nor I had slept much, I had said, "Mama, I wonder if we couldn't have twin beds instead of that double one. You see, Lyle and I aren't used to sleeping together." I couldn't decide whether it was those words "sleeping together" which embarrassed her — they embarrassed me: lying there with Lyle in that room which had been my girlhood's room I sometimes felt very strange and even furtive, as if I should get up and lock the door — or whether she assumed that there was something indecent about my proposal, but in either event her reply had been icy. "I had that bed moved in there especially," she said, "because your old one wasn't big enough. However, we can go down to Harris and Kramer's and trade it in for twin ones, if you like. And if that's what Lyle prefers."

"I prefer it, too, Mama."

"It seems very odd." Odd that we shouldn't occupy the same bed? Or odd that we should occupy the same room? "It certainly seems very odd. . . ."

Mama. Mama. I remember Mama. . . . Ever since I could recall, she had been large, plump-armed, matronly bosomed, black-velvet-band-throated, and had worn her hair in the same style, a pompadour which through the years had gradually progressed from black to gray to yellow-white. I suppose a psychiatrist would have had quite a field day with her, but he couldn't know her as I did and do — and neither he nor I could ever know her as Papa did. I think that in many ways she always wanted me to remain a little girl, and certainly we had been happiest together then. But when it became more and more apparent that I was unavoidably destined to grow up, or at least to grow larger and taller, every milestone of my adolescence became the occasion for a battle, and although she always lost the battle she went down fighting. The day I first began to use lipstick openly, the day she caught me with my first (she thought) experimental cigarette, my first beau, my wanting to go away to Iowa City instead of being just a home girl, the night she had detected hip-flask gin on my breath after a Fair Grounds dance (mine had been the tag end of the flapper era), and of course above all my determination to go to New York — I remembered all those things, and what each of them had done to her; and to me. But (and could a psychiatrist equate this, please?) I also remembered her when she was kind, and gentle, and unexpectedly intuitive: those mornings when she used to come in and sit on my bed for "a good talk," that letter she had so surprisingly written me when I married.

Mama. Mama. A whole book could probably be written about Mama. But it could never be written by me. Either I understood her, understand her, too well, or not enough.

So the omens weren't too promising, what with Mama and the house and that *Argus* office. Yet all those things, as I began to discover — and I hoped Lyle too — were only a part of the town. You go away, and you think that what you leave behind you doesn't change. But it does change. Or at least Ammon had. At first glance Main Street might look more or less the same as it had been when I left it, but it really wasn't. The windows of Adelbert's Grocery might still be decorated with fly-spotted crepe-paper ruffles, but on their other side was a wall-wide frozen-foods cabinet, and if you wanted to — and could afford them — you could eat asparagus in January and strawberries in March. The price board at the Liquor Store listed Mumm's Champagne (1928) and sherry from Spain, and although the most popular purchases might be Old Featherstone and Dixie Dew Gin, the fact remained that the others were there if you desired them. And on the desk at the Ammon Hotel were timetables for the United Air Lines, which would take you to San Francisco, and Pan American, which would eventually take you as far as Rio de Janeiro.

"It's really quite — modern, in a way, isn't it?" I said. But I said it casually, for I didn't want to build up either my own hopes or his. After all, what was a strawberry? What were timetables, even? Anybody could look at a timetable.

"Yes," he said. "In a way."

"I expect it's due to the radio," I said, "the way everybody says. To the radio and the movies and the Hollywood influence." I almost added "and to magazines like *Panorama*," but I didn't.

"I expect so. You know, I wish spring would hurry up and come.

I'd like to try out that golf course. It doesn't look bad at all. And Orin Netcher was telling me they've got a pro out there who used to be . . ."

Of all the things modern in Ammon, I suppose Orin and Irmadee Netcher were the most modern: gayer than the Lalique-style glass behind the beer bar in the hotel's Corn Room, brighter than the chromium fixtures in the lobby of the Hawkeye, more glittering than the permanent-wave machine in Nettie's Beauty Salon. They "took us up," and in, and I was glad and grateful, for in doing so they rescued us from the Fern and Zelda Hauberg set, who had also threatened to take us up but who played a brand of bridge which made me feel as if I had six thumbs. Orin and Irmadee were above bridge. Poker, yes, and for stakes that made my head swim, and sometimes Russian bank or, whimsically, parchesi. But not bridge. "Bridge is for people who talk about their 'kiddies,' " said Orin grandly.

Together they represented an almost incestuous amalgam of the second generation of the Netcher-Tupper Manila County Savings and Trust, where Orin was assistant cashier and unless something very peculiar transpired would one day be president, the day depending on when Mr. Tupper decided either to die or to retire, and they of course lived on Gold Coast Row, a name which they laughed at much more good-humoredly than those who had first conceived it. Their house was small and of no particular period, just white and green-shuttered and good, and it was beautiful both inside and out. ("Whatever people may say about Irmadee," observed Mama, who said a lot because she considered her and Orin to be fast, "she has lovely taste. Did you notice her drapes?") The Early American pieces in the hooked-rugged living room were genuine, not reproductions, and so was the gate-legged magazine table with its symmetrically arranged columns of the current *New Yorker, Vogue, Town and Country, Arts and Decoration, Fortune, Esquire,* Orin's fraternity bulletin, and an only slightly obsolescent *New Republic*. During our first visits the week's *Panorama* was prominently displayed too, but later on it tactfully disappeared.

The house also featured the only Rumpus Room — "We just call it the Joint, though," explained Irmadee — in Manila County, as well as the only domestic slot machine, and we spent a good deal of time there, surrounded by the travel posters ("Wind Thru the Storied Rhine . . . Visit Gay Vienna") for which Orin had sent especially to Cook's in Chicago, and at the bar which was hung with French lithographs, in French, of little boys standing somewhat startlingly by brooks and wearing nothing but big straw hats and impish grins.

"My God, what hit me?" Lyle moaned, on waking up one morning after our first evening in that bar. "We might as well face it. We're out of our class with those people."

"You had a good time though, didn't you?" I said, prompting. I was feeling none too bright myself — and I certainly hoped Mama hadn't heard us coming in — but I did want him to like them. Together they and their house and their conversation formed a cool spring bubbling in what I had feared he might find a desert.

"Sure, I guess so. I must have."

"Irmadee thinks you're terribly attractive." What she had actually said was "sexy." "She told me so when we were in the bathroom."

"I don't know why she took you into the bathroom to tell you. She didn't seem to be shy about anything else. What a bawdy dame. Knows all the four-letter words, and keeps using them."

"Well, she always was one for the shock technique. She was the first girl in town to smoke a cigarette openly on Main Street."

"That's no reason why she should ask if our love-life's satisfactory, is it? Or go on about how wonderful hers and her husband's is."

That had taken me a little aback, too, but I didn't let him know it. "Now don't be prudish. You're supposed to be a city boy." I reverted to my campaign. "And she is striking, you have to admit that."

He yawned. "Um-hum."

"When we were kids she used to be so fat that they called her Tubby, but she told me she hasn't tasted a potato since she was eighteen years old. She sort of reminds me of Carole Lombard, to look at." She reminded herself of Carole Lombard also, she said, though she didn't mean to look at. Just in her ways. "I suppose I'm the Carole Lombard type," she had apologized, when she couldn't

180

remember which was higher, a straight or three of a kind. "You know, just a screwball. Utterly mad. All helter-skelter." And yet on the surface she appeared to be an exceptionally efficient housewife, hostess, and mother, her menu-filed, ledger-lined kitchen desk being the control center of a miniature factory whose operations were planned by her and executed by an amiable Swede named Gretel.

"I wish they'd shut up about *Panorama,* though."

"They mean it to be flattering, dear. To them you're a celebrity."

"You mean I was." Again he yawned. "Where'd she get that dress? I'll bet she didn't get it here."

"She didn't. Marshall Field's."

She sent to Marshall Field's for almost all her clothes, and for the twins' too, despite the fact that Sam Wiebert, who managed the ready-to-wear in Heflin and Wiebert's, had been heard to say publicly, "How would she like it if we banked by mail with the Continental Illinois instead of at the M.C.S. and T.?" The twins were six, and they looked adorable in their mother-daughter dresses. One was named Jennifer and the other Wendy, for although Orin and Irmadee had been victimized by their own parents at christening they had taken care to be more considerate of others: if they ever had a boy they planned to call him either Christopher or Robin, said Irmadee, though not both.

They knew Chicago like a book, for they went in at least twice a year, taking a suite-with-parlor at the Palmer House and spending considerable time — and no doubt money — in the Congress Balloon Room and at the Edgewater Beach. They went to Des Moines even oftener, of course — to see Kit Cornell or the Guild or Tallulah on tour — although they were inclined to be rather contemptuous of Des Moines: "Just an overgrown small town," was the way they described it. Chicago was different, however (New York they dismissed as being "full of Heebs"), and the impression was somehow left that Chicago was where they really lived, Ammon being a sort of suburb to it. In fact they had lived there once, briefly and experimentally, before the arrival of the twins. "I was walking along Michigan the other day," said Irmadee, in the manner of a confirmed commuter, "and I saw the darlingest . . ."

"If we ever get a civilized airport here," announced Orin, mixing stingers behind the bar, "I'd like to have a little plane of my own. A Piper Cub or something like that. Just a two-seater. Then Dee and I could run in every week end or so, if we felt like it. We could paint that North Side a permanent red, and of course we have a lot of friends out in Winnetka and Evanston. Or we could even pop down to New Orleans for the Mardi Gras or up to Mackinac for . . ."

I looked at Lyle, again with hope, because such vision and the carelessness with which it was offered — Buck Rogers was at last here, right here in this very knotty-pine-paneled basement — took my breath away and I believed might take his too.

I was having a good deal of trouble with my breath during that winter and oncoming spring, for most of the time I seemed to be holding it. Evidence was piling up which could not be ignored. By some strange process of immediate osmosis this town, or part of it at least, was obviously not only abreast of the times but a step or two ahead of them. Passengers looking pityingly out their windows during the Husker's four-minute stop couldn't see them, but there were kitchens here which were every bit as complicated and functional as those in the Good Housekeeping Institute. Several of the more enterprising business firms, including the Hawkeye and Mulch's Drug Store and the Welsbach Funeral Home, were completely air-conditioned. And progress was not confined merely to the material and physical. It extended to the cultural and intellectual. *Eyeless in Gaza* might be banned in Boston, but if you were over twenty-one and she liked you you could get it at the Carnegie Library simply by asking Miss Rand for the key to the Permission Shelf. And both the juke box in the Nite Spot and the Six Cats (until recently the Six Jazzmaniacs) who officiated at the monthly dances at the country club were swinging "Loch Lomond" almost as soon as Maxine Sullivan was and while it was still hardly more than number nine on the Hit Parade.

I held my breath, I held my breath. All during the slow, snow-and-thaw-and-snow-again drag of winter and on into spring I held my breath. The way to determine the soundness of a foundation is to

182

subject it to pressure, so that is what I did, becoming my own counterespionage agent. Riding beside Lyle in the rumble of Orin's canary-yellow convertible in the freezing bitterness of February, I said, "They're really not very practical for Iowa winters, are they? Convertibles, I mean. And canary-yellow. Isn't that sort of collegiate?" To which he merely replied, "He let me handle her once. She drives like a dream. Makes your father's sedan seem like a Stanley Steamer."

There were several of those litmus tests, some of them bordering on the brutal. But I wouldn't spare myself, or anyone else either. I wanted to know. I had to be sure. "I do wish Orin would stop explaining why at the last minute he decided to go to Iowa City when his credits were all accepted for Princeton," I said. "And does Irmadee always have to hum 'The Sweetheart of Sigma Chi' as if it were the national anthem and dedicated to her, personally?"

"For a childhood playmate of theirs," he said, "you certainly have developed a fine set of fur-bearing claws. After all, you ought to be a little more tolerant. Remember, all little boys can't grow up to go to Harvard. And some of them may even wish they hadn't."

That was what I wanted. That was what I sought. I was a Penitente. Scourge me. . . . And he was a candidate for conversion, and I would try him ruthlessly: stick needles into his slightest syllables, light fires under his most random glances. Orin and Irmadee, Fern and Zelda Hauberg, the Pete-and-Paul-Schauffler crowd, Main Street itself, they all went into my crucible for his assaying, and they all came out unscarred, unscathed. "Fern and Zelda are putting a wine vault into their cellar," I said. "Did you ever hear of anything more ridiculous?" A rich opportunity for him, surely. But all he said was, "Why ridiculous? That's where wine is supposed to be kept, isn't it? As the old Connoisseur, I ought to know." And at another time, from me: "I hear they're talking about installing parking meters on Main Street. Next thing, they'll be zoning new buildings to an eighty-story limit." And from him: "Those parking meters are a very sensible idea. Traffic down there on Saturday nights is worse than Times Square." And my "Mama told me she can't understand why you haven't been asked to join either the

Rotary or the Kiwanis, and she hopes you aren't hurt. Isn't that killing?" And his "Well, I don't know as I understand it either."

And then came the day, oh happy day, when his novitiate was over and he took his vows. It was a day in lilac-scented May and we were waiting on the front porch for Orin and Irmadee to pick us up and take us out to the country club for golf. I don't recall exactly what it was I had said — something about Orin's always making it a point to be fashionably late, I think — but he turned to me from where he had been watching Papa pushing Johnny in the swing under the elms (my old swing, exhumed from the garage and equipped with new ropes) and said: "Listen, you've been talking like a God-damned snob lately. This is your town. Don't you like it? And these people are supposed to be your friends. Don't you like them either? If you don't, just come out and say so. But don't keep on with that continual dig-dig-dig."

If he had presented me with a diamond necklace, I couldn't have been more appreciative and delighted. Finally and at last I let my breath out, permanently.

"Say that again," I said, because it had been music to me.

"Huh?"

"What you just said." I smiled, in a state of beatitude. "Don't you see? It's been you. All along it's been you. I was afraid you might be . . ."

"What?"

"Oh, I don't know. Bored, maybe. And maybe kind of suffocated."

"Suffocated," he repeated. "Now there's a pompous word for you. What gave you that notion?"

"Why not? I love Ammon, every bit of it. But you're new here, and you aren't accustomed to a small town, and — "

"Do I looked bored?" he said. "Do I act suffocated?"

"No, of course you don't. But — "

"Well, then stop this incitement-to-violence or whatever it is you've been doing. If I was fed up, you'd know it."

And that was true enough: I always had known it.

"Oh, you have no idea what this means — " He was seated in the hammock, and I went toward him. Leaning down, I kissed him, even though I was aware that Mrs. Old Art Bruer was sitting on her porch down the block with her mother-of-pearl opera glasses conveniently placed on the wicker table beside her. "Oh, darling," I said. "Oh, darling."

He smiled up at me. "You better throw away all those sharp little knives and flush that acid down the drain," he said. "You better wake up to yourself and relax." And then, hearing the quadruple notes of Orin's musical horn, he rose. "Here they are. Let's go." And he walked to the edge of the porch and raised his hand in an Indian salute. "Hi, neighbors!" he called. "What cooks?"

So at last I did relax, because I could at last afford to, and for the first time I began really to enjoy Ammon — not just to dissect it and analyze it and weigh it on Lyle's scales, or on what I had erroneously judged to be his scales. Summer was here, full summer — June, with Papa's peonies raising their round, ragged heads in tawny splendor in the side yard; July, with Mama in white voile wielding a palm-leaf fan on the front porch after Callie's Sunday afternoon fried-chicken-and-mashed-potatoes, and with Papa in suspenders and with a handkerchief tucked in at his collar getting up from his rocker to look at the thermometer and then resuming his rocking and saying, "Well, sir. Good corn weather. 'Knee-high by the Fourth of July,' they always say. But she's dry. Mighty dry."

And she was dry, parched-dry, because there was a drought everywhere in the Middle West that year and everything was dry — everything except people's skins and their underwear and the moisture-pebbled porcelain of the toilet cabinets in their bathrooms. It was what was called "cyclone weather," though there was no cyclone. The air was murky with a fine brown silt that blew in from the dust bowls of the Dakotas and Nebraska and powdered all it touched — the leaves on the trees, the girls' summer dresses, even Mama's black-walnut furniture in those big, dark, cool rooms whose windows she kept tightly shut and whose shades were drawn from dawn to dusk.

Small-town Iowa in summer — hot, humid, uncomfortable, but despite all that beautiful too, though it has yet to bear the Keats to celebrate its beauties. And a Keats would be the one to do it, for there is sensuousness there: colors and smells and sounds. There is no moon so full and round and platinum-pale as the Iowa moon, no scent of fresh-cut clovered lawn so sweet, no Fair Grounds crickets so loud, no nights so still, no stars so near. Slow steps of strollers on the sidewalk beneath the shadows of branches, the glow of cigarettes in the dark, the faint whiz of tires on Number 60, the hiss of the popcorn man's wagon up on Main Street, and the leafy quiet of Manila Street. A dog's bark. A light going out in an upper window. A distant voice crying, "Barbara-Jean? Barbara-Jean? Time to come in now, Barbara-Jean. . . ." The old folks and the little folks are in bed (Johnny on his sleeping porch, with screened moonlight silvering his cheek), and the young folks are out hell-raising either at the Nite Spot or at the country club. . . . Iowa in summertime.

> . . . an' the livin' is easy,
> Fish are jumpin', an' the cotton is high —

But at the moment the song was not a pastoral for Iowa or for anywhere. At the moment it was a threnody of woe, a self-dedicated dirge, and it came from Irmadee's alligator-skinned, pocket-type radio, propped at the tip of her white-dabbed nose as we lay stretched out flat on our stomachs alongside the new concrete swimming pool. She shut the little door and there was silence, except for the screams and shouts of eighty-nine children splashing in the warm green waters. Ours were there too: Jennifer and Wendy at the shallow end in duplicates of their mother's dirndl bathing suit, and Johnny paddling on the steps while Callie watched.

"I can't stand it," said Irmadee. "That's all they've played on practically every station ever since Monday. That and 'The Rhapsody in Blue' and 'The Man I Love.' Why don't they play the gay ones? 'I Got Rhythm,' and those?"

Yes, I thought. Why don't they? . . . Though "I Got Rhythm" was never really gay to me now, for whenever I heard it I saw a dead, slim-ankled, white-shod foot tapping.

Reaching for her sun lotion, she began to smear her face and to lower her shoulder straps, preparatory to a shift in posture. She had an earnestly earned and highly becoming tan which probably would

186

have been the envy of Malibu, "Isn't it tragic?" she said. "Isn't it *sickening?*"

"Yes," I said. "Yes, it is."

She turned, sat up, clutched modestly at her straps, and then lay down again on the striped air cushion, squinting upward through dark glasses. Whatever site at the municipal pool she chose she converted into her own cabana: there were the air cushion and the radio, and there were also three different lotion bottles, two pairs of sun glasses, a manicure case, cigarettes, lighter, magazines, books (currently *The Flowering of New England* and *Murder in Mayfair*), and occasionally a thermos of martinis in case she felt thirsty — "They sort of pick you up along in the middle of a hot afternoon," she said.

"You know," she said, "when Orin and I first heard about it the other night we went down into the Joint, just the two of us, and he opened a bottle of Scotch and we began to play the 'Rhapsody' on the Capehart, and I bawled like a baby. So did he. I guess we were both a little drunky before we were through." She lifted a wrist across the sun, to clock herself. "But it's like Orin said. 'Dee,' he said, 'Gershwin wrote for *us.*'"

"I suppose he wrote for a lot of people."

She went back, in a not unpleasant nostalgia. "Mm, the times we've heard them playing him out at the Edgewater Beach or in the Balloon Room. . . . 'Somebody Loves Me.' That was our favorite. In fact it's our song. You know?" She exposed another quarter inch of her breasts. "What's your and Lyle's song? I don't mean just Gershwin. I mean which is *the* song?"

"I don't know," I said. And I didn't. We had had so many.

Her head turned lazily on the cushion's pillowed top to glance at a scrawny, olive-skinned twelve-year-old girl in a red suit and a white rubber helmet who was poised at the end of the diving board. The girl went up in an expert jackknife, and then down. A splash, though not much of one, and then the white helmet reappearing.

"Sylvia Wurzberg," she observed, groping for a cigarette. "Orin says they oughtn't to let her in the pool. It's a disgrace, he says."

"Why?"

"That's what I ask him. 'You shouldn't be so prejudiced,' I say. 'After all, there's only the one family here. Judas, what if you had to live in Des Moines? The place is crawling with them.'" She snapped her lighter shut, and blew smoke upward. "And all the men who trade at the Fad say Moe Wurzberg couldn't be sweeter to do business with. You get full value for your money, and there's no question that his ties are much cuter than the ones at the Haber-dash."

I looked from the red suit, now reascending the diving tower ladder, to the edge of the pool where Callie was leaning down to admonish Johnny — black straw hat with the wired cherries bobbing on it, blue cotton dress with dark stains at the armpits, broad feet in their bunion-bulged black shoes. I heard her stern voice: "Johnny, don't you go down another step. You hear me? You hear me now?" . . . A phrase came to my mind: "the minority races." Well, they were certainly a minority in Ammon. But the Wurzbergs had each other, and a synagogue only sixty miles away, while Callie had no one. However, she was much more contented now than she had been during the winter, for she had not only discovered a family of Negro farmers who lived west of town and who sometimes asked her out, an obligation which she repaid by taking them to Mulch's for sodas when they came in on Saturday afternoons, but she had also become a member of the Holy Rollers, who held forth two nights a week in a ramshackle across-the-tracks structure which in its time had been first a tannery and then a paint warehouse. The Holy Rollers were white, and mostly Scandinavian, but they seemed to be at least a partial substitute for Father Divine — and if you were holy and rolled, and shrieked and sang, apparently they didn't mind what your color was, and Callie didn't mind either. "They don't sing good, Mis' Ellery," she said, "but they sing loud. And they got the Lord in them just the same."

Still, as Irmadee had pointed out — not that it was news to me — Callie was a very unusual person. "And I know darkies," she had said, "and I love them, too. After all, I didn't spend a whole year at Ward-Belmont for nothing. But they really ought never to leave the South, poor things. They're so much happier there." Which might have been true in general, although it didn't happen to have been true of Callie in particular. Not the way I'd heard it.

"You must have come across a lot of them in New York, Amy." I turned. It was Irmadee again. "How do you get along with them?"

"Who?"

"Kikes."

I rolled over onto my back, for I too was trying to tan. "All right with some. Not with others." I glanced down aslant at ten red toenails. Mine. "My best friend is married to one, and I get along with him." Usually.

There was a coolness in her voice, for she had once been my "best friend" and I think still regarded herself as such. Perhaps she was now again, too: I wasn't sure. "Oh, yes. That Natalie you're always talking so much about." But she forgave my perfidy, and her instant of resentment passed. Propping her cheek up on her elbowed hand, she looked at me. "You know, kiddo," she said — in moments of intimacy she occasionally lapsed into the speech of an earlier, purer, pre-Chicago day — "I notice you mention this Natalie a lot and that Kendrick man and people like that, but you never say anything about the Royal Archers. The *Panorama* people. Lyle worked for him. Didn't you ever meet them?"

Still looking down at my toes, I wiggled them. "Oh, yes."

"Socially?"

"Yes."

"Were you ever at their home?"

"Yes."

"What's it like?"

"It's beautiful. Regency, mostly."

"Um-hum. That's nice, too." Leaning over, she dropped her cigarette into the pool's gutter. "What's she like?"

"Who?"

"Mrs. Archer. There's a photograph of her in this month's *Bazaar* where she's over in Salzburg, in Austria, and she looks stunning. Wearing a dirndl, too. So simple."

"Well, I wouldn't say she was simple."

"Oh." She paused, dubious. "Snooty, hm?"

189

"No, not exactly. She's hard to describe."

"I suppose she's one of those women you have to get to know."

"I suppose so."

"I'd say she looks as if she'd be good in bed, anyway. Royal Archer must have himself a time."

"I wouldn't know."

She was silent. Reaching her arm over the side, she let her hand drift in the water, swishing forth, swishing back. "Lyle was awfully young to be the editor of a big magazine like *Panorama,* wasn't he?"

"Yes, he was."

"Well, personally I think you're just as well off here. Better off, probably. Don't you?"

"Yes, I think we are."

"That's what I always say to Orin whenever he begins to gripe about what a hick town this is. I always say, 'That's all very well, Orin. I'd like to go back and live in a nice apartment up on Sheridan Road, too, and be able to go to the Drake for cocktails every afternoon and to Chez Paree and Ambassador East and places like that. But the fact remains that we have our house here and the club and you've got your responsibilities at the M.C.S. and T., and — well, that time we did try it you know we weren't really contented there.'"

"How long did you and Orin live in Chicago, Irmadee — Dee?" I asked, for although they mentioned their residence there often, they were usually vague about its details.

"Oh, more than a year."

"On Sheridan Road?"

"Well, not *right* on it." The brown of her arm was sun-shimmered as it moved eel-like in the green waters. "Orin had a very good position with the Connover Trust Company, but it was really too big an organization and he prefers one that he can have at his finger tips. And the personnel man there was a Mr. Feinstein who was simply impossible to work with. A horrible person. An utter bastard." She withdrew her arm, and cupped her hands behind her head. "No, say what you will about it, there's no place like Ammon. . . ."

Closing my eyes against the sun, I let bright hotness eat into me. No place like Ammon. No, I thought, there probably wasn't. But I decided definitely that, attractive though she was, I didn't really consider Irmadee to be my best friend after all. . . . And then I felt a wet finger tapping my shoulder. "But we do have fun, in our crazy way, don't we? And we'll have more fun this fall, too, just you wait. Parties in the Joint and stuff. We always collect a gang together and drive down to Homecoming, and you and Lyle'll have to come along. Believe me, we raise the roof. . . ."

Summer. Iowa in summer. Blossoming, blooming richly, fading. Even in a country which is mostly country there are different ways of sensing the passing of summer and the coming of autumn, and mine was the town dweller's way. The walls of corn lining the highways were tall and green, and then gold, and then a dry, rustling brown, and after that, suddenly one day, a stubble. There was the first frost, and leaves drifting along the gutters of Manila Street, and then the smoky smell of those leaves burning in bonfires. The distant piping of the calliope from the Fair Grounds, the exodus of the college crowd, coal scuttling down chutes, storage tanks being filled with oil, the screens coming off, the storm windows going on, back-yard clotheslines sagging with the garments of winter, Johnny's first pumpkin that he identified as a pumpkin, Mama saying, "You may be needing extra comforters tonight, Amy. . . ."

Irmadee was right. We did have fun that fall. There were exclusive parties in the Joint and less exclusive ones at the country club, where Orin and Irmadee were the first to dance the Big Apple — which they had brought back from Chicago — and later the first to stop dancing it. They brought other things back from Chicago, too: a raccoon-collared three-piece ensemble, completely zippered, for Irmadee; a re-enactment of the juicier lines of *The Women,* the stage play, which they had seen performed by a company which everyone agreed was much superior to the original New York company; accounts of looping the Loop (but really!) with Winnetka friends; and a report of one day having watched and listened to President Roosevelt dedicate a new bridge up on the Drive. "All the fuss and to-do it's stirred up," said Irmadee. "Hell, it didn't seem to us to be so much, though we had to admit it was sort of thrilling to realize that we were looking at the President of the United States, himself, in person—whatever you may think of him. As a matter of fact we couldn't even stay for the finish, because we were meeting friends at the Stevens for drinks. When we left he was just getting into that quarantine part. It's a beautiful bridge, though, and it's going to save loads of time and traffic when you want to go from the Drive to . . ."

We went down to Homecoming and duly raised the roof, and as November gave way to December I began first secretly to ponder and then openly to discuss the possibility, next spring, of our at last being in a financial position to raise our own roof, a physical one. As a temporary measure, living with Mama and Papa had worked out much better than I had ever dreamed it would—but then, so had everything—yet naturally and inevitably there had been certain periods of stress and friction. Mostly with Mama. Sometimes between Callie and Mama, although their shared adoration of Johnny could be relied on to make a truce when all else failed. Always between Lyle and Mama, despite his most winning efforts to make her "come round." Obviously she had no intention of ever coming round, as far as he was concerned. Her attack was seldom frontal — merely allusive and oblique—but her barrage was constant. However, he had apparently been able to condition himself to it. And, as he said, why not? Other people had. "After all," he said, "she's been sniping at your father for thirty-four years, and he's thrived on it. I guess I can stand her sniping at me for one. And this way we pay our rent and they get the extra income and everything's dandy. More or less."

"Then you think we can?" I said. "Build, I mean? In the spring?"

"I shouldn't be surprised. If we can get an FHA. And if your father doesn't fire me."

"Fire you. As if he would. He thinks you're wonderful."

"So?"

"Of course he does. He told me so himself. He says you've taken so much of the burden off of him, and that the *Argus* had never had a better man. All the men in the shop like you, he says, even Alf. He says you're a born editor."

"Me? I'm not doing any editing. I'm just the guy who writes up the locals and cracks the whip over the country correspondents so they'll get their copy in on time, that's all." But evidently I had pleased him, for he went quickly on. "Still, it's not at all a bad little sheet, you know. And praise from Alf is praise indeed. I've always thought he was queer for that lino, and never even knew people existed."

One of the reasons, one of the many reasons, why I looked forward to having a house of our own was that we would find it easier to entertain there, for although we had made partial payments on our indebtedness to the Netchers and the Haubergs and others by taking them to dinner at the club or to the Corn Room in the Hotel, such festivities weren't quite the same as private ones. Occasionally we had had Irmadee and Orin and the Diederdocks in for poker, and Zelda and Fern for bridge, but those evenings had required considerable finesse, because we played for money and we served drinks, neither of which was approved by Mama. Not that she ever made any outright complaint. In fact usually she didn't even put in an appearance. However, no one could remain unconscious of her presence, for she sat among the sputtering radiators of the sun porch audibly coughing and rustling the pages of her magazine until it was time for her to rise and make her exit by a tortuous and invisible route which included switching out the lights in the front hall, clinkingly transferring the empty soda bottles from the pantry shelf to the head of the basement steps, and noisily ascending the back stairs.

But the gathering I suggested for Christmas Eve, and to which she graciously assented, would be different, I felt — if only because it would be Christmas Eve and because she would have her own group, mostly the ladies of the Altar Guild, to divert her from Lyle's and mine. And there would be carols instead of cards, and although there would be liquor it would be in the form of punch rather than highballs and might therefore seem more innocuous, might even seem to be in the tradition of Dickens. "I thought we could have just sort of open house, Mama," I said. "You know, people drifting in and out. And it won't last long, because most of them won't want to stay up late on Christmas Eve anyway. Callie can fix trays of sandwiches, and there'll be coffee, and this punch Lyle makes is awfully tasty — it's from an old family recipe that a bishop gave his grandmother to serve at christenings."

"It all sounds very nice, dear," she said, musing and already mentally drawing up her guest list. "Let's see. There'll be the Trost girls, of course, and the Young Art Bruers, and the Old Art Bruers if they feel up to it — though Mrs. Old may not — and Dr. Pletch, if he isn't working on his sermon, and . . ."

The Old Art Bruers felt up to it all right, even Mrs. Old, and so did the weather, which co-operated by beginning to snow again in great fleecy flakes which guaranteed to make an already white Christmas even whiter. Late in the afternoon, before the others came, we hung the red-paper bells throughout the downstairs and trimmed the tall tree in its corner, looping it with tinsel somewhat tarnished after twenty years of use and crowning it with the one-winged pink-and-blue angel, and after Johnny was in bed arranged the presents — most of them for him — around the cotton at its foot. Mama even relented so far as to let Lyle build a fire in the fireplace, though as a rule she didn't like open fires because they were so dirty. "Very pretty to look at," as she said, "but what they do to my curtains and the ceiling is quite another thing."

Irmadee had lent us their big Tom-and-Jerry bowl from the Joint, along with its gothic-in-gilt-lettered mugs, and Lyle stood before it in the pantry, surrounded by rum bottles and nutmeg and the beaten whites of eggs. The pantry was a sanctuary for him, because neither Mama nor Callie would deign to enter it while he was engaged in the mixing of what they both united — one of their rare unitings — in terming "that stuff." Standing beside him, I gazed out at the snow as it fell soft and white and silent in the light from the bulb over the garage. Except for last year, which had been quite different, this was my first Christmas in Ammon since I had first gone to New York, and as I stood there I remembered the white, Middle Western Christmases of my childhood and adolescence, tomorrow's turkey in its pan on the back porch, the smell of sage and cranberries, the piled-up drifts, the glistening, squeaky sidewalks, the hoarfrost on mittens and stocking caps, the tongue stuck daringly against the bright blade of a skate. . . . And now here it all was again. But better.

"Here. Taste this," he said, and I did and it was wonderful.

"Too strong? Not strong enough?"

"Just right," I pronounced, critically. "Perfect."

He reached again for one of the rum bottles. "O.K. We'll make it perfecter." He had already been doing some sampling on his own, and his voice was gay. And I wanted him gay, because he had certainly earned the right to be if anyone had. "You know, maybe I'll tie one on tonight, in a refined way. What would you think of that?"

"Why don't you?" Drinking very much very often was one thing I never had to worry about him. I imagine I probably had Mrs. Ellery to thank for that. "It'd be good for you. Relax you."

"Hm. She eggs me on, she does. My own dear wife. My spouse. . . . Eggs. Eggs. Who mentioned eggs?" Drawing one of the crockery bowls toward him, he dumped its foamy contents into the punch and then ladled some of it into one of the gilt-lettered mugs. He lifted the mug, and bowed. "I give you peace-on-earth-good-will-toward-men. Including Hitler and your mother."

I smiled. "Next Christmas our own house," I said. "Our own pantry. And a fire in the fireplace all the time, even in our bedroom."

"You bet," he said, and again lifted the mug. "I give you next year. And the year after that. And the one after that and that, and that. And so on, infinitum."

From the front part of the house came the jangle of the doorbell and, from the vestibule, an arch voice crying, "Mistletoe! Look, Fern, mistletoe!"

"That," said Lyle, placing the empty mug back on its tray, "would be our flirtatious friend Zelda. The amorous and insatiable Mrs. Hauberg."

Another jangle, and another voice, two almost identical voices: they were starting to come now. "Ooh-hoo?" and "Anybody home, lady?"

"And those would be the sprightly sisters Trost. The Whoops kids." He showered a final sprinkling of nutmeg over the bowl and then, picking up the tray, turned toward the pantry door. "Hark, the herald angels sing. It's time for wassail and many a merry Noel. Come Donner, come Blitzen, let's throw up the sash."

There was many a merry Noel, and he was merriest. Standing beside the cherry-wood upright while Mrs. Pete Schauffler played the accompaniments and Mrs. Paul Schauffler acted as page turner, he led the others in "Good King Wenceslaus" and "O Tannenbaum" and "Adeste Fidelis," although Mama was heard to remark to Dr. Pletch (but not heard by the Diederdocks and the Herkles, I trusted) that she had never cared particularly for "Adeste Fidelis" as it always seemed to her to be such a Roman Catholic hymn. At first there were two separate and distinct groups, Mama's friends and ours — Papa managed to shuttle between them — but the punch and Lyle's joviality did a great deal toward welding them together. In spirit, at least. Physically they continued to remain more or less apart, with Mama and the Trosts and the Guild ladies at one end of the room and with Zelda and the Diederdocks and Irmadee, seasonally charming in a holly-sprigged red-and-green dinner dress, at the other. But variance in ages and interests seemed to be no barrier to the men, who all hovered together. Their bond was that they were men.

"Now, come on, folks! Raise your voices high!" urged Lyle, scooping his mug into the bowl. "Sing!"

We sang; even Papa, who could recognize only one tune — "Red-Wing, My Pretty Red-Wing" — and had never been able to master that. I looked at Lyle, and my heart went out to him warmly for the way he was working to make the party go. And it wasn't easy, and wouldn't have been for anyone, because the elements were so diverse: the dumpy dowdiness of Mrs. Young Art Bruer contrasted with Irmadee's Chicago chic, the flowing bowl on the doilied table which had never held a flowing bowl before. I tried to picture him as he would have been in this gathering a year ago: strange, alien, ill-at-ease, perhaps even supercilious. So much adjustment to so many things in such a short space of time. And yet although he had changed in that way, he hadn't changed in others; for he was still the handsomest, the brightest, the ablest man in this room, in this whole town — or in any room in any town. Who would have thought on that dreary, rainy morning when we had first alighted in Ammon that he —

"Amy." It was Mama, who had risen and had stealthily made her way over to me and now was bending toward me where I sat on the sofa between Irmadee and Myrtle Jasperson, nee Gannett. Her voice was pitched to a confidential, this-is-in-the-family tone, though less successfully than she intended. "I believe Lyle has had quite enough," she said. "Don't you?"

"Oh, he's all right."

"No, dear. I mean it. The ladies are noticing that he —"

"Mama," I said. "Please. Christmas comes only once a year."

"So does Santa Claus, poor old man," interjected Orin, who was weaving near by and who didn't see Mama but did see me; perhaps saw two of me. There could be no doubt that he had had enough, and probably had had ever since early afternoon. Orin was in good form.

"Orin!" giggled Irmadee, warningly. "Judas! Watch yourself! You're not at home, you know."

But Mama either hadn't heard or didn't understand, and in any case she was single-purposed. She leaned lower toward me. "You'll have to do something. He was tippling all the time he was making that stuff. He —"

"Please, Mama. Please."

She straightened, her lips tightening. I could gauge her mood by the way the cords were standing out above the black velvet band around her neck. "Like mother, like son, apparently," she said, and, turning, started back toward her camp.

"Hey, what's this, what's this? Secrets?" Looking upward, I saw that Orin had moved closer and that his red eyes were blinking down at me. He called toward Lyle. "You got a skeleton in your closet, Lylie?" he said. "You come from a long line of lushes?"

"Now Orin," said Irmadee, "don't be disgusting. And if you keep pouring all that rum on top of martinis and Burgundy and brandy you're going to feel perfectly terrible in the morning. Remember last Christmas, you know."

I was looking at Lyle. Had he heard? At first I decided not, for he was at the punch bowl and his back was toward us. But as he turned I saw that his hand holding the mug was trembling, and I knew he had heard. Rising, I went toward him. But Orin was following me; or accompanying and escorting me, rather, his arm companionably around my waist. "You going to read the riot act to him, Amy?" he was saying. "You going to give him hell?"

Irmadee's voice floated after us. "Orin, don't be such a dope. Come back here and sit down. If you can."

I suddenly realized that the room had become very quiet, except for the neigh of Mrs. Old Art Bruer's breathing and a pair of antiphonal "tchk-tchks" from the Misses Trost and from Mama a murmured, "If he were in his own home and this were New York City, I should certainly never have opened my mouth. But this doesn't happen to be his own home and it isn't New York City and — "

"Darling," I said, and extended my sherbet glass — there hadn't been enough of the mugs to go round. "Darling, I'd like another drink, please."

"Well, what shall we have now?" said Mrs. Pete Schauffler, frenziedly thumbing the pages on the music rack. "How about this one?" She struck a chord and began to sing, in her mellifluous, throbbing alto. " 'We Three Kings of Orient — ' "

Her words and her song died, and the chord with them, as he made no move to take my glass but instead set his own mug down on the piano top with such force that I wondered why the china didn't break. He looked at Mama. "Did it ever occur to you that I might wish I did have a home," he said, "and wish that it was in New York City — or anywhere else that's a thousand miles from here?"

I glanced quickly and instinctively at Papa. Papa was usually good at coping with situations like this, although so far as I knew he had never actually been faced with a situation like this. But he was standing in front of the fire, his hands behind him and his thin legs straddled, and he was saying nothing.

"Lyle," I said. "I want a drink. You have a drink, too."

" 'Three Kings of Orient,' " said Mrs. Paul Schauffler. "Yes, that would be good. Oh, that would be very good. Or how about 'Jingle Bells'?"

"Did you hear me?" said Lyle, still looking at Mama. "Did you?"

"Amy, dear," suggested Mama, "perhaps it's time your friends would enjoy a cup of nice, hot coffee. If you would be so kind as to go out and speak to —"

"Did you hear me?"

Until that moment, she had never even glanced at him. But now she did, penetratingly. "Yes," she said. "I heard you. And so did everyone else."

"Now look, fella," said Frank Diederdock, who was the head of the K.C.'s and who was generally acknowledged to stand an excellent chance of becoming mayor, even if he was a Catholic, "this is Christmas. We're having fun —"

"My God," said Lyle. "You call this 'fun'? This waxworks?"

Orin's hand fell on his shoulder, soothingly if fumblingly. "Keep your pants on, Lyle," he advised. "All this is probably my fault. But can't you take a joke — ?"

Lyle's shoulder jerked away, and the hand pawed at nothingness. "Not your jokes," he said. "I'm fed to the teeth on your jokes, clean, dirty, any kind, because I've heard them all at least once before from somebody else, usually when I was about fifteen, and at least twice from you." He reached for his mug, on the piano top. "And I'm fed up with the Manila County Savings and Trust, too, and the whole damned Sigma Chi fraternity and all its chapters, and the entire city of Chicago, especially the North Side." He tapped at the stiff shirt front of Orin's dinner jacket, which was one of the few double-breasted dinner jackets in town and the only one of any description in the room. "But do you want to know what I'm fed up with most? It's the Balloon Room. My God, am I fed up with the Balloon Room!"

"Well!" said Irmadee, rising.

"Well!" repeated Mrs. Young Art Bruer, rising also, though for a different reason. She nudged Mrs. Old Art Bruer, who, though interested, was fortunately not too good in her hearing.

The hand that wasn't holding the mug was in his pocket . . .

jingle-bells, jingle-bells: jingle-keys, jingle-keys. He looked around at the circle of faces. "Are there any questions from the audience?" he said

"Yes," said Irmadee, throwing a gold-spangled black veil over her head. "You're very smart, very clever, very New Yorky — for a man who couldn't keep a job there and who had to come back and sponge off his father-in-law." She shoved a little at Orin, as if to steer him toward the door. "But may I ask if you don't like it here, why don't you go back where you came from?"

"For the same reason you and Orin don't go back to Chicago, probably," he said. "Because I got licked, that's why." He came toward her. "But it's very interesting, your mentioning fathers-in-law when everybody knows that you and Orin have lived off the two of yours for years and always will."

She was tugging now, instead of shoving. "Don't just stand there, Orin. Come on. We're leaving."

"However, if you want to go into the subject of relations," he continued, "let me tell you that there was a time when my father could have bought your father's M.C.S. and T. and never even missed what he paid for it. He could have bought the whole of this jerk town, this whole damned county — "

"Oh, Lyle," I said. The rest was all right, I supposed. But not the money. I wished he hadn't said that about the money. "Don't, Lyle. Please."

He looked at me then, and he looked around at all the others, and after that he looked back at me.

"I'm sorry," he said, to me. To me alone. "I'm sorry." And he hurried across the room, past all the ladies with their red faces and Mama with her white one, and disappeared into the vestibule, and a moment later I heard the storm door slamming and then his quick tread on the porch steps and then a fading crunching on the snowy walk and then nothing.

"Amy, dear," said Mama. "Now if you'll just have Callie bring in the coffee — "

"Oh, it's getting so late," said Mrs. Paul Schauffler. "I do think we ought to be going."

"Yes, I think so too," agreed Mrs. Pete Schauffler. "The children are bound to be up early for their presents, you know, and . . ."

But Irmadee was far ahead of her — already at the cloak closet and reaching for her fur-trimmed galoshes while Orin leaned waveringly against a wall in whose substantialness he seemed to have none too much confidence. He was humming: "Jingle-bells, jingle-bells — "

"Shut up, Orin," said Irmadee, in an aside, and added brightly, "Well, good night, Mrs. Hardin. We've had such a lovely time. A really lovely time. . . ."

And so they went, all of them, and they all said they had had a lovely time and they all clustered around the cloak closet and they said, "Are those your rubbers, or are they mine?" and they all said "Merry Christmas" and some of them said "We brought a little giftie for you. It's really nothing, but I'll just leave it right here by the tree," and they trooped out onto the porch and Mama called "Be sure to watch those steps, lady. They may be slippery," and their voices rang in the night and then there was the low grind of cold motors turning, turning, turning, and finally catching and starting, and then they were gone.

Standing in the living room, I saw the porch light go out, heard Mama close the storm door, the inner door, then the vestibule door, and after that saw her come back into the room, where she began to go around collecting mugs and glasses and ash trays.

"Such a mess," she said. "Such a mess. And look — somebody left a cigarette burning on the top shelf of Mother Pepperdine's whatnot."

Papa had taken up his position in front of the fire again, which was now dying. He started forward. "Let's leave the cleaning-up until morning, Mother," he said. "It's time we got to bed."

She hesitated. "Well — all right. Not that it will be any easier in the morning than it would be now. It never is." She headed toward the dining room. "I might as well just take these things out, though." At the portieres, she paused. "Good night, Amy."

"Good night, Mama."

"Before you go up, you'll be sure that the fire's out, won't you?

I don't like the idea of leaving it burning. Any one of those sparks might —"

"Yes, Mama."

She disappeared. Papa reached for the poker, its brass tip still unblackened because it was so seldom used. He started to remove the hearth screen. "A nice thing, a fire," he said. "It's cheerful."

"Let it go, Papa. I'll fix it."

He stood looking down at the glowing logs for a moment, and then replaced the screen and put the poker back. He turned toward the front hall. "Well, sir. You coming up?"

"Not just yet."

He came toward me, and he put his arms around me. I was taller than he was, and always had been, ever since I was sixteen years old.

"Good night, Amy," he said. "Good night, daughter."

I clung to him. "Oh, Papa. Papa . . ."

He patted my shoulder, and I felt the straggle of his mustache against my cheek. "Don't stay up too late," he said. "And don't think too much. Night's no time for thinking." And then he continued on toward the hall, and I heard him begin to climb the stairs, slowly. And at the same time I could hear Mama climbing the back stairs, less noisily than usual. Although I was unable to see either of them, I could picture them meeting on the landing and then finishing the flight together, a big woman and a little man, and going along the upper hall together and into their room together, as they had every night for thirty-four years.

"Mis' Ellery?" Callie had appeared by the portieres, her face skeptical. "Mis' Hardin say not to clean up in here until tomorrow. She mean it?"

"Yes, Callie. Just leave it."

She shook her head. "My land," she said. And then she withdrew. "Well, good night, Mis' Ellery."

"Good night, Callie."

I glanced at the mantel clock. Hardly ten-thirty yet. Not really late. . . . Well, I decided, I might as well do a little cleaning up after all. So I began to gather up the rest of the glasses and the mugs. I gathered them all up and took them out into the kitchen, making several trips, and gathered up the punch bowl and its tray and the ash trays, too. I rinsed out what was left in the bowl — there wasn't much — but I didn't bother with the glasses and the mugs: just stacked them for Callie to take care of in the morning.

Back in the living room, I turned out all the lights except those on the tree and, drawing up a chair, sat in front of the fire, or rather the embers of the fire. Ashes dropped, crackling. I must have sat there quite a while, looking down into the glow and up at the row of six orange-bulged, candy-caned stockings dangling from the mantel edge: Papa's and Lyle's brief socks, the one black lisle and the other brown wool; Callie's mysteriously long black cotton; Mama's gun-metal silk; Johnny's tiny white knit; my flesh silk. Then suddenly I rose and, going to the cloak closet in the hall, opened its door and pulled at the light chain and looked into it. Yes, there they all were: his hat, his scarf, his overcoat, all there on their hanger and hook with his galoshes standing below them. Pulling at the light chain again and closing the door, I went to the window and lifted the curtains aside and stood gazing out at the all-night window candles and the few decorated outdoor trees of Manila Street. The snow was still fall-ing, but not in fleecy flakes now — thickly and steadily, blizzard-like. The drifts were mounting higher, and in the multicolored light cast by the Gannetts' tree next door, I could see that the foot tracks on our walk were already covered over and that in the street the tracks of the departing cars were covered over also.

I was afraid, and I knew it, but I refused to admit that I was afraid. Snow, I thought. Snow is harmless enough. Nothing can happen to anybody in the snow, except maybe a bad cold coming from not wearing a hat and overcoat. Nothing can happen even if — if any-body wants something to happen, hopes for it, seeks it. Snow is so soft. It's not like — concrete, six inches of concrete and a forty-two-story plunge down onto it. . . . I leaned my forehead against the icy pane, and into my mind came patches of a conversation, two differ-ent conversations, although the speaker had been the same: "So much ego he had. Too much. And so when the crash came and he was wiped out, I wasn't enough for him. Nothing was enough for him, because he felt that he himself was nothing." That and the same

203

voice saying, encouragingly, "So cheer up. He's like Vincent in so many ways. He may be like him in that way, too."

Letting the curtains fall back, I turned away. Papa was right, I told myself — night's no time for thinking. And, as a distraction, I bent toward the radio and switched it on, tuning its volume low. Out from it, in a moment, came the intricate harmonizing of a female trio. A record, probably; or a transcription:

> *Bei mir bist du schön,*
> *Please let me explain . . .*

I stood looking down at the yellow eye of the dial, which glowed in the shadows of the corner like a cat's eye in the night. What any right-minded station was doing playing that song on Christmas Eve I certainly couldn't imagine — perhaps as a relief from carols, or possibly through force of habit — but anyway it was.

> *I could say BEL-la, BEL-la,*
> *Even say VOON-derbar . . .*

"That Yid song," Orin always called it, and no doubt it was, but not even the slick overarrangement employed by the trio could keep the brooding and the wailing out of it. The Blues. The Jewish Blues. . . . And momentarily I thought of Ben, and of Natalie, and wondered where they were in New York now and what they were doing. For they weren't living in Washington any more, to Natalie's great delight. Ben had become thoroughly disillusioned with what he pronounced to be the timidity and half-measures of the New Deal, even its fast-dissolving Brain Trust, and was back teaching economics again. Not at N.Y.U., though, and not as an assistant professor. At Columbia, and as an associate professor. A step up.

> *Bei mir bist du schön,*
> *I've tried to explain . . .*

I switched the knob to silence, and once more there was only the fall of the embers in the grate and the ticking of the clock above it. That was no song for me. Not now. Not tonight. I didn't want to hear the Blues tonight, Jewish or any other denomination, and I didn't want to hear any joyous carols, either. . . . I'm going upstairs,

I decided. I'm going upstairs and to bed and I'm going to sleep.

So I did. That is, I went upstairs and to bed, first glancing in on Johnny, lying warm and woolly in the boarded-up chill of the sleeping porch. Mama's and Papa's door was shut, and from behind it came the sound of Mama's heavy breathing, the long rhythmic intake of the *enhhh* and the even longer outlet of the *anhhh* which I probably would have called an outright snore if it had come from anyone else. Undressing and crossing the hall to the bathroom and then crossing back again, I turned out the light in our room and went to the windows and opened one of them a few inches — snow was banked solid in the storm-window slot, and a bitter wind whistled in. I touched the drift and again looked out into the blizzard and down onto Manila Street. Except for the snow-blurred bulbs on the lighted trees, the only light I could see was the one in the Senior Netchers' bedroom window. What were they talking about in the bedrooms of Manila Street tonight, the lighted one and all the dark ones too? What were they talking about in the bedrooms of Gold Coast Row? I knew. I knew.

I got into my bed and shivered between the icy sheets. And then, just as they were warming a little, I heard sounds downstairs — the storm door being quietly opened and shut, the stomp of snowy feet in the vestibule, and after that a soft tread on the stairs.

Thank God, I thought. Thank God.

He came into the room noiselessly, or almost noiselessly, tiptoeing, and began to undress in the darkness. For a while I pretended to be asleep, but all the time I was watching the shadow of his movements through half-closed lids. Coat being shouldered onto its hanger in the closet, the unknotting of a tie, the paleness of a shirt coming off, the metallic click of coins and keys being placed on the bureau, the flap of trousers being shaken briefly and then hung, the small thud of one shoe and then the other.

"You ought to have something hot before you go to bed," I said, in that bedroom whisper which after a year had become automatic to both of us. "You might have caught cold."

"I'm all right," he said. "I had some coffee up at the diner. And I called the taxi to bring me back."

"Is it still snowing?"

"Mm. Bad."

He tiptoed out into the hall, in his pyjamas, and I could see a slanting ray as the bathroom light was switched on. And then the ray was cut off as the door closed, softly, and then after a while it was on again, and off again, and he was tiptoeing in. He closed the door behind him, and got into his bed, shivering a little just as I had, squirming down in search of warmth. We lay in silence.

"Where were you?" I said, then.

"Walking."

Whispers, whispers. . . .

"Walking where?"

"Oh, just around."

Whispers.

"You ought at least to have taken your overcoat."

"I know."

Then, from him: "I'm sorry about the dramatics."

"It's all right."

"No, it isn't. I shouldn't have talked to your mother that way. Our being here probably hasn't been any easier on her than it has on us."

"It doesn't matter. She's — well, she's Mama."

More silence. Then: "I'm not sorry about what I said to Orin and Irmadee, though. They had it coming. They've had it coming for a long time."

A long time. Yes, probably ever since he had met them. And undoubtedly he felt that the town had had it coming for a long time, too: ever since he had stood there in the rain at the station. . . . My address for the past year might well have been "Mrs. Lyle Ellery. Fool's Paradise. C/o Postmaster." A well-populated locality, Fool's Paradise, and this had been the second time that I had taken up residence in it, the other time having been that deceptively happy period when I was carrying Johnny.

"Lyle, why didn't you tell me?"

"Tell you what?"

"How you really felt. How you've always felt."

The sheets rustled, the comforter moved. "Oh, I don't know. I'd washed out on you before. I decided that this time I wouldn't. I decided I'd make a go of it."

"You've never washed out on me. Not really."

"No? Thanks."

"What's been the worst — your job on the paper, or the town, or living here with Mama and Papa?"

"All of it together, I suppose. It just — got me." There was a pause. "You were right in the first place. You said it wouldn't work. But I had the idea that being on a small-town newspaper might be sort of romantic. So I learned that it isn't."

"Maybe if we had a house of our own — "

"Huh." In the darkness I knew there was a smile, a wry, dry smile. "You think either of us can live here now, anywhere in this town — after tonight?"

No. No, I didn't think it.

I heard him sigh. "You know, sometimes I wonder if it ever happened to us. Sometimes I think maybe I dreamed it."

"What, dear?"

"*Panorama*. Me and *Panorama*. All of that. Like a rocket I was, I guess. Up it goes and then — phtt — out it fizzles." Again that sigh. "The industrious but unfortunate apprentice. The boy grows older, and falls flat on his face amid the alien corn. . . ."

Faintly there came a chiming: the courthouse clock striking. I listened to its heavy, slow, spaced strokes. It had been after eleven when I had finally come upstairs. This would be twelve.

"It came upon a midnight clear," he said. "And how clear it was when it did come." And then he turned over, with a final whisper. "Good night, darling. And a Merry Christmas."

"Merry Christmas."

The last chime struck, the twelfth chime. I lay in darkness and in stillness. Silent night, holy night. . . . Then suddenly, throwing back the covers, I got out of my bed, stood, and after that bent down and crawled into his, beside him. I put my arms around him, and I held him close.

"Do you love me, darling?" I said.

I felt him turn, felt his warmth, felt his lips.

"Yes. Yes, I love you."

"Then love me."

His arms drew me tighter to him.

"I'll love you," he said. "I'll love you now. I'll love you always."

In the gray overcast of nine o'clock on the morning of New Year's Day he picked his way across the hard-packed ruts of a completely deserted Main Street and headed toward the *Argus* office. Although there was no one in the street and no one on the as yet unshoveled walk, it was evident that there had been only a few short hours ago, for the walk still bore evidences of recent revelry. Scattered in front of the arched entrance leading up to the Firemen's Hall were a swirl of confetti, some loose curled strands of paper streamers, the brown broken glass of a whisky bottle, the torn frill of an orange crepe-paper cap, a spiral-striped cardboard horn, a wooden noise-maker-whirler, and a pool of vomit, greenish-yellow in the snow. The Firemen's Ball had been only one of many parties held the previous evening, although by no means the most select. That one had taken place at the country club and we had been scheduled to attend it and, along with other choice spirits of the inner clique, to have preceded it by attending a cocktails-and-buffet in the Joint, the latter invitation having been issued as far back as November. We had not made an appearance at either gathering. Irmadee's invitation had not been officially withdrawn, either by telephone or by note, nor had we withdrawn our acceptance of it. We just hadn't gone, that was all. We understood. They understood. There was no need for anything more.

Skirting the greenish-yellow pool, he continued onward to the *Argus* office entrance, and all that was what he saw and all this is what he did and felt and thought.

He unlocked and opened the door, on which the shade was drawn and in the corner of which was a placard reading "Closed Dec. 25 and Jan. 1," and went in, passing the circulation-and-advertising counter and continuing on to the room he shared with her father. The room was so cold that he could see his breath in it, and the first thing he did was to go to the radiator, twist its knob, and kick at its paint-blistered ribs. There was a slight iron response, a subterranean clanking, but not much else: no warmth, anyway. Well, that meant that Kelly had forgotten to bank the furnace, as usual, and it also meant that the pipes might be frozen. So what? So he'd keep his coat on, and his muffler, and his hat too.

There were two desks in the office, one a roll-top, which was her father's, and one a glassed flat-top, which was his. Seating himself at the flat-top, he pursed his lips and gazed meditatively at a neatly squared sheaf centered on the glass, the copy submitted in advance for next week's issue by Miss Ethel Huber, who combined the functions of bookkeeper and society editress. He leafed the first page:

AMMON SOCIETY

Mrs. Arthur Bruer, Jr., entertained the ladies of the St. James Altar Guild last Tuesday in her home on Manila Street at a Yule supper. Those attending were Mrs. Arthur Bruer, Sr., Mrs. Rev. Pletch, Mrs. Herschel Tupper, Mrs. John Hardin. . . . ["*Must Run,*" had been penciled on the margin in Ethel's Palmer Method script.]

Hm. Oh, yes, that was the evening he and Amy had been able to come downstairs and sit in the living room. Most of the other evenings during the past week they had spent at the Hawkeye, sometimes staying on through both shows.

Mr. and Mrs. Fern Hauberg feted the members of the Pot-Luck Bridge Club at their home on California Street at a buffet dinner on Wednesday. A delicious repast was served, after which cards were enjoyed. Those playing included Mr. and Mrs. Frank Diederdock, Mr. and Mrs. Peter Schauffler, Mr. and Mrs. Paul Schauffler . . .

Well, no need to read who else played. He could have listed them blindfolded, and so could any constant reader of the *Argus*.

One of the gay parties of the Yule season was that given on Thursday by Mr. and Mrs. Erwin Mork at their home on California Street . . .

"Gay" was the word all right, if what he had heard was true. Orin had been sick all over Estelle Mork's new two-toned rug and had passed out in the bathroom and Irmadee had had to put cold cloths on his head. But you would never see the names "Mr. and Mrs. Orin Netcher" in any society notes in the *Argus,* and those who didn't know otherwise might think they were either lepers or hermits. "That crap," was the way Irmadee referred to the column, when she didn't employ a more Anglo-Saxon term. "If that Huber hag ever puts Orin and me in it, I'll sue her."

A large turnout is anticipated for the New Year's Eve dance at the country club, for which the Six Cats will supply the music. Among those who have already made reservations and who are expected to welcome the New Year in by tripping the light fantastic are Mr. and Mrs. Fern Hauberg, Mr. and Mrs. Frank Diederdock . . .

Ah, but not Mr. and Mrs. Lyle Ellery. That is, they had made reservations all right and had even bought tickets — at this moment still in the center drawer of Amy's dressing table — but they hadn't welcomed the New Year in by tripping any light fantastic. They had slept it in, and even in their sleep they hadn't welcomed it.

He turned to the last page, and as usual saw at its bottom Ethel's crisp " — 30 — " She was a demon newspaperwoman, Ethel was. But an even better bookkeeper.

He tossed the pages aside. Take it away, Ethel, he thought. Take it away and keep it away. From now on it's your baby, and whatever you want to do about commas and semicolons and the spelling of the word "mousse" is between you and your Maker.

Bending downward, he pulled out a drawer and began to empty its contents onto the desk. A textbook — *The Editorship and Management of the Rural Weekly,* an unconsulted memento of that period when he had thought that he might prove to be a modern-day Ed Howe or a smaller-scale William Allen White. He dumped it into the wastebasket. A chatty and intimate mimeographed letter, some months old, from his class agent soliciting a contribution to the Class Fund. His eye caught a few phrases: ". . . dire need . . . desperate straits . . . this Recession period through which we are now being forced . . . to our jubilee throng, must all pull together . . ." Dire need? Desperate straits? Well, no doubt those were relative terms. Crumpling the letter, he threw that in the wastebasket also. John Harvard was a good man, but he would have to wait his turn: another John came first.

He straightened as he heard the air-wheeze of the street door closing. Now who could that be, at nine o'clock of a New Year's morning? Alf maybe? Come down to see if by some miracle his precious lino had risen from its cement bed and fled off during the night? But Alf wouldn't be sober enough to walk yet. . . . Then he heard the slow shuffle of footsteps coming down the hall, and he knew who it was. Her father. The old man. And he looked at the pulled-out drawer. Well, they had agreed they wouldn't tell him until tomorrow, when the holidays — ah, such holidays — would be officially over, but apparently he might as well tell him now.

The steps were shuffling nearer, and then the slight, black-coated, muskrat-capped, muskrat-gloved figure stood in the doorway.

"Well, sir," he said, entering. "Cold in here. Looks like Kelly's failed us again."

"Yes," he said, opening a second drawer and continuing with his clearing-out and cleaning-up. "Looks that way."

"Not too reliable, that boy," said the old man, going toward the roll-top and seating himself at it and beginning to pull off the muskrat gloves. "We'll have to speak to him."

Not "we," he thought. You.

There was a squeak as the swivel chair was turned to face the roll-top. He went on with his work — old letters to tear up, receipted bills to discard — and didn't glance at him. Sooner or later the old man would notice what he was doing, and then would begin to ask questions. And would be answered, surprisingly. Or possibly not surprisingly.

Papers rustled, and the light, reedy voice spoke. "I see Mrs. Ericson's got her Mott Creek Notes in ahead of time, for a change."

"So?"

"Mm. And here's some new boiler plate. 'The Origin and Development of Hybrid Seed Corn,' with cuts. I expect Henry Wallace has something to do with that." A pause, and an examination. "Well, it looks quite informative. And there's considerable interest in this hybrid business around here. You may be able to use it sometime."

Not me.

"He knows corn all right, Henry does. And he's been a good

Secretary of Agriculture, too, for a Democrat that was a Republican. But when he began to tell 'em to kill their hogs and plow-under their grain they didn't like it much. And I don't blame them." A cough, another chair squeak, a drawer opening. "No man wants to be told when to stop planting oats and start planting flax. At least not on his own farm and not by somebody who's sitting at a desk off there in Washington, D.C."

Finally he did turn to the roll-top and, rising, went toward it. He might as well get it over with now.

Standing by the scuffed, nicked, varnished wood, he looked downward. The blottered surface of the desk was like a rat's nest — but then, it always had been. However, it was even more like a rat's nest now than ever before, because there were things strewn over it which he had never seen — rusty fishhooks, an elk-toothed watch fob, a silver dollar with a hole drilled in it, a dusty stack of poker chips spilled over the well-worn calfskin binding of *Memories of Shiloh*.

"A lot of junk, I suppose, isn't it?" said the old man, without glancing up. He was fingering into a pigeonhole and withdrawing a rubber-banded pack of photographs. He slipped the band off: William McKinley, General Grant, Theodore Roosevelt, Lillian Russell, Fay Templeton, Olga Nethersole. He picked out Lillian Russell, held her up, surveyed her. "Actresses don't look like that any more. And you know, maybe it's just as well they don't. She's too stout. Her and this Ginger Rogers — just compare 'em. She couldn't ever dance like Ginger Rogers can, even if she tried."

"What is this?" he said. "Your annual New Year's Day house cleaning?" If it was, a decade or two seemed to have been skipped.

"No, not exactly." The photographs were dropped into a brown leather satchel on the floor, and were joined there by a souvenir inkstand (empty) from the Chicago World's Fair of 1893 and a toy ebony elephant lettered "G.O.P." with its trunk broken off. "I'm retiring."

"From what?"

"From the paper. From the *Argus*."

"Who's going to run it?"

Another pigeonhole was yielding other photographs—the old man when he had been a younger man, wearing a Spanish-American War uniform and with a palmetto tree behind him; a high-chaired baby which might have been Amy; a nine- or ten-year-old girl who definitely had been Amy, dressed in a middy skirt and blouse and with her hair in a Dutch bob and with a big bow on it; a slim, shirtwaisted, high-pompadoured, frizzle-banged, and very pretty young woman who by a great effort of the imagination could have been—yes, must have been—Mrs. Hardin.

"Who's going to run it?" For the first time the weak blue eyes had turned from the litter of the desk and were looking up at him. "Why, you are, aren't you?"

He was caught off guard for an instant, and then he saw the whole plan—the well-meant but impossible plan—at once; all of it. So that was the idea: the transference of responsibility, presumably followed in due course by the manly shouldering of it. Oh, these characters, he thought, these corny, corny characters here among the corn. In certain ways he was even rather fond of the old man, although there had been many occasions when he had been irritated by him: the old codger was a kind, good-intentioned, ineffectual muddler. But he was no David Harum, or even a Scattergood Baines. No Mr. Fix-it. At least not for him, Lyle Ellery, he wasn't. It had been nice of him to try, and ingenious of him to devise, but Lyle Ellery wasn't having any.

"No, thanks," he said. "Not me."

"Why not? You've got a wife and child to support, and I've got Mother—and I think I've earned me the right to take things easy. Sounds very sensible the way I see it."

"Maybe." He nodded toward the flat-top desk and its pulled-out drawers. "But I'm retiring, too."

"Where you going?"

"Back to New York."

"What you going to do there?"

"I don't know yet."

"How you going to live? How's Amy going to live? How's Johnny going to live?"

"I don't know. But I'll find something. You needn't worry. They won't starve."

"I never imagined they would." The chair swung around and tilted back, the buckled overshoes five inches from the floor and a puddle dripping from them. The preliminaries were over: obviously this was going to be heart-to-heart, man-to-man. "You don't like a small town much, do you, Lyle?"

"No. Not this one, anyway."

"Neither do I, sometimes. A lot of times, as a matter of fact. For about thirty years I was always surprised to wake up each morning and find myself still living in one, though by now I'm more or less used to it." The thumbs were twiddling. The tone was conversational. "That Flatiron Building — is that still standing?"

"What Flatiron Building?" As always, the old man's talk had the unity and coherence of an absent-minded bird brain. Not that he was a bird brain, really. It was simply that although his editorials were well-reasoned and well-written — with an archaic and often florid formality — his speech seemed to flop around in carpet slippers.

"In New York City. On Twenty-third Street, I think it was."

"Oh. I don't know. I guess so."

"Yes. Twenty-third Street, that was it. Right near Madison Square Garden. There was a gold figure up on top the Garden. Diana. A man named Stanford White designed it. Not the figure. I mean the building itself. He was shot and killed later. A nasty business. Quite a scandal at the time."

Dodder-dodder. But the least he could do was be civil and listen. He owed the old man that much, anyway. Maybe more. . . . So he reached for a cigarette.

"You go to the Garden much?"

"Not much. It's moved uptown. In the Fifties. And it's all changed now. Prize fights, ice shows, rodeos—all that."

"In the Fifties, hm? Yes, I expect it would have. They said the whole city was going to move up that way." The thumbs separated, and fingers drummed on the blotter. "I once was considering going to New York to live myself, you know." He hadn't known. In fact he hadn't even known he had ever been there. "Thought I might get a job with Pulitzer on the *World* or Reid on the *Tribune*. Or the *Sun,* if I could. But then I came back here and married Mother and—well, she didn't believe she'd care for it."

He waited, becoming almost scientifically interested in the ramblings of that mind, which was as stored with oddments as the pigeonholes of this desk.

"Ever read *Main Street,* Lyle? That Sinclair Lewis book?"

"Yes."

"A lot of boobs in it, aren't there? Mossbacks."

"Yes."

"A lot of boobs in Ammon, too—hm?"

"Well . . ."

"Sure there are. Old Herschel Tupper. The Art Bruers, all of 'em. People like that." Pushing the muskrat cap back on his head, he got up and began to amble around the room, leaving melting snow wherever he stepped. He stood in front of a stuffed pike hanging on the brown-painted wall, and gazed up at it. "The biggest fish I ever caught," he said. "One of the biggest ever to come out of Okiboji. Biggest pike, that is." And he turned. "I never could figure that book out. Of course it was written fifteen-twenty years ago, but Ammon wasn't like that town, that Gopher Prairie, even then. And it certainly isn't now. . . . Do you think?"

"No. No, it isn't." The old man was right. It might be better or worse, but it wasn't like Gopher Prairie.

"Of course things might be different up Minnesota way." He returned to the swivel chair and sat down again. "That girl in it, though. That Carol Ken . . . Kenni—?"

"Kennicott, I think. Carol Kennicott."

"Yes, that's the one. Well, sir, she was real. And you know who she reminds me of?"

He hazarded a guess, assuming that the conversation must still have something to do with the situation at hand. And maybe the old man was right in that also. Maybe he was a modern, male Carol Kennicott. Not that it mattered. "Me?"

"No. Not you." He appeared to be even rather surprised at the answer. "Amy, that's who she reminds me of. Only this Carol, she came to Main Street from someplace else, and Amy she was born and raised there and went away from it." A pause. "And came back to it."

"Yes." Was dragged back — for one reason or another.

There was a silence.

"She's a good girl, Amy. A fine girl."

"I know."

"Funny. Now you take her, and you take her mother . . ." The reedy voice stopped, and then went on. "Not that her mother wasn't a fine girl too, and isn't a fine woman. A better woman never lived. But they're different."

Thank God.

The small, frail, blue-veined hand reached down and pulled at a tall drawer. It stuck, and he pulled again. When it opened he drew out a — picture, was it? Something in a frame anyway, with a strand of wire looped across the brown paper of its back. Then it was turned around, and there beneath the dusty glass covering it was the contents page of the first issue of *Panorama* — Vol. 1., No. 1. And the words "Editor in Chief. Lyle Vincent Ellery" were neatly underlined in blue pencil.

"I was mighty proud of that," said the old man.

Tossing his cigarette into the brass cuspidor, he turned away, quickly — had to turn away. His eyes sought out a lightish square on the brown paint. So that was what had once been hanging there, and had been removed. He had sometimes wondered.

"I was proud of it, too." Did the old man know why he had left *Panorama?* He had a curious feeling that he did, although he had never mentioned it and wasn't mentioning it now.

"It was the kind of thing I'd have liked to do when I was your age. Something new. It took — originality. It showed what you had in you."

" 'Had' is right."

The framed page went into the brown satchel also; carefully, face down. Then the old man sat up again. "You know what it was like?" he said.

"What what was like?"

"You and *Panorama*."

"Like a dream, I guess."

"Maybe that's the way it strikes you now. But then it was like somebody going up onto a great, big, high diving board and making a wonderful dive — a swan dive or something. And then — and then belly-flopping." He paused. "And you know why? Because maybe you never learned to swim. Maybe you never learned to swim in New York and maybe you haven't learned here."

He put his hands into his overcoat pockets, and turned away from the roll-top. Words. Platitudes. A simile which might be apt enough — as to that he didn't care to speculate at the moment — but which was still merely a simile. . . . Damn it. God damn it. He wasn't going to be waylaid and maneuvered by any foxy grampa, even Johnny's grampa.

"Why don't you learn to swim here, Lyle?" the voice said, from behind him. "Or try to learn. Why don't you stay? The pond isn't as big — but the water's just as wet. Why go back and flounder around there and maybe — maybe go under?"

He faced him again. "I couldn't stay even if I wanted to. Not after the other night. Do you know how many people have said Hello to me up here on Main Street during the past six days? Exactly four. And one of them was Silly Willy, who says Hello to lampposts."

The gray mustache was being smoothed. "I didn't say it would be easy, did I?"

"And supposing I did stay," he continued. He was becoming argumentative now, becoming really irked. He'd show him that what might seem very simple in theory was quite another thing in practice. "Just supposing. What would I have? A tank-town weekly paper that everybody laughs at. What would I be? Its editor. It isn't — " And there he halted, for what he had been about to add was "It isn't good enough." He fingered out another cigarette, and felt himself flushing a little. He hadn't meant to hurt the old man. "I'm sorry," he said. "I oughtn't to have said that."

But the rejoinder was calm enough, and unmindful. "What

would you have if you went back to New York? What would you be there?"

He shrugged. What would he have and be? He hadn't dared think ahead that far, and neither had Amy. WPA again, perhaps? Well, something. The main idea was to get out and get away from here. Because you could — well, although he had once pretended to deride the notion, the fact was that you could suffocate here.

The old man swiveled around and tapped at the glass-fronted shelves containing bound volumes of back issues of the *Argus*. "There's one thing you ought to get straight, though," he said. "Not everybody laughs at the *Argus*. Oh, Orin and Irmadee Netcher and a few of those do, I know, but there aren't many of them. And even the ones who do laugh read every word of it, from the front page to the courthouse reports and the legal notices." He swiveled back. "Ever been with Orin on *Argus* day when he goes to his box at the post office and takes out both it and the *Chicago Tribune*?"

"Well, I —"

"Watch him sometime. See which he opens first. Watch Judge Anson when he's got both his *New York Times* and the *Argus*. Notice which one he sticks under his arm and which one he shakes out and begins to read." The thumbs were twiddling again. "As a matter of fact, *Panorama* comes out on *Argus* day, too. But it isn't read until after the *Argus* is read. Not in Ammon, it isn't. Not in the whole of Manila County, either. It has to wait. Everything has to wait — even the *Des Moines Register*."

The old man got up, stomped his feet, and stooped for the brown leather satchel, which he placed on the chair. "No," he said, "if it's a public you want, the most devoted one in the whole world, you've got it here. I know, because I've had it for forty-two years." He was sweeping what was left on the desk into the satchel. "And now I'm going to turn it over to you, if you want it. Or if you don't want it, to anybody who does. Me, I'm not going to do anything but read up some on Gettysburg. I've already read quite a bit on it, but I still haven't got it clear in my mind."

He watched him as he opened and shut drawers, searching for final treasures. What were these coming out now, these scores of little string-tied packets? Oh, check stubs. The pink check stubs of the Manila County Savings and Trust.

"You'll miss it, won't you?" he said. "The *Argus,* I mean."

"Miss it? I'll be glad to get rid of it. I'm tired." The old man turned, his arms filled with the packets. "Know what these are?" he said. "The stubs for every check I've ever written. And you know what I'm going to do with them?" With some sense of drama, he showered them all into the wastebasket. "Going to burn 'em with the trash. Or Kelly will. After he gets through reading them."

The satchel's brass clasps were slid shut. The muskrat gloves were being put on.

"Well, sir. I guess I've had my say."

He knew that he was waiting for a comment, for an answer. But he had no answer to offer him.

A silence. Then: "Give you a lift back to the house?"

He started toward the flat-top desk. "No, thanks. I've still got some clearing-up to do."

"See you later then."

"That's right."

Standing by the desk, he looked down at its glass, while the slow steps shuffled outward. He remained standing there, without glancing around, expecting to hear the street door opening and closing. But it didn't. Then he did glance around, and he saw that the old man had paused in the hallway and was looking in at the room. Not at him. At the roll-top, and at the pike, and at the black leather couch and the glass-fronted bookcase. At his life.

Tired? The liar, the liar. . . .

"Well, sir. I'm off."

And he was off then, really. Steps growing fainter down the hallway. The sound of the street door opening, its lingering asthmatic sigh as it shut.

Alone in the room, in the building, he began to pace the sun-faded, ink-stained carpet, which was so worn in spots that its nap had completely disappeared, leaving only frayed threads. He made a complete circle of the room, and was starting to circle it a second time when he stopped by the clutter of the exchange table on which were piled copies of rival weeklies and an indiscriminate collection of magazines, ranging from *Ballyhoo* to *Wallaces' Farmer.* A familiar green attracted his eye, and his hand went toward it — *Panorama,* the current issue, on its cover a photograph of two men in a warm handclasp, the one big and bald, the other small and Chaplinesque. "The Men of the Year," said the caption, and beneath it, in parentheses, "Where Is America's Strong Man?" But it wasn't the caption or its subtitle which held his attention, or the picture either: it was a line printed in the lower left-hand corner — "2 Million Circulation." Two million, he thought, and he picked up a copy of last week's *Argus.* There was no circulation statement in it anywhere, but he didn't need one. He knew what it was: 3236. Including the free list for advertisers and those copies mailed out to ex-Ammonites who had retired to the warmer clime of Long Beach, Calif., taking their bodies with them but not their hearts.

He tossed both magazine and paper back onto the table.

Once more pacing, he found himself standing by the old man's wastebasket and gazing down at the mound of check stubs. Suddenly, on impulse, he stooped and scooped up a handful. He began searching for a year, a particular day in a particular month in a particular year. Leafing through the small, square, perforated-edged pages, he found the track and trailed the scent. "Sept. 2, '32. Repub. State Comm. $3.50 (Camp'g)" — no, it had been later than that. "Nov. 28, '32. F. M. Herkle, M.D. $5.00 (Cold)" — and it had been later than that, too. "Jan. 8, '33. Gertrude Hardin. $15.00 (Mother's birth.)" Well, this was the year, anyway. He thumbed a few more pages. Yes, and there it was — the month and the day. Leaning against the roll-top, he stood studying the figures:

No. 3986....................
Mar. 1, '33.
To Amy ~~Hardin~~ Ellery
For Wedding Pres.
___
Bal. Bro't For'd ...... $ 629.31
Am't This Check .... $ 225.00
___
Bal. Car'd For'd .... $ 404.31
(~~Bank Cls'd.~~ Check O.K.)

He let the thin booklet drop back into the wastebasket and then, abruptly, on another impulse, picked up the wastebasket and started toward the door. . . . He didn't want Kelly to read that. He didn't want anyone to read that. In fact he was ashamed of having read it himself, for somehow it had been like prying into a private and personal diary, with those neatly inked figures more eloquent than any words could have been.

Going down the wooden stairs into the basement, with one hand on the railing, he reached the bottom and turned to the right, into the furnace room, usually an asbestos inferno and now not even tepid. He opened the door of the furnace, seeing only the faint red of cinders, and dumped the contents of the wastebasket into it and stood there watching. Finally some of the loose leaves of the check stubs began to burn, and the others to smolder. . . . How many thousands of dollars are in there, he thought, and how many thousands of hours? How much does the editor of a country weekly make during a lifetime? And how much does he spend? And what does he spend it for?

The booklets were catching the flame now, the fire burning. He glanced tentatively toward the shovel and the coalbin. Should he try to stoke it up? No, the hell with that. That was Kelly's business, not his. Nothing in here, or in this whole building, was his business any more.

Or is it? he thought. Or is it?

He went out and started to climb the stairs again. And then, halfway up, he paused, looking down into the empty print shop from which drifted up the never-quite-gone smell of hot lead, now cold. Alf's lino. The press. The folding machine. The type rack. The machines for job work: County Fair posters, programs for the American Legion's annual home-talent play, Funeral Mass announcements for Father Benedict, Commencement and Baccalaureate programs for the members of the Senior Class of the Ammon High School, and their first — and usually their last — calling cards. . . . The shop seemed very quiet now that the pumping, clicking lino was still and the press also, the rollers not rolling, the cylinders motionless. Only the swift scurry of a mouse, that was all.

His hand on the railing, he went on and up and back into the old man's office. . . . Whose office? Well, it would always be the old man's office, no matter who might occupy it.

Returning the empty wastebasket to its position by the roll-top, he went toward the flat-top and, seating himself, began to put back the things he had removed from the drawers. As his hand reached outward, it brushed against the desk calendar, and he looked at it. "Dec. 31." Smiling a little, and appreciating the symbolism of the gesture, and even being self-conscious about it, he lifted back the page, expecting to see the "Jan. 1" beneath it. A new leaf. But there was no leaf: only the blank brown metal of the stand itself. . . . Well, he thought, and maybe that's a kind of symbolism too.

He picked up a pencil and drew a memorandum pad toward him. "Get new cal.," he wrote, and then, after a moment, added, "Give Kelly hell."

How do I know that he wrote that, felt all that, thought all that? Because he told me most of it — some of it soon afterward, some not until a long time afterward — and I have guessed the rest. . . . But my father never told me any of it, not a word, not a single word.

My father was a wonderful man.

VII

ALTHOUGH I APPRECIATE THE FACT
that it will come, it has never been quite credible or conceivable to
me that I shall ever really die. Others have died and will die —
statesmen and poets and people I pass in the street — but not me.
However, there are moments, usually in the small hours of the
night, when a sharp beacon swings round and picks me out and I
realize that I too will die eventually, and when I do I suppose that
someone (who?) will ink still another entry onto the gilt-scrolled,
yellowing genealogy page in the Pepperdine family Bible which
was handed down to Mama and which Mama will in turn hand
down to me. "Amy," that unknown recorder will write . . .

Amy, daughter of Gertrude (Pepperdine) and John Hardin. Born
Ammon, Ia., June 15, 1907. Died (where? when?). Married Lyle Vin-
cent Ellery, New York, N. Y., Mar. 4, 1933. Mother of John Hardin
Ellery, born New York, N. Y., April . . .

But what that writer won't add, because he or she will have no
way of knowing about it — in fact nobody knows about it except
Dr. Herkle, Callie, Lyle, and me — is that I was also almost the
mother of someone else. So in a way that part of my obituary will
always be incomplete, and even if that unknown hand were able to
fill in what is missing it still couldn't determine the sex. Not even
Dr. Herkle was able to do that, for I had been carrying the baby
less than four months at the time I lost her. I say "her" because
although I had no more proof than anyone else I nevertheless was

certain and always will be certain that it would have been a her. A girl. A daughter, as I had been a daughter. "Eva" I was going to name her. . . . I never grieve about her now, any more. I used to, occasionally, but I haven't even thought of her for a long time. It is only at intervals when I see little girls of six or seven, starched and fresh and pretty—at least I like to believe she would have been pretty—that I sometimes think, "She would have been about that age now. Eva." And at other times, though rarely, when I see them even older—sixteen, seventeen, dressed for their first formal parties and wearing their first low necklines and their first high hair—I find myself musing, "How would Eva have looked with her hair up? And what color would that hair have been?"

All that isn't really important, though. It is just an episode which probably ought to be put in for the record. It happened during our second summer in Ammon, and after it happened Dr. Herkle said, "Well, Amy, your mother had only one child, and it looks to me as if you're going to have only the one, too. Still, better one than none, eh?"

Better one than none? There was a time when I was to wonder about that. . . .

However, as I say, it isn't actually important, and when Lyle counseled, "Now you're to forget this, do you understand? It's not something for you to brood over. It wasn't born, so it couldn't die. It was just one of those things you see in medical-book illustrations, and they would have weighed it in ounces, maybe grams," I obeyed him and I did forget. And, I repeat, this isn't at all important— except perhaps for Johnny. Because I think he would have enjoyed having someone to play with. I know I would have enjoyed that, when I was little.

But I wish she could have had a grave. One Eva should have, anyway.

The roll-top desk remained where it was, an anachronism and a monument, and the brass-plated pike on the wall remained also, but almost everything else was changed. The color of the wall itself was changed, from an intestinal brown to a light cream. The fiendish and frustrating sectional bookcase was replaced by one with open shelves. The frayed carpet came up, and a smooth, dull-finished, diamond-patterned "composition covering" went down. The torn tan shades went off and Venetian blinds went on, not only in the windows in the sanctum but throughout the whole building. The mice which for years had roamed almost at will and had made their nests wherever they chose, from the print shop in the basement to the drawer where Ethel Huber cached her chocolate bars — must have been very, very surprised at what was taking place, and no doubt indignant. And dust which had lain undisturbed for a quarter of a century found itself suddenly being swept away while its former habitat was ruthlessly and antiseptically scoured. Even the much-gashed black-leather couch disappeared, and its bleeding horse-hair with it. There was no time for naps now. . . . As Mama said, "He may kill the paper — time will tell as to that — but apparently it will be buried clean. You have to give credit where credit is due."

The only comment Papa offered on the renovation was, "Well, sir. It certainly peps the old place up, doesn't it? I'd forgotten that wainscoting was originally that color." But although he seemed to approve, he seldom went to the office any more, seldom even went uptown. Most of his time he spent at home in his den, slouched in the Morris chair and getting up on Gettysburg; or, when spring came, rocking on the front porch with his book in his lap. Though often not reading it.

So the office looked different, and the paper itself began to look different also. Alf's lino was sold to the ironmonger's for junk (Alf cried, Lyle said) and in its place stood a new one, and the type it set was no longer Minion, whatever that was, but 8-point Paragon, whatever that is. Something more legible, evidently. "They may not like the *Argus* the way I run it," said Lyle, "but at least they're going to be able to read it. We'll set the heads in 42-point Erbar and the subheads in 10-point Regal. Old Art Bruer can throw away his magnifying glass if he wants to. All he'll need are his nears." And out with the old lino went the old folding machine, and its successor really folded. And whole packing boxes filled with boiler plate went out, too. "I don't see why our subscribers should be much interested in ready-print rehashes of the San Francisco fire or how they change the guards in front of Buckingham Palace or how long it took to build the Eiffel Tower," said Lyle. "I know I'm not interested. And I'm not interested in being fed any free ready-print, either — whether it comes from some government agency, the N.A.M., or the C.I.O. The *Argus* is listed as 'Independent,' even on its own masthead. All right, it'll be independent."

And it was independent, on local issues — which were the only ones Lyle undertook to discuss in his editorials; and even those issues he had to study up on before arriving at an opinion. But once that opinion was arrived at, there could be no doubt about it. Papa's editorials had been inclined to center on such not too current topics as the Spirit Lake Massacre of 1857 and Pickett's Charge and the way the first robins build their nests in the spring, but Lyle's were contemporary and sometimes controversial. The composition of the school board, the membership of the city council, the estimates submitted for the repaving of Main Street and the questionable need for it, the long-term sewage bonds, the wisdom of renewing the Nite Spot's beer license — the *Argus* spoke its mind on all those things, and spoke it decisively. Some people didn't like what they read; others did. But they read.

I don't mean to imply that either the paper or the plant came to resemble the *New York Times,* but they were undeniably more modern than they had ever been before — and more modern than those of most of the other weeklies in the counties around were still. Nor do I mean to imply that any of this happened overnight, because it didn't: it was a slow process. But the results were there. The building, the machines in it, the staff, they all took on new life. Kelly kept the furnace stoked to such a roaring pitch that Lyle finally had to tell him to relax a little. Alf grumbled about the strange lino at first, but both he and the other men in the shop discovered that the new equipment was capable of producing twice the work — and much better work — in half the time, and with less physical exertion on their part. And perhaps most enthusiastic of all about the general speed-up was Ethel Huber, who had always considered herself as being essentially a *Front Page* type and who found the altered regime much more to her liking. Seated in her front-office igloo, surrounded by her ledgers and her adding machine and her typewriter and with three pencils stuck in her graying shingle-bob and a cigarette dangling from her lips, she took to lifting her green eye shade long enough to shout, "Copy! Here, boy! Copy! Rush!" The boy was Kelly, and sometimes he rushed and more often he just came. But he got there.

"All these newfangled machines are very nice," Mama had said, when they began to make their appearance, "but may I inquire where he's getting the money to buy them with?"

"From the M.C.S. and T.," I said. "He went to Mr. Tupper and borrowed it."

"Well, I will say that's very Christian of Herschel," she said. "Very Christian indeed. After the scene Lyle created with Orin and Irmadee, not to mention practically everyone else in town. That's turning the other cheek."

And probably it was turning the other cheek, although it was also turning 5½ per cent interest.

I don't suppose people in a small town relinquish their grudges any more willingly than the residents of any other place do, but they may relinquish them a bit more quickly, if only because it is so inconvenient and embarrassing to do otherwise. When you unavoidably pass an enemy at least six times daily on Main Street, the chances are that sooner or later either you or he is going to speak. Perhaps not very heartily at first, or ever, but one of you is likely to relent, nevertheless. I know that was true of Irmadee and me, and I expect it was also true of Lyle and Orin — and Lyle and everybody. What I got from Irmadee to begin with was the cut complete, followed gradually over a period of weeks by a cold nod, then a warmer nod, including something which might have been a smile, and after that, in State Department progression, the first "Hello," then "Hello, Amy," and "Hello, Dee. It's beginning to thaw, isn't it?" and finally a mutual stopping and a "Where have you and Lyle been keeping yourselves? We were saying only the other day that we never see you any more. I hear you have your own house now. We'd love to see it."

"We'd love to have you see it. How about coming to dinner Thursday?"

"Grand."

"Let's say seven, then."

"Swell. See you at seven on Thursday. Thanks so much."

"We'll be looking forward to it."

"So will we. . . . So long. Be good."

" 'Bye."

And she goes down Main Street her way and I continue up it my way. But we both know that although an armistice has been arranged, the old feeling, the old intimacy is gone — and that it will never come again. . . . However, and this may be another cause why wounds heal more swiftly in Ammon — though their scars run just as deep — whereas in a city you can go out and form new friendships with people of your own age and your own interests, in a small town there is usually no reservoir of new friends to draw upon. So you try to keep the ones you have, or had.

"Your own house" was the flattering phrase Irmadee had used in referring to it, but it was our own only in that we were renting it, and had been renting it ever since the furniture which we had had in storage in Jackson Heights arrived. There were several reasons why we had abandoned our plan to build, the most practical one being that Lyle's *Argus* loan was enough for him to carry and we didn't want to take on the additional payments necessary for an FHA. But even if we had had the funds, I wouldn't have wanted to build, or even buy. Things looked all right on the surface — Lyle was settling down, digging in — but they had looked all right on the surface before, and I didn't want to be fooled again. This new "readjustment" might prove to be a real and permanent one, or it might not, but in either case I had been twice bitten and therefore was more than several times shy. "We might as well just take the Bitzer place for now," I had said, after inspecting it and a few others. "Later on we can begin to think about buying or building, if we still feel like it. And it's a nice house, and when we get our things in it it'll look even nicer."

It was a nice house, too, although not nearly so large as those on

228

Manila Street or so new as those on Gold Coast Row: Gold Coast Row was operated along seigneurial lines, and no rentals were available there. A green-trimmed white clapboard — two-storied, three-porched — the house stood well back on a deep lawn over near the Catholic Cemetery, in a section of town which while certainly "good" was perhaps not much more than that. But I had liked it when I had first seen it (what was almost more important, so had Callie: "I get awful tired traipsing around Mis' Hardin's kitchen," she said. "This one's human-size"), and I liked it even better after we moved in. Well-proportioned rooms, plenty of closet space, an abundance of baseboard outlets, a nice fenced-in yard for Johnny — and it was all our own. Yes, even though it was legally Mr. Bitzer's it was still our own. No Papa. No Mama. Especially no Mama. . . . And there was a fireplace and at night it almost always had a fire in it, even when the weather didn't strictly warrant one.

"Holy spit, it's stunning," was Irmadee's generous verdict, following her first tour of it. "Simply super. And such lovely padded headboards. Where did you get those? Not at Harris and Kramer's, I bet."

"Oh," I said, "we had them." And again I thought of Laura's little man. Jackson Heights had been degrading enough as the repository for the fruits of his talent, but at least he would have known where it was. But he never would even have heard of Ammon, Iowa. To him it would have represented the ends of the earth.

"And that mahogany chest in the living room with the silver tray on it. Where did that come from? I saw one just like it advertised in the *Tribune* — Field's Antique Department."

"That was Lyle's mother's."

"Were those alabaster lamps hers too?"

"No, they were a wedding present."

"Well, the whole place is just perfect, Amy. You've really done wonders with it. You should feel very pleased with yourself."

I looked around, and I did feel pleased with myself — mainly because of my foresight in not having consented to selling all our things when we moved West, as Lyle had wanted to do. Of course in a sense it actually hadn't been foresight, because I had never

229

imagined that they would find their way here, to this town and this house. My argument had been that we probably wouldn't be staying in Ammon, and so I had said, "No. Let's just sell some and store the rest. You may not like it out there, you know, and we might be coming back. . . ." And he hadn't liked it, but he was growing to like it now—if he wasn't, I would never trust my own judgment again—and we weren't going back.

"Of course it's too bad you couldn't have bought or built on California Street, near us," added Irmadee, sympathetically. "But you know how silly and snobbish they are out there, with that funny Gold Coast Row of theirs. 'If people can only afford to rent,' they say, 'we don't want them.' It's so ridiculous. So small-town. . . ."

I doubt if Lyle ever worked any harder in his life than he did during that first year when the *Argus* was under his editorship; not even when he had been planning *Panorama*. Anyone would have had to work hard in order to reshape the paper's format and style to the extent he did, and he had the further handicap of having to work to win not only the support and confidence of the town but even its friendship. He succeeded better with the paper than he did with himself, I think; at least at first. Nobody ever slapped him carelessly on the back as he was walking along Main Street and said, "Hiya, Lyle! How's it going, fella?" Nobody ever dropped in at his office during the afternoon and said, "How's about coming over to the Smoke Shop for a beer?" And Orin didn't even tell him dirty stories any more.

"But that's all right," he said, well aware that he was not popular in the way that Frank Diederdock and the Schauffler brothers were popular. "As long as they keep on subscribing to the *Argus* and as long as the merchants keep upping their advertising linage—and they are upping it—I'd just as soon let somebody else be the hail-fellow-well-met. It's the paper that's important."

Important? It was the paper which was coming to be his life. And I was glad, for it had been some time since he had seemed to have a life. The masthead now read "John Hardin, Publisher," but below that was "Lyle Vincent Ellery, Editor." It was his paper, to do with exactly as he wished. Before, he had just worked there.

"We're publishing for Ammon and Ammon only," he said. "Well, for Manila County too, of course. But that's as far as our field goes —no farther. They can get their state news from the *Des Moines Register,* and their national and world news from that and the *Chicago Tribune* or any one of a dozen daily broadcasts. Or even from *Panorama,* if they can wait a week. But they can't get Manila County news anywhere except in the *Argus*—and there they'll get it all."

"You could try running sort of a column summary, though, couldn't you?" I suggested. It wasn't that I was advocating it: I just wanted to appear intelligently interested. What I was really thinking about was that he had mentioned the name of *Panorama* offhandedly, without even noticing it, without wincing. The patient was recovering. "I mean, you could put down just a line about Howard Hughes flying around the world and this Wrong-Way Corrigan man when he—"

"No," he said. "In the first place, just a line wouldn't cover it. And in the second place, once you begin that you've got to go on to everything else. You've got to say 'Hitler took over Austria this week' and 'Dewey's got the goods on Hines' and 'Whitney goes to Sing Sing' and all the rest of it. The New York papers give whole pages to that bank clerk because he stands for half a day on a window ledge in the Gotham and can't make up his mind whether or not to jump. Well, that's fine—for New York. But for the *Argus* the story isn't worth one slug. But let somebody burn down the courthouse—and it might not be a bad idea—and I'll put out an extra. I know my limitations."

"Don't say that. You haven't any limitations."

"Well, I know what I can do, and do better than anybody else— put it that way. If it sounds better."

"It sounds much better."

And that was the way the *Argus* was run, and run with increasing profit and even a small steady increase in circulation. That September there was the Sudeten crisis and two never-to-be-forgotten weeks when there was a conference in Munich, but you won't find any mention of it in either of those weeks' issues of the *Argus:*

instead you will find headlines dealing with the proposed enlargement of the Ammon Municipal Airport, and editorials ardently supporting it — and not even the name "Czechoslovakia." In October the state of New Jersey as well as most of Manila Street was thrown into a panic by a Halloween broadcast, but the only reference to it in the *Argus* is a sly invitation in the "About Town in Ammon" column to "Ask the Misses Trost how they feel about the Men from Mars. Ask Miss Bertha especially." In December a man supposedly named Coster turned out to be really named Musica, and the resulting drug-and-money scandal shook Wall Street. But not Ammon, and not the *Argus*. Ammon and the *Argus* had their own scandal: Charlie Sechendach, who had been County Assessor for twenty-two years, was discovered to have embezzled ten thousand dollars of county funds and in consequence went home an hour later and got into the bathtub with all his clothes on and cut his throat.

"News?" said Lyle, once. "Did I ever complain because there wasn't enough news in a small town? It's all over the place. I wish I could print sixty pages a week instead of sixteen."

"You know what you're developing through that paper?" I said. "You're developing community spirit."

His tone was defensive. "Oh, I wouldn't say that. Ammon's full of community spirit. It's always been a live — "

"I didn't mean you were developing it in Ammon. I meant you're developing it in you."

He looked at me, and he laughed. "In me? Don't be silly. You know me. I — " And then he stopped. "I guess maybe I am a little different from the way I used to be, at that. Now that you mention it."

"Yes, you are."

"Better?"

"Ah — why, of course better. What else?"

And that was what I began to tell myself as the paper's entrenchment grew firmer and his with it. Of course he was different and of course he was better. What else? And yet — and yet there were certain qualities which he had once had and which now seemed to be either diminishing or disappearing entirely and which I . . . well, missed. Not that they had necessarily been good qualities: some of them had often been exasperating. But for me they had set him apart from all others. And there were other qualities which he had never had before and now was beginning to manifest, and those I found a little curious, a little strange. Sometimes merely funny, sometimes not. Different? Yes, different.

One of the funny ones, to me — yet nice too, of course — was when he came home one evening early that autumn, looking fairly sheepish, and said, "Guess what. They've asked me to join the Kiwanis."

"Oh, dear," I said, for I had heard him on the subject of the Kiwanis before, their pre-lunch songs and post-lunch speeches. "And I suppose there's no way you can get out of it, is there?"

"Get out of it?" His surprise was genuine. "Well, as a matter of fact it's sort of an honor, you know. I mean, it's not the Rotary, naturally — they get the older crowd — but they have a pretty up-and-coming bunch of fellows down there. Frank Diederdock and — "

"You singing 'That's Where the Tall Corn Grows,' " I said, and I began to laugh. "Darling, I can hardly wait. I hear they wear little paper caps and — "

Suddenly I stopped, and my laughter too. "What's the matter?"

"That's sort of a snooty attitude, isn't it?" he said. "You sound like Irmadee. After all, Orin's a Kiwanian too. Never misses a meeting, either."

I wanted to laugh again then, and yet in another way I was touched, moved. . . . He was — he was proud. And why shouldn't he be? This was something which he had had to earn: it was a token that he had at last been accepted. I made my face sober.

"I think it's awfully nice, Lyle. Really I do."

"No, you don't," he said. "You think it's corny. Well, maybe it is and maybe it isn't. But it's no more corny than when Kendrick goes to the Dutch Treat, is it? You get chicken cutlets and green peas at both places, only he used to pay more for them at the McAlpin than I will at the Corn Room, that's all."

"But I didn't mean to — "

"I know what you meant. And I can't say I like it. We're making

233

our living here, and I don't see why the town should be ridiculed just because it's small. It's not — "

"Look, honey. I knew Ammon before you ever even heard of it."

"I wonder if you did. I wonder if you know it now." He shrugged. "Satire's pretty easy, you know. It's like when Orin stands around the Joint mimicking the farmers who come into the M.C.S. and T. 'I swan,' he says, as if they were all Lum-and-Abners, and 'By cracky.' They don't say 'I swan' and 'By cracky.' And even if they did, what about it? More than half the deposits in the bank belong to those farmers. And they worked a hell of a lot harder to earn their money than Orin ever worked to get his."

"Now just calm down," I said. "Just calm down. And go join the Kiwanis, if you want to. I think it's fine."

And he did join it, and changed its button in his lapel every time he changed suits.

That was one of the funny things, more or less. There was something else, however, which I regarded as being not so funny. I was willing to grant that perhaps I had been wrong and he had been right about the Kiwanis, but on the other I wasn't willing to grant anything. Particularly the "Yes" which he was seeking.

It began casually enough on a Sunday morning when we were seated in the living room surrounded by the spread-out pages of the *Register,* while Johnny sprawled on the floor "reading" the comics and droning "A-Tisket, A-Tasket," which had ever been a nursery rhyme but which that winter had been revived and set to music for adults, with jive added to it. And Johnny was jiving too, erratically, in treble.

"Reverend Pletch was in the office yesterday," said Lyle, from over the edge of the editorial section. "He's a nice fellow, when you get to know him."

I was looking at the rotogravure: Brenda Frazier in sepia and much white tulle. "That's what everybody says."

"He was telling me he makes it around the course in the low nineties. That's not bad."

"Um-hum." Glamour Girl, I was thinking. What would it be like to be a Glamour Girl? Kind of fun, I should imagine.

There was a rustle of the paper as he creased it and folded it on his lap. "Amy, what do you say we start going to church?"

I glanced across at him, and I couldn't believe it. It wasn't that either of us was agnostic. It was just that — well, we never want to church, and except for the occasion of Johnny's christening (and I had been the one who had insisted on that) had never even been in one together. I had stopped going when I had first been living in New York, and he had stopped while he was still in college. We weren't certain why. We had just stopped, independently. "Strayed," they call it.

"Who?" I said.

"You and me — and Johnny later on."

"Why?"

"Well, it'd be sort of a nice thing to do, don't you think? And it would please your mother."

Please her? I would probably be hauled into the Ladies' Guild in two minutes flat — there had already been a series of hints — and be sitting between the Trost girls embroidering luncheon cloths three minutes later.

"Since when have you become so anxious to please Mama?"

"Oh, it's not that so much." He stretched, with a laziness which seemed to me to be rather studied. "But you know, you sit here on Sundays and you look out the window and watch other people going, and you think, 'Well, it probably wouldn't do you any harm to go, too.' And as editor of the *Argus* I've got a certain position to maintain, and — "

"Oh," I said, at last seeing the light. "So that's it. The *Argus*."

"Partly, yes."

"Good for circulation, hm?"

"Of course if you're going to take that attitude — "

"Papa never goes to church, and he maintained his position all right."

"There was talk, though. And plenty of it."

I looked at him, and again there was that impulse to laughter — and that counter-impulse to something other than laughter. "Oh, Lyle," I said. "Lyle."

"What?"

I turned another page of the rotogravure. "I can think of a lot of good reasons for going to church, but you haven't mentioned any of them. And until you do, I think I'll just stay home. But you can go if you like."

"No," he said, after an instant of pondering, "that wouldn't look well."

"Then let's not discuss it. I mean, it doesn't seem to me to be the sort of thing you can discuss. Either you feel it, or you don't."

There was a silence: hurt. "All right. I didn't intend to make an issue of it. Forget it."

"I think I will."

But I didn't. I couldn't. I couldn't forget that or any of a number of other things I saw, and heard, and sensed. I don't know the order of their occurrence: I just know they were there. A gesture, a phrase; inclinations, disinclinations; a pattern being formed, a mold being set. What had been a way of doing things yesterday was today a habit and tomorrow would be — what? Routine? Whatever it was, the effects seeped into all the levels of our life, personal, domestic, social. We didn't see nearly as much of Orin and Irmadee as we had before, and that was understandable enough — but the reason was not due to any lack of invitations on their part but to Lyle's reluctance to accept them. "They drink too much," he said, which was undoubtedly true. "They're always helling around and staying up till all hours. Orin may not have to have a clear head in the morning, but I do. And of course Irmadee sleeps till noon."

"They've asked us so many times," I said. "It's getting embarrassing."

"Let it be. And another thing, frankly that gutter talk of Irmadee's is pretty hard to take." Which was undoubtedly true also. "She may think it's cute, and I suppose it's all right when you're younger. But I don't like it."

All right when you're younger. . . . At what age should the fresh breeze of morning become a little cold, a little raw, and begin to whistle slightly? By what clock does the noon sun lose its warmth?

"Well, I don't suppose we ought to retire *too* much into a shell,"

I said. "Maybe we ought to start seeing a little more of Fern and Zelda."

"Yes," he agreed, "they're a nice couple. Their bridge stakes strike me as being a bit high, but I think they'd be willing to shave them down a bit if we asked them. A twentieth of a cent seems about right to me. Even a fortieth. After all, it's the game itself that's the thing, not the money you win or lose at it."

So we began to see a great deal of Fern and Zelda. Quite a lot, in fact. As he said, they were a nice couple.

All those things were small things, probably. But there was something else which was more important than any of them; to me, at least. I couldn't talk about that, though. Not to anyone. If the Library had had that kind of books, I might have consulted them; but it didn't. And even if it had, I would have been too embarrassed to have asked Miss Rand for them. Perhaps I should have tried to speak of it to Dr. Herkle, or maybe to Mama, or even to Lyle himself. But I just couldn't. And of course I couldn't speak of it to Papa either, although I could and did edge around the general topic of some of the other things.

On an afternoon in late February Papa sat with me in our glassed-in, heated porch through whose windows a wan sun filtered. He often strolled over in the afternoon, to take Johnny for a walk or to sit in the kitchen querying Callie on the Civil War place names of her native Georgia or sometimes just to sit. Today he was just sitting, relaxed back in the wing chair which had come to be known as "Grandpa's chair." And I was on the sofa, knitting.

"Warming up a bit," he said. "Soon be spring."

"You'll like that, won't you?" I said. "You can go down to the river and fish."

"Oh, I don't know," he said, putting his feet up on the ottoman. "I don't think there are any more fish in that river. Never was much of anything except minnows anyway."

"How's Mama?"

"She's fine. She's got her Guild ladies today. Wednesday, you know."

"That's right. So it is."

The week's *Panorama* lay on the table beside him and, picking it up, he began to leaf through it. Lyle bought *Panorama* regularly now each Friday at the Smoke Shop, although we didn't "take" it in the sense of subscribing to it: his rancor might have mellowed, but he still couldn't bring himself to allowing his name to flow with millions of others through the machinery of the circulation department, even though its present staff probably wouldn't have recognized it. . . . There was the sound of pages turning.

"Well, sir, I see Congress has decided not to waste any more money on fortifying that Guam island out there. Roosevelt, he won't like that much." More pages turned. "But then, he's always been hepped up on the Navy. Kind of a hobby with him, I guess."

I kept on knitting, and didn't say anything. The simplest way to conduct a conversation with Papa was to wait until it showed indications of stabilizing itself to a definite trend.

"Remember during the World War when they wanted binoculars and I sent mine in?"

"Yes, I remember it well." They had been a very primitive type of binoculars, and I had sometimes wondered to what use the Navy had put them.

"I've still got the letter he wrote thanking me. His signature's right there. 'Franklin D. Roosevelt. Assistant Secretary of the Navy.' Didn't know me from Adam, of course. Maybe sometime Johnny might like to have it as a keepsake."

"I'm sure he would, Papa."

"I don't know why I didn't throw it away at the time, because he was a Democrat then and he still is a Democrat. Calls himself one, anyway. But I just stuck it in there in the desk, never thinking he'd ever be President." He placed the magazine back on the table. "Though *Panorama* certainly doesn't have much to say for him even if he is President, does it?"

"No, it certainly doesn't."

He twiddled his thumbs. "Bitter. Very bitter. Vitriolic. Always has been."

No. Not always. . . .

We sat in silence, while I knitted. Papa was easy to be silent

238

with, for he had his own world in which he moved around at his leisure, picking things up here, laying them down there. I suppose it must have been somewhat like an attic or storeroom, that world, filled with all sorts of different relics, some of them dating back a long time: Bull Run, which he had only read about and had heard Grandpa Hardin speak of; Las Guasimas, which he had seen.

"Lyle ever talk much about *Panorama* these days?" he said, then.

"No, not much. He reads it, I think, but he doesn't talk about it."

"Um-hum." A pause. "What was she like, Amy?"

"Who?"

"This Archer woman."

My needles froze, and I glanced up at him. Then the needles began to weave again. "Oh — it's hard for me to say." I knitted on for a while and then went on to something else which was hard for me to say. "Papa, Lyle's done awfully well with the paper, hasn't he?"

"Yes, he has. Mighty well. He's really made a go of it."

"He's changing, though. Has changed."

"People do." One ankle on the ottoman crossed itself on the other. "And you approve, don't you?"

"Oh, of course I do."

He nodded. "Mother, she used to say 'You live and you learn.' Still does say it, now and then. And she's right, too."

I let my knitting — it was a sweater for Johnny — lie idle on my lap, and I looked over at him. . . . Was I doing to Lyle — or had I done it already — what Mama had done to him? The dreams which had once been dreams, quick and eager, and which now were hardly even memories. "Richard Harding Davis," I remembered him saying, and saying it more than once. "He was on the *New York Herald*. I saw him once, when I was visiting New York that time. He was stepping out of a hansom cab on Fifth Avenue, all togged out in a silk hat and a coat with a cape on it. A fine-looking man."

Suddenly I got up from the sofa and went over and sat down on the ottoman. "Papa," I said, "I didn't mean to clip his wings. I never wanted to do that. In any way."

His hand came out and patted my arm. "Now, Amy," he said. "Now, daughter."

Leaning forward, I placed my head against his shoulder. I was eight years old again, and in trouble.

"What is it?" he said.

"So many things."

"Tell me."

"I can't. I don't know how."

"Could you tell Mother?"

"No."

His arm went up, around my waist. "You work things out in your own way, Amy," he said. "And you'll find a way, I know you will. You're a bright girl. You always were."

I shook my head. "This doesn't have anything to do with brightness. It's . . ." I rubbed my face against his coat. "Oh, Papa. Papa."

At that moment there came the slam of the front door and the small pounding of racing steps, and glancing upward I saw Johnny standing in the archway — some thirty inches and some thirty pounds of red wool snow suit and red cheeks, with dark hair coming out from under his helmet and dark eyes bright. Lyle in little.

"Hi," he said.

"Well, sir," said Papa. "Look who's here. . . ."

Always his advice has stood me in good stead, and it did now, too. "You'll find a way," he had predicted, and I began to think, "Well, maybe he's right. Maybe I can." And a few days after that I thought perhaps I had found a way. I found it in a short story in a magazine.

I don't remember which magazine it was or what author, but I do remember that the title of the story was "Never Ask My Love" and that the color illustration showed a woman seated before a dressing-table mirror wearing an evening gown and with her hair in the new upswept style. After finishing reading it, I decided, skeptically, "Now that's not very probable. It's even silly, and it could happen only in fiction." But somehow the story refused to leave my mind, and the more I thought about it the more I began to wonder, and to meditate, and to speculate. It was about a woman named Leslie who had been married several years and who was about to have a wedding anniversary and whose husband (she called him "Bart," for Herbert probably) had —

But I guess that it was really about me, so I'd better tell it that way.

First things first, and therefore after an interval of laying out the groundwork I started with Callie. "Callie," I said, "Saturday is Mr. Ellery's and my anniversary, and I was wondering if we couldn't plan a special dinner."

"Sure, Mis' Ellery," she said, co-operatively. "Who you goin' to invite? Mist' and Mis' Hauberg? Them Netchers?"

"Oh, I didn't mean special that way. There'll be just the two of us." The presence of Orin and Irmadee might lead to too much excitement, that of Fern and Zelda to not enough. "I meant a special menu."

"You want chicken? A nice roaster?"

"Well, I was thinking of something perhaps a little more unusual. Filet mignon, possibly."

"You can't get good filets here, Mis' Ellery. You know that. We tried."

"Then how about squab with wild rice? And maybe we could get some asparagus and you could make some of your hollandaise. And I thought that before dinner you might serve some of those canapés you —"

She was already reaching for her grocery pad. "I know what you want, Mis' Ellery," she said. "You want the kind of company dinner we used to have on Sutton Place like when Mist' and Mis' Archer came. Ain't that it?"

"Yes," I said, for that was it. "Yes, that's it exactly, Callie." I couldn't have put it better myself. And I wouldn't have tried.

"Just for two?"

"Yes, just for two."

So much for Callie. Next, Nettie. Nettie of the Beauty Salon. The preliminaries to this transaction also had to be arranged in advance, by phone:

"Nettie, could I take over your Saturday morning for a manicure and a facial and a shampoo? The works, I want."

"Oh, honey, you know what my Saturdays are. I could split you up among the girls, but —"

No, thanks. I'd been split up among the girls before. "Please, Nettie. Just this once, as a favor."

"Okie-doke, Amy. I'll squeeze you in somehow."

"Oh, and Nettie, you know this new upsweep do?"

"Sure do, honey. I wear it myself — around the house."

"I think I'd like to try it."

"All righty. . . . You going formal? What is it? The country club?"

"No," I said. "No, it's a private party."

So much for Nettie. And so much for a stop at the Liquor Store and a purchase of a bottle — all right, two bottles — of its best champagne. And so much for getting out my black chiffon and looking at its limpness and deciding that, limp or not, it still was better than anything else I had, or than anyone else in town had — except Irmadee — and after that pressing it. And getting out Lyle's dinner jacket and leaving it at the Mode Cleaners to be pressed also. So much for all that, including cleaning my silver slippers. So much, too, for considering taking the car — we had our own car now, a Chevrolet sedan which made Papa's seem prehistoric — and driving down to Hansen's Greenhouse and buying flowers. But considering that was as far as I went. After all, the flowers were a risk I would have to face, along with the possibility that Lyle might forget the date entirely; for I wasn't going to mention it to him in any way. Bart had forgotten his and Leslie's. However, Leslie hadn't made a scene about it, hadn't even referred to it. Very quietly and very serenely, she had simply smiled and had said, "Well, Bart, lover, shall we dine now?" And if necessary, that is what I would do too.

But it wasn't necessary, for on Saturday afternoon Hansen's truck delivered a long white cardboard box with almost two dozen red roses in it and with them was a card saying, "Happy anniversary. Love from Lyle." I put some of them in the living room and some on the table, and one I saved for the black chiffon. . . . This was beginning better than Bart-and-Leslie had ever begun: I only hoped it would end as well.

When he arrived home I was already seated, or arranged rather, in the living room, all dressed (I ought to have been: I had started at four), and when he opened the front door and saw the dress and the fire in the hearth and me sitting by it he stopped with his hand on the knob and said, "Now there you have a picture. A real picture."

"Hello, darling," I said.

Closing the door, he went to the closet and hung up his hat and overcoat and took off his rubbers. "Thought you'd fool me, didn't you? But I knew there was something up." And then he came toward me and, leaning down, kissed me. "You look beautiful," he said.

"Thank you, darling. And thanks for the roses."

His hand cupped my chin. "Bet you'd thought I'd forgotten, didn't you?"

I shook my head.

"Say — your hair. I like it that way."

I smiled up at him. "Do you?" Bart hadn't even noticed Leslie's hair, at first.

He straightened. "Who's coming?"

"Nobody."

"But why the — ?"

"It's just for you. Aren't you enough?"

Again he kissed me. "You bet I'm enough. Two's company, hm?" And he headed toward the stairs. "Be with you in a minute. You can get out the mixings any time. This demands a toast."

It certainly did, but there weren't going to be any mixings — just champagne. Champagne before dinner, champagne with dinner, and maybe champagne after dinner. And roses, roses all the way.

"Oh, darling," I called, for although I had planned to let him discover it himself, I decided now as I saw him mounting the stairs that I'd better give him warning. "The studs are already in your shirt. It's all laid out."

Halting, he turned. "Oh, now look," he said. "Fun's fun, but — "

"Please."

He hesitated only a fraction of an instant, and then he shrugged, smiling. "O.K. Why not?" He continued up the stairs. "Hope nobody takes it into their head to drop in, though. They'll think we're crazy."

I sighed in relief: another hurdle passed. And then I turned toward the entrance to the dining room, where Johnny had suddenly and breathlessly appeared, his face slightly greasy. "You know what I ate for supper?" he said, coming forward. "I ate a pigeon. Part of a pigeon. Callie cut me off some."

Johnny was another hurdle, and one Leslie hadn't had. He was a dear, darling little boy and I loved him very much, but the fact remained that this happened to be one occasion when I felt that I could do without him very well.

"Now, Johnny," I said, drawing him closer and wiping his face, "remember, when Daddy comes down you can stay just ten minutes and no more, and then I'm going to take you upstairs and put you to bed. Now you know you promised."

"Uh-huh. It was a pigeon just like the kind that walks around on the walk. . . ."

Well, I don't suppose there is much need for me to go into the details of that evening, because they were probably obvious and inevitable from the start — to anyone except me. I don't think it was anybody's fault, really. It wasn't Johnny's, for he was true to his promise and when his ten minutes were up (well, twenty) he permitted himself to be withdrawn with hardly any fuss at all. It wasn't Callie's either, for all through the serving of dinner — and it was a beautiful dinner — she voluntarily imposed a rigorous silence on herself, so different from her customary review of the doings of the day, and if that silence was occasionally interrupted by a titter and a giggle who could blame her?

And it certainly wasn't Lyle's fault, because he did his best, too, and tried to enter into the proper spirit. During the champagne cocktails his toasts were lavish and well-worded, and were punctuated at intervals by kisses, and when we went in to dinner he drew my chair back with a flourish. But somewhere after the consommé, between the squab and the salad, the dinner began to die; and by the time the chocolate soufflé arrived it was dead. And I knew it was dead. This might have worked out very well for Leslie and Bart, or for Norma Shearer and Robert Montgomery, or for Joyce and Garry of the "Joyce and Garry" program which Callie and I did our dusting by — but it wasn't working for me.

And yet I refused to admit defeat, for by now I was becoming stubborn. I think I would have given almost anything if there had been a country club dance to go on to, and even more for a night club — any night club, the cheapest, tawdriest kind you could find around Forty-second Street. But the monthly country club dance wouldn't be held for another three weeks, and the nearest night club of any description was sixty miles away. That is, unless you could call the Nite Spot — beer and a juke box — a night club. And some people did.

"You know what we might do?" I said, brightly, after coffee. Oh, I was so very bright. "We might turn back the rug and dance a little."

"Swell," he said, and immediately began to move back chairs.

So we danced. We had a little trouble getting the right music at first — "Flat-Foot Floogie" was too bouncy, and "Three Itty Fishes" was for Johnny — but eventually I dialed to Eddy Duchin. Eddy Duchin playing "My Heart Belongs to Daddy" from the Persian Room at the Plaza. A good tune, with rhythm in it, and with that Duchin piano.

"That's more like it," he said, drawing me to him.

"Eddy Duchin," I said, after a moment. "Remember?"

"What?"

"You know. The Central Park Casino."

"Oh — sure."

The turning, the swaying, the spinning, the dipping.

Then: "You still know how to dance, Mr. Ellery."

Now why that "Mr. Ellery"? I asked myself. Why this sudden attack of the cutes? Not that it was so sudden either: this whole experiment was pretty cute.

"So do you."

The music stopped, and fifteen hundred miles away there was the patter of hands clapping and a buzz of conversation. . . . He applauded also, with great gaiety.

"Wonderful, isn't it?" he said. "And just think — no cover charge."

"Yes, wonderful."

We danced again, and then again, but by the beginning of the

245

third dance I was starting to feel self-conscious — or even more self-conscious than I had been, rather. "Let's just sit this one out," I said, and, stooping, began to turn back the rug again.

"All right," he agreed, and started pushing the chairs into their original positions.

We finished our tasks — I the rug and he the chairs — at exactly the same instant and, straightening, stood. . . . This house is very quiet, I thought. And it was: only the intermittent clatter of Callie as she finished up the pots and pans in the kitchen. It was much too quiet.

"Would you like to call somebody up?" I said. My flag came down then. The towel, the sponge, I threw them both in. "Have them come over for a while?"

"Sure." Quickly, and yet not too quickly. "That is, if you would."

"Well, there's still a whole bottle of champagne left. . . ."

He was already on his way to the phone. "How about Orin and Irmadee?" he said, and I knew that the suggestion was a concession on his part — a concession to my mood, or what was left of it.

"Fine, if they're not busy. It's Saturday night, though, and —"

"Oh, I forgot," he said, his hand on the phone. "I ran into Orin on the street this afternoon, and he told me they were going in to Chicago tonight for a week or so."

It was time for me to make a concession, too. "Then how about Fern and Zelda? A little bridge, maybe."

"O.K. I'll try 'em."

And he did. Standing by the mantel and looking down into the fire, I heard his end of the conversation: "Fern? . . . How are you, boy? . . . Fine. . . . Look, do you and your lady feel up to losing some money tonight? . . . Oh. Oh, I see. . . . Say, that's a shame. . . . You tell her to take care of herself, see? . . . You bet. Well, Mother and I were just sitting around here and we thought we'd give you a buzz, that's all. . . . So long, Fern. And tell Zelda I hope she's better."

"Zelda," he said, relaying the news hot off the wire. He replaced the phone. "She's laid up with a cold. Herk thinks it may be the grippe."

I looked up from the fire. "What did you just say?" I said.

"It's Zelda. She's got a — "

"No, I mean to Fern. What did you call me?"

He came toward me, puzzled. "Call you? What do you mean? I didn't call you anything."

"Yes, you did. You called me 'Mother.'"

He was silent for a moment, and then he reached down toward a cigarette box. All the cigarette boxes were filled to the brim that evening, all the ash trays gleaming. "Oh, I was just kidding."

"Well, I wish you'd stop kidding. That way, anyway. My name is Amy." And it means "beloved," in case you've forgotten.

He lighted his cigarette, and shook out the match. "I'm sorry. I won't do it again."

"You'd better not."

He flicked the match into the fire. "I said I was sorry, didn't I? As a matter of fact, what's wrong with the word 'mother'? You are one, and . . ." But he didn't go on. The words died.

We stood by the fire. It is very curious. Open fires are nice, but you can grow to dislike them. Perhaps it's because if you've seen one, you've seen them all.

I reached my hand out to his sleeve. "I shouldn't have snapped at you like that," I said. And then I let the hand go up to his cigarette, and I took it from between his lips and puffed at it. That seemed to me to be one way of trying to re-establish the right note of nonchalance. "Look, why don't we go up to the Hawkeye?"

He gestured at my dress and at his white shirt front. "Like this?"

"It'll take me only a minute to change. And nobody will notice you if you keep your overcoat on."

He hesitated. "Well . . . do you feel like going?"

Cigarette in hand, I was moving toward the stairs. "Sure. Why not? All we'll miss are the ads, probably. We'll still be in time for the second showing of the feature."

"What's playing?"

I was climbing the stairs now. "This Bob Hope in something," I said. *"Thanks for the Memory,* it's called." And then, because I couldn't resist it, I added, "It should be a howl."

I knew that my irony was unfair — after all, as I say, it wasn't

247

his fault — but I needn't have worried that he might be offended by it. "Well, I guess we could use a laugh," he said, and as I rounded the landing I heard him call, "Better put on your galoshes. It's pretty slushy out."

So I changed, and I did put on my galoshes, and as I hung the black chiffon in the closet I noticed the scar of a small rip in the bodice, a rip made long ago and mended long ago. I pushed the dress back on the rod, yanked out the light, and closed the closet door. . . . The hell with Leslie, I thought. The hell with Bart, too.

Which anniversary was that? That was the iron one. The one after the wooden one.

Mr. and Mrs. Benjamin Liebermann of New York City arrived on the Husker last Tuesday to spend several days as the house guests of Mr. and Mrs. Lyle Ellery. The Liebermanns have been vacationing in California this summer and are en route to their home in the East, where Mr. Liebermann is a member of the faculty of Columbia University.

Thus Ethel Huber in the "Locals" column of the *Argus,* in the restrained prose which Lyle had enforced on her, and for once Ethel got everything right, even the spelling of the name. But she couldn't be expected either to know or to appreciate the background leading up to the item. That had begun several months earlier, as far back as May, when I had received a letter from Natalie saying that Ben's Aunt Fanny had died and left him her whole estate, which was a sizable one and which included not only a box at the Metropolitan on alternate Saturday matinees but also a surprising number of shares of American Telephone and Telegraph stock.

. . . It was a dirty lowdown capitalist trick of her [wrote Natalie] to thrust all that on Ben, but I'm glad to say that he's facing it courageously. Anyway, we're off to California for the summer, because Ben's been reading *The Grapes of Wrath* and wants to investigate conditions among the migratory workers — and I guess that ought to teach Aunt Fanny all right, all right. Incidentally, we're also going to investigate conditions at the San Francisco Fair, Yosemite, Del Monte, the Santa Barbara Biltmore, Lake Arrowhead, and probably Hollywood. We'll be heading east again in late August and it occurred to me that if you and

Lyle would care to harbor two earnest, tired, tanned social researchers we could arrange to . . .

So now it was late August and they were here, and neither of them had ever looked better to me. In fact neither of them had probably ever looked better to anyone, for there was an air of travel first-class about them and both were brown and each had a newly acquired California wardrobe, which in Ben's case ran to doeskin slacks and brightly checkered sports coats with tremendous shoulders and with scarves tucked in at the neck in lieu of ties. ("More results of Aunt Fanny's nasty unearned increment," explained Natalie. "We just don't talk about it.") They had done California from its redwoods to Coronado, with a side trip to Salinas where Ben had taken notes on Okies, and Natalie was enthusiastic about it. "A wonderful place," she said. "All the men are eight feet tall and look like Joel McCrea and all the women go around with their stomachs bare. It couldn't be more interesting."

But Ben seemed to have little to say about anything he had seen, even Okies. From the very moment he arrived he was strangely silent, curiously quiet. And that wasn't like Ben. It wasn't like Ben at all.

"What's the matter with him?" I said, as I sat watching her unpack in the spare room that first morning after Lyle and Ben had gone uptown. "He seems so sort of depressed. With this windfall of his, I should think he'd be walking on air."

"Well, Ben's had a blow, you know. We must all be very kind to him."

"Blow? Did he care that much for his aunt?"

"Oh, he couldn't stand her." She picked up one of the most beautifully tailored jackets I have ever seen, and shook its folds. "No, it's this Russian-German nonaggression pact. You see, the Great Red Father has crossed Ben up."

"Oh, that." It was the news of the week. "How is he taking it?"
"Big."

"I suppose he would, feeling the way he did." I started to smile. "You know, it's really funny, isn't it? Comic, I mean. He —"

She stood with the jacket over her arm, and she wasn't smiling at all. In fact she was as grave as I had ever seen her. "It isn't very comic, actually," she said. "I thought it was at first, too. But it isn't. Not for him." She went toward the closet. "I imagine it's like losing your religion. That is, he hasn't lost his yet — he still maintains that Stalin must have something up his sleeve — but he's beginning to wonder. And it's tough on him. Really tough." She shrugged. "Never having had much religion myself, or many ideals either, I can only guess how tough. And yet I suppose that in a way they're like love — it's better to have had them and lost them than never to have had them at all."

"What's Ben's attitude now?"

"I don't believe he knows yet. He's waiting for the Party to make up his mind." She sighed. "I wish he could sit down for a nice long talk with Earl Browder. That'd clear things up for him."

I sat there on the bed in silence. No, it undoubtedly wasn't funny, for Ben.

Stooping toward a suitcase, she went on with her unpacking. "It's easy enough to laugh at him," she said. "I know, because I've done it myself — too often. 'Ben-baiting.' It was a game, fun." She lifted out a pile of lingerie. "But the fact remains that he was on to Hitler and Mussolini when a lot of other people — you and I, too — considered one of them to be just a Chaplin clown and the other a buffoon on a balcony. It's simple for us to say now that they're a threat to world peace, but they were just as much a threat then. And Ben knew it. And said it."

And that was true, and I knew it was true. Ethiopia, Austria, Munich (I had heard him on the subject of "appeasement" long before Munich), Czechoslovakia, Albania, even as far back as the Japs in Manchuria, Ben had always tried to make people realize what all that meant and where it might lead. Tiresome? Yes, he had often been tiresome. A monomaniac? Yes, that too. But he had been determinedly anti-Fascist from the very start. Including Spain. Yes, Spain. . . . And with a feeling of guilt and shame I remembered myself standing there at that cocktail party in Georgetown listening to that tense young woman in the gold lamé blouse discuss Franco. How — how flippant I had been about it. How pert, and impertinent. A whole issue had been there before me, and I had allowed a personality I hadn't particularly liked to blind me to its gravity. And now I was blushing for it — too late.

Mea culpa, Ben, *mea culpa* — and this is probably as good a place as any for me to acknowledge it. I have disagreed with you since and I will undoubtedly disagree with you again — but you were an anti-Fascist long before it was even fashionable, much less compulsory ethically, to be one. You were aware and alert. Your eyes and your ears, if not your mind, were open. Mine weren't. And Lyle's weren't. *Mea culpa,* Ben.

"However," said Natalie, shutting a bureau drawer and pausing in front of the mirror to draw out her lipstick, "let's let current events go, and talk about something pleasanter. You, for instance." She glanced around the room. "This is a nice house you have here."

"We like it."

"Are you happy in Ammon?"

"Wonderfully."

"Lyle too?"

"Oh, yes."

"Really?"

"Yes, really."

"No more — babies?"

I hesitated. "Well . . ." Should I tell her about Eva? And then I decided against it. "No. No more."

She fingered her lipstick, and looked down at it. "They're perverse little things, babies," she said. "When I remember all those years Ben and I tried not to have one, and didn't — and then when I think of all the times since when we've tried to have one, and haven't. . . ." She was quiet for an instant. Then, tossing the lipstick onto the bureau, she turned. "Well, now why don't we take Johnny and go out for a walk or something? You can show me the town."

"Fine," I said, rising. I went toward the door and she joined me there, and we walked along the hall together.

"Amy," she said, "what in God's name have you been doing to your hair?"

"My hair? Nothing."

She linked her arm through mine as we started down the stairs. "Exactly what I thought. . . ."

We gave a party for them — Orin and Irmadee, Fern and Zelda, the Pete-and-Paul Schaufflers, and a few others. When I invited Irmadee I decided I'd better caution her a little, and so I attempted to — as subtly as I could; which wasn't very subtly. "Dee," I said, "I know how you and Orin feel about Jews, but Ben is one and so — well, I'd appreciate it if you didn't use the word 'kike' or 'Heeb' or anything like that. Do you mind?"

"Judas," she said, "do you suppose we're *completely* stupid? We'll be just as courteous to him as we would be to anyone, believe me. I assure you, we both know how to treat a house guest."

"Well," I said, "I just thought I'd mention it, that's all."

And they were courteous — more than courteous. They too had been to California during the summer, having gone out to San Francisco to see the Fair and to Hollywood to see the Trocadero, and when Irmadee discovered that Ben was interested in both the migratory-worker problem and *The Grapes of Wrath* she put herself out to discuss them with him. "We went in to Chicago and took the Chief," she said, sitting beside him on the sofa and balancing her plate on her lap, "and you know it runs right along Highway 66, the same road the Joads traveled in the book. We used to sit there in our compartment (we couldn't get a drawing room) and look out at all those awful, broken-down cars piled up with mattresses and things and filled with Okies and — well, we got to feeling as if we were a part of the book ourselves. You know? That's what Orin said, in fact. 'Dee,' he said, 'Steinbeck writes for *us*.'"

It seemed to me that Ben's eyes were glazing slightly.

"Steinbeck," she continued. "Steinbeck. That name. I wonder. Is he — ?" And then she quickly and even convulsively reached for her glass. "Well, and what do you think of this funny little town of ours, anyway?" she said. "Isn't it dear?"

Which was as close as either she or Orin came to a blunder,

except when Orin was talking with Natalie and happened to remark that something was "not quite kosher" — but he immediately,
and very politely, said, "Oh, I beg your pardon."

"It was a lovely party, Amy," said Natalie, when they had all
gone and while we were picking up the glasses and preparing to go
upstairs. "Thanks a lot."

"Well, it wasn't as large as the one you gave for us when we were
visiting you. But still . . ."

"They're a good crowd," said Lyle. "They mix well."

"That pretty one in red," she said. "Mrs. — Netcher, is it?"

"Yes. Irmadee — Dee."

"I don't like to criticize, or to seem narrow either — but where was
that girl raised? In a pool hall? She really made me blush. And
I didn't know I could any more."

"Well, she's spent quite a bit of time in Chicago."

"Around Cicero, I should imagine. With the Capone set."

"She's not representative of Ammon," said Lyle, hastily. "Not
representative at all. She doesn't even buy her clothes here."

"I didn't think she did," said Natalie, and for some reason looked
at me.

I stood with a tray of glasses in my hand, and faced toward the
kitchen. "Anybody care for a nightcap?"

"Oh, I don't think so," said Lyle, yawning. He glanced at his
watch. "It's pretty late now." He moved toward the stairs. "Want
to turn on the news, Ben? See if there're any developments?"

"No," said Ben. "No, thanks." And he also moved toward the
stairs.

Natalie watched him as he went, watched him until both he and
Lyle had disappeared. "Poor guy," she said. "Poland and Danzig
— and with both Stalin and Hitler sharpening up their knives and
saying, 'Will you carve, or shall I?' His Christ and his Antichrist
— chums and buddies. And being a Jew doesn't make it any easier
for him. He won't sleep a wink." And then she turned to me. "I
believe I'll take you up on that nightcap suggestion."

We had them in the kitchen, with her leaning against the sink
and me against the oilclothed table. We discussed the party and

the people for a while — she had liked the Diederdocks very much — and then, pointing with her glass, she abruptly said, "That's an elegant refrigerator you've got there. New, isn't it?"

"This year's," I said. "Next year's, I guess, technically. The latest model, anyway."

She drank. "What year model is that dress you're wearing?"

"Why, it's — " I glanced down into my glass, and then up. "Look, you've been making a number of cracks about my appearance. My hair, and so on. Do I seem dowdy to you?"

"Frankly, yes. A little. You've let yourself go."

"Well, we can't all take trips to California and — "

"I'm not talking about styles alone. Or even style. It's — " Suddenly she placed her glass on the sink behind her, and came toward me. "Oh, Amy, Amy," she said. "I could cry about you — about you and Lyle both. I've been wanting to cry practically ever since I saw the two of you there at the station."

I waited a moment, and then lifted my glass and sipped. "You needn't cry. We're happy."

"You're not."

"Well, Lyle is. And if he is, I am."

"That's complete nonsense, and it makes me sick to hear you say it. And even if he is happy, he has no right to be." She was standing in front of me, her arms folded. "Small towns are wonderful — for some people. I think this one would have been wonderful for you, if you'd never left it. But it should never be wonderful for a man like Lyle, especially at his age. And it isn't. The whole setup's wrong. He may have learned some things here and he may have made a success, but it's turned him into a stuffy, stodgy — "

"No," I said. "No. Don't say that." I didn't want to hear words like that, even from Natalie.

She made a gesture. "All right, I won't say it. Because I don't have to. You know it." Turning, she went back to the sink and picked up her glass again. . . . I finished my drink in silence. I had been looking forward to a girls-together talk with her. But not like this. Not like this.

"Listen," she said then, "would you object if I tried to do a little blasting?"

"It wouldn't do you any good." Or me.

"Maybe not. But would you object if I tried?"

I hesitated. "No."

"I think I will then." She went toward the door leading into the front hall. "Good night," she said. "And no hard feelings. I hope."

"None."

I rinsed out my glass, and after that reached for the light switch. As I did so I noticed the refrigerator, and my hand went out toward its smooth, white surface. I touched it. . . . It was a de luxe refrigerator, and I was proud of it. What's wrong about having a de luxe refrigerator? I thought. And what's wrong with being proud of it? A refrigerator you use every day. A print dress you wear just for special occasions.

Then I flicked the switch and went upstairs.

So Natalie tried her blasting — what she called her "Lazarus act" — beginning the next morning. I must say she chose a momentous day for it, the Friday when the German *Wehrmacht* crossed the frontier into Poland and their *Luftwaffe* bombed Gdynia and a blitzkrieg started. *Wehrmacht, Luftwaffe,* blitzkrieg, they were new words to me, the first of many new words I was to learn: there is nothing like a war for enlarging the vocabulary. Ben sat at the breakfast table, silent, wretched, unable even to eat. Lyle was deep in the *Register,* and as I looked across at its black headline I thought, "Will it come, really? After so many false alarms?" And I decided, "No. Something will happen. Something has always happened before to avert it, and it will happen again now. Peace in our time — they can scorn and ridicule the phrase if they like, but it's all I ask. And peace in Johnny's time. After that, it won't matter so much."

Such were my thoughts: what Lyle's might be, I didn't know. But Natalie was launching a blitzkrieg of her own, briskly. "Lyle," she said, "I don't believe I told you that Kendrick's starting a new magazine, did I?"

"Mm?" From behind the headline.

255

"Well, he is. Next spring or summer. He's calling it *Chic*."

"Oh, God," groaned Ben. "All hell starts to break loose, and she talks about *Chic*."

"He's going after the low-budget, younger-set glamour trade," she continued, unperturbed. "I understand he's trying to collect a staff together. Freddie Wheaton's going to be advertising manager, but what he's really looking for is a managing editor."

Ben stared at his untouched coffee, and put his head in his hands: I did hope he wasn't going to be sick. "All this and Freddie Wheaton too," he said.

"The man doesn't have to be a fashion expert. But he does have to be a magazine expert. He — "

The barricade of Lyle's paper crashed down, and I saw a gleam of triumph in Natalie's eyes. But he wasn't looking at her. . . . He was looking at Ben. "This Smigly-Rydz fellow, or however you pronounce it," he said. "Is he supposed to have anything on the ball?"

Well, it went on like that for the whole of the two days that remained of their stay. The Manila County Fair had opened, and we took them to it — but although we wandered past the livestock pens and up the Midway, Natalie might just as well have been walking around Grand Central's editorial zone. She employed the attack direct and the attack indirect: she sallied, infiltrated, smoke-screened, and ambushed. She spoke not only of Mr. Kendrick but of almost every other magazine publisher I had ever heard of — and some I hadn't, because apparently they were new since our day. She spoke of *Panorama,* much of *Panorama,* and of Stanley Tremaine, who was still editing it although she said he might not be for long because it was rumored that he had ulcers. ("That Fascist bastard," said Ben. "I hope he's got a million of 'em. He's a Red-baiter and — " And then his lips were suddenly sealed again.) She spoke of New York, in general and in detail. "A very nice Fair," she said, sitting in the grandstand and watching the trapeze artists. "Very nice. But you ought to see the World of Tomorrow. That French Pavilion. Oh, my." She spoke of the new apartment she and Ben were taking on Central Park West. "It's on the thirtieth floor, and it has a terrace where you can get the most spectacular view of the whole city," she said. "And we've got loads of room, in case anybody ever wants to visit us and sort of — look the view over." Satan she was, with that view of hers. But mostly she spoke of magazines, magazines.

She sang a siren song. . . . But nobody heard it. Well, I heard it. But it wasn't meant for me.

"Natalie's become kind of insular in her point of view, don't you think?" said Lyle to me, in private. "A lot of New Yorkers do, if they stay there long enough."

"Yes," I said.

"I never imagined it would be this hard," said Natalie to me, in private. "Don't you suppose I'm making any dent at all?"

"No."

So they went, on Sunday afternoon. Sunday afternoon, September third. We knew there was a war in Europe by then, of course. Officially. There had been a war ever since five o'clock that morning, our time, and somewhere guns were going and somewhere planes were rising. But I don't think I fully realized it until we were driving to the station and the car radio (none of us had dared to move from a radio during the past forty-eight hours, excepting Ben, who refused to listen at all) brought us a tired rebroadcast of the tired voice of a tired old man. And it was difficult to realize it even then, in this September sunshine and driving along the Sunday leafy quiet of Manila Street:

". . . satisfactory assurances to the above effect have been given by the German Government and have reached His Majesty's Government in London, a state of war will exist between the two countries from that hour."

No such undertaking was received by the time stipulated and consequently this country is now at war with Germany.

It is a sad day for all of us, but for none is it sadder than for me. . . .

Sad? I thought. Sadder? Yes, no doubt. But was this a moment to be claiming comparatives and superlatives of sadness? When you are sad, you are sad — and words won't make it any sadder. Or the past any better or the future any brighter.

Yet this definitely is not real, I thought again. I'm not sitting here beside Lyle, with Natalie and Ben in the back seat. I've never even met Lyle, or them either. It's 1914 and I'm seven years old and it's August instead of September and I'm playing jacks on the front porch and I can see Papa coming up the walk — dimly, very dimly — and he is calling to Mama — faintly, very faintly — "Mother? Mother? Germany has invaded Belgium! Well, sir, it's on! There's a war in Europe. . . ."

And well, sir, it was on again. Belgium, Poland, *der Kaiser, der Fuehrer* — take your choice.

"Turn it off, Lyle," said Ben, from behind me. "Turn it off."

But it was I who turned it off, and I moved closer to Lyle.

There was a short laugh from Natalie. A strange time to laugh, surely. "It just occurred to me," she said. "You know where our mutual friend Laura Archer was when last heard of?"

I didn't know, and didn't care. Nothing seemed farther away from me than Laura Archer at this particular moment.

"She was sitting in Bayreuth beside Frau Goering, listening to *Götterdämmerung.* Herr Goering is the one who operates the Flying Circus. For all I know, they may still be listening to it."

"Well," said Lyle, after a moment. I thought he might possibly have been thinking about Laura, but evidently he hadn't been. He was stating a generalization — and a program, too. "It's not our war."

"That's right," said Ben. His voice was very tight: there even seemed to be a note of sullenness in it. "It's not our war." And then the voice cracked a little, and although I couldn't see them I knew that his hands were clenched. "Oh, Jesus, Jesus — "

"Now, baby," said Natalie. "Now, baby."

"Those Peaceways ads," said Lyle, over his shoulder. "I guess they never ran any of them over there, did they? You know, the one showing the basket case and the one about the butcher and the baby. I guess they never formed any Veterans of Future Wars groups, either." He swung the wheel, and the car veered off Main Street, toward the station. "But we did, and I've got a hunch nobody's going to forget them. You can't train a whole generation to pacifism — choke it right down their throats — and expect them to throw it overboard the minute they hear a bugle. No matter what the bugle's blowing for — or against."

I didn't like this talk, any of it. I didn't like the entire subject. Our war? Who had ever suggested even the remote possibility of this being our war? So, reaching out, I switched on the radio again. Swirling past a newscast, several newscasts, past symphony and past swing, I finally settled on something which could be agreeable to everybody, even Ben. Something neutral — a wise and cackling voice: "Bergen, I'm gonna mow 'em down. So help me, I'll mow 'em down. . . ."

"Well," said Natalie, "now that's better."

The train wasn't yet in sight when we drew up to the graveled platform of the station, but its whistle could be heard from around the bend, down by the trestle. The bags were got out, and Ben looked around him. "Porters?" he said. "No porters?"

"No, dear," said Natalie. "No porters. This is where you learn another meaning of the labor act."

We each took a bag, and started toward the place where the Pullmans would be stopping. "We've had such a grand time," she said, as we walked. "I wish we could do it all over."

"Come again," said Lyle. "Come often."

I could see her lips compress grimly as she glanced at him. She wasn't finished with him yet. She might have been detoured momentarily by the outbreak of a war, but she wasn't finished. However, she was almost finished, because she had to be. The train was in view now, and again its whistle sounded. There was a humming on the rails.

"Good-by, Amy," she said, as we stood among the bags. Her lips brushed my cheek. "And thanks."

"Thank you." And although I didn't stress the "you," I knew she knew that I meant "for trying."

Turning to Lyle, she kissed him too. "You clod," she said. "You stupid clod."

He smiled. "There you go. Always the charmer — "

"I'm not joking. I mean it."

The smile faded. "Say, what sort of a farewell to a host is this?"

"Let it go, Natalie," I said. "Let it go."

"I won't let it go." The yellow length of the cars was slowing to a halt now, and there was the grinding, straining of iron and the clank of couplings. Then with a final shudder the train stopped, and after that there was the hiss of steam. . . . She continued to look at him. "I could kill you."

Ben was indicating the bags to the white-coated porter. "Now don't go sticking your nose into other people's business," he advised.

She ignored him, her gaze still on Lyle. "Don't you realize that they still talk about you in New York?" she said. "The way you started *Panorama* and what you did with it. The way you began with just an idea — your idea, and one that nobody had ever had before — and built it up into a million circulation. Don't you realize that?"

"Natalie, please — " I began.

"What's the matter?" she said, but she didn't take her eyes from him. "Are you afraid of him? Well, I'm not. When I see waste, I'm at least going to have the satisfaction of pointing it out. And that's what this is — all waste. His life and yours too."

The porter had swung the bags into the car entrance, and Ben was tugging at her sleeve. "Come on," he said. "You can write it. They don't stop here long."

Turning, she put one foot on the portable step. "He does, though," she said. "He stops here forever. And after that beginning he made, too." She was climbing upward now, with Ben and the porter following her, and she was speaking over her shoulder. "He's smug, self-satisfied, and he's stale — God, is he stale! He's a stuffed shirt. And not even a big stuffed shirt. Just a little one."

The train was beginning to move. I couldn't look at him: I couldn't bear to. Instead, I looked up at her as she stood in the vestibule.

"Once upon a time there was a bright young man," she called down, above the screeching of steel, "and where is he now? What's become of him?" Her finger pointed. "There he is. Right down there. That mute, inglorious . . ."

I waited just an instant. Long enough, I thought. Then I took his arm. "Come on, dear," I said.

But I don't believe he either heard my voice or felt my hand, so I let the hand fall away. Turning, I started back toward the car, and behind me there was the heavy *unh-unh . . . unh-unh-unh* of the engine. As I walked onward, slowly, the bull on the Bull Durham sign on the barn opposite seemed to smirk at me. Once I glanced around and saw that he hadn't moved. He was watching the train as it gathered speed. The red-illuminated "Husker" circle on the rear of the observation car was far down the tracks, and again the whistle went. Then there were only the empty tracks themselves, and the humming was gone.

I had forgotten to shut off the radio, and the first words I heard as I opened the car door and climbed in were "Premier Daladier has announced . . ." I turned the knob, and there was silence. And if there is anything more silent than a small-town station on a Sunday after the train has gone, I don't know what it is.

I sat alone. For a long time I sat alone. Minutes, maybe.

Then I heard a crunching on the gravel, and the door opened and he got in and settled himself behind the wheel. But he made no move to start the motor. He just sat.

I put my hand on his knee. "Don't pay any attention to her," I said. "You know how she is. She never means half what she says."

"It's true, isn't it?" he said, at last.

"What?"

"What she told me."

"Oh, darling — please. Don't brood about it."

"Why not? You have been." He looked at me. "Haven't you?"

"No. Of course I haven't. I'm happy. You are too."

His finger traced the circle of the wheel. "That bright young man," he said. "I wonder what ever did become of him. I haven't thought about him for a long while. Years."

Oh, I wished he wouldn't, I wished he wouldn't. . . . And if I

261

could have had Natalie there then, I think I would have throttled her.

"What happened to him, Amy?"

"Well, he — he became a good husband and a good father." I paused. "Is that bad?"

"Not in itself. No."

"All right. Then he found security. And it wasn't easy for him to find it."

"Security," he repeated, and he seemed to lift up the word, square it, weigh it. "I wanted more than that." Immortal longings. Immortal longings. . . . "Only for myself at first, probably. But then for you — and later on for Johnny, too."

I was silent. "Well," I said, "you live and you learn." And immediately after I had spoken the words I knew they were an echo. "That isn't me talking," I thought. "That's Mama. I don't want to be like Mama. And I don't want him to be like Papa — in some ways." And I took his hand. "Yes," I said. "It was true, what she told you. Most of it, anyway. It's true of me, too."

A meadow lark sat on the fence across the tracks, and it sang.

He was gazing upward, at the rear-view mirror. "Look at us," he said. "We're middle-aged."

"No, we aren't. Not really. We just — "

"Yes, we are." He turned to me. "Look at that hat. You oughtn't to be wearing a hat like that." And he took it off.

I glanced down at the brown felt. "It's not a bad hat. When Sam Wiebert sold it to me he told me that — "

He tossed the hat into the back seat. "I don't care what Sam Wiebert told you. It's no hat for you. You probably oughtn't to be wearing a hat at all, in September on a Sunday afternoon. Certainly that one isn't good enough for you."

I smiled. This I liked. This I could use more of.

Reaching his arm out, he put it around me. "If you must wear a hat, it should be like the one Natalie had on. Or — well, like Irmadee wears."

I was still smiling. "Marshall Field's?"

He shook his head. "No," he said. "Saks Fifth Avenue. Or Lilly Daché."

I waited. I wasn't going to cue him. Natalie might, if she liked, but I had no intention of it.

"This town," he said then, his hand warm on my shoulder, "maybe that isn't good enough either. Any more. Though it taught me more than any other town ever did, big or small, including Cambridge, Massachusetts." And he edged closer toward me. "You know, your father said something to me once about learning to swim — I'll tell you about it some day. Well, I think I've learned. And I think I'd like to go out a little deeper. A lot deeper."

I wasn't certain exactly what he was talking about then, at that time, but I knew that whatever it was had brought an exuberance and vitality into his voice which had long been absent.

"I can do it. We can do it. We —" His sentence broke off and, leaning down, he kissed me. "There's a time to settle down and there's a time to get up. There was a time to come to Ammon and there is a time to leave it. So saith the prophet."

I let my head fall against his shoulder, and for the second time that day time rolled back. I was in a taxi and he was beside me and he was all full of his first excitement about his plan for a picture magazine, and he was saying, "Miss you? Every day and every hour. Nights and noons and all the time. . . ."

"Lyle," I said. "Lyle, do you know what we're doing? We're parked in front of the station and we're necking."

He made no answer right away, and when he did he said, "So we are, so we are," and his hand left my shoulder. For an instant I wished I hadn't spoken. But it was all right, for the hand went out toward the ignition key and turned it. "And I expect we can find a better place for it, don't you?"

"Yes."

His foot reached for the starter, and pressed on it. The motor whirred, then purred.

"Amy," he said. "Let's go home, shall we?"

"Yes. Yes, let's. Yes."

So he backed the car around, and we headed home, fast. It wasn't even twilight. The sun was still shining.

You can forget a war, even after it has begun. Yes, you really can. You can forget all about it. And although perhaps you shouldn't, I think it is good that you can.

VIII

I THINK THAT IN CERTAIN WAYS I came to understand Ammon better and love it more during those months when we were preparing to leave it than I ever had before, even during all those years of my childhood and girlhood. I think too that in those same ways — ways of tolerance and patience and adaptability — I had probably never either understood or loved it nearly as much as I had claimed. To me it had always been a place to escape from, and always there had been that feeling of "The others have to stay. I don't." And then economic pressure had forced me to return, and my escape had been cut off, and there had been a period when I knew that I also had to stay — presumably forever. But now that I was free to go again, or soon would be, I realized that had it been necessary I would have been willing to remain. More than willing: happy. Lyle wouldn't — not any more — but I would. So when I say that I "grew up" in Ammon, I should also add that at last I grew up to it. A long-retarded growing up, I suppose it was. Yet I'm glad it finally came.

Therefore Lyle was the one who was eager to get back to New York now, and I was eager only because he was. I was anxious to leave, but on the other hand I would have been content not to — a good state, a Biblical state: whither thou goest . . . But we both knew that in any case we wouldn't be able to make the move at least until spring, for in the first place Lyle's M.C.S. and T. loan wouldn't be completely paid up until then — though when it was the paper

265

would be in a far better condition financially and physically than when he had taken it over — and in the second place when he did go back he wanted to go back to the right job. And it wasn't going to be with Mr. Kendrick, either, he said, for although he might have succumbed to Natalie's angling in general he had rejected the specific bait with which she had begun. "Somehow I doubt if I'd have much to offer on a magazine called *Chic,*" he said, "even if Kendrick would want me, which isn't likely. The thing for me to do is try some long-distance casting around to see what's available — maybe an ad in *Printers' Ink* or *Editor and Publisher.* I can afford to take my time. We have the winter."

Yes, we had the winter, and it was a good winter, one which bore the promise of spring in it for all of us, including Callie. Until I told her that we were going back, I had never heard one word of complaint from Callie during her exile from the asphalt pastures of Harlem — and she uttered no actual complaint even then. But when I did tell her there was relief, so much relief, and the way she expressed it gave me some small conception of how much it must be relief from. "Oh, Mis' Ellery," she said, "you know, the sisters they write me" (somebody wrote her, for laboriously penciled envelopes addressed to her arrived regularly, and they couldn't very well have been from Everett because Everett had never even learned to write his name) "and they always telling me about this new Heaven we got up there on the Hudson, and I say to myself, 'How about you, Flowin' Balm? You ever going to see it?' And now I will." Her eyes shone with a rare excitement. "The Redeemer Delivereths" (the formal name of the Holy Roller congregation) "they very nice people, but they ain't the same as your own folks."

So Callie was looking forward to a return to her heaven, and Papa was looking forward to a return to his, which was the roll-top desk. He had had enough of "retirement," which he had never wanted anyway, although he refused to admit that he had never wanted it. For the time being he had even had enough of Shiloh and Antietam, and Gettysburg too. "A man ought to keep on at what interests him most," he said. "That's what Lyle's going to do. He's going back to New York and magazines. And I'm going back

266

to the *Argus*. Or maybe I ought to call it the *New Argus*, because that's what Lyle's turned it into. Bigger and better than ever."

I smiled. We were seated on the sun porch again, and again it was winter and again I was knitting, though the size was now larger. "Maybe I ought to call him 'the new Lyle,'" I said. A combination of the new and the old, with the best of each. "Because that's what you've made him into. Bigger and better than ever."

"Me?" he said, in feigned surprise. "You mean Ammon."

"Yes, Ammon too. But you started him."

He shook his head. "I didn't do anything. I wanted a rest, and I took it. And now I've had my rest, and I'm getting back into harness. That is, when Lyle gets out."

"You saved him, Papa. You really saved him."

"Oh, bother, Amy. Bother." He twiddled his thumbs, and nodded sagely. "It's like Mother always says. 'You live and you learn. . . .'"

Lyle didn't want to announce that we were even considering leaving until he had some assurance that we had something definite to leave for, but of course the word spread round — through Mama via the Guild Ladies, I suspected. (Mama's own attitude was one of dubiousness, tinged with reluctant tribute: "Now that he's finally managed to get on his feet," she observed, "it does seem so risky for him to gamble with the future. He left New York because he was a failure, didn't he? What does he want to go back now for?") And when the news did leak out, I was surprised — and I think Lyle was also — to learn how genuinely he was going to be missed. Not I, the native. He, the stranger; or rather he who had once been the stranger.

The comments from people we knew were pleasing but more or less socially obligatory — Frank Diederdock's "We'll hate to see you go, fella"; Orin's "You bastard, the old burg won't seem the same"; Zelda's "Lyle was one of the few men here who understood Blackwood." But it was the homage from people we didn't know, or knew only slightly, which really amazed me. Callie's colored farmer family sent in a freshly killed and expertly cleaned chicken for us to have one Sunday, and when I started to give her the money to pay them for it she said, "Oh, no, Mis' Ellery. It's a present — for Mr. Ellery. He was the one that made the Hawkeye keep on letting us in after Mis' Cartwright went up there and said her grampa had been born in Virginia and she was a D.A.R. and she didn't think it was right." And one day on Main Street a leather-cheeked old woman stopped me to tell me that she had lived in Manila County for sixty-five years ("I knew your Ma when she was a Pepperdine") and that although my father had run a good newspaper she thought my husband ran an even better one. "He was the first to give us country ladies a chance at the Fair with our dahlias," she said. "Always before, the Ammon ladies took all the prizes, because they don't have much else to do but raise dahlias. And so he came out in the paper and said there ought to be two classes, one for town and one for country, and after that there were. He's a good man, Mrs. Ellery. A just man. Churchgoer or no churchgoer, he's a just man."

Those were only two instances, but there were others — many others. The Kiwanians were talking of a plaque, he was invited months in advance to deliver the Decoration Day address ("Be glad to, if I'm still here," said he, who abhorred public speaking), and smaller towns throughout the county sought his presence at civic celebrations, such as Mott Creek's Husking Day and Minota's Sauerkraut Festival.

"You know what?" I said. "They like you."

"Yes, I think they do," he said, and after a pause added, "And I'm not sure which is odder — that, or that I like them. Because I do like them. I like them fine. And I think that when I go, a part of them will go with me — and stay with me."

There was still a war on in Europe that winter, but it was generally agreed to be a phony war, and it seemed to me that Irmadee summarized the situation very neatly and wittily — and at the time I thought quite originally — when she remarked that what had begun as a blitzkrieg had turned into a sitzkrieg. There had been predictions that if there were another war, it would prove to be the swift and final juggernaut which the Jules Vernes of the Sunday supplements had for years been ghoulishly and lovingly envisioning. And yet compared to the first one, now relegated to the position of "the other war," this war was really very tame stuff. In fact after the first flurry caused by the sinking of the *Athenia* and the seizure of the *City of Flint* had passed (names, names, long-forgotten names, forerunners of the *Reuben James* and the *Greer* and the *Kearny*), I decided that perhaps I would be able to ignore the war almost entirely. The whole business was not only undramatic and anticlimactic: it was a bore. A bore to be received gratefully, of course, in its present and some said permanent form; but a bore nevertheless. Germany had taken over what it wanted of Poland in three weeks and Russia had got into and almost out of Finland in three months — but I somehow couldn't regard either Poland or Finland as being very significant. To me and my generation there was only one theater of war, the one made familiar by the other war — France. But France had her Maginot Line and, like Frenchmen, I had been nurtured on descriptions of its impregnability. . . . All that is history now, I know, ancient history — and history has no surprises in retrospect. But it has many of them while you are living it.

It was a campaign year, and accordingly Papa was experiencing his quadrennial blooming of excitement, for Papa looked forward to the circus of campaign years as some people look forward to circuses themselves. And this year was even more than ordinarily promising because the political pendulum was due to swing again toward the G.O.P. — and to Papa the G.O.P. was what the Ladies' Guild was to Mama. Unlike Mr. Kendrick, he was opposed to Roosevelt not so much because of his New Deal program as because he was a Democrat. "And now he'll be going out," he said happily, "and if we name the right candidate we've got a good chance that another of 'em won't be coming in. The rascals. He won't run for a Third Term — the country wouldn't stand for it. Nobody's ever run for a Third Term. Not even McKinley would have. Yes, sir, it looks like next fall we'll be able to move Thanksgiving back to where God meant it to be."

"Who will be the candidate, do you think, Papa?" I said. "Republican, I mean."

"Mm, young Dewey might do — he's been a good gang-buster, and he makes a nice appearance. Or maybe Taft."

"And the Democrats?"

"Oh, I don't suppose it matters much, since it can't be F. D. R. He was their vote-getter — he and that WPA of his. Though I must say we at least got the swimming pool and the new post office out of the WPA." His expression changed to one of sourness. "And that thing on the wall in the post office."

That thing on the wall was a mural, an imitation Grant Wood, already cracking and peeling. Its intent was presumably to celebrate the dignity of the farmer, but all it succeeded in doing was to insult and irritate all the farmers who looked at it. Not to mention the farmers' wives.

"You know, Amy," he continued, and there was something approaching wistfulness in his tone, "that's about the only fault I've got to find with Lyle. He ought to take more interest in politics. He's got kind of a blind spot there."

"I know, Papa." And he always had had, even back in the *Panorama* days. "But you see, he's so busy now getting the *Argus* ready for you to take over and trying to get himself located in New York."

"How's it coming? New York."

"It's coming fine. We think."

And it was. He had run an advertisement in both *Printers' Ink* and *Editor and Publisher* ("Experienced magazine man originally responsible for successful publishing innovation wishes to return to New York area. . . ."), and although there had been only a few replies from each, out of them there were two which looked fruitful. One was from a small-format digest magazine, but that he discarded as representing a field already too well plowed. The other was from *Newsreel,* one of the many picture magazines which had followed in *Panorama's* wake — but one of the longer-lived and more successful ones. "I think that's our best bet, if we can come to terms with them," he said. "I've still got a lot of ideas for a picture magazine that that Tremaine on *Panorama* has never even thought about. But I'm not going in there as any office boy, or as any caption writer either. If they want me, they'll have to pay for me."

"Well, don't make it too high," I advised. "Confucius say — "

"Confucius say much too much. No, I'll have to dicker a bit — I imagine they expect me to — and then we can settle on a golden mean."

So he dickered. *Newsreel's* first letter had been an inquiry rather than an offer, and it had arrived in December, a bland and guarded "feeler." But when they discovered that the "experienced magazine man" was the pioneer among all picture-magazine editors, their interest obviously quickened, and although they still made no definite offer it was evident that they wanted him. ("You see," I said. "Natalie was right. They do remember you.") By February they had reached the stage where they were starting to mention money, and by March they were mentioning almost enough money. I began to approach our post-office box with the same nervousness with which the Misses Trost were answering the telephone's ring that winter, never knowing whether or not it might contain our Pot o' Gold. But although I was gratified by the self-confidence Lyle was displaying in having named a figure and sticking to it, I was also becoming a little uneasy. He wanted the job, wanted it more than he was willing to acknowledge, and I hoped he wasn't going to lose it through overindependence.

"They've come part of the way," I said to him along in April, on the day when he told me that he had paid the final installment on the M.C.S. and T. loan and that it would be very convenient for *Newsreel* to flash the green light any time now. "Maybe you ought to come part of the way, too."

"No," he insisted. "If I'm not worth that extra thousand a year to them, I'm not worth anything. Anyway, I've got a feeling that there'll be some hot news in a few weeks."

There was, though not concerning *Newsreel*. In a few weeks it was the middle of May, and from then on for a solid month there was so much hot news — blared from radios, blazoned in headlines — that no one could assimilate it. In fact I could hardly believe it, even though it was there at every station on the dial and on the front page of the *Des Moines Register* each morning as I picked it up with the milk. Had we ever labeled the war as "phony"? Had I ever considered it "tame"? Well, if so, it seemed to be making up for lost time. Now we learned what blitzkrieg really meant. Now we learned how it worked.

This is my history, not that of a war, so all I can do is try to record a part of what I felt and thought during that lifetime of cataclysm which was being so handily compressed into a pocket-size six weeks. Belgium was invaded, and Chamberlain gave way to Churchill, and I thought, "Churchill? But he's an old man. Why replace one old man with another old man?" Wilhelmina and her family fled from The Hague, and I thought, "The Hague. In school we used to be taught that The Hague was 'the home of Peace.' Now will they unlock the dikes and flood themselves and the enemy too, as the strategists always said they would?" Louvain was taken, and I thought, "Will they burn the books again? Those books we used to contribute our dimes and nickels for?" The King of the Belgians surrendered, and I didn't know what to think. Norway surrendered also, and Paris, and I thought, "I never saw Paris, and I always wanted to. Now it's too late." And Italy entered the war, and I thought, "But it's not too late for that. Oh, no. Not too late for the jackal. Not too late for the dagger in the back and the kill. Just in time." And finally, at least it certainly seemed final enough, there was an armistice in a railroad car in the Forest of Compiègne. "A pretty name, the Forest of Compiègne," I thought. "That's another place I would have liked to have seen. Lyle was there once, and he said it was just like any other forest. And yet . . ."

Why hadn't we ever gone? I asked myself. Back in those days when we had had plenty of money and were living in New York where all we would have had to do was hail a taxi and ride cross-town to a ship, why hadn't we gone? While all of it was still there. The cathedrals and their spires and their windows and all the rest.

Lyle was silent during most of those weeks, and that was understandable, because a lot of others were silent also: the phrase "stunned silence" took on a meaning. But he was increasingly irritable, too — partly, I thought, because he had had no word from *Newsreel*. On Decoration Day he was to have made the address for which he had long been scheduled and on which I knew he had long been working, but on the very morning of the day itself he declined to go ahead with it, and as a result we had a small argument. Decoration Day had always been important in Ammon, a time of family reunions when people went out to place flowers on graves and then returned to their front porches for picnic suppers of cold fried chicken and potato salad. In short, a very enjoyable and sociable occasion, and he should have felt—and at the time had felt—honored to have been selected as the orator of the day.

"They asked you way last winter," I said, when he told me at breakfast that he wasn't going to speak, "and it doesn't seem right for you to back out at the last minute."

"What can I say?" he said. "What the hell can I possibly say?"

"But your speech is all done. It's finished. You told me it was."

"Sure. Finished and junked." He passed the *Register* over toward me. "Look at that."

I looked, and saw a headline: "British Pocketed at Dunkirk."

"What can I say on Memorial Day when that's happened the day before?" he persisted. "I ask you. What can anybody say? I'd get up on a platform with a lot of bunting on it, and I'd gag. I'd have to."

I understood what he meant, of course, and I put the paper aside. "Lyle," I said. "Lyle, it's not our war. You've always said it wasn't."

"Yes, I know." He rubbed his forehead. "I know."

For a moment I didn't say anything, and then I reached for my coffee again. "Well, if you'd rather not speak, all right," I said. "They can get somebody else."

They did. They got Papa, who had performed the same office many times before. He put on his Spanish-American War uniform and gave an address on Gettysburg, with passing references to San Juan Hill. An irrelevant and obsolete topic on that particular Memorial Day in that particular May? Perhaps. But if I had to hear oratory, I couldn't think of any other topic I would have preferred —and I could think of several that I definitely wouldn't have preferred. The past can be comforting, if only because it is past.

So those catastrophic weeks went on, and at last they ended and there was no place left for the Germans to advance — no place except across the Channel, and that was expected momentarily. "After they've had a little recess," people said. "After they've stopped to change their oil." It had been a whirlwind campaign. . . . And while it had been going on, a whirlwind campaign of a different sort had been in progress — Wendell Willkie's. In early spring I had never even heard his name, but by mid-June it seemed to me I was hearing it everywhere, most of all from Papa. Papa had been for Willkie ever since he listened to him on "Information Please." "A very able fellow," was his considered verdict. "Very bright and wide-awake. He's a credit to the Republican Party." Than which, in Papa's view, there was no higher praise. "The *Register's* for him. I'm for him. And I've an idea that a lot of the delegates are going to be for him. How about the *Argus,* Lyle?"

"I'm not sure that this year's candidates matter much," said Lyle. "It looks as if the man to beat is Hitler."

"Well, Willkie's no pussyfooter on that," said Papa. He looked meditative. "I see *Time* Magazine calls him a 'utilitycoon.' Now how do you suppose they pronounce that?"

In our living room in June with Johnny, who found it a tedious form of entertainment, I listened to Willkie being nominated at Philadelphia, and then in July, in Mama's living room with Papa, I sat listening to Roosevelt being renominated at Chicago. ("We want McNutt!" was the insistent, defiant chant. "We want McNutt!" But what they got was Henry Wallace.) Papa was incredulous, and yet in his own way jubilant. "He's really going to do it then," he said. "He's really got the brass to come out and try and be a Third Termer. Well, sir, I've been waiting forty years for the Democratic Party to hang itself by its own halter, and at last they've done it. They've cooked their goose right there — this is the straw that'll break the donkey's back. It's going to be Willkie in a walk. Hm, Amy?"

"What, Papa?"

"Willkie, I said."

"Oh, yes."

I couldn't concentrate on what he was saying. Nor had I been able

274

to concentrate on the convention, either this one or the other one. So much noise here, so many brass bands, so much shouting and parading — and such an ominous quiet across the sea. Though not on the sea, or in the air over it.

"She's a lovely looking woman, Mrs. Willkie," said Mama. "She'd make a First Lady we could be proud of. And I'll venture that she'd be no gadabout like some I could mention."

"Yes, Mama."

There was a word abroad in the land that summer which had at first been spoken in conversational, reasoning tones but which now was beginning to rise to a roar. The word was "Isolationism." It was a word like a wind, and at the start the wind had blown steadily and confidently, even when the Neutrality Act had been revised and the arms embargo repealed to a "cash-and-carry" basis; but now it was mounting to a hurricane force — and nowhere more so than in towns like Ammon. Today it is a principle which has few defenders. Then it had many, and although some were special pleaders most were activated by legitimate, sincere, and understandable motives. At least in Ammon. For in Ammon you could always look out your window east or west and reflect on the comforting thousands of miles to either sea and the further thousands of miles of those seas beyond.

There were those who classified all who displayed isolationist tendencies as "either imbeciles or traitors," but that was a theory I couldn't subscribe to then and even with the advantage of hindsight can't subscribe to now. I think most of them were just human. Foolish, yes, and myopic, even blind. . . . I say "them," but I suppose I should say "us," for I was hardly less blind than the others. In a way my blindness was far more indefensible than theirs, because although events were forcing me to look ahead and see — if only dimly — I was deliberately refusing to face what I saw. I turned my head aside, in a score of ways I turned my head aside. That is, until that July afternoon when I could turn it aside no longer.

I had been uptown that day and on impulse had stopped in at the *Argus* with Johnny, who immediately raced downstairs to Alf and the presses. Lyle had stepped out for a moment, Ethel Huber said, and so I decided to wait for him in his office, and as I walked back toward it I passed a group of farmers who were.clustered at the front counter talking about Lindbergh. "Lindy, he says . . ." they said. "Now you take Lindy. . . ." But I turned my head aside from that too, because I didn't want to hear what Lindy said and I didn't want to hear what those who disagreed with him said either. I wanted neither pro nor con.

Hard sunlight slanting through the Venetian blinds was gilding the scales of the pike on the wall to iridescence when I entered the room, that room which was as familiar to me as any in my whole life. But the pike and Papa's roll-top — its cave bare and a little forlorn — were almost the only things which had remained unchanged since those faraway days when I had used to come here for consolation, counsel, and occasional quarters for banana splits. If these walls could talk, I thought, looking at them, what confidences and adolescent perturbations they would echo back to me: "Papa, Fern Hauberg wants me to wear his signet ring. Do you think I ought to, Papa? . . . Daddy, Mama still won't listen to my going to New York. And I've got to get to New York, Daddy. I've simply got to. I'll die if I don't. Can't you coax her?" And perturbations of a date later than adolescence: "His name is Lyle Ellery. Oh, it's nothing serious. Nothing serious at all. We're just — friends."

Standing at the flat-top desk, I gazed down at three wire baskets — "In," "Out," and "Pending." Atop "Pending" lay a printed leaflet lettered "The Yanks Are Not Coming," and I picked it up. On the cover was a meticulously penciled script: "Lyle. Thought this might be of use to you. Yours. Ben." I fingered the leaflet, although neither its message nor the fact that Ben was circulating it was news to me, for I knew from Natalie's letters that he had long since come to a decision about the war. "It seems it's a capitalistic, imperialist war," she had written, "and he says the hell with it. It also seems that Helsinki was a different kettle of fish entirely. Say what you will about dogma, it certainly saves a lot of wear and tear on the emotions."

"The Yanks Are Not Coming," I thought. Well, it was a good

slogan. Evidently *Panorama* thought it was a good slogan too, for it had used it to head the lead editorial in its last week's issue. Strange bedfellows, Ben and Mr. and Mrs. Royal Archer III. But what did that matter, if they both were right? . . . Then as I was about to replace the leaflet in the basket I noticed a letter which had been lying beneath it. The letterhead was one I had seen before and, bending toward it, I started to read. I had begun only the first sentence — "Dear Mr. Ellery: *Newsreel* has decided to meet your salary demands in full, and therefore we are pleased to offer you —" when my eyes lifted to the dateline. "July 2." July second? I thought. But that had been almost three weeks ago, and hardly a day had passed during those three weeks without my asking, "Don't you think it's strange you don't hear from *Newsreel?* Do you suppose maybe they've lost interest?"

Gradually, standing there with the letter in my hand, I began to understand a lot of things. I began to understand Lyle's evasive replies to my questions, I began to understand his silences, and his moodiness, and his irritability, and I also understood why the letter had been filed under "Pending" — and perhaps why Ben's leaflet had been filed there too.

There was the sound of a step and, glancing up, I saw him standing in the doorway, looking at me and looking toward the letter. Then, coming forward, he sank into the chair in front of his desk.

I put the letter back into the basket. "Have you answered this?" I said.

He shook his head.

"Don't you think you ought to?"

He nodded.

"What is it?" I waited, and still he didn't speak. "Don't you want the job any more? Don't you want to go to New York?"

He hesitated, and then he looked up at me. "You know what it is," he said.

I turned away and went over to the roll-top desk and sat in Papa's chair. I swiveled around with a squeak, then back with a squeak. "It's not our war," I said stubbornly, parrot-like.

"I realize that. But I'm thinking of the time when it might be."

"What does that have to do with your turning down a job you want?"

He was silent for a moment. "Because maybe there's a job here, too. One I don't want, one nobody wants, probably. But one that needs doing."

"But Lyle, what could you possibly accomplish here in Ammon? No matter how you may feel."

"I've won friends, or think I have. Maybe I can influence people."

"In what way?"

He rose and began to roam the room. "Don't you see? We happen to be living in what they call 'the heart of the isolationist Middle West.' And I happen to be running a paper."

I understood what he was getting at then; understood his aim, but discredited its range. "Such a little paper, though."

"Yes, but who reads it? The very people I'd like to get at, or at least somebody ought to get at. To wake 'em up, shake 'em up, scare hell out of them if necessary."

"Oh." My tone was scornful. There was a word at that time which we all were armed against, if against nothing else, and now I used it. It was a word of unutterable stigma. "Oh," I repeated. "Propaganda."

"Propaganda — information. Call it what you like." He leaned against the exchange table, and I heard the jingling of keys. I suppose that was the first time I had ever heard those keys jingle in anger against something which might affect others besides himself. Not that their sound was any sweeter to me because of that. "You know, your father told me something once. 'If it's a public you want,' he said, 'you've got it here.' And I've learned it's true. But what am I supposed to do with that public now? Leave it to the *Chicago Tribune* and *Panorama* and their propaganda? And to Ben's?"

I got up and went to the window and stood looking out at Main Street, lazy in the summer sun. For the first time I saw it as not just one Main Street but as a thousand of them.

278

"The interventionists have their propaganda, too," I said. "Let Anne Morgan fight for France, if she likes. I don't want to. And I don't see why you should want to either."

His voice continued behind me. "Who says I'm an interventionist? I'm not thinking of France — it's too late for that. I'm not even thinking of England, because it may be too late for that also. But I am thinking of ourselves."

I turned. "I'm a pacifist," I said. "And so are you. Or you used to be."

He had gone back and had seated himself at his desk again. "I still am. But that was taught me. And apparently it isn't as strong as the instinct for self-preservation. That I was born with."

"Self-preservation? Oh, now, Lyle. That's alarmist talk. That's — "

"It's not alarmist. It's common sense. It's written on the wall — a lot of walls." He looked over at me. "I've an idea that it may be later than we think, Amy."

I came toward him, and my glance went toward Ben's leaflet, there in the basket. "Well, if you believe the *Argus* could do something, why not let Papa do it? He's all for Willkie, and certainly Willkie's not isolationist. He's — "

He shook his head. "I've thought of that, too. But your father's old, and getting older. His spirit might be willing, but his flesh is weak."

There was only one thing for me to say then, and I knew it. So I stood behind him and placed my hands on his shoulders and said it. But there was no enthusiasm in my voice, nor did I attempt to simulate any. "All right," I said. "You win. We'll stay."

His hands came up and took my wrists. "You're not too disappointed?"

"You're the one who's disappointed."

"And surprised, too, I guess," he said, shrugging. "It's funny, really funny. Me with a Cause. I wasn't built for Causes. I'm not the type." Smiling, he glanced up at me, over his shoulder. "But now is the time for all good men to come to the aid of — all good men."

I leaned my chin against his head. "Poor Callie," I said. "And poor Papa too, in a way. He's been champing at the bit."

"I know." He sighed. "Nobody's going to get much fun out of it. Including me."

"Do you have a program yet?"

He nodded and, opening the center desk drawer, withdrew a typewritten sheet of paper and handed it up to me. "See that? Beginning with our next issue, that goes up on the masthead."

I took the paper, and read — read aloud:

In our unity, our American unity, we will pursue two obvious and simultaneous courses: we will extend to the opponents of force the material resources of this nation and, at the same time, we will harness and speed up the use of those resources in order that we ourselves in the Americas may have equipment and training equal to the task of any emergency and every defense.

"Roosevelt?" I said.

"Yes. Roosevelt." He reached for the paper, and looked at it. "He said it first. He said it best."

There is nothing deader than a dead issue, and today those editorials contained in that whole year's volume of back numbers of the *Argus,* gathering dust there on the open shelves beneath the gelid gaze of a stuffed pike, are filled with dead issues. But they weren't dead then, at the time Lyle was writing about them. Then they were alive, burning, controversial. And the words he used were alive and burning, too. . . . There are occasions when the time and the place and the man all come together, and that was the time and Ammon was the place and he was the man — if only because there was no other.

"I've won friends," he had said. "Maybe I can influence people." Well, I think he influenced some all right, a good many in fact, but in the process he also made enemies. Overnight the *Argus* shifted from a policy of never mentioning the war — never mentioning it at all, in either the news or the editorial pages — to one of, it sometimes seemed, seldom mentioning anything else. And there were those who didn't like it. For instance some of the farmers up around Little Germania didn't like it, and when Lyle began to publish material from the Committee to Defend America by Aiding the

Allies several of them canceled their subscriptions. "But you can't blame them, I suppose," he said. "The Germany they remember meant Kriss-Kringle and *Kaffee-klatsches*. It didn't mean concentration camps."

Yet that was a loss which he could and did sustain with equanimity. What bothered him more, much more, was when, as a result of the *Argus's* support of the Burke-Wadsworth bill and conscription, he lost the friendship of Judge Anson, whose only son had been killed at twenty-one at Château-Thierry and whose daughter's only son was now turning twenty-one himself. The Judge stormed into the office and shook his cane at him and called him a warmonger, and it depressed him for days. "I can imagine how he feels," he said, "and I know how the boy feels. At least I know how I would have felt at twenty-one if somebody had wanted to take a year out of my life for military training."

"But you'll come under Selective Service too, if they pass it," I said, in an attempt to comfort him. At least I hoped it might comfort him: it certainly was no comfort to me. "Won't you?"

"I'm thirty-five, practically over the wire, and I have a wife and child," he said. "The draft won't affect me. And yet I've got to plug for it. No matter what the Judge calls me, I've got to plug for it."

And so he did plug for it, and on registration day in October he stood in line at the Legion Hall along with all the other men in town in the twenty-one-to-thirty-six age group, even Silly Willy, and later in the month on drawing day it was he who said to Kelly, "What did you tell me your order number was, Kelly?" and when Kelly replied "158" clapped him cheerfully on the back and said, "Well, Kelly, you're a local celebrity. We'll put your picture on the front page. Because down in Washington this morning they reached into a goldfish bowl and you'll never guess what was the very first number they drew out. Yes, sir. 158. Congratulations, Kelly. Nice going."

"Thanks, Mr. Ellery," said Kelly, hollowly. "Thanks."

"Ah, what a lucky boy. We'll have to give you a farewell party."

"Thanks."

We did give him a farewell party, too, and the staff presented him with a gold wrist watch, and at the party Ethel Huber got un-accountably and melancholically drunk and revealed amid tears that she had always been in love with Kelly and had hoped that some-time when he got a little older he might marry her but now he never would because he was going off to be a soldier and there was going to be a war and he was going to be killed in it. . . . It was an anti-climactic embarrassment to everyone, especially to Ethel and no doubt to Kelly also, when he was returned from Fort Des Moines three days later because he had hemorrhoids. However, he still had the wrist watch.

I say that Lyle's editorials influenced a good many people, and yet I have no actual proof that they did. Nor did he, and the absence of such proof often discouraged him. "I hammer along week after week," he said, "and sometimes it seems to me as if I might just as well be shouting down a rain barrel. And now Judge Anson says he's going to form a chapter of America Firsters here, and he's already lined up Herschel Tupper and the Schaufflers and several others to join it. He's even got Orin. What am I developing — an audience, or an opposition?"

"Maybe both," I said. For at least he had converted me: I no longer made any attempt to turn my head aside. "And maybe the one produces the other."

Yes, he had converted me — and the blitz which had begun on Britain that autumn helped him. With Johnny by my side I used to sit at the radio listening (with the feeling that I was eavesdropping) to transatlantic conversations between British parents and their evacuated children, and although I was aware that some claimed this too to be propaganda I had no way of steeling myself against it. Those trite and tragic questions-and-answers spoken so brightly and vivaciously in strange accents from across the sea, punctuated by the roar which of course was only static but which always made me think of the crash of bombs: "Peter? Mummie here. How are you, darling? . . . Oh, splendid. Yes, we're all very fit. . . . You're learning to play baseball? Oh, how thrilling. But you won't forget cricket, will you? . . . Much love, dear. . . ."

"Much love," I sometimes thought. What would I have found

to say to Johnny if he had been three thousand miles away from me and the drone of German bombers only a few thousand feet? . . . Well, I suppose I would have said just that: "Much love." But would I have been able to pitch my voice to that particular blitheness? I hoped so. I hoped so.

Irmadee was a constant listener to those conversations also, and they had much the same effect on her — but more galvanically. For although London might be able to take it (but for how long?), Irmadee couldn't. Always of an Anglophilic bent — she hadn't named the twins Jennifer and Wendy without reason — she was gradually achieving a state of personal and individual cobelligerency, open and declared. She knitted furiously in behalf of Bundles for Britain, the fall suit she brought back from Marshall Field's was R.A.F. blue in color and smartly military in cut, and even such an item as a story in a motion-picture magazine concerning the departure of David Niven from Hollywood to join his regiment ("I just happened to pick it up at Nettie's when I was under the dryer," she explained apologetically) could inflame her to a sympathetic fury. "I get just *sick* about it," she said. "Believe me, if I were a man I'd go straight up to Canada and enlist. And look at Orin — joining that America First thing and all the time quoting Lindbergh and Verne Marshall over in Cedar Rapids and that General Wood. But I'll get even with him for that, just you wait."

"How?" I said.

Her tone mingled quiet triumph with a daring and defiant iconoclasm. "I'm going to vote for Roosevelt. At least he's had the decency to send them those destroyers. So I'm going to vote for him, and I don't care who knows it."

A house divided. . . . But there were many houses divided then. Manila Street was one long open forum, Gold Coast Row echoed with argument. The election came and went, and Papa at least had the satisfaction of seeing Iowa as a whole return to the Republican fold even though Manila County was among the minority which went for Roosevelt. (Could that have been an index that Lyle's words were bearing weight? He liked to believe so, and yet there was no way of being certain.) I had thought that after the election was over the controversy might subside, but instead it grew even more turbulent, for as the old year died a Fireside Chat proclaimed America to be "the arsenal of democracy" and as the new year was born a battle began to be waged — in addition to the faraway Battle of Britain — regarding Lend-Lease.

It was with Lend-Lease, I think, that Lyle really hit his stride. He wrote an editorial on the arsenal-of-democracy theme and the necessity for the passage of H.R. 1776 (a symbolically numbered bill, surely) which was reprinted in the Sunday *Des Moines Register,* and that recognition seemed to spur him on to an even greater intensity. *Panorama* of course was opposed to Lend-Lease, and he derived a certain grim enjoyment from reading its polemics week after week and then rebutting them in the columns of the *Argus.* "It's probably like a gadfly on the hide of a rhinoceros," he said, "and they'll never even be aware of it, but at least it's fun for me. You know, sometimes I wonder who's editing that thing these days — Tremaine, or Gerald L. K. Smith. And who's publishing it — Roy Archer, or Fritz Kuhn."

"Perhaps Laura is," I said. It was a name I could utter with an almost complete objectivity by now.

At first I thought he intended to ignore the reference. "It's certainly peculiar. Anybody can get a break in *Panorama* just so long as he's an obstructionist. It doesn't matter whether it's the Jehovah's Witnesses or Joe Lash. But when it comes to a question of preparedness, even for self-defense — " And then he stopped short. "She was smart, wasn't she, Amy? Laura."

"Yes."

"She was smart, and I was stupid." He was silent, musing. "In a lot of ways."

It was a strange time, that time, unsettling and unsettled. We weren't at war, and yet we weren't at peace. All through that winter and on into the spring groups of farm boys were collecting in the early morning in front of the courthouse to wait for the bus that would take them to Fort Des Moines, and when they returned on furlough uniforms ceased to be a novelty along Main Street. They were much better-looking uniforms than those I remembered, I

decided — those spiraled puttees which were always becoming undone, those square, broad-brimmed campaign hats which had made
their wearers resemble Boy Scouts. That is, they were much better-
looking if you happened to have a taste for uniforms at all. But even
if you didn't, there they were, in increasing numbers. Uniforms, and
the Guild Ladies rolling bandages for the Red Cross, and the formation of "Civil Defense" units (Irmadee attempted to organize an
Ammon Air Raid Warden service, but its reception was lukewarm),
and the Defense Bonds which seemed to be simply another issue of
the old Liberty Bonds (was "Any Bonds Today?" to be our current
"Good Morning, Mr. Zip-Zip-Zip"?) — what sort of peace was this?
If and when ASCAP and the broadcasting networks finally settled
their differences and "Jeanie with the Light Brown Hair" gave way
to something more contemporary, would we be hearing streamlined
recapitulations of "Pack Up Your Troubles"?

I have been here before, I thought. I have heard it all before, and
seen it. . . . When I was very young.

Yes, it was unsettling and unsettled — and confusing, too. And
that Saturday night in June when we sat with Orin and Irmadee in
the Joint drinking Scotch-and-soda and surrounded by those travel
posters advertising the enchantments of gay Vienna and the storied
Rhine and other places which held no enchantment any more, even
if one could have gone there, was perhaps as confusing as anything,
for it was on that night that we listened to the first accounts of Germany's invasion of Russia. To Orin it meant merely one more
argument for his isolationist stand: "Let 'em knock each other out.
What do we care?" he said. To Irmadee it meant a moment of
perplexity and then a stanch acceptance of a not-quite-welcome ally:
"They're Reds, of course," she said, "but if they can fight, that's what
really matters. Don't you think so, Lyle?"

"If they can fight and win, yes," he said. He shook his head. "But
they haven't a chance, not a chance. The experts give them just about
three months."

"I can't understand it," I said. "I mean, why do you suppose they
made that pact in the first place?"

He shrugged. "It looks as if maybe Ben was right all along. He said there must have been a reason for it, and I guess there was. Only he took the reason purely on faith, without knowing what it was. Nobody knew. Except Stalin."

"I wonder what Ben's attitude will be now."

"I doubt if you'll have to wonder for long."

And I didn't. During those weeks that followed, when the Germans were surging eastward and fanning out into the Ukraine and up toward Kiev and even Leningrad, I had a letter from Natalie:

. . . I ought to have written before [she wrote] but things have been spinning around here, and they've had me dizzy. I went to bed on June 22 under the impression that this was a capitalistic, imperialist war and I woke up on June 23 to be informed by Ben that it's no such thing. It's a war against Fascism. You'd hardly recognize him now. He's got back all his old vim and vigor—no more red spots before the eyes, and he's able to do all his own housework. He says why don't we get in there and pitch, too? Are we going to stand by and let Russia fight our fight? But he's also infatuated enough to say that he thinks Russia may be able to hold out. However, I expect that's like any religion. Once you embrace it, you have to embrace the possibility of miracles also.

I still wish that Lyle hadn't turned down the *Newsreel* thing, and I still hope that sometime, somehow . . .

Hope? Well, she might as well put that particular hope away. I had, and Lyle had also.

Then there came that day in August—that day of significance for me and, for another reason, for others. It was Callie's day off, and I was alone in the house with Johnny that afternoon. That is, I was in the house and he was somewhere outside it, near enough for me to hear the grind of his scooter. Drawing the bedroom shades against the glare, I had partially undressed and had lain down, not intending to sleep but merely to rest. The afternoon was hot, swelteringly hot, and as I lay there I could feel moisture on my palms and forehead. The heat and the semidarkness and the sounds of summer—somewhere a lawn mower, a fly buzzing against the ceiling, the drone of the scooter—must have lulled me into drowsiness, for the next thing I knew I was swimming up from a void and half-opening my eyes and a voice was coming toward me. Johnny's voice. He was standing by the bed, leaning his elbows on it and cupping his face between his hands.

"You look funny when you're asleep," he said.

"Oh, Johnny." I turned my cheek against the dampness of the pillow. "And I was having such a nice nap. You ought never to stare at people when they're asleep. It isn't polite."

"There's a man downstairs. He wants to see Daddy."

I yawned. I was barely back to consciousness yet. "Didn't you tell him Daddy was up at the office?"

"Uh-huh. But he says he isn't. He says he went there first. He says his name is Loyal Archer."

Again I yawned. "Not Loyal, Johnny. Royal. . . ." And then I was awake, all of me and all at once. Sitting erect, I swung my legs over the side of the bed. "You mean he's downstairs? Here?"

He nodded. "Uh-huh."

Getting up, I went toward the closet. "You go down and tell him I'll be there in a minute."

So he went, and I took a shower and dressed in what I believe must have been an all-time record for me. I didn't even have time to think much, and those thoughts I did think were only two, repeated over and over. Why is he here? I thought. And is Laura with him?

He was seated on the sofa when I came down, and Johnny stood at his knee examining the intricacies of a flat gold oblong which was a combination cigarette case and lighter, and he looked at me over the top of Johnny's head as I came forward. Then he rose. I had forgotten that summer suits could be tailored like that and that russet shoes on such small and well-shaped feet could be so obviously expensive and hand-bespoke. He was still debonair, still slight and lean, still brown. . . . But he looked older, much older, and that silvered-temple effect which I had once admired was now completely snowy.

"Hello, Amy," he said.

"Hello, Roy." Odd that the name should come out so automatically and easily after so long.

He smiled down at Johnny, who usually held himself aloof from strangers but evidently hadn't from him. Odd, too, to see Roy Archer alongside a child: he was a person I never would have connected with children. "This is a fine boy you have here."

"Thank you." I was remembering our last meeting, there in the clublike atmosphere of his much-leathered office. Johnny had been a fine boy then too, although I had no way of knowing that he was a boy. He had simply been a burden. I turned toward him. "Johnny, why don't you go outside and play for a while?"

He left, with a prompt if not overly characteristic obedience, first depositing the gold cigarette case back on the sofa, and we were alone. Picking up the case, Roy opened it and extended it toward me, but I shook my head.

"That's right," he said, fingering one out for himself. "You don't smoke, do you? You never did."

"Not often." Seating myself, I gestured toward the sofa. "Sit down, Roy."

But he continued to stand. He lit a cigarette, and I could see by his movements that he was nervous, unsure of himself. Royal Archer III unsure of himself? This was something new. However, I made no effort to help him. It wasn't that I harbored any resentment against him, or ever had. I knew that Lyle still did. Lyle had never forgiven him for cutting him out from *Panorama,* no matter how justifiable the cause, and since then — or rather ever since the magazine had set itself up as the militant champion of isolationism — Roy had come to symbolize everything which he himself was arguing against. . . . But I had never been able to learn how to dislike him, much less hate him. And I was offering him no assistance now only because I knew that he must have had a reason for coming here and that nothing I could do or say would divine it.

"Well," he said, stooping toward an ash tray. "I suppose the first thing I ought to do is offer my congratulations. I think it's fine, Amy. I really do."

"What is fine?"

Straightening, he looked at me. "Have I beaten the news?"

"I don't know what you're talking about, Roy," I said. "What news? And why congratulations?"

"Because —" And then he stopped. "No," he said. "Lyle will

want to tell you himself. You see, I flew to Des Moines and got a plane there to bring me up here, and I assumed you would have heard by now."

Rising, I went toward him. "Heard what? If it's something good, I don't see why I should have to wait until — "

From outside there was the sound of a car door slamming, and his glance went toward the wide front windows. He moved toward them. "It is something good," he said, "and you won't have to wait any longer." He nodded. "Look."

I looked, and through the glass I could see our sedan at the curb and Lyle coming up the walk — hurrying up it, excitement in his every movement. He was in his shirt sleeves and his tie was undone, as if he had just risen from his desk. Forgetting Roy's presence entirely for the moment, I went swiftly toward the door, opening it just as Lyle was opening the screen on its other side. We almost collided, but he didn't notice that, and neither did he notice my face or the anticipation on it. In fact I doubt if he was in a condition to notice anything. He had a telegram in his hand, and he waved it in front of me. He was panting a little.

"Get out the smelling salts!" he said. "Prepare to be flabber-gasted!"

But I was prepared already. "Darling, what — ?"

He was trying to catch his breath. "Did you ever hear of the Ed Howe Award?" he said, and then, seeing my look of blankness, immediately went on: "Well, did you ever hear of the Pulitzer Prize?"

I was trying to grasp the telegram, which he was tantalizingly holding up just beyond my reach. "Lyle, you haven't been given a Pulitzer — ?"

"No, but it's the equivalent." Then the telegram came down, and he thrust it toward me. "There you are," he said. "Read that and see how far our little candle threw its beams."

My eyes descended progressively from the date line — New York — to the address — Lyle Vincent Ellery, The *Ammon Argus,* Ammon, Iowa — to the signature — William Chapman Ferris, Chairman. Chairman of what? I wondered. And after that I returned to the body of the message. Phrases stood out three-dimensionally from the pasted strips: . . . AM HAPPY TO INFORM YOU THAT THE SELECTION COMMITTEE HAS CHOSEN YOU TO RECEIVE THIS YEAR'S ED HOWE AWARD FOR THE EDITORSHIP OF THAT WEEKLY NEWSPAPER WHICH HAS SERVED ITS COMMUNITY MOST USEFULLY AND HAS BEST MAINTAINED AND FURTHERED THE AMERICAN TRADITION OF RURAL JOURNALISM. . . .

I read it once, then started to read it again, and the second time the letters began to blur. I knew it was an honor, but it was only afterward that I realized how important an honor it was: every weekly paper in the forty-eight states coveted the annual Ed Howe Award, and out of them all the *Argus* had been chosen. Lyle and the *Argus*. . . . I looked up at him. "Oh, Lyle," I said.

He had put his arm around my waist now and was guiding me into the living room. "You know what this means, don't you?" he was saying. "That is, aside from the five hundred bucks, which we can use, and the kudos. It means that somebody's been reading what I've been writing, and listening to it. It means — " And then, glancing up, he saw Roy standing in the center of the room, and his arm fell away. For an instant he halted, frozen. Then he went forward. But he made no move to extend his hand.

"Well," he said. "Well."

"Hello, Lyle," said Roy. "I heard about it yesterday. Congratulations."

There was no pretense of Lyle's being hospitable, even civil. The old hostility was there, and when he spoke his voice had the fine edge of irony in it. "Have you come all the way out from New York to tell me that?" he said.

Roy crushed his cigarette out on a tray. I didn't know why I should be feeling a sudden impulse of sympathy toward him, but I was.

"No."

"I didn't think so." Lyle had taken the telegram away from me, and now he creased it and placed it on the mantel. "All right, what is it? What do you want? Because you want something, I know."

Roy waited a moment before answering. "I want you to come back and edit *Panorama,* Lyle."

As we stood there side by side, my arm instinctively linked itself under Lyle's. He turned to me, and made a flourish with his hand, indicating Roy. "I give you Mr. Rudolf Hess, come a-riding on a Trojan horse," he said. And then he turned to Roy again. "No, thanks. You go peddle your paper, and I'll peddle mine."

"You haven't heard me yet."

"I don't need to." He paused. "But did you really imagine I'd be that much of a sucker?"

Roy's face had become suddenly puzzled, as if he had been ready for almost any reaction except this one. "Sucker?"

"Yes, sucker," continued Lyle. He went toward a chair and sank into it. "Only what I can't understand is why you should want to bother. I'm such small fry. So I've won a prize — what of it? A bare three thousand people read what I write, while almost three million read what you write. You, or that Tremaine, or . . ." He allowed the remainder of the sentence to go unfinished. "You needn't worry. I'm no menace to you, and even if I were you couldn't buy me off."

Roy stood gazing at him. He began to smile, slowly. "I'm glad to see you haven't lost your self-confidence," he said. "You want to hang onto that. It's valuable."

Lyle made no answer. But it seemed to me that perhaps — just perhaps — he was beginning to feel himself to have been a little premature, even silly.

Then Roy's smile faded. "I've changed, Lyle," he said. "And I want the magazine to change, too."

Lyle glanced at him shrewdly, suspiciously. "What's changed you?"

"A lot of things." He was silent. "I've read those editorials of yours. I borrowed them from the Howe committee, and I've read them all."

"You mean *they* influenced you?"

"No. I'd been — converted already."

I saw that Lyle was watching him closely. "A pretty sudden switch, wasn't it?"

"Not as sudden as you think."

There were only the three of us there in that room, and yet in a way there were four. But neither of them had as yet mentioned the fourth. So I did. "Roy," I said, "what does Laura have to say about this?"

His eyes remained focused on Lyle as he answered. "Nothing, any more. About this or anything else. From now on, I'm the policy-maker."

Lyle's voice was skeptical. "Since when?"

"Since Laura went to Lisbon."

"Lisbon? What's she doing in — ?" And then he stopped, for he didn't need to go on. He knew, and I knew too.

Roy spoke quietly. "Maybe she's got to Paris by now," he said. "She always wanted a 'strong man,' and so she's gone where the strong men are." Although he wasn't smiling, there was a sort of wintry humor in his tone. "Yesterday New York. Today Europe. Tomorrow the world. . . ."

Looking at him then, I remembered how once I had thought of him as an elegant figurine of Eros, fragile and yet strong. But Eros was tired now, Eros was old — and disillusioned. . . . And I watched him as he went toward Lyle and stood beside his chair. "The idea of the magazine was yours to begin with, Lyle," he said, "and since then you've picked up some other ideas. I want those ideas. I want you to tell ten thousand Ammons what you've been telling this one." He paused. "There'll be a clean sweep. Tremaine goes out — almost everybody. And you can name your own salary."

Lyle's hands were locked together, and he was staring at them. He didn't lift his head. I think he was still thinking of Laura. I know I was. I was thinking of the long road she had traveled from Butte, Montana, and where it had taken her. She had always been seeking "a leader." Now she had found him.

"It isn't easy for me to ask a favor of you," Roy continued. "You probably realize that. But I want you to come back. Will you?"

"I — I'll have to think about it, Roy," said Lyle. But he still didn't look up.

"All right, think about it. And let me know." Roy picked up his hat and headed toward the door. "Only let me know quickly. Because there isn't much time left now. . . ." Opening the door, he started to go out. Then he paused. "There's just one thing I'd ask. I'd like to change the color of the cover. Not green any more — something else. You wouldn't object to that, would you?"

"No."

Then he went out. After the door had closed I went to the windows and stood watching him as he went down the porch steps. Johnny was waiting below with his scooter, and I saw Roy stoop toward him and say something. Then he straightened and continued on down the walk, with Johnny trailing behind him on the scooter.

Turning, I looked at Lyle, still sitting there in the chair. At last he raised his head.

"Well, Amy," he said, "what do we do?"

I went toward him. "You know what we do."

I say that day had significance for me — for both of us — and it did. And it had significance for others also, or at least I hope it did. For it was on that day, as we learned later, that a conference at sea began between Churchill and Roosevelt and the Atlantic Charter was formulated. But we didn't know about that then, of course. We didn't know about a lot of things.

❧❧❧ IX ❧❧❧

Yₒᵤ CAN LEAVE AND GO A LONG, long way and stay a long, long time. You can come to regard the name as merely a postmark on an envelope or a date line in a newspaper story, and the memory and knowledge of the skyline can fade in your mind to the point where it becomes little more than a symbol — what the Eiffel Tower is to Paris and the Sphinx to Egypt. Those soaring buildings no longer have any reality or dimensional quality. They aren't solid structures of stone and steel which you once walked past daily, and entered and ascended and worked in and lived in, as commonplace and familiar as the houses on Manila Street and the Baker Block on Main Street. They are cardboard cutouts, mere silhouettes, useful as the trademark on a life-insurance calendar or the introductory and establishing shot in a motion picture but having no other meaning. New York? What is New York? It is the source of shoes and ships and stock-market quotations. It is a pictorial background for perfume advertisements and fashion layouts. Yes, a background and a backdrop — that is New York. A façade, a convention, a legend, perhaps even a myth. And where is it? It is that dot up there on the map. They print the words in large letters, but you'll notice that the island which is its heart is so small that they can't even show it.

Such is New York when you are away, a long time away. It isn't really real any more.

But when you come back, when you come back . . . The waking

in the morning and looking out the Pullman windows at the broad Hudson, its bluffs misty and particolored in the autumn sun. Today's *Times* and *Herald Tribune* lying on the table at breakfast in the diner. Not day before yesterday's *Times* and *Herald Tribune,* or last week's, but today's. The billboards racing past: "1000 Rooms, 1000 Baths" — "Dance to Guy Lombardo in the Grill" (Guy Lombardo *himself,* mind you, not just a phonograph record or over the radio) — *"Life with Father.* Empire Theater. Second Year" (and now I can get to see it, before it closes) — "Radio City Music Hall" (Radio City is where Daddy's office is, Johnny).... And then Harmon, and the porter begins to reach up and down and under for the bags. And after that the suburbs start to flash by — Scarborough, Tarrytown, Ardsley, with commuters' trains at the platforms and with passengers sitting in them reading their papers just as if this were an ordinary day and they were bound for an ordinary place. How can they sit there like that, so calm and unmindful? Don't they realize they're going to New York?

"Brush you off, ma'am?"

"Yes, thank you. The little boy too, please."

The Bronx now, and 125th Street, and fleeting, kaleidoscopic glimpses into private lives. A man in his underwear, stretching and scratching. A plaster polychrome Virgin in a niche with a candle burning before her. A pillow on a window sill and a plump-armed woman leaning on it, already stationed for a day-long vigil. A cat leaping up on a kitchen table to lap at a saucer. And through the narrow lanes of the side streets, beyond the fretwork of fire escapes, a glimpse of green. . . . See, Johnny — through there. That's Central Park.

"Mother — look. The train's going down. It's going under the ground."

"That's right. We go into a tunnel."

And the train slanting down, and concrete walls rising to cut off the daylight, and the clicking roar of the tunnel, and the blinking of signals green and red. And then the train gradually begins to slow, and standing in the corridor with the piles of luggage beyond you stoop to the window and see pillars passing by, a forest of pillars, and the train noses among them to find its berth. And does. And halts.

"Grand Central! All out! Grand Central! Last stop!"

The last stop? Yes, for me the first and last stop, the only stop, after a long detour at a way-station. This is New York again. This is home again. This is where I was originally going, and this is where I have finally got. Once when I was twenty-two I stood in a corridor here waiting for that vestibule door to open, and my heart leapt then and my heart leaps now.

"Johnny. Do you know something, Johnny?"

"What?"

"This is where you were born."

"Here?"

"Yes, here."

And in a way I too.

So we came back to New York, in the autumn of Pearl Harbor.

On the surface there were many changes. On the surface and under the ground. The trolley tracks had been torn up from Madison Avenue, and the El was being torn down on Sixth, and a new subway had been opened on Eighth, and in front of Rockefeller Center — no longer rivet-ridden, at last completed — trees had been planted. Trees on Fifth Avenue, real trees with real leaves, now yellowing and falling. But all those things were mere minor alterations in an old acquaintance, an old love. Basically nothing had changed at all — except possibly ourselves. We could afford a river view once more, and we had one — framed in the windows of the apartment we leased on Eighty-ninth Street. It was the same river of which we had had a fractional view from Tudor City, and a wide view from Sutton Place, and over which we had ridden daily while en route to and from Jackson Heights, but now I felt that I had a better perspective on it. In fact I felt I had a better perspective on the whole city, and that Lyle had also. We may make mistakes again, I thought, but I doubt if they'll be the same mistakes. We may encounter difficulties, but they probably won't be the same difficulties. And whatever they are — whatever awaits us around this bend, beyond that hill, behind this door — I think we can meet them.

Such were my thoughts in those last months of peace, in that autumn of Pearl Harbor.

But what can be said about Pearl Harbor now, at this date, except that it happened? It is the dividing line in most lives, the zone change, and so it is in mine, and yet the day itself, the Sunday, is as cold and distant to me now as a steel engraving of any other historical event. I have since been informed with minute exactness what almost all those I know were doing at the particular moment when they heard the news, and how they heard it and what they felt and what they thought and what they said, and according to each of them that one instant became permanently and uniquely frozen into the dramatic — to Mama coming out from church, to Papa climbing the post office steps, to Orin and Irmadee sitting down to a hungover brunch, to Fern washing his car and Zelda washing her hair. And I suppose it comes back to me as being dramatic, too. And yet it somehow comes back as a static kind of drama — a set piece, a tableau, a still life from which both motion and emotion have been evaporated.

What we were doing was giving a cocktail party, our first since our return — our housewarming. I'm not certain who it was who happened to twist the dial from one station to another, but I do know that at one moment the buzz of conversation was rising briskly above a muted version of "The Hut-Sut Song" and that at the next it had completely died in the face of catastrophe. There were perhaps twenty-five people present, and seconds earlier they had been laughing and talking and moving about and seconds later they were to be talking and moving about again, though not laughing. But now at this one instant, this frieze on the walls of memory, all are arrested and motionless, as if engaged in childhood's game of "Statue." The pretty girl from *Panorama,* wearing the red dress, is motionless, and so is the ardent and amorous young man with her. Natalie sitting in the wing chair is motionless, and the smoke from her cigarette curls forever upward. Ben is about to set his glass down, and never does. Lyle is reaching for the cocktail shaker standing atop the mahogany chest, but he never grasps it. Mr. Kendrick sits on the sofa flanked by the two alabaster lamps he had once given us, and his jaw always hangs gaping in their pink glow.

That is the way it is and always will be to me, like a single frame in a motion-picture reel which the projectionist has suddenly and capriciously stopped. And then the machine starts again and the figures move again.

I moved, too. But not immediately. Around me I could sense the progressive reactions which I myself was experiencing, those swift and universal reactions of shock, disbelief, momentary panic, and finally gradual realization and acceptance. And already — yes, already — the inevitable patterns were being established: molds sliding neatly into the grooves which were waiting for them. From Mr. Kendrick came a raging "He said he hated war, and now look what he's got us into! He provoked 'em! They're bastards all right, but the fact is he provoked 'em!" And across the room there was even a kind of satisfaction in Ben's voice as he said, "Well, we're in it now, sure as shooting. And about time. Now we can form a united front. . . ."

Sure as shooting. Yes, that was it. Sure as shooting.

I had a tray of canapés in my hand, which is a silly thing to be holding at the moment a war comes, though probably no sillier than any other, and replacing it on a table I headed out toward the hall. Why the hall? I didn't know. Did I intend to turn to the left, toward Callie and the kitchen? Or to the right, toward Johnny and the bedrooms? I turned to the right. Going down the hall, I paused at Johnny's door and opened it. He was hunched over his play table, biting his tongue and industriously engaged with crayons and paper. He glanced upward. "Is the party over?"

"No, not yet. Are you all right?"

"Sure. I'm all right."

I hesitated. What would it mean to him even if I did tell him? He was little more than six and a half years old. Let him learn about it later — the later the better. If possible, though I knew it wasn't, let him never learn about it at all. So I started to close the door again.

"Be good."

"I am good."

"You're very good."

Then I found myself going into our bedroom, and once there I realized that I had left the others because I had wanted to be alone a little. And although I might be the hostess, this was one party where no hostess would be needed to stimulate and guide conversation. This party's conversation would take care of itself. So I seated myself in a boudoir chair and let my head relax back against its edge and gazed up at a ceiling I didn't see.

That was where Lyle found me, there in the chair. I looked up and saw him standing in the doorway, leaning against it with his hand on its frame. How long he had been there I didn't know.

"Roy and I are going to have to go up to the office in a little while," he said. "We'll probably have to rip up the whole issue."

"All right."

Then he came forward, and stood beside the chair. "You feeling O.K.?"

"Of course."

"Then why the retirement?"

"Oh — no reason."

Placing his hands on the arms of the chair, he bent toward me. "What are you doing in here brooding? What are you thinking about?"

"You."

"Why?"

"You know why."

"Um-hum. I guessed as much." He took my hand, fondling it. "Now, look, I'm no more martial than the next man, probably less. But you wouldn't want me not to practice what I've been preaching, would you?" I made no answer, and he began to smile. "Just where have you been seeing me, anyway? Inside a tank? Or down in a submarine, maybe? Or was it in the cockpit of a bomber, heading up for the wild blue yonder?"

"You can laugh, if you like — now." The fact was that I had been seeing him in all those places, and worse.

He did laugh, briefly. And then he perched himself on the arm of the chair, his arm around my shoulder. "Now let's be reasonable. I'll be getting into it, yes — that's inevitable. In my particular case, what with the soapbox I've been up on, it's even obligatory. But there are different kinds of war, and the chances are that mine will be the dull kind, not the dangerous kind."

"How do you know? How can you tell?"

"Because it's the only way it makes sense. They'll reclassify me and draft me and I'll probably end up sorting out shoelaces behind a counter in some Quartermaster's depot in Oklahoma. Or maybe I can get a commission, and they'll prop me up in front of a typewriter at 90 Church Street or in the Munitions Building down in Washington." He soothed my shoulder, caressingly. "After all, I'm crowding forty and — let's face it — I'm a tired old man."

Suddenly I reached up and pulled him down toward me, tightly, possessively, even fiercely.

"Not to me you aren't," I said. "Not to me. . . ."

We were all white-collar people and for all of us the war began as a white-collar war, although for some of us it wasn't to continue that way. Except for Callie's Everett, whom I never met and who always remained a rather legendary figure to me, there were few among my personal acquaintances who went to work in what had once been termed "defense" plants and which now, overnight, had become "war" plants. Everett went on the swing shift in a Jersey City ball-bearing factory, and thereafter I heard even less about him than usual. And Papa wrote that he had lost Kelly to a turret lathe in an aircraft factory in Wichita. But otherwise conversion seemed to be taking a gradual and typical form. Ben's collar remained white, or at most striped, as he labored among the pamphlet-filled rooms of the Outpost headquarters of the Office of War Information, and later on a snapshot from Irmadee indicated that Orin's was white above his Navy blues at Great Lakes. (Orin in the Navy, I thought. Wouldn't you know Orin would choose the Navy?) And Lyle's collar was white at first also, a stiff starched white with a black silk tie, but it didn't stay white for long because he had barely got into uniform when a newly issued Army regulation prescribed khaki with a brown wool tie.

"Khaki, mind you," he said, when the order came out. "Just like a real soldier, practically. From now on it looks as if it'll be really rugged."

"Do all captains have to wear khaki shirts now?" asked Johnny. "Would Colin Kelly have had to wear one too?"

"I don't know," he said. "Colin Kelly was a different kind of captain. I don't know what he'd have had to do."

"Now, darling, no more of that," I said. "Please."

"All right, all right."

Yes, he was a captain and we were among the lucky ones, for he was subjected to no training and I had to follow him to no camps. He was directly commissioned, and in company with a vinous-nosed lieutenant colonel named MacArthur (no relation) he spent his days in a small, mauve-walled, bronze-lamped suite of offices on Fifth Avenue where he attempted to "co-ordinate" the magazines — more especially the picture magazines — with War Department policy. No one seemed too certain what the co-ordination should consist of, particularly the War Department, but apparently someone wanted it done and so he did it. The Fifth Avenue office was his post, and he rose in the morning and went there just as if he had been going to his office at *Panorama,* the chief differences being that he received considerably less money and wore a uniform, and he came home at night. Bataan might be falling, and finally Corregidor, but Captain Lyle Ellery, AUS, came home at night. Every night.

We had every reason to be well content — and yet we weren't.

That is, Lyle wasn't. I knew why, of course: it was due to the inevitable contrast between what he had been doing when war had been only a threat and what he was doing now that it was a reality. At first he was good-humored enough about it. "They also serve who sit," he observed, and when the adjective "chairborne" came into current and jocular usage he employed it freely. But gradually as spring came on his good humor began to be corroded with the acid of frustration. I think I first noticed it on that day when, in a flurry of pride, I bought a small service flag and hung it in the front window, only to have him wordlessly remove it and drop it into the wastebasket. Looking back now, I realize that what he was developing was the general pattern of the home-front soldier's neurosis, the symptoms of which I have since seen evidenced in others, sometimes genuinely and sincerely and sometimes being merely assumed as a social convention. But I didn't realize that it was a neurosis then. At the time, he seemed to me to be simply unappreciative of his good fortune — and mine.

"But we're so lucky," I said, before I had become fully aware of the trend his mind was taking. "Think of the men scattered all over the country at those dreary camps. Think of the ones stationed in Iceland and North Ireland."

"That's just the trouble," he said. "I do."

"Would you be happier if you were miserable?"

"Possibly."

"Well, I wouldn't be."

So archaic and long ago that seems — those words, those attitudes, his as well as mine. But we were new to war then, and we had much to learn. . . .

"Consider the subway soldier," he said once, when Guadalcanal was beginning. That was in midsummer, and his heavy, self-flagellating irony was increasing daily in direct proportion to the gravity of events overseas. "He shoots not, neither does he salute much. But he gets into the movies for half-price, and if he hangs around bars long enough some generous and deluded patriot may offer to buy him a drink. It's a rich, full life."

Roy was with us then — Roy was a definite member of our circle of intimates now — and he spoke sharply.

"There's no need for you to be apologetic," he said. "You're doing your job."

"And what a job. This war isn't going to be won by people lunching with editors in the Oak Room." He gestured at the bars on his shoulder. "Look at me. I'm partly civilian and partly military and yet I'm really neither. I'm a fish out of water."

"So what are you going to do about it?" said Roy.

I held my breath, for that was a question I would never have dared ask, a challenge I would never dare give, fearing what the answer might be. Then I saw him shrug and reach again for the newspaper picture of the Guadalcanal beachhead which had prompted his self-recrimination. "I don't know. Flounder, I guess." He studied the picture. "There seem to be worse ways of floundering, judging from this."

"Much worse," I said. And I hoped he would look at such pictures long and often, because — rightly or wrongly — I preferred him to be as he was and here rather than as he felt he ought to be and not here.

But I suppose what happened was that he looked at those pictures, or at others like them, too long and too often.

He didn't tell me outright that he had applied for a change of duty. He didn't have to, because I guessed it almost immediately when he arrived home that evening on the last day of September, in a self-consciously buoyant and aggressively humorous mood, and announced, "Well, I've wangled some leave — a whole week of it. We haven't been out of town all summer. What do you say we go away someplace? To the country or someplace. Have ourselves a real vacation and forget this here now war."

Leave, I thought, and by that time I had been an Army wife long enough to know what leave could sometimes be a prelude to. But in order to make certain I said, casually, "You couldn't arrange to postpone it for a while, could you? If we took Johnny with us, we'd have to interrupt his school just when he's getting started, and — "

"No, I can't very well postpone it. It's all set. You know how those things are."

I didn't know, but I was at least beginning to suspect. "Well, naturally we wouldn't *have* to take Johnny. We could leave him with Callie."

"Oh, no. He comes with us. The whole damn family. And we'll give Callie a holiday."

"But — "

"Now, look. I don't get leave very often. Don't you think we ought to do it my way?"

"Of course."

So we did it his way, which meant pretending that the leave was just ordinary leave. And on the whole I think it was a good way, probably the best way. Roy loaned us the station wagon from his Southampton house, and with the aid of it and the extra gasoline coupons which Lyle's leave entitled him to we were able to make the drive out to Montauk Point, where we had rented a cottage belonging to some friends of Natalie's. She had warned us that the place was rather on the primitive side, and it was — especially the plumbing — but its isolation and its view of the ocean compensated for that. Anyway, except for the first two days, when it rained steadily, we were on the beach most of the time. We really didn't do much — walked among the dunes, one day rented a boat and went out fishing and caught nothing, went to bed early and rose late. We didn't see a newspaper all during our stay, and didn't hear a radio, and except for the nightly dimout and the neighboring Naval Station and the Coast Guard patrol boats cruising intermittently offshore there wasn't any war at all for us. Lyle didn't even wear his uniform, having temporarily abandoned it in favor of flannel slacks and a sweater. . . . It was a wonderful week. Artificial and contrived, but wonderful.

And then it was over, almost. It was our last afternoon, one of those unseasonably hot afternoons which sometimes come in early October, and because Johnny had been begging all week for a swim in the ocean, which he had never been in, we had let him get into his bathing suit and had taken him down to the beach and now we sat watching him as he played in the surf. As long as I live I'll never forget that afternoon — for several reasons. I'll never forget the cloudless blue of the sky, the bright hard yellow of the beach, the green-and-white of the breakers, and the silence broken only by Johnny's occasional shrieks of terrified delight and the cawing of the circling gulls. By the calendar it was officially autumn, yet as we sat there on a spread-out blanket it seemed to be summer again, the last of summer and therefore the best. Sitting with my arms clasped around my hunched-up knees, I looked out at the sea. No patrol boats were in sight that day, and so there wasn't any war here either. Here least of all. And yet somewhere deep down under those waters there probably were the machines of war, and somewhere far away in the sky over them, and the surf which rolled here was part of the same sea which boomed against the impregnable shores of the fortress Europe. But those thoughts I kept to myself.

Lyle was lying on his stomach with his head propped up between his hands, gazing out at Johnny, who had become sufficiently familiar with the breakers to wade out and daringly plunge into them as they crashed.

"For somebody who learned to swim in the municipal pool in Ammon, Iowa, he doesn't do at all badly in the ocean, does he?" he said.

I had been watching also. Now I smiled, and I glanced down at him. "He's like his father, maybe," I said. "His father learned to swim there, too."

Rolling over on his back, he spread his arms wide across the blanket and his hands ruffled the sand. "Yes — finally." He was silent for a moment, squinting up at the sun. "Remember the first time you ever swam in the ocean? Long Beach? Remember how scared and excited you were?"

"Um-hum." It had been on a Sunday during that summer when he had managed to get a brief job on the old *World,* and I had got up early and had met him at Penn Station. I had even packed a shoebox lunch, which had both amused and embarrassed him because he had never known the kind of girls who brought shoebox lunches.

There was a pause, and then he went on: "Remember what happened that night when I took you home to MacDougal Street?"

I nodded. "Yes, I remember that too." Looking out to sea, I saw a white gull perched unconfidently on the crest of a wave. So little it looked, and so lost. Then its wings spread, and it soared upward. But not to the shore and safety — instead, farther out. It rose higher, and its whiteness merged with the blue. . . .

His hand came out and rested on my shoe, and then it circled my ankle. "That was another first for you, wasn't it? And you were scared and excited then, too." I didn't say anything. Neither he nor anyone else could ever know how scared and excited I had been, how eager and afraid. "But if you could have looked ahead, you'd probably have been even more scared. In fact you probably would have stopped right there. You wouldn't even have begun."

"Oh, yes, I would have. Oh, yes. . . ."

With his other hand he was shading his eyes against the sun — or was it against me? Perhaps it was against me, for he was not normally a demonstrative man and he was rarely given to extravagances of emotion. "There are so many things I've wanted to tell you and ought to have told you and never have," he said. "How can I expect to get them all into one afternoon?"

So it was coming now, at last: the time for pretending was over.

"Why just one afternoon?" There, that was an opening for him, if he wanted to take it.

But apparently he didn't, yet. He had withdrawn his hand from my ankle and had placed it on the sand again, and he wasn't even touching me. Therefore what he said was just that much more remarkable, for although in moments of physical intimacy he could and did use endearments he usually used them then and then only. But now he lay alone and apart, with nothing to prompt his speech except the mind and the heart. "Where would I be without you?" he said. "Nowhere. What would I be? Nothing. And yet all I've done is take and all you've done is give."

I didn't look at him. I couldn't. . . . But if words could be weighed like gold, those would have been of a price which no one could have paid, no king and no country. And I recalled something his mother had once told me: "Don't love him too much. Try to love him as little as you can, and still get along. Because you'll never get as much as you give, never in a million years." But I had got as much, and it hadn't taken any million years, either.

Leaning over, I kissed him. "It isn't true," I said. "Just take my word for it. It isn't true at all."

He made no answer, but he took my hand and placed it on his shirt front. He lay looking up at the sky, and I relaxed back and lay looking at him. For a time there was only the sound of the gulls and the surf.

"Darling," he said then, "I've got some news for you. I'm going overseas."

"I know."

"I sort of had an idea you did."

"When?"

"Tuesday."

Tuesday — three days.

"Where?" Not the Pacific, I hoped. Anywhere except the Pacific, because the Pacific was where all the action was. Elsewhere, there was just waiting.

He pointed eastward. "That way."

"England?"

"Mm."

After all, it had been a silly question, for there was no place he could be going in that direction except England — or Iceland.

Suddenly he turned and held me close, his cheek against mine. "I don't want to go," he said. "I'm no Eager Beaver. But I have to go. You understand that, don't you?"

"Of course I do."

"And you'll be all right?"

"Of course I'll be all right."

"But you'll miss me?"

"Oh, darling — darling. . . . Every day and every hour. Nights and noons and all the time."

There was a final pressure of his hand on my shoulder. "That's all I need to know. That's enough to keep me going."

And I felt that I had enough to keep me going now, too.

He sat erect then, stood, and brushed sand from his trouser legs. Reaching out his hand toward mine, he pulled me upward. Then he turned and beckoned toward Johnny. "Come on!" he shouted.

"In a minute!"

"No — now!"

I picked up the blanket and took his arm and we started toward the dunes. Once I glanced back over my shoulder and saw that Johnny had at last come out from the water and that he was following us, running. And that is another thing about that afternoon which I shall never forget, the way he ran and how he looked against the horizon of sea and sky. A small boy in red wool trunks, running.

307

A small boy running with the fiery sun about to set behind him.

In a way that was our real good-by, there on the beach, although the official one took place at two o'clock in the morning at La Guardia Field, where he was to board a Clipper. His Army classification was as a "Casual," and a Casual he certainly seemed to be, even to the manner of his departure. He didn't look as if he were setting out for a war. Instead, he looked as if he were going duck hunting, for since the plane was technically a nonmilitary transport and was to land in Eire he wore civilian clothes — his oldest and his shabbiest. But I doubt if his appearance fooled anyone, and I doubt if that of the other passengers did either, for most of the shirts were undeniably Army shirts and not even the most garish of ties could disguise them.

He had said it wasn't necessary for me to come to the airport with him, since the hour would be so late, but I had insisted, and so we rode out in one of the air-line cars in company with three other men and their wives — very young men those were, in their early twenties, and with wives even younger. At least I suppose they were wives: they certainly didn't behave like sisters. I have never seen three couples so completely oblivious of any other presence. All through that journey in darkness there were the soft sounds of whispered endearments, and sighs, and once I turned and was greeted by a lost-and-locked embrace profiled against the light from a passing street lamp — and moments later when I cautiously looked again it was still there.

Which is easier, I wondered, sitting close beside Lyle, to see them go when you haven't even had a chance to have much time together — or when you've had a lot? Neither is easy, but which is easier? And I gazed out at the shadow of the Queensboro Bridge, over which we were passing. Over the river, I thought, as I had thought once before on another occasion. Over the river and through the wood. . . . But we had finally come out from that other wood all right, and surely we would come out from this one too.

With only minutes left we stood in the map-muraled circular waiting room at the airport and studiedly confined our remarks to the prosaic and commonplace — insurance premiums and my allotment and what to forward and what not to forward and the comparative efficiency of V-mail and air mail. But those topics exhausted themselves, and for the first time I began to think that it might have been wiser of me not to come. I glanced around the waiting room, whose atmosphere seemed almost like that of peacetime. People going "abroad." Well—abroad, overseas, there didn't appear to be much difference. There was even a convivial party of flask-equipped drunks, as at a midnight sailing in those far-off days when there had been midnight sailings, and one woman was in evening dress.

"Maybe I ought to have worn an evening dress, too," I said. "After all, it isn't as if I didn't own one."

"And I suppose I could have worn a black tie—or even a white one. Gone off in full fig."

"I wish you had. You look like a tramp. A regular old tramp. That hat, that coat—you're a disgrace to the service."

There was a silence, and suddenly I found myself wanting him to be gone. If he had to go, let him go now. Let the whistle blow or the loudspeaker blare or whatever the signal for the departure might be. But let him go and let it be over and done with. These final minutes were doing no one any good, neither him nor me.

The signal was a bell and just then, as if in answer to my request, it rang—and immediately and contrarily I wished it hadn't. It rang twice. There was a flurry of movement around us.

"Well," he said, "I guess this is it."

"So soon?"

And then he took me in his arms. "Good-by, my darling. . . ."

But the rest of it was no different from a million other good-bys which were being said then and millions more which were to be said later. It was a good-by, that was all, and at the end of it I watched him go down a corridor, watched him until he disappeared, a baggy-trousered, unpressed man wearing a battered felt hat and what was obviously an Army officer's trench coat from which the shoulder insignia had been removed.

There ought to be a band, I thought. The least there ought to be is a band, and maybe some banners. Drums and a bugle, anyway. Trumpets, even.

And after that I turned and started home. That was at two o'clock on the morning of Wednesday, October fourteenth, and for two reasons — because of what it took away from me and because of what it brought — I date time from that hour. And the rest is like steps going down.

I have dreaded this part, and now that it is here I realize that I don't know how to tell it, I don't know how to make it real. Maybe that is because it looms too large and cuts too deep. The rest I can handle, but this defeats me. Yet it is with me now in memory as it was with me then in fact and it is a part of me and so it must go in.

This is the way it began. I think and always will think that the real beginning took place there on that last afternoon on the beach at Montauk, but this is the way it began for me.

"Good night, Jim," I said, and "Good night, Mrs. Ellery," the night man answered, sleepily, and heading up the hall toward the apartment door I heard the elevator sigh shut behind me and its fading drone as it descended. Then the drone ceased abruptly, with a subterranean spasm, and all was quiet again, the vacuum quiet of three o'clock in the morning. But in my ears I seemed to hear the roar of airplane motors, and although I was progressing pedestrianly enough along this dimly lighted strip of gray carpet I was also aboard a Clipper, winging northward, northward and eastward. I had never even seen a Clipper, except in photographs, and I knew that they certainly couldn't bear much resemblance to the only plane I had ever actually ridden in, which had been an exhibition barnstormer at the Manila County Fair when I had been sixteen. Yet now, through some mysterious chemistry, I was in a Clipper soaring high above a dimmed-out coast line and heading out across the Atlantic.

Pausing at the door, I fumbled for my key and then inserted it into the lock and turned it. . . . Now comes the worst moment, I decided analytically; even worse than watching him walk down that corridor. This entering for the first time and knowing that he isn't in and that he won't be coming in, this knowing that he isn't even on the same continent any more. But once it's over, once it's past, you'll be able to do it a thousand times again without even ever giving it a thought. You'll get used to it.

So I opened the door, and I went in. It wasn't bad. It wasn't bad at all. Just a sort of empty feeling.

I'm not sure what I expected to see — the table lamp lit in the foyer, probably, and the rest all darkness. What I didn't expect to see was a broad shaft of light from the hallway slanting out into the living room and Callie's angular figure outlined against it, Callie wearing her brown blanket bathrobe and with her bony ankles bare above her huge felt slippers.

I reached for the wall switch, and flicked it. Twin pools of pink welled up from the two alabaster lamps on their tables.

"You shouldn't have waited up for me, Callie," I said. "It's late. You ought to be in — "

And then I stopped. Beyond her, farther down the hallway, I heard a whimpering wail, a kind of moaning.

"Mis' Ellery," she said. "Johnny, he's sick. He's been sick all night."

I moved toward her. Ever since our return from Montauk he had had a slight cold, but it had seemed so trivial — sniffles mostly — that we had paid little attention to it. It was a cold, that was all. In his time he had had many of them.

"What's wrong?"

I could see that she was frightened, and she didn't frighten easily. "I don't know. He's only got two degrees of temperature, but he threw up all his supper and his head's as hot as fire." She turned in toward his room, where the night light was burning. "You just look at him, Mis' Ellery. You just look."

I did look. He lay sprawled diagonally in the bed, drowsily awake and uttering those small noises. His face was flushed, but his lips were pale. I placed my hand on his forehead, and it was as she had said it was — like fire. And it was damp with sweat. His whole body was damp, his pyjamas dark with wet.

"Mis' Ellery, I'm scared."

But I wasn't, yet. I don't know why: I just wasn't. And I remember thinking, "I'm glad this happened after Lyle left rather than before. It would have worried him."

I bent toward the bed. "Darling, what's the matter?"

"I hurt."

"Hurt where?"

"All over."

"He's been so cross," said Callie. Reaching out, she placed a pink palm against his cheek — and he shrank away. "See? He don't want me even to touch him."

"Does your head ache?"

"Yes."

I pulled back the covers. "Sit up a minute, dear. Let me look at you."

"No."

"Please, dear."

"No, I don't want to."

"Now, Johnny." Putting my arms around him, I started to draw him upward. He lay back, protesting and rigid, as I lifted him. "You've got to let me — "

And then he screamed. . . . Always I hear that scream. Sometimes I awake in the middle of the night and hear that scream, and when I do I can still feel his dead weight as he lay there stiff in my arms.

I try to piece all this together now, and I realize that it was at that instant, when he screamed, that I felt the first sharp jagged flash of fear. And yet I managed to stifle and suppress it as I had managed before. Because I had experienced that same fear often, though always fleetingly: I suppose there are few parents in my generation who haven't been haunted by it at one time or another. He had been seven in April and now was seven and a half, and in all those seven and a half years I doubt if he had ever complained of a chill or a fever or an ache when I hadn't for a fractional instant thought, "Maybe it's — " But I never permitted myself to use the word, or the words, even in my mind. I always censored the end of my thought. And I censored it now.

But Callie didn't. Her voice was hoarse. "Mis' Ellery, he couldn't maybe have — ?"

I spoke quickly, not even allowing her to finish. I probably spoke curtly, too. "We'll have to try Dr. Wenner, from downstairs," I said. "Go get Jim and ask him to bring him up."

"Now?"

"Yes, now."

She left swiftly, her slippers shuffling, and I remained standing by the bed, gazing downward. Then I took off my coat and hat and placed them on a table, and after that I drew a chair up beside the bed and seated myself on it. There'll be a little wait, I thought. It will take time for her to get Jim, and more time for Jim to rouse the doctor, and still more time for the doctor to rouse himself. There'll be a little wait, and meanwhile there's nothing you can do. Except not think. That you can do. As Papa always says, "Night's no time for thinking."

But I did think, I couldn't help it. Tell me, where is fancy bred, in the heart or in the head? For me, sitting there and leaning forward and listening to the heavy rasp of that uneven breathing, it seemed to be bred in both. The mind conjured up images and the heart reacted to them. As vividly as if someone had laid an icy hand on my shoulder, I felt the cold clutch of panic.

"Johnny," I whispered. "Johnny."

He stirred slightly, but either he didn't hear or he couldn't.

Rising, I went to the window and, pulling up the shade, looked up at the sky, or at as much of it as could be seen between the buildings. The night was clear and, for New York, even starry. A good night for flying. A good night for . . . Then I turned and went back toward the bed again. This can't be happening, I thought. I'm dreaming it. I've come home and have gone to sleep and now I'm having a nightmare in which the worst imaginable aspect of Lyle's absence is presenting itself. All I have to do is wake up and it will all be over. I'll be able to sit down tomorrow and write him about it. "After you left I had the most awful dream," I can write. "I dreamed that I came home and found that that little cold of Johnny's had developed into — "

Leaning down, I touched the fevered flesh — and I knew that it wasn't a dream.

313

"Johnny." I spoke the name aloud now. "Johnny, Johnny."

I knelt and prayed then, I who had neither knelt nor prayed for many years. I had almost forgotten how to pray, but I did the best I could.

Steps going down, down.

That was the longest night of all, and the day it gave way to was the longest day. Most nights have a definite end and most days have a definite beginning, but those had neither. They were continuous, the one blending into the other with no line of demarcation except that the electric bulbs eventually paled against the blatant sunshine flooding through the curtains. The doctor appeared, a stubble-chinned, sleepy, and disgruntled man wearing a purple-brocaded robe over green-striped pyjamas, and I watched him gently try to bend that dark and sweat-pebbled head which wouldn't bend and I saw him draw his finger down the arm and saw the red trail it left. I heard the city waking and the building too — the brisk rattle of garbage cans in the street below, the hum of traffic mounting, the thud of windows being shut, the slam of doors in the hall outside. The doctor was neither sleepy nor disgruntled now: instead, he was kind and considerate. He asked questions, and I answered them — "Yes, doctor." Oh, the many times I was to speak that phrase, not only to him but to the others who came after him. "Yes, doctor. Yes, doctor." The room was gray, then pink, then yellow-bright. Meanwhile people came, people went — that first and emergency doctor, another doctor, a nurse, and the room which had been a boy's room altered to a sickroom, with a sickroom's quiet and a sickroom's smell. And with each passing minute I knew, I knew, I knew. Why didn't they know too?

And then they did know. They made the spinal-fluid tests in the first pale light of daybreak, and by the time the sun had begun to inch in and the shrill canary in the next apartment had begun to greet the day the ambulance had come and they had taken him to the East Side Medical Center.

Both Natalie and Roy were with me in the consultation room at noon when the formal diagnosis was presented to me. Although the

314

doctor who made it was young he seemed permanently tired, and what he had to say he said as if by rote. It wasn't that he was unsympathetic. It was just that he had undoubtedly said the same thing so many times before that it had come to be automatic to him. His name was Kusick, and he was Roy's recommendation. According to Roy, he was the best man in the city. . . . As I was to discover later, he certainly must have been one of the most expensive.

He was seated at his desk, a thin, sallow man wearing a surgeon's smock. His words were rapid and staccato, as if he were anxious to deliver his statement as quickly as possible. "Now your boy's name is — ?"

"John. Johnny."

"Yes." He swiveled round in his chair, facing me. "Well, Johnny has poliomyelitis. You're probably already aware of that, aren't you?"

"Yes, doctor."

"Now you have a lot to be alarmed about," he said, "but I don't want you to be alarmed by the word 'poliomyelitis' itself. In fact I want you to repeat it over and over until you get used to it. Say 'infantile,' say 'polio,' say anything you like. But don't let the word itself defeat you." He paused. "Do you understand what I'm trying to tell you?"

"Yes, doctor."

He snuffed out the cigarette he had been smoking. "Unfortunately, it's respiratory, so that has to be our first concern. We'll cross the other bridges when we come to them." For the first time he hesitated. He was a frank and realistic man, and I respected him for that, although it didn't necessarily make me like him any better: I could have used some professional blandishments then, even knowing they were blandishments. "If we come to them," he added.

Then I asked a question which must have seemed as silly to him then as it did to me later. But I was still a novice in the disease, and my education was only beginning. "Will he be paralyzed?"

He glanced at me in surprise, but his voice was patient enough. "He's paralyzed now, from the waist down. Both legs. That isn't the question we have to ask ourselves now, at the moment. That we already know. But the respiratory phase — that's something else again."

Natalie was standing beside my chair, and I felt her hand press on my arm, either in consolation or in shock. I looked up at her and across at Roy and then back at the doctor — and I didn't really see any of them. And it was then that I recalled Dr. Herkle's attempt at comfort when he had told me that I could have only the one child, the one I had, and his brisk geniality as he had said, "But one's better than none, eh?" And it was then that I wondered — is it? Is one better than none? If the one dies?

I tried to fortify myself, and at last I managed to get the words out, the words the doctor was waiting for. "Will he live?"

The narrow, white-garbed shoulders lifted. "I don't know."

"When will you know?"

"Maybe today, maybe tomorrow — maybe not for weeks." He rose. The interview was over, and his relief was obvious. It couldn't have been much fun for him either. Bending toward me, he took both my hands in his, his clinical detachment vanishing. He seemed much less formidable now, and he smiled, a dark, warm, Semitic smile. "Now you go home. You hear me? You let Mr. Archer and your friend here take you home. If you can pray, pray — and if you can't, just hope. All right?"

"Yes, doctor."

So they took me home. I remember that drive. I remember it well. We sat in silence on the gray upholstery of the wide back seat of Roy's car, and as I looked through the gleaming glass it seemed to me that I had rarely seen such a beautiful October afternoon. It seemed to me, too, that I had rarely seen so many children — boys especially — in the streets. They ran, they walked, they tossed footballs, they ostentatiously and arrogantly hopscotched over lines chalked on the pavement. A troupe of agile acrobats they were, block after block of them, and I hated them all. Why were children being allowed to play in the streets in midafternoon? Why weren't they in school, where they belonged? Where were the truant officers? What did we pay taxes for?

"He's cold, that doctor," said Natalie, finally. "He undoubtedly knows his business, but he's cold."

Roy nodded. "He probably has to be."

She reached for a tasseled cord, and fingered its fringe. I imagine all three of us had the same thought in mind, but it was she who first spoke it. "Amy, how about Lyle?" she said. "Don't you suppose you ought to cable him?"

I made no answer. Once more there was the vibration of airplane motors loud in my ears. It rose above the purr of the car and drowned out the noise in the streets. And then I glanced at my watch. Two o'clock — he had been gone just twelve hours. Two o'clock here on a bright afternoon: that would mean seven o'clock there in a blackout. He would be landing very soon now. The motors gave a final flutter and then died away. . . . Well, it seemed to be very simple, keeping the mind from worrying about the possible dangers of a transatlantic flight. All you have to do is let your child contract infantile paralysis. That accomplished, anything else seems like a breeze.

"Or would you rather wait?" It was Natalie again.

"What?"

"I said would you rather wait. Until you — know a little more."

"I'd rather wait."

"Did he give you an APO number?"

"Yes."

"Well, then you know how to get in touch with him."

"Yes."

She opened her mouth as if she were about to add something more — but she didn't add it. And for the rest of the ride there was only silence again.

So it started, the waiting.

I suppose I must have slept sometime during those weeks which followed. I suppose I must have eaten, too, and brushed my teeth and bathed and performed the other necessary functions pertaining to the body. I probably even put lacquer on my fingernails and rouge on my lips and debated whether to wear this dress or that one, and when people smiled at me I may even have smiled back.

317

I do know that eventually I received a terse safe-arrival cable from Lyle, and that I replied to it with one of those equally terse and blessedly stereotyped E.F.M. messages: Nos. 35–38, "Fondest love darling loving greetings from all of us." Yes, I blush to admit that I sent that, and later at intervals I sent others, including Nos. 32–56, "All my love dearest my thoughts are with you." Standardized and codified emotion, and all for sixty cents. But the more banal and noncommittal they were the better, and in time, had they continued, I might even have been reduced to the idiocy of "Hearing your voice over the wireless gave me wonderful thrill" (No. 136). Perhaps he would think I was being economical, or possibly just lazy and unimaginative, but in either case it didn't matter.

Once I sat down and tried to write a letter, but I couldn't even bring myself to the point of starting it. That was after the news of the invasion of North Africa had come, and from the very first moment when I picked up the paper and read of the landings I had a feeling that he was not only there, either at Algiers or Casablanca or Oran, but that he had known all along that he was going to be there. "England?" I had said, and he had pointed eastward and had said, "Mm." And he had gone to England, but only as a point of embarkation for somewhere else. His war had started in earnest at last, the Real Thing. "I'll probably never hear a shot fired in anger," he had once assured me. Well, I had an idea that he was hearing plenty of them now.

So now he is in Africa, I thought, staring at a blank piece of paper, and what shall I tell him? Civilians are advised to write chatty, cheerful letters filled with intimate detail. But what kind of intimate detail can I supply? Shall I tell him that I go to the hospital once a day and that sometimes I'm permitted to stand in the doorway to Johnny's room and sometimes not? And that sometimes he knows me and sometimes he doesn't? And that when he does, it's even almost worse than when he doesn't? Should I be lightly humorous about the night nurse's volubility concerning her complicated love life or should I be interestingly statistical about the day nurse's accounts of how many polio cases she has attended and how many lived and how many died? Or should I simply enclose a picture of an iron lung and say, "This is where Johnny is. Having miserable time. Wish you were here"?

In the end I didn't write anything. I merely sent off another E.F.M. No. 66, that one was, and I suppose thousands of them were being sent then. "God bless you and keep you safe," it read, and for once the words said all I wanted them to, nothing more and nothing less.

Steps going down.

I don't want to protract those weeks. They were protracted enough as it was. But gradually the word "respiratory" was used less and less, until finally it wasn't used at all, and at last the time arrived when the day nurse — a vivacious type — could brightly and triumphantly announce, "He's coming along just splendidly. He's going to be all right." A comparative phrase, "all right." What it meant, in Dr. Kusick's more accurate translation, was that he wasn't going to get any worse. He might not get any better, but at least he wasn't going to get any worse. And he wasn't going to die.

It was Thanksgiving Day, raw and rainy, and by then I was allowed not only to enter the room but to sit beside the bed. I sat there now, in the late afternoon, trying to give thanks. But thanks for what? I found myself thinking. For the absence of the iron lung, and the presence of the plaster casts? For the threat of death lifting, and the realization of despair settling? Count your blessings, I thought, and so I attempted to. After all, I told myself, your son was stricken and he hasn't died, your husband has seen battle and he has survived — so far. Isn't that enough? What more do you want or expect — in this particular year of the world's history? So count your blessings and keep your peace.

I looked at Johnny's face, thin and wasted on its pillow and tinted a greenish yellow by the bed light which had already been switched on above his head. As a special concession in honor of the day I was being permitted to watch him eat his supper, which was turkey. But he obviously had no appetite, and his fork scratched listlessly against his plate. I tried to make conversation. It wasn't easy.

"Would you like to keep the letter?" I said. It was a letter from

319

Lyle, his first from Africa. "Shall I put it here on the table so that you can read it again?"

Except for the intermittent scratching of the fork there was silence. In fact there had mostly been silence for the past half hour. He wasn't a "good" patient; he never had been. He was like Lyle in that way. He was like Lyle in so many ways.

I made a new start. "Guess who's coming to see you today. Natalie and Ben and Mr. Archer. And then I'm going out with them and we're going to have turkey too."

There was no response to that either. Instead, after a moment, he pushed his tray away.

"Don't you like it, honey? Aren't you hungry?"

"No."

He lay back, looking at the ceiling, and his hands were quiet on the coverlet. I sat just outside the circle of light, and I was grateful that he couldn't see my face as clearly as I was seeing his.

"What's the matter, Johnny? What are you thinking about?"

"I'm tired of being in bed. I want to get up."

"You'll be getting up some day." Maybe.

"When?"

"Well — I don't know."

He had turned his face away from me now, and I saw only the dark profile of his head. He had a well-shaped head, and that was Lyle's also. His head and his eyes and the very way he walked — or had walked.

"Mama." He rarely called me "Mama." Usually it was "Mother."

"Yes, dear?"

"I almost died, didn't I?"

"Now that's all over. You're to forget about that."

But he went on, persistently. "My legs did die. If my legs died, why didn't the rest of me die, too?"

"Darling, these things take time." I fell back on the jargon of consolation. "You have to — have patience." And who am I to counsel patience for him? I thought. I'm not lying there and he is.

Then I saw his shoulders begin to twitch convulsively, and I knew that he was crying. It was the first time he had cried. He had sulked and had been petulant and often darkly moody, but until now he hadn't cried. For a moment I didn't move. I was well aware that this was an occasion when I ought to be controlled and impersonal and kindly corrective, but I didn't know how to begin.

"I want to go home," he said. "I want to go home."

Rising, I went toward the bed and seated myself beside him. "Johnny — don't. Please don't."

The sobs continued, and all my firm resolves not to give way either to fruitless pity or to even more fruitless self-pity deserted me. Leaning over, I took him in my arms, half a child, half soft warm flesh and the rest hard and unyielding plaster. "Darling, darling," I said. "You mustn't. You can't give up now. You have to be brave. You have to have hope. . . ." Yes, I said all that, and more too — but they were just words without conviction, and I knew it and he probably knew it also. They weren't real in the way the casts on his legs were real.

The door opened then, and there were brisk steps and the flapping of starched skirts. It was the day nurse, Miss Fairfax. Her expression was usually sweet to the point of saccharinity, but as she saw us there her set smile disappeared and her face stiffened with polite disapproval.

"This won't do at all, Mrs. Ellery," she said. "It's very bad for him."

"I know." I stood. "I'm sorry."

Stooping, she removed the tray and began to straighten the sheets. "Your friends are here. But I don't believe we'd better have any visitors. Not today."

"All right." I looked toward Johnny again, but he didn't turn his head. Slowly the sobs were subsiding.

"See?" said Miss Fairfax. "He's feeling better already. He was just a little tired, that's all."

I got out of that room somehow and, leaving him to her efficient, antiseptic ministrations, started to walk down the corridor. There is a time for friends, but this wasn't one of them. I didn't want to see Natalie and Ben, or Roy either. They were good and they were loyal, but I didn't want to see them. I didn't want to see anyone except the one person it was impossible for me to see.

They were standing in the carefully calculated chintzed cheerfulness of the visitors' room, and when I appeared in the doorway they came toward me. They had presents with them — the shaggy blooms of chrysanthemums, a pile of bright-jacketed books, oblong packages which looked as if they contained games. Good samaritans they were, all of them, and I should have been more gracious than I was. But all I did was sink onto a sofa and begin to fumble at my compact.

"You've been crying," said Natalie, accusingly.

I nodded. "So has he."

"It's just as well," said Ben, firmly. "An emotional release — you'll both feel all the better for it."

Natalie seated herself beside me on the sofa. "Look," she said, "hasn't this lasted just about long enough? When are you going to break down and tell Lyle what's going on?"

I drew a lipstick around my lips. "Why should I tell him? What good would it do?"

Roy spoke gently. "They might send him home for a while. A sort of — compassionate leave."

"Send him home to do what? To hold my hand?" I stuffed the compact back in my purse. "Johnny isn't going to die. He's just going to lie there, that's all. What could Lyle possibly do that isn't being done now?"

"Well, at least tell him what's happened," said Natalie. "At least let him know."

"Did he let me know that he was going to Africa?"

"What does that have to do with it?"

"A lot. He didn't want me to worry — and I don't want him to worry. The least I can do is try to spare him — "

"Spare him!" she interrupted, and made a gesture of impatience. I suppose she had been restraining her disapproval for so many weeks that she at last had to let it out. "That's exactly the sort of attitude I'm objecting to. Why don't you be realistic and face a few

322

facts? You're in no position to be sparing anyone, least of all him. If you ever needed his help, you need it now."

"And he needs mine." I rose. From their silence I could tell that both Roy and Ben were in agreement with her and that the matter had probably been discussed among them before. She was being kind, she was being well-meaning, they all were being kind and well-meaning, but they hadn't thought it all out as I had — for long days and longer nights. They might believe that they knew all the answers, but the fact was that they didn't know any of them. Not as I did. And suddenly I felt a rising and unreasoning resentment against the three of them. I glanced round at their earnest, good-intentioned faces. "Don't you see?" I said. "Don't any of you understand? I *can't* tell him. I can't possibly."

For an instant none of them answered. Then Natalie said, "Listen, gallantry is all very fine and you're being very noble. But you're also being very foolish. You — "

I found myself starting to tremble. "Do you think I like being 'gallant'?" I said. "Do you think I enjoy being 'noble'? And don't you realize that I'd give all the rest of my life if when I go into that room Lyle were here to go in with me? Do you imagine for one minute that I'm doing what I'm doing for *fun?*"

And after that I turned and left her, left them all. I had to. I hurried down the endless corridor, toward the elevators, and I even started to run a little. And I was beginning to cry again and I knew that I had spoiled my make-up again and all for nothing.

That was the evening I wrote him my first letter, the first of that long, long series of letters which were compounded of lies, all lies. And this is what I wrote:

Thanksgiving Day

DARLING:

We've had our turkey and Johnny has just gone off to bed in an overstuffed condition and the frost is on the pumpkin and the fodder's in the shock. . . .

Steps going down, down, down.

⇛ X ⇚

THAT ENTIRE YEAR IS FOREVER LOST to me. Like other years, it must have had a winter and a spring and a summer and an autumn, but I don't remember any of them. And yet it was a year which will be judged highly important and even decisive, for it was the one during which Africa was won and a part of Italy and the one when the Russian tide turned and the stepping-stones of the islands of the Pacific began to be bridged, slowly, arduously, confusedly, bloodily. But I have said before that this is my history, not that of a war, and for me it remains a year of almost total blankness. I look back now and think, "What happened then? There are twelve whole months. Surely all of them can't have been completely empty of incident. What did you do, aside from grow older — and more than twelve months older?"

Well, what did I do? I subleased the apartment, furnished, and moved from seven rooms on Eighty-ninth Street to two on Bank Street, which is only a few blocks and a lifetime from MacDougal Street. I returned to work as Mr. Kendrick's secretary. I borrowed three thousand dollars from Roy, and Papa sent me five hundred. Mama came East for a month of solace and tears and I dutifully piloted her through Macy's and to the top of the Empire State Building and took her to see *Oklahoma!* I went to the dentist and I read *A Tree Grows in Brooklyn* and I belatedly acquired the cigarette habit and eventually reached the point of a package a day. I lost eight pounds. I —

But there is no use in my trying to dredge up any of those things, because they were all externals, even the eight pounds. This is what I really did. I sat beside Johnny's hospital bed in the presence of a disaster I could see and touch, and then I went home to type out those fictional fabrications for Lyle, any one of whose many possible disasters — to be encountered anywhere on the long road that led from the Kasserine to Bizerte and on to Sicily — I could only imagine. That was where my true life lay, my inner life, in those daily visits to the hospital and in letters, the ones I sent and the ones I received. Everything else was a waste and a waiting.

No, I cannot render any accounting of that lost year. And I suppose the reason I can't is that my spirit was petrifying during it as rigidly as Johnny's legs had petrified. I suppose, like them, I withered. I suppose that in a way I even died.

This was December. This was the season of influenza, and a fetid closeness in Madison Avenue buses, and a slush speckled with a thousand varieties of soot and grime. This was the time when the outdoor cages in the Central Park zoo were deserted and wind-swept, when subway platforms were a miasma of coughs and sneezes and puddles formed from dripping umbrella tips, and when overage and 4-F Santa Clauses were beginning to take up their stations on street corners, there to shiver disconsolately while their barrel organs whined "I'm Dreaming of a White Christmas." This was December, when it seemed as if the sun had disappeared from the universe, never to show its face again.

At the end of the day I sat at the same desk in the same office where I had so often sat before, while through the doorway I could see Mr. Kendrick talking on the telephone to Charlie Belden, his income-tax consultant. I could not only see him, I could hear him, and so could anyone passing in the hall, for time had not mellowed Mr. Kendrick and when he made mention of that-man-in-the-White-House, as he was making mention now, his mood was ever vindictive and vituperative. "God damn it, Charlie," he was bellowing, "I know it's not your fault, but that man and his Morgenthau are nailing me right to the cross, that's what they're doing. They're

325

crucifying me. They're . . ." But I didn't need to listen any longer, for I had heard all the rest of it many times before and would undoubtedly be hearing it many times again. In fact I felt that if I were to shut my eyes a whole decade would be erased: I in this room, Mr. Kendrick in the next one complaining about Roosevelt. This is where I came in, I thought. This is where I came in.

But a decade ago there had been no magazine called *Chic* and no Junior Misses for it to cater to, and it was the current issue of *Chic* which I was now leafing through. It was filled with pictures of girls in their teens — so completely and currently in their teens that they seemed to be not so much individuals as a type, and a caricature of a type at that. Which came first, I wondered idly, Sinatra and swooning — or these phenomena called bobby-soxers? Do they like all those things because they are fourteen, or do they like them because they happen to be fourteen and are expected to like them? Do they copy the fashions, or do the fashions copy them? Certainly nobody had ever made a cult — much less a Big Business — of Irmadee and Zelda and me and all the rest of us when we had been fourteen. We had just been fourteen, that's all, and at the time no one had regarded it as being particularly remarkable or eccentric of us.

From the other room there came the crash of the phone being slammed down, and in a moment Mr. Kendrick came out from his office, hat on head and overcoat over his arm. He was glowering. Sometimes I wondered how his arteries had managed to survive three terms of Roosevelt. And yet in a way he seemed to thrive on his obsession, and perhaps he even would have felt a little lost without it.

"Just talking to Charlie Belden," he said, unnecessarily.

"Yes?"

He began to shoulder himself into his overcoat. "Yes. Taxes going up again. Good grief, what do you suppose they *do* with the money? You know, I wouldn't be surprised but what Eleanor's caching a lot of it away somewhere."

"Oh, now, Mr. Kendrick. Really." Although his harp had but one string, that string was capable of infinite and often fantastic variations.

"Well, I wouldn't put it past her. How can you tell? Maybe she's got a secret strongbox off there in the Kremlin."

Laying aside the copy of *Chic,* I reached for a sheet of paper and rolled it into my typewriter. I shrugged. "A war is expensive."

He was buttoning up his overcoat and arranging his scarf. "If it wasn't a war, it'd be something else. It always has been, right from the start. 'Soak the rich' is his motto. So what's he going to do when there aren't any more rich? What's the country itself going to do?"

I didn't answer, knowing that he didn't really expect me to. His phobia had long since reached the self-nourishing stage, and any questions he asked were likely to be purely rhetorical, for he had all the answers before he asked them. . . . I began to type. "Darling," I typed, almost automatically because it was for perhaps the hundredth time. The hundredth? Two letters a week for a period of over a year. Yes, it would be about the hundredth. And each one was just as difficult as the first had been.

He was putting on his gloves. "Time to shut up shop. Aren't you going home?"

"I thought I'd write a letter."

He shook his head disapprovingly. "You and those letters of yours. I swear I don't see how you do it. What on earth do you tell him?"

"Oh, I — make up things."

"What kind of things?"

I hesitated. "All sorts of things." Happy things, mostly. Good things. I looked down at my fingers as they rested on the typewriter bar. "You'd be surprised. I've really become quite an accomplished liar."

He was silent for a moment, and I felt his mood change. Not many people knew Mr. Kendrick as I did. Not many people knew his capacity for sympathy, even a kind of tenderness. When I had come to him and had applied for a job — any job — he had merely nodded toward my old desk and had said, "There you are. It's been waiting for you. And it's yours as long as you want it." I had almost begun to cry then, I had been that touched. I had cried a good deal during those early months, though I didn't any more. Neither did Johnny.

327

That was the trouble, or one trouble. Sometimes I felt I would prefer to have him cry rather than just lie there as he did.

"Where is he now, Amy?" he said.

"Lyle?"

"Yes."

"Naples. Or at least he was the last time I heard from him."

"Naples, hm." Turning, he faced the wall where he had had a large map hung whose pins and ribbons and tiny flags he rearranged daily in accordance with the morning headlines. It was his toy and his joy, that map, and whenever he stood before it he seemed to be regarding himself as a latter-day Clausewitz. He stooped and extended a finger. "Right there. Right there he is."

"Yes." Open my heart and you will see, carved inside of it Italy. Hands plunged into his overcoat pockets, he stepped back and surveyed the map admiringly. "By George, we've come a long way, haven't we?" he said. And then his eyes roved upward, toward the column of swastikas spiking the outline of France, and after that darted swiftly over half a world and settled gloomily on the Pacific, still pockmarked with Rising Suns. He sighed. "But we've still got a long way to go yet, too." There was a silence, and then he brightened. "However, we'll get there. It may be slow, but we'll get there."

I smiled, and was unable to resist a deliberate taunt. There was so little that seemed humorous to me in those days that I was quick to seize whatever opportunities came my way. "Despite the Commander in Chief?" I said.

He snorted. "Commander in Chief! What does he have to do with it?" He tapped significantly on the sands of Africa, and nodded toward the Solomons. "It wasn't Roosevelt who was responsible for all that. It was Marshall and King, Eisenhower and Nimitz and MacArthur. Men like that. Men who've got the know-how. Big men."

I nodded, solemnly but politely. "And who was it who appointed most of the big men?"

But he ignored the query, and again concentrated his attention on the map. I could see by his air of sober meditation that he was in his George-Fielding-Eliot phase. "You know, I've been giving a lot of study to this Second Front thing lately," he announced, "and I've just about decided where it's going to be."

"Where, Mr. Kendrick?" I said, co-operatively.

Dramatically he pointed a finger at the coast of Norway. "It's going to be right there. That's the only logical place. You just wait and see."

Norway, I thought, and looked toward its fiords. Well, maybe — maybe not. Certainly it was as good a guess as any. Better than mine, anyway, if only because I had none.

He left then, having delivered himself of his sage prediction, and I turned again to my letter. Each time I wrote it seemed to me that I was always having to explain something. I had had to explain why I had chosen to sublease the apartment and take a smaller one ("It seems so much more sensible"), and why I had returned to work ("It keeps me occupied, and Mr. Kendrick needed someone"), and now I was faced with having to explain why I hadn't sent any photographs of Johnny. "I'd like to see how he's growing," Lyle had written. "So get out your Brownie and start to work. You don't need to try anything fancy. Just a snapshot will do."

Just a snapshot, I thought. How about a sheaf of X-rays? . . . Well, he had mentioned the pictures before and had then apparently forgotten about them. Maybe he would forget about them again. Meanwhile I could always say that I was sending them under separate cover, and they could always be conveniently lost. And if not that, then I could devise something else. After a year of such letters I felt capable of devising almost anything.

But at the moment my inventiveness seemed to be lagging, and I sat for a long time without writing anything. Outside, in the corridor, there was a steady patter of feet heading toward the elevators and the repeated exchange of "Good nights." I dreaded this pre-dinner hour. I dreaded all hours, but this one most. And yet I preferred to spend it here in the office rather than in the apartment on Bank Street. It was a comfortable and even cheerful apartment, and Callie insisted on coming in several evenings a week to cook for me, but somehow I had never got quite accustomed to it. Perhaps that was because it and its alien furniture held no associations for me.

Yet its very anonymity had been one reason why I had moved, in addition to the all-compelling reason that I had been unable to afford not to. You can pretend you're just a Village girl again, I had thought. But since then I had learned that I was too old to be a Village girl.

I smoked one cigarette, and then another, and after that I found myself rising and strolling toward Mr. Kendrick's map. I stood looking at it, especially at the row of pins which divided the Italy which had been won from that which had still to be won. Naples now, and probably Rome next. But there was still a far distance to be covered before Rome would be reached, and even farther to the northern border. Yet presumably this was a country which had "surrendered." And I recalled the wildly jubilant crowds in Times Square in September when that surrender flash had first come through, the confetti and the cheers and the confident celebrators climbing lampposts and proclaiming that old Mussolini was gone and old Hitler was going and that the war was practically all over except for the shouting, their shouting. And for a few brief dizzy hours I too had allowed myself to believe that it was practically over. But it wasn't over. It wasn't nearly over.

Bending down, I placed my hand on the word "Naples." Oh, darling, I thought. Oh, my darling. Are you here? Are you here where my hand is?

There was the click of the door opening, and quickly I turned away, heading briskly back toward my desk. Whoever it might be, I didn't care to have them find me mooning over a map. Not even if it was just the cleaning women.

But it wasn't the cleaning women. It was Natalie, followed closely by Ben, and both were chanting a determinedly breezy "Surprise! Surprise!" From the manner of their entrance I knew they had a purpose in mind, and even before Natalie spoke I suspected what it was. This would be the Cheering-Up-Amy Act. This would be a visitation from the Society for the Relief of the Heartsore.

It was. "Come on, get your bonnet," she directed. "We're going on a party, and you're coming with us."

"Party?" I said. "What party?"

330

She seated herself on my desk, while Ben lingered by the map. "Oh, nothing special. Just a select group of friends. You remember what friends are, don't you?"

Presumably that was an oblique reference to the fact that it had been weeks since I had called her. "I've been busy," I said. "You know."

"Sure. I know." She brushed open the collar of her mink, which represented another of Aunt Fanny's legacies. "Nevertheless, we've decided it's high time you got out of this rut you're in, or slough of despond or whatever. So come along now. And no arguments."

"Oh, I can't. Thanks just the same, but—"

"Yes, you can." Picking up the typewriter hood, she dropped it over the machine, covering Lyle's letter with it. "Whatever you're doing can wait. And you need a little extra-curricular activity. You're going stale, hiding yourself away like this. You need to get drunk or something. Light wines and dancing."

"Well . . ." And why not? I thought. Perhaps that was exactly what I did need, although I had tried to get drunk once before and had merely managed to get sick. That had been some months earlier when Orin had been in town — or "in port," as he had termed it — and we had made an exhaustive tour of Fifty-second Street together, an extrovert j.g. and his introvert girl-friend. Still, this might prove more successful. At least it was worth investigating. "All right," I said, rising and reaching for my purse. "And if you thought you were going to have to coax me, you're much mistaken."

"Now that's better," she said, and then added, as I went toward the mirror, "What news from the Major?"

"Nothing much. He wants to know what a zoot suit looks like and if I've ever seen one."

"Oh, dear." Then she hesitated, and after that asked casually, "How's Johnny?"

"Oh — about the same."

"Any more improvement in the left leg?"

"No, that's about the same too." I had always disliked people who made that evasive and irritating answer, "about the same." Yet there was nothing else for me to say. He was about the same, even though he was at last able to flex his left leg now. And I knew that he would always be about the same. And, what was worse, he knew it also.

Ben was as engrossed in the map as if he had never before seen one. "Just look at those Russians, will you?" he said now, with the pride of personal proprietorship. "Just look at that advance. Kharkov, Kiev — there's no stopping 'em." He cast a triumphant glance toward Natalie. "And remember when everybody, including a certain party who shall be nameless, said they were licked before they even began?"

"I retract, dear," she said, humbly. "I retract everything. Rub my nose in it, if you like. The fact is that Stalin's a jolly good fellow, which nobody can deny."

Momentarily mollified, he examined the map again. "But how about this so-called Second Front we're always hearing about? Are we ever going to get on with it, or aren't we? All this shilly-shally — and meanwhile Russia's practically fighting the war alone."

Shilly-shally? I thought, gazing at his reflection in the mirror. Did he call Italy "shilly-shally"? Had Africa been shilly-shally? For an instant I felt a surge of anger at again hearing his chronic complaint. "Perhaps they have to get ready for it," I said. "After all, Russia took a little time to get ready too, you know. Remember?" And then my anger began to ebb as I thought, "Now why be so malicious? The truth is that you're resentful because he's a civilian and here and safe and Lyle isn't." So I made my voice more conversational and less heated. "As a matter of fact, Mr. Kendrick was saying just this afternoon that when it does come it's going to be in Norway."

"Norway?" said Ben, contemptuously. "That's nonsense. It's even ridiculous. When it comes, *if* it comes, it's going to be — " and abruptly he halted. "However, I don't suppose I ought to say. It's Top Secret."

"Oh, come, dear," invited Natalie, winningly. "Surely you can trust us."

He glanced around him, and lowered his voice confidentially. "Well, I happened to hear about it up at the OWI from somebody who'd just come from the Pentagon and who had it straight from the brother-in-law of a man who'd talked to General Marshall himself. Only a handful of insiders know about it, of course, the very high brass, but — "

"Darling, this suspense . . ."

With another furtive glance around, and with eloquent pantomime, he stepped closer to the map and pointed to the Bordeaux area, though he zealously avoided mention of any place name. "There you are. Right there. It's all laid on — if they ever get around to it."

Lipstick in hand, I again gazed toward the map. There? Yes, it could be, it could be. Though if half a million men were scheduled to be killed, did it matter particularly where they were killed? Norway, Biscay — they'd be just as dead at either place.

It was as if there were a sudden chill in the room, and a sudden shadow, and as if Natalie felt it too. She got down from the desk. "That's enough of that," she said. "Let's go."

Putting the lipstick back in my purse and giving a final adjustment to my hat and wishing it were my good one, I turned from the mirror. "All right, I'm ready." I headed toward the door. "Come on. Let us be gay."

We were quite gay. Natalie had referred to "a select group of friends," but when we arrived at the Barberry Room, whose entrance seemed curiously familiar to me even though I couldn't recall ever having been in it, there were at least six couples waiting for us, seated at two tables which had been pushed together, and several more came in later. I never did get all their names, either then or afterward, although Ben was punctilious about the introductions. According to Natalie, it was a spur-of-the-moment gathering — "We throw these every once in a while since we Came into Money" — and the guests represented accretions ranging from the OWI to Ben's N.Y.U. days and back again, by way of the Columbia Club and Aunt Fanny's attorneys. "They're nice people, most of them," she said. "You'll like them."

And they were nice and I did like them. They were well-informed, intelligent, attractive in varying degrees, friendly, and articulate.

Especially articulate, and about so many diverse topics — Tarawa and *The Voice of the Turtle* and Red Cross pressure points and Ernie Pyle and the coal strike and the lamentable scarcity of Scotch. Theirs was a civilized, well-rounded conversation and point of view, and I enjoyed it. More than that, I envied it. They seemed to be managing to take the war in their stride. Why couldn't I?

"You're — Mrs. Ellery, is it?" said the man next to me, a rotund lieutenant colonel with the Pearl Harbor and the American Theater ribbons linked modestly across his chest.

"Yes, it is. And you're Colonel — ?" Time had been when I wouldn't have been able to identify him as Colonel anything, but I had come to be an expert on insignia.

"Beecher. War Department." He cleared his throat, rather militarily. "Mrs. Ellery, have you seen *Oklahoma?*"

"Oh, yes, I have. It's enchanting, isn't it? My mother was visiting me not long ago and we went together and she . . ."

And, as easily as that, we were off.

This is very good for me, I thought, sitting in blue-mirrored murkiness and sipping my martini and discussing *Oklahoma!* and kindred subjects. I should do this oftener, get about more, see more people. Natalie's right. I've been too much a hermit, too much alone.

And then gradually I began to sour. Was it due to that first martini and the one which came after it? Or was it due to the Colonel's fashionable absorption in a game of gin-rummy with the man on his left? I didn't know then and I don't know now. Certainly neither circumstance ought to have been responsible. The drinks should have exhilarated me instead of depressing me — and, inexplicably, antagonizing me — and the Colonel's withdrawal should have been a relief, since he had on the whole proved somewhat fatuous. But for some reason there came to be too many voices at the table, not only at the table but in the whole room, and they were all talking too much and too glibly and detachedly about too many things. Even when they spoke of the war it was in calm, reasoning tones, as if they were analyzing an intricate problem in chess. And there were too many bangles on too many wrists

334

and too many well-tailored civilian shoulders and too many peanuts mounded on too many little dishes and too much popcorn.

Isn't there any unhappy medium in war? I suddenly found myself thinking. Isn't there any middle ground between all this, where there is too much of everything, and Tarawa, where there is nothing? Yes, and between all this and Naples, where there is only a little more than nothing?

A voice was coming at me, a pleasant voice. ". . . wondered if perhaps you might be interested." It was a woman across the table, and she was leaning toward me. "In the A.W.V.S., I mean. We're always anxious for more volunteers, and if you'd care to—"

"No," I said shortly—shortly and rudely. "No, I can't. I haven't time." And immediately I regretted my rudeness, though it was too late by then, for she had turned away, clearly conscious of the rebuff and quite justifiably frigid. I started to lean toward her again, and then leaned back. In a moment I'll be pouring out all my troubles to her, I thought. In a moment I'll be telling her that I have a husband who has been overseas for more than a year and that there are a million reasons why I want him back again, aside from the usual one, which is that I want him to make love to me, and not to mention what may be a unique one, which is that his son has infantile paralysis and he doesn't even know it yet. In a moment I'll be weeping maudlinly on her shoulder and she'll be comforting me and murmuring, "Now never you mind, my dear. Things are tough all over."

"Another drink down there?" called Ben, from the far end of the table.

"Yes, please." And as I turned I noticed Natalie looking at me reprovingly. Her lips were moving, and I was able to read their message: "Now don't just sit there. Talk. Enter In." And I nodded obediently.

But just sit there was exactly what I continued to do, for somehow I found it impossible to enter in. The drink was set before me, but after one sip I didn't touch it, for I realized that no amount of drinks would do me any good in my present antisocial state. And no soft music would do me any good either, and there was soft

335

music. From a piano in a corner came the sound of adroitly manipulated chords, and after that "Smoke Gets in Your Eyes." I listened, though no one else seemed to. "Smoke Gets in Your Eyes" and then "Where or When" and then "What Is This Thing Called Love?" and after that "Night and Day," all played insidiously, artfully, for calculated effect. Bar music, it was; polite, genteel mood music — and if you didn't happen to be in the mood it would soon get you there. Not one of the songs held any particular significance for me, and yet somehow they all did. . . . They shouldn't be permitted to play things like that in wartime, I thought. It's demoralizing. There ought to be a law.

Then I became aware of a pale hand being raised across the dimness of the room and of a wrist waving gaily in my direction. Someone who knew me? Straining my eyes, I saw two men seated at a wall table, one a civilian and the other an apple-cheeked young soldier, a sergeant. It was the civilian whose hand was raised. He smiled and bowed, and I uncertainly smiled back. Oh, yes, now I recognized him — and I bowed in return. It was Glen, one of Mrs. Ellery's friends, and looking not one day older than when I had first met him. But with a soldier? I'd always been under the impression that it was usually sailors.

Perhaps it was due to seeing him, or perhaps it was due to the bar music, but all at once I knew why the entrance and location of this place had seemed familiar to me. I had been here — either here or somewhere very close in this same block — once long ago with Mrs. Ellery when the premises had been occupied by a speakeasy. Glen had undoubtedly been here with her too, and many times. Did he ever think of her? What if he were to turn to that young sergeant he was so animatedly conversing with, that sergeant who must have been running around in knee pants at the period I was remembering, and say, "There's a rather interesting thing about this room. It's haunted. There's a ghost here . . ."?

I looked down into the amber depths of my drink, and for an instant I seemed to see her face. There's a lot you don't know, I thought; at least I assume you don't know it, though maybe you do. Anyway, there's a lot you've missed. And I'm glad you missed it.

Suddenly I pushed my chair back from the table and got to my feet. This is too much, I thought, this is really too much. You're no longer fit for human society. First misanthropy, then galloping melancholia, and now visions — hallucinations, even. What next? You'd better get out of here. . . . And so I moved down the table toward Natalie and bent over her shoulder. "I'm sorry," I said. "Would you mind very much if I ran out on you?"

She glanced up and around at me, surprised. "But we're all going on to dinner together. We — "

"I know. But . . ."

Surprise gave way to sympathy. "The prescription didn't work?"

I shook my head. "No. Not very well. Maybe another time."

"All right," she said, after an instant. Her hand came up and patted mine, squeezed it. "Call me, will you?"

"I will. And you'll explain to Ben for me? And apologize?"

"No apologies needed. You tried, anyway."

"Yes," I said, turning. "Yes, I tried."

And I went out.

How shall I describe that hour which followed, or was it an hour or was it more? How shall I describe that emptiness I felt, that weariness, that loneliness? In almost every life there probably comes a time when you say to yourself, "This is the bottom. This is bedrock," and I think that was my time, from the moment when I came out into the street from that bar and, declining the door-man's offer to get me a cab, began to walk, to walk aimlessly, knowing that eventually I would have to return to Bank Street and yet not wanting to, knowing that it would have been better for me to have remained with the party and yet not wanting that either. I don't even remember where I walked. All I remember is the walking itself, slow and directionless, and the snow falling pale against the dimmed-out streets. I suppose there were passers-by, but I wasn't aware of them. I suppose there were sounds, too — voices, traffic, the hum of the city — but my ears were deaf to them. I was on an island surrounded by millions of people, and yet I was alone — walking, walking, and walking. But why, and to what end?

And then I saw it — the name "Naples." Is this an hallucination too? I thought. But it wasn't, for when I lifted my eyes I saw a neoned marquee and I realized that I was standing in front of the Lexington Avenue Trans-Lux and that the word which had loomed out at me like a beckoning beacon was part of a poster: "Liberated Naples Welcomes U. S. Troops." There were other events listed also, but those I didn't even notice. Could he be there? I thought. Could he be there waiting inside for me on a strip of celluloid curled in a tin can? Could it be possible that I might be able to get a glimpse of him? It had happened before to others — people sitting in darkened theaters and miraculously sighting the image of the beloved ten thousand miles away and suddenly crying out "There he is! Look — there!" Why couldn't it happen to me?

I didn't even hesitate. Swiftly I went toward the box office, put down my money, and pushed against the turnstile.

See Naples and live.

The improbable adventures of a vociferously and emotionally unstable duck were in progress as I entered the gray twilight and seated myself, and although ordinarily I might have enjoyed them it seemed to me on that occasion that they would never end. The audience watched the screen in sober silence, as if at a ballet. Then, having survived indignity and infinite catastrophe, including trial by fire and a ton of bricks, the indomitable fowl strutted off into the horizon for a well-deserved week's rest and recuperation, and a brass fanfare announced the start of the news program. There was a clearing of throats and a shifting of knees as the audience prepared to leave a world where bullets never killed and knives never cut and to return to the world of reality. The stern, grave voice of a commentator sounded: "Naples. Veterans of Pantelleria and Sicily, American Forces parade while Neapolitans gather to greet . . ."

I leaned forward. An armored column rumbling along a broad avenue. Faces under helmets, masses of faces. Men marching. A girl tossing a garland of flowers, and an old woman's tears, maybe of grief, maybe of joy, maybe of both. (But hadn't garlands been strewn before Hitler, too, from Prague to Paris, and hadn't there been tears there also? How else do you greet the conqueror?) More helmets, more faces. Abruptly I sat up straight, and held my breath. There — there, that pair of shoulders. But no, the face turned and it was merely another face. I slumped again. A truck now, packed with waving arms and upstretched hands. Smiles, hundreds of smiles, but never the smile for me. Men, thousands of them, but not the one man.

Then it was over, and I relaxed apathetically back in my seat, weak with disappointment. I ought to have known better. The whole idea had been silly. And yet, I tried to comfort myself, rationalizing, I had seen the streets and buildings he had seen, was seeing. I had seen the city. That should be something, shouldn't it? And it was, but not enough; not nearly enough.

Well, I thought, that's that. Now up. Now out. Now home.

Rising, I skirted past a row of jutting knees and started up the aisle, while around me I heard the commentator's omniscient voice resuming, amid a patter of applause: "The Big Three confer at Teheran. President Roosevelt, Premier Churchill, and Marshal Stalin meet to discuss . . ." As I continued up the aisle I glanced over my shoulder and saw them as they sat together. Again faces, but these I knew. These the whole world knew. The cherubic man with his cigar, the smiling man with his tilted cigarette holder, the equally smiling man with his solid, stocky figure and folded hands. There they were, the giants. There they were, the hope of humanity.

At the rear of the theater I paused and, leaning against the rail, stood idly, watching. What did I see? I saw what everyone else saw — two men wearing gold-braided uniforms and a third wearing a striped, double-breasted business suit. The President sat in the center, flanked by the other two, and he was laughing. And now he was turning to his right and now to his left, and the others were laughing also. The hand gestured upward with the cigarette holder, while the other hand brushed against something which was propped against his chair. What is it, I thought — that stick? Oh, yes, his cane. He has to have his cane with him because — because . . .

Suddenly I found myself seeing nothing else except that cane. The others blanked out before my eyes, and all that was left was the cane and its owner.

A cripple, I thought, a paralytic. Until now I had never particularly heeded the fact that the President was a cripple, even though I had watched scores of newsreels similar to this one and had always been vaguely aware of the sustaining arms and the special railings and ramps and all the other paraphernalia of physical dependency. Sitting in theaters, I had dutifully but rather absently dropped coins into baskets passed during the annual March of Dimes campaigns; I had read of the Birthday Balls, though I had never felt any inclination to attend one; I had grown accustomed to the yearly photographs of movie stars being received at the White House, with moppets and glamour girls beaming toothily into the camera and with Mickey Rooney squatting cross-legged in the front row. But I had accepted all that as being merely a sort of tradition. Aside from the virtues inherent in any worthy charity, none of it had any special meaning or message for me.

But it had now, it had now. My hands gripped the railing in front of me. A cripple, I thought again, a paralytic — and yet he sits there laughing. He can't even get up out of that chair unaided and he can't take a step without the dragging weight of steel braces supporting him, and yet of those three great men he is the dominating one. For years and years he has been a cripple. He can't even dress himself, and for every movement he makes he pays a price which the unafflicted can probably never even imagine. But his heart and his head have made him a whole man. His spirit has given him his strength, and now a beleaguered continent — even the world — is depending on that strength. They look to him for guidance. He is the symbol of their hope.

And it was then and there, as I stood in the rear of that theater, that he became the symbol of my hope too.

Oh, Johnny, I thought — will you be able to see it? Can I make you see it?

What I got was no miracle and where I went was no Lourdes. Orthopedics and the slow, monotonous routine of physiotherapy are much the same whether they are practiced in a tall, smoke-grimed building in New York or in a one-story, white, sun-dappled pavilion in Warm Springs, Georgia. The massages and the packs and the daily exercises are much the same also. Even the swimming exercises are the same, the only difference being that in New York the pools are artificially heated while at Warm Springs the water flows at natural temperature from somewhere underneath the rising crest of a pine-covered mountain. Casts, pulleys, wheel chairs, crutches, braces, presumably they are identical no matter where they may be employed. There are doctors as capable in New York as there ever were at Warm Springs, there are nurses as efficient.

Yet there is an additional something at Warm Springs which is available nowhere else. I can't analyze it, I can't even describe it — but it is there.

I took him down by train in January, accompanied by Callie, who displayed considerably more interest in the therapeutic potentialities of the project than she did in her long-delayed return to the land of her fathers. ("I ain't so keen to go south, Mis' Ellery," she admitted candidly, when I expressed surprise at her lack of enthusiasm. "I been south.") From other quarters the counsel I received was mostly on the pessimistic side. Mama wrote that she was certain the Warm Springs doctors couldn't hold a candle to the clinic at Rochester, which had done such wonders for Mrs. Old Art Bruer's gallstones; Papa hinted that maybe Dr. Herkle might be as good as anyone at this stage; and while Dr. Kusick didn't actually advise me against the move he did warn me not to expect too much from it.

"It's not a faith-healing center, you know," he said. I hadn't told him the underlying reason for my going — I hadn't told anyone, including Johnny himself — but I think he had surmised it. "They'll give him exactly the same treatment down there that we've been giving him here. And tissues are tissues."

"I know," I said.

He shrugged. "Well, that's all right then. Just so you aren't building yourself up to a letdown. Or the boy either."

"So far as he's concerned," I said, "it'll be just another hospital. If there's anything more to be found there, he'll have to discover it himself."

"Good," he said, nodding. "That may save you both a lot of grief."

No, I can't say that I was given any particular encouragement in the venture — except by Roy, and his approval was not only welcome but necessary because it was to him that I turned, again, for the money. "A change of scene and climate," he said, as he sat at his desk in his *Panorama* office and reached for his checkbook. "A good idea. It'll be good for you and it'll be good for Johnny." He paused. "Of course you realize that there are complications. Once you write Lyle you're going to Warm Springs, he's bound to — "

I shook my head. "He won't even know. He's been addressing his letters to the office. I'll have Mr. Kendrick forward them, that's all."

"Oh." He fingered his pen. "Well, if that's the way you want it."

"It is," I said. "I've gone this far. I might as well go a little farther. . . . So many lies. A few more won't matter much."

He smiled. "I shouldn't imagine you'd be very good at lying. Are you?"

"I've come to be." I made an attempt at a lighter note. "And of course being a woman helps, I suppose. I understand we've acquired rather a reputation for it."

His smile faded, and his gaze was reflective. "Quite justifiably, I should say," he said, after a moment. "Judging from what personal experience I've had. Though mine may not have been exactly representative."

There was a bitterness in his voice, and yet it was a detached bitterness. I hesitated. "Roy," I said, "do you ever hear anything of her?"

"Laura?"

"Yes."

He didn't answer immediately. "She was in Vichy for a while," he said, then. "Now I don't know where she is. It doesn't really matter, anyway. Not to me at least."

Didn't it? I was inclined to doubt that. And then, as if he had been able to read my mind, he looked at me and added, "You don't believe me, do you? Sometimes I can't believe it myself. But it's true. It seems I've been delivered. It seems I've been exorcised."

342

Abruptly his mood altered as he tore out the check and handed it over to me. "There you are," he said, smiling again. "And incidentally, that's not a loan. Call it Lyle's leave-of-absence pay, or accrued interest on his original invention, or my personal contribution to the March of Dimes. Call it whatever you like — only don't try to pay it back."

I looked down at the check, which was for just twice the amount I had asked. For an instant I felt tears starting, but I managed to restrain them. I mustn't cry, I thought. It would embarrass him terribly. He's not used to women who cry. I'm sure Laura never cried, though she may learn to.

"Thank you," I said, and would have said more if I could have found the words. But at the moment I couldn't even trust myself to go on.

"For what?" He had come around from the desk and was looking down at me. "For letting me help you in the only way I can help you?"

Getting up from my chair, I folded the check and put it in my purse. "It's funny," I said. "I used to be afraid of you, because you were so cold and distant. I used to be awed. And now — "

"And now?"

Suddenly, on impulse, I kissed him. "Well, now I'm not." And after that I hurried toward the door. As I went out I glanced back and saw that he was standing where I had left him, a little man, a lonely man. And I realized then, for the first time, that although his kindness and generosity had been partly motivated by a fondness for Johnny and a liking for Lyle, there was something more to it than that. But how much more there was I would never know, because he would never tell me.

The only reason I gave to Johnny for his removal to Warm Springs was that "it'll be warmer down there, and you'll be able to get some sun." If he had any awareness of the associations connected with the place, he gave no indication of it. His whole manner was laconic. And even after we had arrived and he was installed as a bed patient in one of the dormitories and Callie and I were settled in the small cottage I had rented, he still remained

343

laconic. He submitted himself docilely enough to the rigorous treatments, he permitted himself to be lowered into the tropical-blue waters of the glass-enclosed patients' pool, he did everything he was requested to do. But for several weeks I could detect no change in his attitude, and I began to be discouraged.

There were times when I felt that I didn't even know Johnny any more and that there was no way of my ever coming to know him. When he had been smaller and well he had been normally talkative and often even garrulous, but his long illness had caused him to become uncommunicative and curiously secretive. Sometimes, sitting with him and growing uneasy during his long periods of silence, I seemed to see him less as a boy than as a wizened little old man. He had created a private world into which neither I nor anyone else was allowed to enter. I don't know what that world was like, except that it must have been bleak.

And then there came that one afternoon, that afternoon when I knew that he was at last reacting to the influence — the legend, whatever it was and is — to which he was being exposed. How it had come to him I don't know — perhaps through the other children, perhaps through the medical staff, perhaps through a sort of seepage process, an emotional osmosis — but it had come. Sitting up against his pillows, he looked at me gravely and said, "I think this is a good place. I'm glad we're here."

"Are you?" I said. For him to admit "gladness" about anything was an innovation. "Why?"

"Because this is where President Roosevelt came after he was sick." He made the statement as if he were announcing a remarkable and unique discovery. "Did you know that?"

"Well — yes. I believe I did." I waited. "Who told you?"

"I heard it. I heard them talking."

We sat in silence, and I hoped for more. But for the present there wasn't any more. Then, after a moment of hesitation, I reached into my purse and withdrew a clipping from a magazine article. I had been carrying it around with me ever since I had first chanced to come across it some weeks earlier, and now I decided that the moment had come for me to show it to him. I hadn't dared to do it

344

before because I hadn't been sure that he was ready. But it seemed to me that the ground was now prepared, the seed sown.

"Do you want me to read something to you, Johnny?" I said.

"What?" he said, glancing toward the clipping.

"It's something President Roosevelt said when sombeody asked him how he manages to do as much as he does. I'd like you to listen to it. Will you?"

He nodded, and I read. That is, I pretended to read: actually I had repeated the words over so many times that I knew them by heart. " 'Once I spent two years lying in bed, trying to move my big toe. That was the hardest job I ever had to do. After that, anything else seems easy.' "

He stretched out his hand for the clipping, and I gave it to him. I could see him studying it.

"Can I keep it?" he said, then.

"I want you to keep it. I want you to think about it."

He fingered the clipping, and then opened the drawer in his bedside table and tucked it inside. After that he relaxed back on the pillows again, and sighed. But it was a different kind of sigh from the many which I had so often heard him give. There seemed to be a kind of satisfaction in it, and a determination.

"He knows what it's like, I guess," he said. "Doesn't he?"

"I guess he does," I said. "You both do. You and the President of the United States."

He smiled. It had been such a long time since I had seen him smile like that.

"Say, that's something, isn't it?"

And that was the beginning.

I saw him come back to life that winter, and in more ways than one. Day by day as the thin, pale southern sun warmed into spring and took on heat I saw his tissues strengthen and grow firm. I saw him begin to laugh again, and, in school, begin to learn again and to take an interest in his learning. I saw him progress from a bed patient to a cast patient, and then the casts were removed and he was fitted with his braces. He was living with us at the cottage now, and he went to and from the clinic and the pool by means of his wheel

345

chair, pushed either by me or by Callie. He was a little boy again — and yet not so little either. Almost as tall as my shoulder he was, when he stood. But of course he couldn't stand yet, at least not unaided and even then not for long. But he would be able to eventually. I knew that now — and so did he.

But how can you trace the healing of a branch which has been snapped and then mended and which at last begins to grow again? All you can do is watch it with wonder.

Lyle had been transferred to a staff job in London by then, and that was a source of relief to me too because I knew that even despite its sporadic bombings London must be a good deal safer — not to mention pleasanter — than Anzio would have been. That is, his transfer was a source of relief to me until the spring wore on and the papers began to be filled with hints as to a coming invasion. And where would it be coming from? It would be coming from the only place it could come — from England. From then on, I began to wish that he had remained in Italy. I scanned his letters minutely to see if between the lines I could glean any hint as to his future duties, and found none. He had never been the most informative of correspondents, and now he was even less so. Well, I understood how that could be. I understood what it was to be in the possession of a secret.

Then at last it came, what the world had been waiting for. D-Day, doomsday, whichever it was to prove to be, it was here. It was here and I sat on the front porch of the cottage in the hot morning sunshine of Georgia in June listening to the radio, both fascinated and afraid. From other porches and open windows all down the street came the amplified blare of analyses and prophecies and the sonorous platitudes of the experts, all of it so far based on a few bare communiqués. Normandy, Normandy. . . . I suppose my thoughts were the same as those of millions of other women on that June morning. Is he there? I thought. Is he there? And, like millions of others, I was certain that he was.

Up the walk I saw Johnny coming toward me in his wheel chair, propelled by Callie. I watched the chair as it moved closer. What if this should be Providence's little way of balancing the scales? I asked myself. What if the debt incurred for this straighter body and those squarer shoulders should now at this moment be in the process of being paid on a Normandy beach by one who doesn't even know that they were once less straight and less square?

Rising, I went down the steps to help Callie pull the chair up the boards which served as a ramp.

"Any more news?" he said, as I pulled and Callie pushed. He had been so excited ever since breakfast that it had been only with difficulty that I had finally got him started off for his morning therapy.

"No. They just keep on repeating the same things over and over."

The chair at anchor, Callie seated herself on the top step, panting a little, and cast a speculative glance toward the chatter-chatter of the radio. "I bet you he's there, Mis' Ellery," she said. "I bet you anything he's there. I was telling Johnny. I just feel it."

I felt it too, but I wanted no affirmation of my feelings. What I really wanted was a refutation of them. So I tried to divert the conversation. "How did the treatment go, Johnny?"

"O.K."

"Did you go in the pool?"

"No. We just listened to the news." He too was looking at the radio now, and when he spoke again it was with the normal reaction of any nine-year-old boy — and I suppose that as long as it continues to be a normal reaction there is small hope for the human race. "Boy!" he said, his eyes shining, his tone frankly envious. "Boy, what a place to be!"

Yes, I thought, what a place to be. . . . And suddenly, unable to listen to the commentary any longer, I turned and went inside, closing the screen door behind me. But the disembodied voice followed me and echoed in the green dimness of the shade-drawn room. After the glare of the sun, a shower of iridescent stars danced before my eyes, and momentarily I felt a little dizzied. I ought to be praying, I thought. In fact I suppose I really am praying, and have been all morning, only I just haven't happened to be praying in words. But what words can I use? What words would be good

347

enough now, at this of all hours? Please God. . . . Well, that's the old way, and it's probably still the best way. A simple prayer, but not a small one.

Then, as I stood there, there was the shrill burr of the phone ringing, and I groped for it. "Hello?" I said.

"Amy? Amy?"

It's this dizziness, I thought, passing my hand over my forehead. I stayed out there in the sun too long. That voice, it — it sounds so much like Lyle's.

"Yes? Who is it, please?"

There was a laugh at the other end of the wire, and it was the laugh which really identified him for me. "Darling, don't you know me any more?"

There was an instant then when I couldn't even speak. To have heard his voice again at any time, after so long, would have been enough; to hear it now, on this particular day, was almost too much. Faintly — the connection was a bad one — I could hear him saying, "Are you still there? Amy? Amy, are you O.K.?"

"Oh, Lyle," I managed, at last. "I — I can't even talk."

"Now take it easy, take it easy. Sit down or something. Or are you sitting already?"

"I am now," I said, sinking into a chair. The first shock was passing. "Lyle — Lyle, where are you?"

"I'm in Washington — just flew in this morning on a temporary mission, a courier job. Look, what are you doing down there anyway? When I called your office they gave me this number but that's all they did give me. Is this part of your work?"

"Yes," I said. "That's it. It's part of my work."

"Well, you can just drop it and grab a plane and hurry right up here."

I thought fast then. I had to. "Darling, couldn't you come down? You could get a priority and I couldn't. And Johnny's here — I brought him with me — and, well, I just think it would be easier that way. Don't you?"

He hesitated, and for a moment I thought he had guessed the truth. But he hadn't, for when he spoke his tone was natural and

348

easy. "Sure, I'll do that then. I'll come today. How do I get there? What about schedules?"

"Can you get to Atlanta by four o'clock? If you can, you can catch a train there that'll bring you in here at six."

"Consider it done. I'll see you at six tonight. All right?"

"All right? Oh, if you only knew . . ."

"You'll meet me?"

"Yes. Yes, I'll meet you."

"And you think you'll be able to recognize me?"

"Yes, and I think I'll be able to recognize you."

And then it was over, and as I sat there with the phone still in my hands I thought, "Was that real, or did I dream it?" But I knew it was real. And as I looked out through the screen door I saw Johnny in his wheel chair on the porch, bent close to the radio and listening, and I knew that was real too. This is the day you have been longing for, living for, I thought — and now it's here and you're afraid. Then, replacing the phone and rising, I went toward the door and stood at the screen.

"Johnny," I said. "Johnny, I've got some wonderful news for you. . . ."

And for you, my Lyle, I've got some news that isn't so wonderful. But how am I ever going to be able to tell it to you?

All during that long day of waiting I formulated phrases, a hundred different sets of phrases, ranging from the gradual preparation of "I don't know how to break this to you, but . . ." to the stark factuality of "Johnny has polio," but as I stood there on the station platform in the pink wash of the evening sun of summer and watched the train inch to a halt and then saw him coming down the car steps all the phrases deserted me, every one of them, and as I went toward him and then felt his arms around me I stole the moment for myself, myself alone.

"Oh, darling," I said. "Oh, darling. . . ."

His hands on my shoulders, he stood back and looked at me. "You're thin," he said, accusingly. "What have you been doing to yourself?" And then he glanced around him. "Didn't Johnny come with you?"

'No, he's waiting for us." I linked my arm through his. "Come on. I've got a taxi."

He was still glowing with the returning soldier's ebulliency at the wonder of being home again, and as we rode along in the taxi he said what they probably all said. "I can't believe it," he said, sitting close beside me and holding me in his embrace. "I just can't believe it. I'm not really here. I'm still in London, or I'm at a south-coast port, or I'm even in Normandy — but I'm not here in good old Zone Interior."

"You might have given a person some warning you were coming, you know."

"I couldn't. I didn't know it myself until two hours before I took off from Prestwick."

"How long can you stay?"

"Well, I've got ten days' leave and then — " He smiled. "Look, let's not talk about that. Let's talk about you. What's this job you're doing down here, anyway? I thought the only industry in Warm Springs was infantile paralysis."

It was coming now. I felt it coming. "It is — just about."

"Don't tell me that Kendrick is going to try and smarten it up for the readers of *Chic*. I doubt if they'll — "

And then I said it. But I couldn't look at him, I couldn't bear to. Leaning against his shoulder, I turned my face against the wool of his blouse. "Darling, I'm not with the magazine any more. I haven't been since January. I've been down here all the time. With — with Johnny."

For a moment I thought perhaps he hadn't heard me, or at least hadn't grasped the significance of what I was saying, because he didn't speak. Then there was an abrupt tension in his body, a sort of convulsive movement. "Johnny?" he said. "With Johnny?"

I nodded.

He was silent.

"When?"

"Oh — a hundred years ago. The night — the night you went away."

He waited an instant. "How is he?"

Reaching my hand up, I touched his cheek. "Better. So much better. He's going to be all right, I think. He's going to be—" And then suddenly I clutched him, and despite all my resolves not to I began to sob. "Oh, Lyle! Oh, my darling. . . ."

I was able to talk after that, to talk freely. I tried to cushion him, to prepare him. And yet even as I talked I knew that no words could really prepare him. And when the taxi drew up in front of the cottage I could tell from the whiteness of his face and the tightness of his jaw muscles that he was making an attempt to steel himself. We got out, he paid the driver, he lifted out the canvas bag he was carrying, and together we headed up the walk toward the porch. Johnny was sitting there in his wheel chair, and Callie was standing beside him.

He mounted the few steps, and then set his bag down.

"Hello, Johnny," he said. "Hello, old man."

They were both nervous and both embarrassed, and it couldn't have been much easier for Johnny than it was for Lyle.

"Hello, Dad."

Lyle put out his hand, and Johnny took it. They shook hands formally, solemnly. Then suddenly Lyle stooped and held him tight, and kissed him.

"Good boy," he said. "Good boy."

Ten days, each of them gold, and then a month during which he was on temporary duty in Washington and came down to Warm Springs every week end, and after that three more days of leave—but of them all I choose only one day, the day he left to return overseas. Not to England this time, and not to Italy. This time to France . . . "Somewhere in France." The phrase had a familiar ring to it. Time had been when most people had said that if and when France ever again became available as a battleground we would all probably consider ourselves lucky. Well, it was a battleground now all right, a bloody battleground—St. Lô and Caen—but I wasn't so sure that it was such luck after all. Not for those who were there, or who were going there.

With Lyle pushing Johnny in his wheel chair and with me beside them, we meandered along a gently graded walk, past the broad lawns of the Foundation and beneath its pines. Despite all the improvement it had wrought in Johnny's condition, I had never been able really to succeed in enjoying Warm Springs. To me it always remained an institution, and the presence of so many bent bodies and twisted limbs was a constant reminder of disaster. But Johnny had come to love the place, he was a part of it, and now he was giving Lyle a personally guided tour. Georgia Hall, the infirmary, the pools, the theater, he had proudly and proprietorially shown them all. But he had saved the best for the last.

We had left the Foundation and now were on a mountain road that led toward a ravine, and ahead of us was a white board fence. "There it is," said Johnny, pointing. "Right behind there. That's where the President stays when he's here. The Little White House, they call it."

"Mm. Very interesting," said Lyle, with more politeness than enthusiasm. His manner was preoccupied, and I knew why. The shadow of his leaving was already descending. A few more hours and he would be gone.

"Before the war," continued Johnny, "they used to have a big Thanksgiving dinner for everybody over in Georgia Hall, and he'd carve the turkey. I guess that must have been something, hm? The President of the United States carving turkey for you?"

Hero worship? Yes, it was a case of hero worship, and it had been for months now. But as Lyle had remarked early during his stay, "Well, if he had to have a hero, he could have done a lot worse."

"Johnny," he said now, veering the chair around and starting back up the road again, "did I ever tell you that I saw him once?"

"Saw who?"

"The President."

The dark head craned around and up, and the dark eyes were wide with amazement, even awe. "You mean you saw President *Roosevelt*?"

"That's right," nodded Lyle. "At Casablanca."

"What was he doing?"

"Well, he wasn't doing much of anything. He was riding along in a car in front of a column of soldiers and he was — well, just smiling and waving."

Johnny shook his head. "And you mean you never even wrote us about it?"

Lyle shrugged. "It so happened that I couldn't very well have written about it at the time, because it was a military secret. And later on I forgot about it."

"How could you ever forget a thing like that?" He had turned and was gazing back toward the white fence. "I'd like to see him once. Maybe I will, too. When he was here before he said he'd be back in the fall if there wasn't a war." He looked ahead again. "But of course there was a war."

"Yes," said Lyle, pushing at the chair, "there was a war. There still is a war."

And at times, I thought, it seems as if there always has been and always will be a war.

In a way I believe that Lyle dreaded the prospect of our last good-by even more than I did — and I was dreading it enough. He managed Johnny's fairly well by forcing a brisk cheerfulness which he obviously didn't feel, and the last thing he said to him as he left him there on the porch of the cottage was, "Now the next time I see you I want you to be up out of this chair and on your two feet and jumping fences. You hear?" To which Johnny replied a military, "Yes, sir." But after that, when we stood together at the station waiting for the train, he allowed himself to relax.

"This is the worst part of leave," he said. "Sometimes I wonder if the rest is worth it."

"Oh, yes, it is," I assured him. "To me, anyway. I can coast for a long time on these past six weeks."

He sighed. "You may have to. It looks as if it's going to be a long, hard pull over there. We've barely begun." And then he brightened. "But still, I may not have to stay for all of it. Something might happen, you know."

"Like what?"

He hesitated. "Like — well, like for instance I might get perma-

353

nent duty in Washington. They've made a few feelers up at the Pentagon since I've been there, and I wasn't what you might call unreceptive."

"Oh, Lyle!" Suddenly I looked at him suspiciously. "You're not just — making it up, are you? Just because you're going now?"

He shook his head. "No, it could happen. Not soon maybe. But — it could be." Smiling, he put his arm around me. "You wouldn't mind a chairborne husband, would you?"

"Oh, it would be so wonderful. We could get an apartment. We could — "

"A tent it would be, more likely. The way Washington is now."

I placed my cheek against his. "That wouldn't matter. We could live in a tree, if necessary." And then I smiled, too. "But are you sure you wouldn't be restless and discontented, the way you were before? Remember all the things you used to say about subway soldiers when you were one of them?"

"I'd try to bear up. You see — I guess I've had it. I can go on. I can go on just as long as they tell me to go on. But just between ourselves, I've had it."

The train had pulled in now, its iron clangor loud in our ears. He kissed me.

"Darling," I said, "was I right?" I had to ask him, I had to know. "Right?"

I nodded. "In not telling you about Johnny?"

For a moment he didn't answer, and then he held me more tightly. "Yes, I suppose so. Yes, you were right. But — but if you ever did it again, I'd — I'd — "

I smothered his words with my lips. "There won't be any 'again.' It's over, darling, or almost."

"Yes," he said, "it's over, or almost."

And then he got on the train and I stood there watching it as it pulled out, and after that I turned away from the station and started to walk back to the cottage. I was alone once more — but now it was different. Now, like Lyle — and like Johnny too — I could go on.

354

⋙ X I ⋘

HERE IS SO MUCH I HAVE LEFT OUT, so much I wanted to put in and somehow forgot, so many nests of trays left dusty and unopened in the attic of memory. That day in Ammon, for instance, when we were still living with Mama and Papa and when Johnny, who was three then, spilled a full box of my face powder all over the bedroom floor and I lost my temper and slapped him, slapped him hard, twice. That I meant to put in. And the mink coat Lyle bought me that first Christmas he was on *Panorama* and which I wore and wore until the hide showed through the matted fur and the NRA label in the collar became so faded that it was almost indecipherable. That I meant to put in, too. And a fortnight we spent in Bermuda in a holiday world made up of cashmere sweaters and Planter's Punches and the clop-clop-clop of horses' hoofs along white stone roads. Then there was the afternoon when I happened to be in Saks and saw Jean Harlow, saw her just as clear as anything, stepping into an elevator with her hair fluffed out around her cheeks like spun sugar. And a day when I was sitting on a bench in Central Park and a pigtailed little girl on roller skates fell down in front of me and when I picked her up and tried to stop her crying by asking her her name she said, "My name's Eva." Things like that. And head colds and newspaper dispatches dated from Rome which began "Virginio Gayda has announced that" and the time in Ammon when Lyle had an abscessed tooth and the first time I ever wore nylons and the time I left a

355

purse with twenty dollars in it on a stool at the soda counter in Schrafft's and when I went back the purse was still there but the twenty dollars wasn't, and — oh, so much more, so much, much more. All that I have left out.

And people, people I haven't even mentioned. A Mr. and Mrs. Houser who lived across the hall from us at Tudor City and who got divorced and then remarried and then got divorced again, though what their current status and whereabouts are I wouldn't know. And Dr. George M. Purdy, who was my obstetrician when Johnny came — and very good too — and who kept a silver tray with chocolate mints on it on the table in his reception room. And a matronly brunette called Rita who clerked in the ready-to-wear at Heflin and Wiebert's in Ammon and who was rumored to be conducting a clandestine affair with Harold Fulmer, proprietor of the Ammon Hardware Company and father of four. And a couple named Willow (Willough?) — just pale and indistinguishable blobs of faces, those, and not associated with much of anything. . . . Names, names. Names on Christmas cards once ranged neatly on the mantel, names carefully inscribed in little leather address books long since worn out and thrown away, names on telephone lists now lost. Names, places, times.

But most of all that is unimportant, I suppose. It is probably what is called "living," and I can leave it out all right. I have left it out, and much more besides. Yet there are other things which I can't leave out, or oughtn't to. And one of them is Orin.

Johnny and I were still in Warm Springs when Papa sent me that marked copy of the *Argus* with its headline, "Local Man Casualty in Pacific." That was in August, when all attention was centered on the great drive in France and the recapture of Paris, and the Pacific seemed very far away, not only in distance but in importance. But it came nearer to me now, now as I read:

According to advice from the Navy Department, Lt. Orin Netcher, USNR, prominent Ammon resident who has been serving as a gunnery officer on a destroyer, has been killed in action somewhere in the Pacific Theater.

On leave from his position as assistant cashier of the Manila County

Savings and Trust Company, Orin was born in this city and attended Ammon High School and the University of Iowa, where he was a member of Sigma Chi. He leaves behind him his widow, the former Irmadee Tupper, and two small children, Wendy Ruth and Jennifer Jean. . . .

I read it all, even though I knew it all. Papa had probably written it himself, since Ethel Huber had now become Captain Ethel Huber, WAC, and was exotically stationed in Cairo, Egypt. I read it to the very last line, which stated that the Manila County Savings and Trust would be closed during the memorial service to be held at the First Presbyterian Church, and then I sat looking at the blur of type and instead seeing Orin, seeing him and hearing him. And with a twinge of shame I remembered how amused and superior and condescending I had been when I had learned that he had rejected the Army in order to accept a commission in the more socially select Navy, and how I had thought "He would. Orin would." He represented much that I had come to disapprove of: he had been bitterly Isolationist, racially intolerant, prejudiced, "insular," smug, and a snob. And now he was dead, and he must have died fighting for a lot of things he not only didn't believe in but was actually opposed to. Yet he was just as dead as if he had spent his adult life orating on the meaning of "democracy" and the Four Freedoms.

And then I thought again, and felt better for the thought. Maybe he had died for something, after all. Maybe he had died to protect and defend the sanctity of the Joint and for a canary-yellow convertible and even for the Balloon Room in the Congress Hotel, Chicago, Illinois. And who was I, alive, to say that his causes were any less real to him than those far nobler were to others? Who was anyone, alive, to say that?

Yet even as I sat there grieving I couldn't help wondering — such are the insuppressible impulses of the mind — if Irmadee would adopt formal mourning and if she would buy it at Marshall Field's and how she would look in it. Very attractive and chic, I imagined. Like Carole Lombard.

That is for Orin. I owe him that. I owe him much more.

*   *   *

It was harvest time. It was harvest time in Georgia, and the land lay mellow in the sun while fallen peaches rotted in orchard alleys and in the mornings a blue haze veiled Pine Mountain. It was harvest time in Europe, too, where the Americans and the British were pushing toward the east — through France, through Belgium, into Germany itself — and the Russians were pushing toward the west — through Yugoslavia, through Poland, into Germany itself. A pincer movement. A lovely, bloody, horrible pincer movement.

And it was harvest time for me also — and for Johnny. It was the harvest of those long hours of exercises and of those hours of clinging to the rungs at the edge of the patients' pool while the legs went splash, splash, splash, and of the enforced rest periods and the whole general drudgery of physiotherapy. Seeing him every day, I probably wasn't aware of how rapidly he was improving, but now and then I would try to look at him detachedly and critically and I would compare his present condition with what it had been two weeks ago, a month ago, and then I would realize that he was definitely getting better. Getting better? He was getting well. I knew it. He knew it.

His graduation from wheel chair to crutches was a signal not only for a celebration but, to him, for something else. It was on an afternoon in early October that he first came hobbling up the walk, followed proudly by Callie trundling the empty chair. He was walking. Yes, walking. Walking with the aid of crutches, but walking. . . . I never would have thought it possible that the sight of a boy on crutches — and that boy of all boys — could start tears of gratitude in my eyes, but it did. And I never thought that the time would come when I would quickly get out a camera and take a picture of him on those crutches in order to send it to Lyle, but I did that too.

"He'll be so proud," I said. "It'll be the best picture he's ever had of you."

"Look at him, Mis' Ellery," said Callie, as he posed by the porch steps. "Ain't he the image of his father?"

Shading the camera with my hand, I looked down into the lens and saw him there — Lyle in little. "Yes, he is, Callie," I said. And

358

he was. He was Lyle — the good and the bad in him, the strength and the weakness.

"Mother," he said, as he maneuvered himself up the steps and toward a chair, "can't we go home now? Can't we go back to New York?"

The question surprised me, because it was the first time he had ever mentioned our leaving. "Why — yes, I suppose so. If you want to."

"He's worried," said Callie. She laughed. "Mighty worried."

"About what?"

She nodded toward Johnny. "You tell her now. You tell her what you been telling me."

His face was earnestly sober. "Well, you see, I've been thinking. New York's your legal residence, and it's Callie's too — and if you aren't there at election time you won't be able to vote."

Election? I had almost forgotten that there was going to be an election. I had ignored the whole campaign. What did the election have to do with — ? And then, suddenly, I understood. "Oh," I said, "I see. You're worried about Roosevelt's chances, is that it?"

"I wrote Dad last week and reminded him about his overseas ballot," he went on briskly, "and with yours and Callie's vote, that'll make three. Three for certain."

"Well, I doubt if three votes are likely to make much difference one way or another."

"They could," he said, frowning. "You never can tell. They could."

Callie placed a calm hand on his shoulder. "Now you just relax. You just relax yourself."

"But it's *important*. You don't want us to change horses in the middle of a stream, do you?"

I smiled. "All right," I said. "We'll go. Don't you worry. We'll be there when the time comes."

And we were there when the time came. By then we were settled again in the Eighty-ninth Street apartment, and therefore our polling place was a small, cluttered cubbyhole of a stationer's shop on Eighty-sixth. The whole operation was Johnny's production. It was he who got us there early and it was he who shepherded us into line with the others, after which he leaned against the wall and shrewdly scrutinized the faces of those ahead of and behind us, as if he were trying to determine the political sympathies of each. To those wearing Dewey buttons he gave a cold stare; to those wearing Roosevelt buttons he gave a warm, benevolent smile.

"Seven Deweys, five Roosevelts," he whispered, leaning toward me. "But you can't always be sure by the buttons."

I was waiting for an immensely patient poll watcher to finish explaining the complexities of the voting machine to Callie, who was none too mechanically minded. "Johnny," I said, "you oughtn't to take all this so personally."

His eyes widened. "Why not? How else should I take it?"

And he was right, I decided. How else should he? How else could he?

So Callie emerged from the booth — smiling triumphantly at her mastery over the machine — and after that I went in. Four terms, I thought, almost awed, as I stood behind the curtain and arranged the knobs and pulled the lever. No man has ever run for President for four terms before, no man in all history. Maybe it will happen sometime again and maybe it won't, but it's happened now and it's — well, unique.

And then I came out and joined Johnny, who limped alongside me and shook his head with grave concern. "Will he win?" he asked anxiously, as we headed toward the street. "Will he?"

"Oh, I think so. I hope so, anyway."

"He win," said Callie, mystically serene. "He always win."

There isn't much more, and except for one interval all the rest was like steps going up. That interval came late in November, shortly after our return to New York, when Papa died and I went back to Ammon to attend his funeral. He died as he probably would have wanted to, sitting at his roll-top desk in the *Argus* office and the beat of his heart stopping as quickly as if a motor had been switched off. For the first time in my life I found Mama unable to meet a situation. It was as if she had lost all sense of authority. She was old, she was old, and suddenly almost senile. "He went off downtown that morning just as chipper as you please," she kept repeating, "and then at noon the doorbell rang and it was Frank Diederdock and the moment I saw him I knew something was wrong. . . . Oh, Amy, your papa's gone, your papa's gone."

Your papa. Always he had been that to her, ever since I could remember, either that or just "Papa." Seldom had he been "John." Yet he became John again as I stood a respectful distance behind her in the tapered quiet of the Welsbach Funeral Home and watched her lean down toward the rouged, waxy face which was no more Papa's face than a colored chromo would have been. I think for that one moment I didn't even exist for her. She wasn't a mother, she wasn't a widow. She wasn't even a wife. She was Gertie Pepperdine, a pretty girl wearing crimped bangs and leg-o'-mutton sleeves, and that white, straggling mustache which she was gazing down at was chestnut-brown and glossy and luxuriant, and those thin, ivory cheeks were pink not with the embalmer's art but with the ruddy flush of youth.

"Dear John," I heard her whisper, as she bent down and kissed the carmined lips, and then she used a name which she probably hadn't used for years — and never in my presence: "Dear Jack. . . ." And after that, in a moment, she turned to me, herself again, Mama again. "Don't you want to kiss him, Amy? Don't you want to kiss your papa good-by?"

"Yes, Mama." I didn't, really. I couldn't. But obediently I came forward and leaned down among the drenching sweetness of the flowers and pretended to kiss him. My eyes were closed, and I was seeing him in many moods — smiling, thoughtful, ponderously deliberative, spryly humorous, drowsing over a book, pecking at his L. C. Smith, leaning back in his Morris chair and steepling his fingers together and uttering a judicious "Well, sir." But I wasn't seeing him as dead, and I never would.

I felt Mama's hand on my shoulder. "Tell him good-by, Amy," she prompted.

"Good-by, Papa. Good-by. . . ."

But that was an interval only, and once I had recovered from it —

361

as much as I ever could recover — from then on the steps continued to rise steadily upward and my heart and hopes with them.

He was coming home. There had been a German counteroffensive in the Ardennes, the Battle of the Bulge, and it had been checked on Christmas Day. Manila and Iwo Jima had been taken and the Rhine crossed, all at a price, and there was fighting on Okinawa. There was a word on everyone's lips which at last people were daring to speak openly, and the word was "Soon. Maybe soon." The word sang, and something inside of me sang with it. Soon. Soon. . . . He was coming home. For months it had been a matter of weeks, and then for weeks it had been a matter of days. But now it was a matter of hours. Soon. Soon. Callie's kitchen clock said it, the lilac bush in the back yard below said it, the rustling leaves on the trees lining P Street said it. Soon. Soon. Soon for everyone, and even sooner than that for me. He was coming home.

But where was home? Home was a place he had never seen — a musty, dank, "made-over" apartment in what must have once been an elegant private mansion which had had a ballroom and a conservatory but which now had merely flats. "Grover Cleveland Slept Here," had been Natalie's comment when she had come down from New York for a week end shortly after we had moved in — and it was quite possible. But that didn't matter. The rooms had atmosphere, a sort of moldy, Southern charm. They also had cockroaches, but they had atmosphere. The windows were tall and shuttered. "Jalousies," the shutters were called. I loved the word. Jalousies. The place was furnished with massive mahogany pieces, much veloured, and outside the living room — the apartment was on the second floor and ran clear through — there was a little wrought-iron balcony. I loved that, too. In fact there was nothing I didn't love, including the lilac bush. Especially the lilac bush. When we had moved in, it had been only bare gray branches and twigs, and I had watched the green fuzz come and then buds and then glossy leaves. And now, standing at the open kitchen window and gazing down into the back yard, I was watching the buds which were ready to burst. Leaning out, I could catch their faint fragrance drifting upward and mingling

362

with the smells of chocolate frosting and frying chicken behind me, where Callie was preparing dinner. A special dinner for a special occasion, this one. For one special occasion definitely, and perhaps — if we were lucky — for another.

It was April. It was April in Washington. It was twilight in April and lilacs were about to bloom. Soon. Soon.

"It's hard enough now, Mis' Ellery," said Callie. "You can stick the candles in."

Turning, I reached for the box and began to embed the rose-budded candles into the rich creaminess of the frosting. One — two — four — ten. Ten candles. Ten candles for Johnny — and a space left for another in the center, just in case Lyle arrived in time. Though he wouldn't, I was sure he wouldn't. Freddie Wheaton was sure, too. Freddie was stationed at the Pentagon in the Air Transport Command, and it was he who had supplied me with the off-the-record information that it would be "sometime the latter part of the week." Probably Friday, he had said. Or maybe Saturday. And this was Thursday.

Callie lifted a skillet and transferred it to the oven. Stooping, she peered into the recess and then slammed the door and straightened. "Well," she announced, "I guess we just about ready." She glanced broodingly toward the cake, and sighed. "It come out good, and now Cap'n Ellery won't even be here to eat it. All the time I was mixing I kept thinking he would be. But he won't."

I had long since given up trying to remind her that there was such a thing as advancement in rank and that Captain Ellery was now a lieutenant colonel. "It'll keep," I said. "We'll save some for him."

"But it won't be oven-fresh. It'll be like a old store-bought cake."

I stepped back and admiringly surveyed the circle of candles. "Well, Johnny will enjoy it, anyway. And so will I."

Going toward her ladder-stool, she seated herself on it and then looked at the clock. "You know where I bet he is? I bet he's hanging around over at that airport again."

"I shouldn't be surprised. I shouldn't be at all surprised."

"Getting himself all tired out, that's what he's doing. 'When your

Daddy gets here, he'll get here,' I tell him. 'And you sitting at that airport ain't going to get him here any quicker.' " She shook her head. "But no, he won't listen."

"Well, it won't be long." Soon. Soon. Soon. . . .

She had picked up a magazine from the shelf behind her, and now she was holding it out in front of her, examining it critically. "My, he looks old, don't he?" she said.

"Who?"

She nodded. "Him."

I moved closer and, glancing over her shoulder, saw that she was looking at the previous week's issue of *Panorama*. On its red-bordered cover was a caped and seated figure. Thin, gaunt face. Sunken cheeks. Tired eyes. A pallor. Beneath was the single word "Yalta."

"Yes," I said. "Yes, he does. Awfully old."

She began leafing through the magazine, and paused at an alluring advertisement of a glass-and-chromium kitchen. " 'Tomorrow Your Dream Deferred Comes True,' " she read, aloud. She soothed the page lovingly. "My," she said, "just look. Just look at that."

I smiled. "Peace, it's wonderful, Callie. Or at least it will be."

"Yes, ma'am," she said, with emphasis.

She turned another page, and then another — a streamlined sedan, a new house set in a garden, a spread of aluminumware, a food advertisement showing a table laden with things which were "shortages" now and which would be taken for granted then. All just around the corner. All waiting almost within grasp.

Her tone was somewhat dubious. "When you think people going to be able to get all this stuff?" she said. "When they going to be able to buy it?"

"Oh — soon." And then — I always had to keep reminding myself of it — I added dutifully, "Of course there'll still be the Pacific. And that may take a long time."

"Mm. That Pacific," she said, with a minimum of enthusiasm.

Turning, I headed toward the living room on what I was fairly sure would prove to be a sleeveless errand, for I wanted a cigarette and I had had the bad judgment to develop a taste for them during a period when there weren't any, or weren't many. The room was

364

shadowy in the oncoming dusk, and I paused as I entered to switch on a lamp. Then I lifted the lid of one cigarette box and after that another. Both were empty. I ought to learn to roll my own, I thought. They say it's quite simple, once you get the knack. All you have to do is to buy one of those little machines. And then suddenly I remembered a package of something called Old Hickories which I had stored away in the desk drawer in case of an emergency. Pulling out the drawer, I picked up the package, opened it, and lit a cylinder of something which tasted like old hickory indeed. Still, technically it was a cigarette and it would serve. Once Lyle was home he would be able to get whole cartons at the Post Exchange, and anyway it was generally rumored that the shortage might be over soon.

Soon. Soon. Again soon. So many things soon, at any hour, at any minute. Peace — and plenty.

The telephone rang then, and in the instant my hand went out toward it I thought again — as I had thought each time it had rung ever since morning — "This could be it. It probably isn't, but it could be."

It wasn't. It was Freddie Wheaton, his voice discreet and very official. "More data on the arrival of a Very Important Person."

"Yes?" I don't suppose there ever was a "Yes?" so eager and urgent.

There was a suggestion of a leer in his tone. "Just what would this information be worth to you, Madam?"

"Oh, now Freddie — don't tease."

"Well, he's due to take off from a certain Unnamed Place at 2100 hours and he ought to be hoving into an equally certain Unnamed Destination sometime tomorrow afternoon. And why I should turn informer just for you I do not know, because I expect I could be court-martialed for it."

"You're a lamb, Freddie! You really are!"

"No, I'm not. I'm a wolf." And he was, half-seriously and half in jest. Ever since he and Blanche had been divorced — "It just didn't work out," he said — he had assumed the attitude of a professional amorist. Now I heard a chuckle at the other end of the wire, and the leer intensified. "The main reason I'm telling you is that I thought you'd want to get a good night's rest, because I have a hunch you won't be getting one tomorrow night. And now good-by —and pleasant dreams to you."

Tomorrow, tomorrow. . . . Replacing the phone in its cradle, I turned and saw Callie standing in the doorway and looking at me expectantly.

"It's tomorrow, Callie!" I said. "It's tomorrow!"

She was beaming. "Oh, Mis' Ellery! Ain't that just —'"

And then I heard it, we both heard it, the tap of Johnny's crutch in the hall outside and the click of the knob as he opened the door and entered. Perhaps I should have noticed his face at once. Perhaps I should have noticed the dragging of his right foot. But I didn't. All I was aware of then, at that particular instant, was that he was home and that tomorrow Lyle would be. Soon. Soon. Almost now.

"Johnny," I said, going toward him. "Major Wheaton just phoned. It's tomorrow. He'll be here tomorrow. He — "

I stopped. I have seen the face of tragedy. I have seen it in the flesh and in photographs — a middle-aged man standing at a Marseille curb and weeping at his country's fall. But I have never seen a face like the face I was looking at now. There were no tears in his eyes. There was nothing at all except a bleak and timeless lostness.

I watched him as he limped toward the sofa and sank onto it, holding his crutch with white-knuckled hands. Then I went over and sat down beside him. I didn't ask what was wrong. He would tell me when he could.

"The President," he said. "The President's dead."

I stared at him, and there was an instant when there was no sound at all in the room. Then I heard Callie's voice — sharp and reproving. "It ain't true," she said. "It's one of those crazy false alarms." She caught her breath, and then went on rapidly, as if her words constituted adequate denial. "It's like the time they said Bing Crosby was dead and he wasn't dead at all. So you oughtn't even to repeat such a thing."

"It's true." A dulled voice, and lifeless. "They announced it over the radio at the airport. I heard it. I heard it myself."

Hesitantly, fearfully, she stepped toward the radio and switched it

366

on. There was a buzz as the machine warmed up, and then there came music — slow and deep. A dirge. I don't know what dirge it was. It was just a dirge. Then she dialed to another station and an announcer was speaking: ". . . at Warm Springs in the cottage which he occupied there. He died at 3:35 this afternoon, and although no further details have as yet been released — "

I motioned to Callie to turn it off, and she did. Then she began to sob. I had never heard her sob before, had never even seen her cry. But now she was sobbing in great, awkward gasps, and she turned away and headed toward the kitchen.

And so, sitting there on the sofa, I watched the breaking of a heart. And then at last he began to cry and I began to cry too and he clutched me and I cradled him. But I made no attempt to comfort him. There was no comfort for him then — or for me either.

XII

This is the lonesome train.

There has been another lonesome train in another April, but not in this century, and that one carried the body of a man mourned by the nation and this one carries the body of a man mourned by the world.

This is the lonesome train and this is the route it takes.

There is a small, clapboarded station in Warm Springs, Georgia, and that is where the train starts, in the warm white sunshine of a morning in spring. It starts slowly, very slowly, while a bareheaded, shirt-sleeved crowd watches in silence. It is the last car they are watching, the car where the flag-draped coffin lies.

The train moves northward, slowly, ever slowly, through a southern spring and through a valley white with dogwood.

At a wayside crossing at noon a farmer and his family sit in a buckboard wagon, watching.

On a country road a group of cars has collected. Their occupants stand on the runningboards, watching.

All through the afternoon the train moves north, slowly, slowly, and at every small town the station platforms are thick with people silently watching.

Sunset comes, and the cars gathered at the roadside begin to switch on their lights. The people in the cars are watching, watching.

The sun sets, there is an afterglow, the sky darkens, night falls. The train is dark now except for the last car, which is brilliantly *lighted from within. The oblongs of light slant through the plate-glass windows and checker the passing trackside with yellow.*

At a small-town station a railroad telegrapher sits motionless at his key, watching. It is full night now, and on the other side of the dusty windowpane a knot of people stand on the platform in the light cast by a single bare electric bulb. They are watching.

The train is now passing through the ramshackle tenement district of a large city. Silhouetted against the lighted windows, and leaning outward with elbows on pillows, are men, women, and children, all watching.

Slowly through the night goes the train, its whistle sounding. Lonesome sound. Lonesome train. . . .

And what of the watchers in the night? What of those who watch the train and what of those who are far from its route, who never hear the whistle, who never see the lighted car? What of them?

In Wichita, Kansas, a man savagely switches off a radio as "My Captain, My Captain" begins to be declaimed in an actor's throaty voice. "Good God!" he says. "Again?"

In a thousand telephone exchanges rows of night operators sit idly in front of switchboards on which no lights flash.

Spring rain drizzles down on a small-town cemetery and rivulets run over the face of a headstone marked "John Hardin. Born Ammon, Iowa, 1872. Died 1944."

A cleaning woman on the thirtieth floor of the Terminal Tower in Cleveland, Ohio, sits back on her heels and gazes meditatively into the suds in her pail.

Lying in bed in his Westchester house, the permanently Unreconstructed Mr. Kendrick is sound asleep and snoring. This is the best night's sleep Mr. Kendrick has had for some time.

The train continues to head north, slowly, and as it passes a road near Charlotte, North Carolina, a farmer and his wife and their year-old baby sit in a small sedan and the wife points at the lighted last car and then glances down at the bundle in her arms and says, "Now you look. You look at that and remember." But the baby doesn't look, because he is asleep. And he won't remember. . . .

But he will be told. He will be told so often that eventually he will believe he remembers.

In a darkened bedroom high above Central Park West, Ben Liebermann tosses restlessly and finally wakes to see that his wife Natalie, in the opposite bed, is awake also and is lying smoking a cigarette. He sees her pale form rising and says, "What's the matter?" "Nothing," she answers. "I just want to get a drink of water." But instead of getting a drink of water she goes out onto the terrace and stands looking across at the Fifth Avenue skyline.

On Manila Street in Ammon, Iowa, Gertrude Hardin whiffles slightly as she sleeps, her hair in curlers and her teeth in a glass on the table beside her. She lies alone in a big double bed, and now in her sleep her hand moves out as if searching. Not there. Not there. Jack, where are you? Jack?

Inside the empty Opera House in San Francisco the massed banners of the United Nations gleam in the darkness.

A victim of insomnia, Royal Archer III puts a robe on over his pyjamas in his house on East Sixty-third Street, New York City, and pads downstairs and goes into his library where he seats himself at his desk beneath a Rivera mural and starts to write an editorial for next week's Panorama. *He is a publisher, not a writer, and he knows it, but this is one editorial he wants to write himself. Using a gold fountain pen, he writes "A Memorial," in a fine, almost feminine script, and then pauses and reflects.*

Perched on a farmyard fence in Windsor County, Vermont, a rooster crows. Light is beginning to break.

In the Palmer House in Chicago Irmadee Netcher lies drunk and struggling for sleep, after a night spent with friends on Sheridan Road. They had all intended it to be a very quiet evening, but it was so monotonous listening to that gloomy stuff on the radio and some of the gang got to exchanging some screamingly funny Frank-and-Eleanor oldies (really outrageous they were) and things went on from there and then they started singing "Home on the Range," sort of burlesque-like but not really mean, and before anybody knew it they were all pretty well on the way to being spiffed. An Army major who was stationed in the Wrigley Building drove her back to the hotel and wanted to come up to the room with her, but she wouldn't let him. She is beginning to fall asleep and to dream about the Major now. It's a nice change from dreaming about Orin. And Chicago is a nice change from Ammon, too. All she was doing there was just moping around the house with the kids and practically working herself into a psychopathic state. A trip like this was due her. And maybe she'll decide to stay on in Chicago. Get a job. Start acting like a human being again. And perhaps later on the Major might . . . After all, you only live once.—Irmadee sleeps. Orin, too.

Light lightening, the eastern sky reddening, the twitter of birds and the plod of milkmen's horses and dew on the lilac bush and all the time the train going slowly northward. It is day.

Yes, the night has ended. It is day. Twenty-three hours have passed. A long time for a train to be traveling such a short distance. A very long time. A lifetime, even. Many lifetimes. Millions.

It is day, and the Capitol dome gleams bright in the clear hot sunshine of an April morning and in the plaza fronting the Union Station massed faces are gathered. They are watching.

So many different kinds of faces, so many different colors, so many ages. Faces are massed along the marble magnificence of Constitution Avenue, too, and at the curb stands an honor guard with fixed bayonets. There are planes overhead and their drone sounds loud, but no one looks at them. The faces gaze straight ahead, watching. Faces lining Constitution and faces along Fifteenth Street and then faces on Pennsylvania Avenue, and all watching. Tears? There are some, though not many. Sobs? A few. But mostly there is only the slow dirge of the music and the clack of horses' hoofs and the grind of iron-rimmed wheels on the pavement.

This is the funeral procession of a President.

It was Callie who saw it first. "He's coming," she said. "I hear it."

Then I heard too, heard the slow ruffle of drums and, looking down the Avenue, saw the nodding, black-bridled heads of six white horses.

We were standing in the densely packed throng of Lafayette Square, and Callie was ahead of me and Johnny at my left and

Lyle at my right. We had been standing there for almost two hours, and the sun was so hot that circles of sweat stains showed at the armpits of Lyle's wool blouse. I realized that Johnny, leaning on his crutches, was white with fatigue and I thought, "He shouldn't be here. He shouldn't be here at all. It's too much for him. I should have made him stay home."

The cortege was in full view now, and I saw it — the horses, the black caisson with the coffin and the colors resting on it. It looked very small, that coffin. Very small for six horses to be pulling.

I had never known that so many thousands could be so quiet. There was more noise from the squirrels scampering among the branches of the trees than there was from all the crowd put together.

Johnny was standing on tiptoe, or trying to, in an effort to see over the heads of those in front of him, and I put out my arm to steady him. The cortege was just about to turn into the circular drive. We were wedged in close to the iron fence surrounding the Jackson statue, whose pedestal was thick with those who had scrambled up on it in order to get a better view. I saw Johnny look at the fence and lift his arm as if he were about to join them — and then the arm fell back and his hand clamped the crutch.

"Go ahead," I whispered. "Don't be afraid. There's nothing to be afraid of."

He hesitated, and then he leaned the crutches against the pickets. Turning, Lyle saw the gesture and made a step to help him upward.

I looked again toward the White House. The caisson was moving up the drive now.

Suddenly I put both palms to my face, and closed my eyes. Anyone looking at me might have thought I was crying, but I wasn't. I was thinking. Don't be afraid, I was thinking. There's nothing to be afraid of. And I found myself remembering something, remembering it as clearly as if it had been yesterday rather than twelve years ago. I found myself remembering my standing with Lyle beside a radio in a Greenwich Village apartment on my wedding day and hearing a voice which I would never hear again say, "The only thing we have to fear is fear itself." I found myself remembering that and so many, many other things, among them my sitting with

Lyle on a bench here in this very same square and our talking of Johnny, who had been just a baby then, and Lyle's nodding toward the White House across the street and saying, "Maybe he'll grow up to live over there. How would that suit you? Along about 1990, say, or 2000." I had been afraid then, on that day, and he had too. I had been afraid so many times of so many things, and I probably would be afraid again. But I had learned something, I decided, I had learned a lot — and from a teacher I had never even seen.

I felt Lyle's hand on my arm, and I opened my eyes just as the coffin was being lifted from the caisson and borne through the door.

Again I felt the pressure of Lyle's hand, and I looked at him. He was smiling, and he nodded upward, toward the statue. And I looked upward too and I saw that Johnny had clambered over the barrier and was clinging to the pedestal, almost atop it.

"I see him!" he cried, his shrill voice breaking the silence of thousands. "I see him!"